THE
PELICAN
BRIEF

Also by John Grisham

A TIME TO KILL
THE FIRM

THE PELICAN BRIEF

JOHN GRISHAM

Large Print Edition

DOUBLEDAY
NEW YORK
LONDON
TORONTO
SYDNEY
AUCKLAND

PUBLISHED BY DOUBLEDAY
a division of Bantam Doubleday Dell
Publishing Group, Inc.
666 Fifth Avenue, New York, New York 10103

DOUBLEDAY and the portrayal of an anchor with a
dolphin are trademarks of Doubleday, a division of
Bantam Doubleday Dell Publishing Group, Inc.

Library of Congress Cataloging-in-Publication Data

Grisham, John.
The pelican brief/John Grisham.
p. cm.
1. Large type books. I. Title.
[PS3557.R5355P4 1992]
813′.54—dc20 91-33235
CIP

ISBN 0-385-42354-3

March 1992
First Edition

1 3 5 7 9 10 8 6 4 2

**This Large Print Book carries the
Seal of Approval of N.A.V.H.**

TO MY READING COMMITTEE: Renée, my wife and unofficial editor; my sisters, Beth Bryant and Wendy Grisham; my mother-in-law, Lib Jones; and my friend and co-conspirator, Bill Ballard

ACKNOWLEDGMENTS

MANY THANKS to my literary agent, Jay Garon, who discovered my first novel five years ago and peddled it around New York until someone said yes.

Many thanks to David Gernert, my editor, who's also a friend and a fellow baseball purist; and to Steve Rubin and Ellen Archer and the rest of the family at Doubleday; and to Jackie Cantor, my editor at Dell.

Many thanks to those of you who've written. I've tried to answer them all, but if I missed one or two, please forgive.

Special thanks to Raymond Brown, a gentleman and fine lawyer in Pascagoula, Mississippi, who came through in the clutch; and to Chris Charlton, a law school

ACKNOWLEDGMENTS

pal who knows the alleys of New Orleans; and to Murray Avent, a friend from Oxford and Ole Miss who now lives in D.C.; and to Greg Block at the *Washington Post*; and, of course, to Richard and the Gang at Square Books.

THE
PELICAN
BRIEF

ONE

HE SEEMED INCAPABLE of creating such chaos, but much of what he saw below could be blamed on him. And that was fine. He was ninety-one, paralyzed, strapped in a wheelchair and hooked to oxygen. His second stroke seven years ago had almost finished him off, but Abraham Rosenberg was still alive and even with tubes in his nose his legal stick was bigger than the other eight. He was the only legend remaining on the Court, and the fact that he was still breathing irritated most of the mob below.

He sat in a small wheelchair in an office on the main floor of the Supreme Court Building. His feet touched the edge of the window, and he strained forward as the noise increased. He hated cops, but the sight of them standing in thick, neat lines was somewhat comforting. They stood straight and held ground as the mob of at least fifty thousand screamed for blood.

"Biggest crowd ever!" Rosenberg yelled at the window. He was almost deaf. Jason Kline, his senior law clerk, stood behind him. It was the first Monday in October, the opening day of the new term, and this had become a traditional celebration of the First Amendment. A glorious celebration. Rosenberg was thrilled. To him, freedom of speech meant freedom to riot.

"Are the Indians out there?" he asked loudly.

Jason Kline leaned closer to his right ear. "Yes!"

"With war paint?"

"Yes! In full battle dress."

"Are they dancing?"

"Yes!"

The Indians, the blacks, whites, browns, women, gays, tree lovers, Christians, abortion activists, Aryans, Nazis, atheists, hunters, animal lovers, white supremacists, black supremacists, tax protestors, loggers, farmers—it was a massive sea of protest. And the riot police gripped their black sticks.

"The Indians should love me!"

"I'm sure they do." Kline nodded and smiled at the frail little man with clenched fists. His ideology was simple; government over business, the individual over government, the environment over everything. And the Indians, give them whatever they want.

The heckling, praying, singing, chanting, and screaming grew louder, and the riot police inched closer together. The crowd was larger and rowdier than in recent years. Things were more tense. Violence had become common. Abortion clinics had been bombed. Doctors had been attacked and beaten. One was killed in Pensacola, gagged and bound into the fetal position and burned with acid. Street fights were weekly events. Churches and priests had been abused by militant gays. White supremacists operated from a dozen known, shadowy, paramilitary organizations, and had become bolder in their attacks on blacks, Hispanics, and Asians. Hatred was now America's favorite pastime.

And the Court, of course, was an easy target. Threats, serious ones, against the justices had increased tenfold since 1990. The Supreme Court police had tripled in size. At least two FBI agents were assigned to guard each justice, and another fifty were kept busy investigating threats.

"They hate me, don't they?" he said loudly, staring out the window.

"Yes, some of them do," Kline answered with amusement.

Rosenberg liked to hear that. He smiled and inhaled deeply. Eighty percent of the death threats were aimed at him.

"See any of those signs?" he asked. He was nearly blind.

"Quite a few."

"What do they say?"

"The usual. Death to Rosenberg. Retire Rosenberg. Cut Off the Oxygen."

"They've been waving those same damned signs for years. Why don't they get some new ones?"

The clerk did not answer. Abe should've retired years ago, but they would carry him out one day on a stretcher. His three law clerks did most of the research, but Rosenberg insisted on writing his own opinions. He did so with a heavy felt-tip marker and his words were scrawled across a white legal pad, much like a first-grader learning to write. Slow work, but with a lifetime appointment, who cared about time? The clerks proofed his opinions, and rarely found mistakes.

Rosenberg chuckled. "We oughta feed Runyan to the Indians." The Chief Justice was John Runyan, a tough conservative appointed by a Republican and hated by the Indians and most other minorities. Seven of the nine had been appointed by Republican Presidents. For fifteen years Rosenberg had been waiting for a Democrat in the White House. He wanted to quit, needed to quit, but he could not stomach the idea of a right-wing Runyan type taking his beloved seat.

He could wait. He could sit here in his wheelchair and breathe oxygen and protect the Indians, the blacks, the women, the poor, the handicapped, and the environment until he was a hundred and five. And not a single person in the world could do a damned thing about it, unless they killed him. And that wouldn't be such a bad idea either.

The great man's head nodded, then wobbled and rested on his shoulder. He was asleep again. Kline quietly stepped away, and returned to his research in the library. He would return in half an hour to check the oxygen and give Abe his pills.

THE OFFICE of the Chief Justice is on the main floor, and is larger and more ornate than the other eight. The outer office is used for small receptions and formal gatherings, and the inner office is where the Chief works.

The door to the inner office was closed, and the room was filled with the Chief, his three law clerks, the captain of the Supreme Court police, three FBI agents, and K. O. Lewis, deputy director, FBI. The mood was serious, and a serious effort was under way to ignore the noise from the streets below. It was difficult. The Chief and Lewis discussed the latest series of death threats, and everyone else just listened. The clerks took notes.

In the past sixty days, the Bureau had logged over two hundred threats, a new record. There was the usual assortment of "Bomb the Court!" threats, but many came with specifics—like names, cases, and issues.

Runyan made no effort to hide his anxiety. Working from a confidential FBI summary, he read the names of individuals and groups suspected of threats. The Klan, the Aryans, the Nazis, the Palestinians,

the black separatists, the pró-lifers, the
homophobics. Even the IRA. Everyone, it
seemed, but the Rotarians and the Boy
Scouts. A Middle East group backed by the
Iranians had threatened blood on American soil in retaliation for the deaths of two
justice ministers in Tehran. There was absolutely no evidence the murders were
linked to the U.S. A new domestic terrorist
unit of recent fame known as the Underground Army had killed a federal trial
judge in Texas with a car bomb. No arrests
had been made, but the UA claimed responsibility. It was also the prime suspect
in a dozen bombings of ACLU offices, but
its work was very clean.

"What about these Puerto Rican terrorists?" Runyan asked without looking up.

"Lightweights. We're not worried,"
K. O. Lewis answered casually. "They've
been threatening for twenty years."

"Well, maybe it's time they did something. The climate is right, don't you
think?"

"Forget the Puerto Ricans, Chief." Runyan liked to be called Chief. Not Chief Justice, nor Mr. Chief Justice. Just Chief.
"They're just threatening because everyone else is."

"Very funny," the Chief said without smiling. "Very funny. I'd hate for some group to be left out." Runyan threw the summary on his desk and rubbed his temples. "Let's talk about security." He closed his eyes.

K. O. Lewis laid his copy of the summary on the Chief's desk. "Well, the Director thinks we should place four agents with each Justice, at least for the next ninety days. We'll use limousines with escorts to and from work, and the Supreme Court police will provide backup and secure this building."

"What about travel?"

"It's not a good idea, at least for now. The Director thinks the justices should remain in the D.C. area until the end of the year."

"Are you crazy? Is he crazy? If I asked my brethren to follow that request they would all leave town tonight and travel for the next month. That's absurd." Runyan frowned at his law clerks, who shook their heads in disgust. Truly absurd.

Lewis was unmoved. This was expected. "As you wish. Just a suggestion."

"A foolish suggestion."

"The Director did not expect your cooperation on that one. He would, however, expect to be notified in advance of all travel plans so that we can arrange security."

"You mean, you plan to escort each Justice each time he leaves the city?"

"Yes, Chief. That's our plan."

"Won't work. These people are not accustomed to being baby-sat."

"Yes sir. And they're not accustomed to being stalked either. We're just trying to protect you and your honorable brethren, sir. Of course, no one says we have to do anything. I think, sir, that you called us. We can leave, if you wish."

Runyan rocked forward in his chair and attacked a paper clip, prying the curves out of it and trying to make it perfectly straight. "What about around here?"

Lewis sighed and almost smiled. "We're not worried about this building, Chief. It's an easy place to secure. We don't expect trouble here."

"Then where?"

Lewis nodded at a window. The noise was louder. "Out there somewhere. The streets are full of idiots and maniacs and zealots."

"And they all hate us."

"Evidently. Listen, Chief, we're very con-

cerned about Justice Rosenberg. He still refuses to allow our men inside his home;
makes them sit in a car in the street all
night. He will allow his favorite Supreme
Court officer—what's his name? Ferguson
—to sit by the back door, outside, but only
from 10 P.M. to 6 A.M. No one gets in the
house but Justice Rosenberg and his male
nurse. The place is not secure."

Runyan picked his fingernails with the
paper clip and smiled slightly to himself.
Rosenberg's death, by any means or
method, would be a relief. No, it would be
a glorious occasion. The Chief would have
to wear black and give a eulogy, but behind
locked doors he would chuckle with his law
clerks. Runyan liked this thought.

"What do you suggest?" he asked.

"Can you talk to him?"

"I've tried. I've explained to him that he
is probably the most hated man in America,
that millions of people curse him every
day, that most folks would like to see him
dead, that he receives four times the hate
mail as the rest of us combined, and that he
would be a perfect and easy target for assassination."

Lewis waited. "And?"

"Told me to kiss his ass, then fell asleep."

The law clerks giggled properly, then the FBI agents realized humor was permitted and joined in for a quick laugh.

"So what do we do?" asked Lewis, unamused.

"You protect him as best you can, put it in writing, and don't worry about it. He fears nothing, including death, and if he's not sweating it, why should you?"

"The Director is sweating, so I'm sweating, Chief. It's very simple. If one of you guys gets hurt, the Bureau looks bad."

The Chief rocked quickly in his chair. The racket from outside was unnerving. This meeting had dragged on long enough. "Forget Rosenberg. Maybe he'll die in his sleep. I'm more concerned over Jensen."

"Jensen's a problem," Lewis said, flipping pages.

"I know he's a problem," Runyan said slowly. "He's an embarrassment. Now he thinks he's a liberal. Votes like Rosenberg half the time. Next month, he'll be a white supremacist and support segregated schools. Then he'll fall in love with the Indians and want to give them Montana. It's like having a retarded child."

"He's being treated for depression, you know."

"I know, I know. He tells me about it. I'm his father figure. What drug?"

"Prozac."

The Chief dug under his fingernails. "What about that aerobics instructor he was seeing? She still around?"

"Not really, Chief. I don't think he cares for women." Lewis was smug. He knew more. He glanced at one of his agents and confirmed this juicy little tidbit.

Runyan ignored it, didn't want to hear it. "Is he cooperating?"

"Of course not. In many ways he's worse than Rosenberg. He allows us to escort him to his apartment building, then makes us sit in the parking lot all night. He's seven floors up, remember. We can't even sit in the lobby. Might upset his neighbors, he says. So we sit in the car. There are ten ways in and out of the building, and it's impossible to protect him. He likes to play hide-and-seek with us. He sneaks around all the time, so we never know if he's in the building or not. At least with Rosenberg we know where he is all night. Jensen's impossible."

"Great. If you can't follow him, how could an assassin?"

Lewis hadn't thought of this. He missed the humor. "The Director is very concerned with Justice Jensen's safety."

"He doesn't receive that many threats."

"Number six on the list, just a few less than you, your honor."

"Oh. So I'm in fifth place."

"Yes. Just behind Justice Manning. He's cooperating, by the way. Fully."

"He's afraid of his shadow," the Chief said, then hesitated. "I shouldn't have said that. I'm sorry."

Lewis ignored it. "In fact, the cooperation has been reasonably good, except for Rosenberg and Jensen. Justice Stone bitches a lot, but he listens to us."

"He bitches at everyone, so don't take it personally. Where do you suppose Jensen sneaks off to?"

Lewis glanced at one of his agents. "We have no idea."

A large section of the mob suddenly came together in one unrestrained chorus, and everyone on the streets seemed to join in. The Chief could not ignore it. The windows vibrated. He stood and called an end to this meeting.

JUSTICE GLENN JENSEN'S OFFICE was
on the second floor, away from the streets
and the noise. It was a spacious room, yet
the smallest of the nine. Jensen was the
youngest of the nine, and he was lucky to
have an office. When nominated six years
earlier at the age of forty-two, he was
thought to be a strict constructionist with
deep conservative beliefs, much like the
man who nominated him. His Senate confirmation had been a slugfest. Before the
Judiciary Committee, Jensen performed
poorly. On sensitive issues he straddled the
fence, and got kicked from both sides. The
Republicans were embarrassed. The Democrats smelled blood. The President twisted
arms until they broke, and Jensen was confirmed by one very reluctant vote.

But he made it, for life. In his six years,
he had pleased no one. Hurt deeply by his
confirmation hearings, he vowed to find
compassion and rule with it. This had an-
gered Republicans. They felt betrayed, especially when he discovered a latent passion for the rights of criminals. With scarce
ideological strain, he quickly left the right,
moved to the center, then to the left. Then,
with legal scholars scratching their little

goatees, Jensen would bolt back to the right and join Justice Sloan in one of his obnoxious antiwomen dissents. Jensen was not fond of women. He was neutral on prayer, skeptical of free speech, sympathetic to tax protestors, indifferent to Indians, afraid of blacks, tough on pornographers, soft on criminals, and fairly consistent in his protection of the environment. And, to the further dismay of the Republicans who shed blood to get him confirmed, Jensen had shown a troubling sympathy for the rights of homosexuals.

At his request, a nasty case called *Dumond* had been assigned to him. Ronald Dumond had lived with his male lover for eight years. They were a happy couple, totally devoted to each other, and quite content to share life's experiences. They wanted to marry, but Ohio laws prohibited such a union. Then the lover caught AIDS, and died a horrible death. Ronald knew exactly how to bury him, but then the lover's family intervened and excluded Ronald from the funeral and burial. Distraught, Ronald sued the family, claiming emotional and psychological damage. The case had bounced around the lower courts for six years, and now had suddenly found itself sitting on Jensen's desk.

At issue was the rights of "spouses" of gays. *Dumond* had become a battle cry for gay activists. The mere mention of *Dumond* had caused street fights.

And Jensen had the case. The door to his smaller office was closed. Jensen and his three clerks sat around the conference table. They had spent two hours on *Dumond*, and gone nowhere. They were tired of arguing. One clerk, a liberal from Cornell, wanted a broad pronouncement granting sweeping rights to gay partners. Jensen wanted this too, but was not ready to admit it. The other two clerks were skeptical. They knew, as did Jensen, that a majority of five would be impossible.

Talk turned to other matters.

"The Chief's ticked off at you, Glenn," said the clerk from Duke. They called him by his first name in chambers. "Justice" was such an awkward title.

Glenn rubbed his eyes. "What else is new?"

"One of his clerks wanted me to know that the Chief and the FBI are worried about your safety. Says you're not cooperating, and the Chief's rather disturbed. He wanted me to pass it along." Everything was passed along through the clerks' network. Everything.

"He's supposed to be worried. That's his job."

"He wants to assign two more Fibbies as bodyguards, and they want access to your apartment. And the FBI wants to drive you to and from work. And they want to restrict your travel."

"I've already heard this."

"Yeah, we know. But the Chief's clerk said the Chief wants us to prevail upon you to cooperate with the FBI so that they can save your life."

"I see."

"And so we're just prevailing upon you."

"Thanks. Go back to the network and tell the Chief's clerk that you not only prevailed upon me but you raised all sorts of hell with me and that I appreciated all of your prevailing and hell-raising, but it went in one ear and out the other. Tell them Glenn considers himself a big boy."

"Sure, Glenn. You're not afraid, are you?"

"Not in the least."

TWO

THOMAS CALLAHAN was one of Tulane's more popular professors, primarily because he refused to schedule classes before 11 A.M. He drank a lot, as did most of his students, and for him the first few hours of each morning were needed for sleep, then resuscitation. Nine and ten o'clock classes were abominations. He was also popular because he was cool—faded jeans, tweed jackets with well-worn elbow patches, no socks, no ties. The liberal-chic-academic look. He was forty-five, but with dark hair and horn-rimmed glasses he could pass for thirty-five, not that he gave a damn how old he looked. He shaved once a week, when it started itching; and when the weather was cool, which was seldom in New Orleans, he would grow a beard. He had a history of closeness with female students.

He was also popular because he taught constitutional law, a most unpopular course but a required one. Due to his sheer brilliance and coolness he actually made con law interesting. No one else at Tulane could do this. No one wanted to, really, so the students fought to sit in con law under Callahan at eleven, three mornings a week.

Eighty of them sat behind six elevated rows and whispered as Callahan stood in front of his desk and cleaned his glasses. It was exactly five after eleven, still too early, he thought.

"Who understands Rosenberg's dissent in *Nash v. New Jersey?*" All heads lowered and the room was silent. Must be a bad hangover. His eyes were red. When he started with Rosenberg it usually meant a rough lecture. No one volunteered. *Nash?* Callahan looked slowly, methodically around the room, and waited. Dead silence.

The doorknob clicked loudly and broke the tension. The door opened quickly and an attractive young female in tight washed jeans and a cotton sweater slid elegantly through it and sort of glided along the wall to the third row, where she deftly maneuvered between the crowded seats until she came to hers and sat down. The guys on the fourth row watched in admiration. The guys on the fifth row strained for a peek. For two brutal years now, one of the few pleasures of law school had been to watch as she graced the halls and rooms with her long legs and baggy sweaters. There was a fabulous body in there somewhere, they could tell. But she was not one to flaunt it. She was just one of the gang, and adhered to the law school dress code of jeans and flannel shirts and old sweaters and oversized khakis. What they wouldn't give for a black leather miniskirt.

She flashed a quick smile at the guy seated next to her, and for a second Callahan and his *Nash* question were forgotten. Her dark red hair fell just to the shoulders. She was that perfect little cheerleader with the perfect teeth and perfect hair that every boy fell in love with at least twice in high school. And maybe at least once in law school.

Callahan was ignoring this entry. Had she been a first-year student, and afraid of him, he might have ripped into her and screamed a few times. "You're never late

for court!" was the old standby law professors had beaten to death.

But Callahan was not in a screaming
mood, and Darby Shaw was not afraid of
him, and for a split second he wondered if
anyone knew he was sleeping with her.
Probably not. She had insisted on absolute
secrecy.

"Has anyone read Rosenberg's dissent in
Nash v. New Jersey?" Suddenly, he had the
spotlight again, and there was dead silence.
A raised hand could mean constant grilling
for the next thirty minutes. No volunteers.
The smokers on the back row fired up their
cigarettes. Most of the eighty scribbled aimlessly on legal pads. All heads were bowed.
It would be too obvious and risky to flip
through the casebook and find *Nash;* too
late for that. Any movement might attract
attention. Someone was about to be nailed.

Nash was not in the casebook. It was one
of a dozen minor cases Callahan had hurriedly mentioned a week ago, and now he
was anxious to see if anyone had read it.
He was famous for this. His final exam covered twelve hundred cases, a thousand of
which were not in the casebook. The exam
was a nightmare, but he was really a sweet-

heart, a soft grader, and it was a rare dumbass who flunked the course.

He did not appear to be a sweetheart at this moment. He looked around the room. Time for a victim. "How about it, Mr. Sallinger? Can you explain Rosenberg's dissent?"

Instantly from the fourth row, Sallinger said, "No sir."

"I see. Might that be because you haven't read Rosenberg's dissent?"

"It might. Yes sir."

Callahan glared at him. The red eyes made the arrogant scowl all the more menacing. Only Sallinger saw it though; since everyone else was glued to their legal pads. "And why not?"

"Because I try not to read dissents. Especially Rosenberg's."

Stupid. Stupid. Stupid. Sallinger had opted to fight back, but he had no ammo.

"Something against Rosenberg, Mr. Sallinger?"

Callahan revered Rosenberg. Worshiped him. Read books about the man and his opinions. Studied him. Even dined with him once.

Sallinger fidgeted nervously. "Oh no, sir. I just don't like dissents."

There was a bit of humor in Sallinger's responses, but not a smile was cracked. Later, over a beer, he and his buddies would roar with laughter when it was told and retold about Sallinger and his distaste for dissents, especially Rosenberg's. But not now.

"I see. Do you read majority opinions?"

Hesitation. Sallinger's feeble attempt at sparring was about to cause humiliation. "Yes sir. Lots of them."

"Great. Explain, then, if you will, the majority opinion in *Nash v. New Jersey.*"

Sallinger had never heard of *Nash,* but he would now remember it for the rest of his legal career. "I don't think I've read that one."

"So you don't read dissents, Mr. Sallinger, and now we learn that you also neglect majorities. What do you read, Mr. Sallinger, romance novels, tabloids?"

There was some extremely light laughter from behind the fourth row, and it came from students who felt obligated to laugh but at the same time did not wish to call attention to themselves.

Sallinger, red-faced, just stared at Callahan.

"Why haven't you read the case, Mr. Sallinger?" Callahan demanded.

"I don't know. I, uh, just missed it, I guess."

Callahan took it well. "I'm not surprised. I mentioned it last week. Last Wednesday, to be exact. It'll be on the final exam. I don't understand why you would ignore a case that you'll see on the final." Callahan was pacing now, slowly, in front of his desk, staring at the students. "Did anyone bother to read it?"

Silence. Callahan stared at the floor, and allowed the silence to sink in. All eyes were down, all pens and pencils frozen. Smoke billowed from the back row.

Finally, slowly, from the fourth seat on the third row, Darby Shaw lifted her hand slightly, and the class breathed a collective sigh of relief. She had saved them again. It was sort of expected of her. Number two in their class and within striking distance of number one, she could recite the facts and holdings and concurrences and dissents and majority opinions to virtually every case Callahan could spit at them. She missed nothing. The perfect little cheerleader had graduated magna cum laude with a degree in biology, and planned to graduate magna cum laude with a degree in law, and then make a nice living suing chemical companies for trashing the environment.

Callahan stared at her in mock frustration. She had left his apartment three hours earlier after a long night of wine and law. But he had not mentioned *Nash* to her.

"Well, well, Ms. Shaw. Why is Rosenberg upset?"

"He thinks the New Jersey statute violates the Second Amendment." She did not look at the professor.

"That's good. And for the benefit of the rest of the class, what does the statute do?"

"Outlaws semiautomatic machine guns, among other things."

"Wonderful. And just for fun, what did Mr. Nash possess at the time of his arrest?"

"An AK-47 assault rifle."

"And what happened to him?"

"He was convicted, sentenced to three years, and appealed." She knew the details.

"What was Mr. Nash's occupation?"

"The opinion wasn't specific, but there was mention of an additional charge of drug trafficking. He had no criminal record at the time of his arrest."

"So he was a dope pusher with an AK-47. But he has a friend in Rosenberg, doesn't he?"

"Of course." She was watching him now. The tension had eased. Most eyes followed him as he paced slowly, looking around the room, selecting another victim. More often than not, Darby dominated these lectures, and Callahan wanted a broader participation.

"Why do you suppose Rosenberg is sympathetic?" he asked the class.

"He loves dope pushers." It was Sallinger, wounded but trying to rally. Callahan placed a premium on class discussion. He smiled at his prey, as if to welcome him back to the bloodletting.

"You think so, Mr. Sallinger?"

"Sure. Dope pushers, child fondlers, gunrunners, terrorists. Rosenberg greatly admires these people. They are his weak and abused children, so he must protect them." Sallinger was trying to appear righteously indignant.

"And, in your learned opinion, Mr. Sallinger, what should be done with these people?"

"Simple. They should have a fair trial with a good lawyer, then a fair, speedy appeal, then punished if they are guilty." Sallinger was perilously close to sounding like a law-and-order right-winger, a cardinal sin among Tulane law students.

Callahan folded his arms. "Please continue."

Sallinger smelled a trap, but plowed ahead. There was nothing to lose. "I mean, we've read case after case where Rosenberg has tried to rewrite the Constitution to create a new loophole to exclude evidence to allow an obviously guilty defendant to go free. It's almost sickening. He thinks all prisons are cruel and unusual places, so therefore, under the Eighth Amendment, all prisoners should go free. Thankfully, he's in the minority now, a shrinking minority."

"You like the direction of the Court, do you, Mr. Sallinger?" Callahan was at once smiling and frowning.

"Damned right I do."

"Are you one of those normal, red-blooded, patriotic, middle-of-the-road Americans who wish the old bastard would die in his sleep?"

There were a few chuckles around the room. It was safer to laugh now. Sallinger knew better than to answer truthfully. "I wouldn't wish that on anyone," he said, almost embarrassed.

Callahan was pacing again. "Well, thank you, Mr. Sallinger. I always enjoy your comments. You have, as usual, provided us with the layman's view of the law."

The laughter was much louder. Sallinger's cheeks flushed and he sank in his seat.

Callahan did not smile. "I would like to raise the intellectual level of this discussion, okay. Now, Ms. Shaw, why is Rosenberg sympathetic to Nash?"

"The Second Amendment grants the people the right to keep and bear arms. To Justice Rosenberg, it is literal and absolute. Nothing should be banned. If Nash wants to possess an AK-47, or a hand grenade, or a bazooka, the state of New Jersey cannot pass a law prohibiting it."

"Do you agree with him?"

"No, and I'm not alone. It's an eight-to-one decision. No one followed him."

"What's the rationale of the other eight?"

"It's obvious, really. The states have compelling reasons to prohibit the sale and possession of certain types of arms. The interests of the state of New Jersey outweigh the Second Amendment rights of Mr. Nash. Society cannot allow individuals to own sophisticated weaponry."

Callahan watched her carefully. Attractive female law students were rare at Tulane, but when he found one he moved in quickly. Over the past eight years, he had been quite successful. Easy work, for the most part. The women arrived at law school liberated and loose. Darby had been different. He first spotted her in the library during the second semester of her first year, and it took a month to get her to dinner.

"Who wrote the majority opinion?" he asked her.

"Runyan."

"And you agree with him?"

"Yes. It's an easy case, really."

"Then what happened to Rosenberg?"

"I think he hates the rest of the Court."

"So he dissents just for the hell of it."

"Often, yes. His opinions are becoming more indefensible. Take *Nash*. For a liberal like Rosenberg, the issue of gun control is easy. He should have written the majority opinion, and ten years ago he would have. In *Fordice v. Oregon*, a 1977 case, he took a much narrower interpretation of the Second Amendment. His inconsistencies are almost embarrassing."

Callahan had forgotten *Fordice*. "Are you suggesting Justice Rosenberg is senile?"

Much like a punch-drunk fighter, Sallinger waded in for the final round. "He's crazy as hell, and you know it. You can't defend his opinions."

"Not always, Mr. Sallinger, but at least he's still there."

"His body's there, but he's brain-dead."

"He's breathing, Mr. Sallinger."

"Yeah, breathing with a machine. They have to pump oxygen up his nose."

"But it counts, Mr. Sallinger. He's the last of the great judicial activists, and he's still breathing."

"You'd better call and check," Sallinger said as his words trailed off. He'd said enough. No, he'd said too much. He lowered his head as the professor glared at him. He hunkered down next to his notebook, and started wondering why he'd said all that.

Callahan stared him down, then began pacing again. It was indeed a bad hangover.

THREE

AT LEAST he looked like an old farmer, with straw hat, clean bib overalls, neatly pressed khaki workshirt, boots. He chewed tobacco and spat in the black water beneath the pier. He chewed like a farmer. His pickup, though of recent model, was sufficiently weathered and had a dusty-road look about it. North Carolina plates. It was a hundred yards away, parked in the sand at the other end of the pier.

It was midnight Monday, the first Monday in October, and for the next thirty minutes he was to wait in the dark coolness of the deserted pier, chewing pensively, resting on the railing while staring intently at the sea. He was alone, as he knew he would be. It was planned that way. This pier at this hour was always deserted. The

31

headlights of an occasional car flickered along the shoreline, but the headlights never stopped at this hour.

He watched the red and blue channel lights far from shore. He checked his watch without moving his head. The clouds were low and thick, and it would be difficult to see it until it was almost to the pier. It was planned this way.

The pickup was not from North Carolina, and neither was the farmer. The license plates had been stolen from a wrecked truck at a scrap yard near Durham. The pickup had been stolen in Baton Rouge. The farmer was not from anywhere, and performed none of the thievery. He was a pro, and so someone else did the dirty little deeds.

Twenty minutes into the wait, a dark object floated in the direction of the pier. A quiet, muffled engine hummed and grew louder. The object became a small craft of some sort with a camouflaged silhouette crouching low and working the motor. The farmer moved not an inch in anticipation. The humming stopped and the black rubber raft stalled in the calm water thirty feet from the pier. There were no headlights coming or going along the shore.

The farmer carefully placed a cigarette between his lips, lit it, puffed twice, then thumped it down, halfway to the raft.

"What kind of cigarette?" the man on the water asked upward. He could see the outline of the farmer on the railing, but not the face.

"Lucky Strike," the farmer answered. These passwords made for such a silly game. How many other black rubber rafts could be expected to drift in from the Atlantic and pinpoint this ancient pier at this precise hour? Silly, but oh so important.

"Luke?" came the voice from the boat.

"Sam," replied the farmer. The name was Khamel, not Sam, but Sam would do for the next five minutes until Khamel parked his raft.

Khamel did not answer, was not required to, but quickly started the engine and guided the raft along the edge of the pier to the beach. Luke followed from above. They met at the pickup without a handshake. Khamel placed his black Adidas gym bag between them on the seat, and the truck started along the shoreline.

Luke drove and Khamel smoked, and both did a perfect job of ignoring each other. Their eyes did not dare meet. With

Khamel's heavy beard, dark glasses, and black turtleneck, his face was ominous but impossible to identify. Luke did not want to see it. Part of his assignment, in addition to receiving this stranger from the sea, was to refrain from looking at him. It was easy, really. The face was wanted in nine countries.

Across the bridge at Manteo, Luke lit another Lucky Strike and determined they had met before. It had been a brief but precisely timed meeting at the airport in Rome, five or six years earlier, as best he could remember. There had been no introductions. It took place in a restroom. Luke, then an impeccably tailored American executive, had placed an eelskin attaché case next to the wall next to the washbasin where he slowly rinsed his hands, and suddenly it was gone. He caught a glimpse of the man—this Khamel, he was now certain —in the mirror. Thirty minutes later, the attaché case exploded between the legs of the British ambassador to Nigeria.

In the guarded whispers of his invisible brotherhood, Luke had often heard of Khamel, a man of many names and faces and languages, an assassin who struck quickly and left no trail, a fastidious killer

34

who roamed the world but could never be found. As they rode north in the darkness, Luke settled low in his seat, the brim of his hat almost on his nose, limp wrist across the wheel, trying to remember the stories he'd heard about his passenger. Amazing feats of terror. There was the British ambassador. The ambush of seventeen Israeli soldiers on the West Bank in 1990 had been credited to Khamel. He was the only suspect in the 1985 car-bomb murders of a wealthy German banker and his family. His fee for that one was rumored to have been three million, cash. Most intelligence experts believed he was the mastermind of the 1981 attempt to kill the Pope. But then, Khamel was blamed for almost every unsolved terrorist attack and assassination. He was easy to blame because no one was certain he existed.

This excited Luke. Khamel was about to perform on American soil. The targets were unknown to Luke, but important blood was about to be shed.

AT DAWN, the stolen farm truck stopped at the corner of Thirty-first and M streets in Georgetown. Khamel grabbed his gym bag, said nothing, and hit the sidewalk. He walked east a few blocks to the Four Seasons Hotel, bought a *Post* in the lobby, and casually rode the elevator to the seventh floor. At precisely seven-fifteen, he knocked on a door at the end of the hall. "Yes?" a nervous voice asked from inside.

"Looking for Mr. Sneller," Khamel said slowly in a perfect generic American tongue as he stuck his thumb over the peephole.

"Mr. Sneller?"

"Yes. Edwin F. Sneller."

The knob did not turn or click, and the door did not open. A few seconds passed, and a white envelope eased from under the door. Khamel picked it up. "Okay," he said loud enough for Sneller or whoever he was to hear.

"It's next door," Sneller said. "I'll await your call." He sounded like an American. Unlike Luke, he'd never seen Khamel, and had no desire to, really. Luke had seen him twice now, and was indeed lucky to be alive.

Khamel's room had two beds and a small table near the window. The shades were drawn tightly; no chance of sunlight. He placed his gym bag on one bed, next to two thick briefcases. He walked to the window and peeked out, then to the phone.

"It's me," he said to Sneller. "Tell me about the car."

"It's parked on the street. Plain white Ford with Connecticut plates. The keys are on the table." Sneller spoke slowly.

"Stolen?"

"Of course, but sanitized. It's clean."

"I'll leave it at Dulles shortly after midnight. I want it destroyed, okay?" The English was perfect.

"Those are my instructions. Yes." Sneller was proper and efficient.

"It's very important, okay? I intend to leave the gun in the car. Guns leave bullets and people see cars, so it's important to completely destroy the car and everything in it. Understand?"

"Those are my instructions," Sneller repeated. He did not appreciate this lecture. He was no novice at the killing game.

Khamel sat on the edge of the bed. "The four million was received a week ago, a day late I should add. I'm now in D.C., so I want the next three."

"It will be wired before noon. That was the agreement."

"Yes, but I'm worried about the agreement. You were a day late, remember?"

This irritated Sneller, and since the killer was in the next room and not about to come out, he could sound a bit irritated. "The bank's fault, not ours."

This irritated Khamel. "Fine. I want you and your bank to wire the next three million to the account in Zurich as soon as New York opens. That will be about two hours from now. I'll be checking."

"Okay."

"Okay, and I want no problem when the job is finished. I'll be in Paris in twenty-four hours, and from there I'll go straight to Zurich. I want all the money waiting for me when I arrive."

"It will be there, if the job is finished."

Khamel smiled to himself. "The job will be finished, Mr. Sneller, by midnight. That is, if your information is correct."

"As of now it is correct. And no changes are expected today. Our people are in the streets. Everything is in the two briefcases; maps, diagrams, schedules, the tools and articles you requested."

Khamel glanced at the briefcases behind him. He rubbed his eyes with his right hand. "I need a nap," he mumbled into the phone. "I haven't slept in twenty hours."

Sneller could think of no response. There was plenty of time, and if Khamel wanted a nap, then Khamel could have a nap. They were paying him ten million.

"Would you like something to eat?" Sneller asked awkwardly.

"No. Call me in three hours, at precisely ten-thirty." He placed the receiver on the phone, and stretched across the bed.

THE STREETS were clear and quiet for day two of the fall term. The justices spent their day on the bench listening to lawyer after lawyer argue complex and quite dull cases. Rosenberg slept through most of it. He came to life briefly when the attorney general from Texas argued that a certain death-row inmate should be given medication to make him lucid before being lethally injected. If he's mentally ill, how can he be executed? Rosenberg asked incredulously. Easy, said the AG from Texas, his illness can be controlled with medication. So just give him a little shot to make him sane, then give him another shot to kill him. It could all be very nice and constitutional. Rosenberg harangued and bitched for a brief spell, then lost steam. His little wheelchair sat much lower than the massive leather thrones of his brethren. He looked rather pitiful. In years past he was a tiger, a ruthless intimidator who tied even the slickest lawyers in knots. But no more. He began to mumble, and then faded away. The AG sneered at him, and continued.

During the last oral argument of the day, a lifeless desegregation case from Virginia, Rosenberg began snoring. Chief Runyan glared down the bench, and Jason Kline, Rosenberg's senior clerk, took the hint. He slowly pulled the wheelchair backward, away from the bench, and out of the courtroom. He pushed it quickly through the back hallway.

The Justice regained consciousness in his office, took his pills, and informed his clerks he wanted to go home. Kline notified the FBI, and moments later Rosenberg was wheeled into the rear of his van, parked in the basement. Two FBI agents watched. A male nurse, Frederic, strapped the wheelchair in place, and Sergeant Ferguson of the Supreme Court police slid behind the wheel of the van. The Justice allowed no FBI agents near him. They could follow in their car, and they could watch his townhouse from the street, and they were lucky to get that close. He didn't trust cops, and he damned sure didn't trust FBI agents. He didn't need protection.

On Volta Street in Georgetown, the van slowed and backed into a short driveway. Frederic the nurse and Ferguson the cop gently rolled him inside. The agents watched from the street in their black government-issue Dodge Aries. The lawn in front of the townhome was tiny and their car was a few feet from the front door. It was almost 4 P.M.

After a few minutes, Ferguson made his mandatory exit and spoke to the agents. After much debate, Rosenberg had acquiesced a week earlier and allowed Ferguson to quietly inspect each room upstairs and down upon his arrival in the afternoons. Then Ferguson had to leave, but could return at exactly 10 P.M. and sit outside the rear door until exactly 6 A.M. No one but Ferguson could do it, and he was tired of the overtime.

"Everything's fine," he said to the agents. "I guess I'll be back at ten."

"Is he still alive?" one of the agents asked. Standard question.

"Afraid so." Ferguson looked tired as he walked to the van.

Frederic was chubby and weak, but strength was not needed to handle his patient. After arranging the pillows just so, he lifted him from the wheelchair and placed him carefully on the sofa, where he would remain motionless for the next two hours while dozing and watching CNN. Frederic fixed himself a ham sandwich and a plate of cookies, and scanned a *National Enquirer* at the kitchen table. Rosenberg mumbled something loudly and changed channels with the remote control.

At precisely seven, his dinner of chicken bouillon, boiled potatoes, and stewed onions—stroke food—was placed neatly on the table, and Frederic rolled him up to it. He insisted on feeding himself, and it was not pretty. Frederic watched television. He would clean up the mess later.

By nine, he was bathed, dressed in a gown, and tucked tightly under the covers. The bed was a narrow, reclining, pale green army-hospital job with a hard mattress, push-button controls, and collapsible rails that Rosenberg insisted remain down. It was in a room behind the kitchen that he had used as a small study for thirty years, before the first stroke. The room was now clinical, and smelled of antiseptic and looming death. Next to his bed was a large table with a hospital lamp and at least twenty bottles of pills. Thick, heavy law books were stacked in neat piles around the room. Next to the table, the nurse sat close by in a worn recliner, and began reading from a brief. He would read until he heard snoring—the nightly ritual. He read slowly, yelling the words at Rosenberg, who was stiff, motionless, but listening. The brief was from a case in which he would write the majority opinion. He absorbed every word, for a while.

After an hour of reading and yelling, Frederic was tired and the Justice was drifting away. He raised his hand slightly, then closed his eyes. With a button on the bed, he lowered the lights. The room was almost dark. Frederic jerked backward, and the recliner unfolded. He laid the brief on the floor, and closed his eyes. Rosenberg was snoring.

He would not snore for long.

SHORTLY AFTER TEN, with the house dark and quiet, the door to a bedroom closet upstairs opened slightly, and Khamel

43

eased out. His wristbands, nylon cap, and running shorts were royal blue. His long-sleeved shirt, socks, and Reeboks were white with royal trim. Perfect color coordination. Khamel the jogger. He was clean shaven, and under the cap his very short hair was now blond, almost white.

The bedroom was dark, as was the hall. The stairs creaked slightly under the Reeboks. He was five-ten, and weighed less than a hundred and fifty pounds, with no fat. He kept himself taut and light so the movements would be quick and soundless. The stairs landed in a foyer not far from the front door. He knew there were two agents in a car by the curb, probably not watching the house. He knew Ferguson had arrived seven minutes ago. He could hear the snoring from the back room. While waiting in the closet, he had thought of striking earlier, before Ferguson arrived so he wouldn't have to kill him. The killing was no problem, but it created another body to worry about. But he guessed, wrongly, that Ferguson probably checked in with the male nurse when he came on duty. If so, then Ferguson would find the carnage and Khamel would lose a few hours. So he waited until now.

He slid through the foyer without a sound. In the kitchen, a small light from the Ventahood illuminated the countertop and made things a bit more dangerous. Khamel cursed himself for not checking the bulb and unscrewing it. Those small mistakes were inexcusable. He dipped under a window looking into the backyard. He could not see Ferguson, although he knew he was seventy-four inches tall, sixty-one years old, had cataracts, and couldn't hit a barn with his .357 magnum.

Both of them were snoring. Khamel smiled to himself as he crouched in the doorway and quickly pulled the .22 automatic and silencer from the Ace bandage wrapped around his waist. He screwed the four-inch tube onto the barrel, and ducked into the room. The nurse was sprawled deep in the recliner, feet in the air, hands dangling, mouth open. Khamel placed the tip of the silencer an inch from his right temple and fired three times. The hands flinched and the feet jerked, but the eyes remained closed. Khamel quickly reached across to the wrinkled and pale head of Justice Abraham Rosenberg, and pumped three bullets into it.

The room had no windows. He watched

the bodies and listened for a full minute. The nurse's heels twitched a few times, then stopped. The bodies were still.

He wanted to kill Ferguson inside. It was eleven minutes after ten, a good time for a neighbor to be out with the dog for one last time before bed. He crept through the darkness to the rear door and spotted the cop strolling benignly along the wooden fence twenty feet away. Instinctively, Khamel opened the back door, turned on the patio light, and said "Ferguson" loudly.

He left the door open and hid in a dark corner next to the refrigerator. Ferguson obediently lumbered across the small patio and into the kitchen. This was not unusual. Frederic often called him in after His Honor was asleep. They would drink instant coffee and play gin rummy.

There was no coffee, and Frederic was not waiting. Khamel fired three bullets into the back of his head, and he fell loudly on the kitchen table.

He turned out the patio light and unscrewed the silencer. He would not need it again. It and the pistol were stuffed into the Ace bandage. Khamel peeked out the front window. The dome light was on and the agents were reading. He stepped over

Ferguson, locked the back door, and disappeared into the darkness of the small rear lawn. He jumped two fences without a sound, and found the street. He began trotting. Khamel the jogger.

IN THE DARK BALCONY of the Montrose Theatre, Glenn Jensen sat by himself and watched the naked and quite active men on the screen below. He ate popcorn from a large box and noticed nothing but the bodies. He was dressed conservatively enough; navy cardigan, chinos, loafers. And wide sunglasses to hide his eyes and a suede fedora to cover his head. He was blessed with a face that was easily forgotten, and once camouflaged it could never be recognized. Especially in a deserted balcony of a near-empty gay porno house at midnight. No earrings, bandannas, gold chains, jewelry, nothing to indicate he was in the market for a companion. He wanted to be ignored.

It had become a challenge, really, this cat-and-mouse game with the FBI and the rest of the world. On this night, they had dutifully stationed themselves in the parking lot outside his building. Another pair parked by the exit near the veranda in the rear, and he allowed them all to sit for four and a half hours before he disguised himself and walked nonchalantly to the garage in the basement and drove away in a friend's car. The building had too many points of egress for the poor Fibbies to monitor him. He was sympathetic to a point, but he had his life to live. If the Fibbies couldn't find him, how could a killer?

The balcony was divided into three small sections with six rows each. It was very dark, the only light being the heavy blue stream from the projector behind. Broken seats and folded tables were piled along the outside aisles. The velvet drapes along the walls were shredded and falling. It was a marvelous place to hide.

He used to worry about getting caught. In the months after his confirmation, he was terrified. He couldn't eat his popcorn, and damned sure couldn't enjoy the movies. He told himself that if he was caught or recognized, or in some awful way exposed, he would simply claim he was doing research for an obscenity case pending. There was always one on the docket, and maybe somehow this might be believed. This excuse could work, he told himself repeatedly, and he grew bolder. But one night in 1990, a theater caught fire, and four people died. Their names were in the paper. Big story. Justice Glenn Jensen happened to be in the rest room when he heard the screams and smelled the smoke. He rushed into the street and disappeared. The dead were all found in the balcony. He knew one of them. He gave up movies for two months, but then started back. He needed more research, he told himself.

And what if he got caught? The appointment was for life. The voters couldn't call him home.

He liked the Montrose because on Tuesdays the movies ran all night, but there was never a crowd. He liked the popcorn, and draft beer cost fifty cents.

Two old men in the center section groped and fondled each other. Jensen glanced at them occasionally, but concentrated on the movie. Sad, he thought, to be seventy years old, staring at death and dodging AIDS, and banished to a dirty balcony to find happiness.

A fourth person soon joined them on the balcony. He glanced at Jensen and the two men locked together, and he walked quietly with his draft beer and popcorn to the top row of the center section. The projector room was directly behind him. To his right and down three rows sat the Justice. In front of him, the gray and mature lovers kissed and whispered and giggled, oblivious to the world.

He was dressed appropriately. Tight jeans, black silk shirt, earring, horn-rimmed shades, and the neatly trimmed hair and mustache of a regular gay. Khamel the homosexual.

He waited a few minutes, then eased to his right and sat by the aisle. No one noticed. Who would care where he sat?

At twelve-twenty, the old men lost steam. They stood, arm in arm, and tiptoed away, still whispering and snickering. Jensen did not look at them. He was engrossed in the movie, a massive orgy on a yacht in the middle of a hurricane. Khamel moved like a cat across the narrow aisle to a seat three rows behind the Justice. He sipped the beer. They were alone. He waited for one minute, and quickly moved down a row. Jensen was eight feet away.

As the hurricane intensified, so did the orgy. The roar of the wind and the screams of the partyers deafened the small theater. Khamel set the beer and popcorn on the floor, and pulled a three-foot strand of yellow nylon ski rope from his waist. He quickly wrapped the ends around both hands, and stepped over the row of chairs in front of him. His prey was breathing heavy. The popcorn box was shaking.

The attack was quick and brutal. Khamel looped the rope just under the larynx, and wrenched it violently. He yanked the rope downward, snapping the head over the back of the seat. The neck broke cleanly. He twisted the rope and tied it behind the neck. He slid a six-inch steel rod through a loop in the knot, and wound the tourniquet until the flesh tore and started to bleed. It was over in ten seconds.

Suddenly the hurricane was over and another orgy began in celebration. Jensen slumped in his seat. His popcorn was scattered around his shoes. Khamel was not one to admire his handiwork. He left the balcony, walked casually through the racks of magazines and devices in the lobby, then disappeared onto the sidewalk.

He drove the generic white Ford with Connecticut plates to Dulles, changed clothes in a rest room, and waited on his flight to Paris.

FOUR

THE FIRST LADY was on the West Coast attending a series of five-thousand-dollars-a-plate breakfasts where the rich and pretentious gladly shucked out the money for cold eggs and cheap champagne, and the chance to be seen and maybe photographed with the Queen, as she was known. So the President was sleeping alone when the phone rang. In the great tradition of American Presidents, he had in years past thought of keeping a mistress. But now it seemed so non-Republican. Besides, he was old and tired. He often slept alone when the Queen was at the White House.

He was a heavy sleeper. It rang twelve times before he heard it. He grabbed it and stared at the clock. Four-thirty A.M. He listened to the voice, jumped to his feet, and eight minutes later was in the Oval Office. No shower, no tie. He stared at Fletcher Coal, his chief of staff, and sat properly behind his desk.

Coal was smiling. His perfect teeth and bald head were shining. Only thirty-seven, he was the boy wonder who four years earlier had rescued a failing campaign and placed his boss in the White House. He was a guileful manipulator and a nasty henchman who had cut and clawed his way through the inner circle until he was now second in command. Many viewed him as the real boss. The mere mention of his name terrified lowly staffers.

"What happened?" the President asked slowly.

Coal paced in front of the President's desk. "Don't know much. They're both dead. Two FBI agents found Rosenberg around 1 A.M. Dead in bed. His nurse and a Supreme Court policeman were also murdered. All three shot in the head. A very clean job. While the FBI and D.C. police were investigating, they got a call that Jensen had been found dead in some queer club. They found him a couple of hours ago. Voyles called me at four, and I called you. He and Gminski should be here in a minute."

"Gminski?"

"The CIA should be included, at least for now."

The President folded his hands behind his head and stretched. "Rosenberg is dead."

"Yes. Quite. I suggest you address the nation in a couple of hours. Mabry is working on a rough draft. I'll finish it. Let's wait until daylight, at least seven. If not, it'll be too early and we'll lose much of our audience."

"The press—"

"Yes. It's out. They filmed the ambulance crew rolling Jensen into the morgue."

"I didn't know he was gay."

"Not much doubt about it now. This is the perfect crisis, Mr. President. Think of it. We didn't create it. It's not our fault. No one can blame us. And the nation will be shocked into some degree of solidarity. It's rally around the leader time. It's just great. No downside."

The President sipped a cup of coffee and stared at the papers on his desk. "And I'll get to restructure the Court."

"That's the best part. It'll be your legacy. I've already called Duvall at Justice and instructed him to contact Horton and begin a preliminary list of nominees. Horton gave a speech in Omaha last night, but he's flying in now. I suggest we meet with him later this morning."

The President nodded with his customary approval of Coal's suggestions. He allowed Coal to sweat the details. He had never been a detail man himself. "Any suspects?"

"Not yet. I don't know, really. I told Voyles that you would expect a briefing when he arrived."

"I thought someone said the FBI was protecting the Supreme Court."

Coal smiled wider and chuckled. "Exactly. The egg is on Voyles' face. It's quite embarrassing, really."

"Great. I want Voyles to get his share of the blame. Take care of the press. I want him humiliated. Then maybe we can run his ass off."

Coal loved this thought. He stopped pacing and scribbled a note on his legal pad. A security guard knocked on the door, then opened it. Directors Voyles and Gminski entered together. The mood was suddenly somber as all four shook hands. The two sat before the President's desk as Coal took his customary position standing near a window, to the side of the President. He hated Voyles and Gminski, and they hated him. Coal thrived on hatred. He had the President's ear, and that was all that mattered. He would become quiet for a few minutes. It was important to allow the President to take charge when others were present.

"I'm very sorry you're here, but thanks for coming," the President said. They nodded grimly and acknowledged this obvious lie. "What happened?"

Voyles spoke quickly and to the point. He described the scene at Rosenberg's home when the bodies were found. At 1 A.M. each night, Sergeant Ferguson routinely checked in with the agents sitting in the street. When he didn't show, they investigated. The killings were very clean and professional. He described what he knew about Jensen. Broken neck. Strangulation. Found by another character in the balcony. No one saw anything, evidently. Voyles was not as gruff and blunt as usual. It was a dark day for the Bureau, and he could feel the heat coming. But he'd survived five Presidents, and he could certainly outmaneuver this idiot.

"The two are obviously related," the President said, staring at Voyles.

"Maybe. Certainly looks that way, but—"

"Come on, Director. In two hundred and twenty years, we've assassinated four Presidents, two or three candidates, a handful of civil rights leaders, couple of governors, but never a Supreme Court Justice. And now, in one night, within two hours, two are assassinated. And you're not convinced they're related?"

"I didn't say that. There must be a link somewhere. It's just that the methods were so different. And so professional. You must remember, we've had thousands of threats against the Court."

"Fine. Then who are your suspects?"

No one cross-examined F. Denton Voyles. He glared at the President. "It's too early for suspects. We're still gathering evidence."

"How'd the killer get into Rosenberg's place?"

"No one knows. We didn't watch him go in, you understand? Evidently, he was there for some time, hiding in a closet or an attic, maybe. Again, we weren't invited.

Rosenberg refused to allow us into his home. Ferguson routinely inspected the place each afternoon when the Justice arrived from work. It's still too early, but we've found no evidence of the murderer. None, except three bodies. We'll have ballistics and autopsies by late this afternoon."

"I want to see them here as soon as you have them."

"Yes, Mr. President."

"I also want a short list of suspects by 5 P.M. today. Is that clear?"

"Certainly, Mr. President."

"And I would like a report on your security and where it broke down."

"You're assuming it broke down."

"We have two dead judges, both of whom were being protected by the FBI. I think the American people deserve to know what went wrong, Director. Yes, it broke down."

"Do I report to you, or the American people?"

"You report to me."

"And then you call a press conference and report to the American people, right?"

"Are you afraid of the scrutiny, Director?"

"Not one bit. Rosenberg and Jensen are

58

dead because they refused to cooperate with us. They were very much aware of the danger, yet they couldn't be bothered. The other seven are cooperating, and they're still alive."

"For the moment. We'd better check. They're dropping like flies." The President smiled at Coal, who snickered and almost sneered at Voyles. Coal decided it was time to speak. "Director, did you know Jensen was hanging around such places?"

"He was a grown man with a lifetime appointment. If he chose to dance naked on tables we couldn't stop him."

"Yes sir," Coal said politely. "But you didn't answer my question."

Voyles breathed deeply and looked away. "Yes. We suspected he was a homosexual, and we knew he liked certain movie houses. We have neither the authority nor the desire, Mr. Coal, to divulge such information."

"I want those reports by this afternoon," the President said. Voyles was watching a window, listening but not responding. The President looked at Robert Gminski, director of the CIA. "Bob, I want a straight answer."

Gminski tightened and frowned. "Yes sir. What is it?"

"I want to know if these killings are in any way linked to any agency, operation, group, whatever, of the United States Government."

"Come on! Are you serious, Mr. President! That's absurd." Gminski appeared to be shocked, but the President, Coal, even Voyles, knew anything was possible these days at the CIA.

"Dead serious, Bob."

"I'm serious too. And I assure you we had nothing to do with it. I'm shocked you would even think it. Ridiculous!"

"Check it out, Bob. I want to be damned certain. Rosenberg did not believe in national security. He made thousands of enemies in intelligence. Just check it out, okay."

"Okay, okay."

"And I want a report by five today."

"Sure. Okay. But it's a waste of time."

Fletcher Coal moved to the desk next to the President. "I suggest we meet here at five this afternoon, gentlemen. Is that agreeable?"

They both nodded and stood. Coal escorted them to the door without a word. He closed it.

"You handled it real well," he said to the President. "Voyles knows he's vulnerable. I smell blood. We'll go to work on him with the press."

"Rosenberg is dead," the President repeated to himself. "I just can't believe it."

"I've got an idea for television." Coal was pacing again, very much in charge. "We need to cash in on the shock of it all. You need to appear tired, as if you were up all night handling the crisis. Right? The entire nation will be watching, waiting for you to give details and to reassure. I think you should wear something warm and comforting. A coat and tie at 7 A.M. may seem a bit rehearsed. Let's relax a little."

The President was listening intently. "A bathrobe?"

"Not quite. But how about a cardigan and slacks? No tie. White button-down. Sort of the grandfather image."

"You want me to address the nation in this hour of crisis in a sweater?"

"Yes. I like it. A brown cardigan with a white shirt."

"I don't know."

"The image is good. Look, Chief, the

election is a year from next month. This is our first crisis in ninety days, and what a wonderful crisis it is. The people need to see you in something different, especially at seven in the morning. You need to look casual, down-home, but in control. It'll be worth five, maybe ten points in the ratings. Trust me, Chief."

"I don't like sweaters."

"Just trust me."

"I don't know."

FIVE

DARBY SHAW awoke in the early darkness with a touch of a hangover. After fifteen months of law school, her mind refused to rest for more than six hours. She was often up before daybreak, and for this reason she did not sleep well with Callahan. The sex was great, but sleep was often a tug-of-war with pillows and sheets pulled back and forth.

She watched the ceiling and listened to him snore occasionally in his Scotch-induced coma. The sheets were wrapped like ropes around his knees. She had no cover, but she was not cold. October in New Orleans is still muggy and warm. The heavy air rose from Dauphine Street below, across the small balcony outside the bedroom and through the open french doors. It brought with it the first stream of morning light. She stood in the doors and covered herself with his terry-cloth robe. The sun was rising, but Dauphine was dark. Daybreaks went unnoticed in the French Quarter. Her mouth was dry.

Downstairs in the kitchen, Darby brewed a pot of thick French Market chicory. The blue numbers on the microwave said it was now ten minutes before six. For a light drinker, life with Callahan was a constant struggle. Her limit was three glasses of wine. She had neither a law license nor a job, and she could not afford to get drunk every night and sleep late. And she weighed a hundred and twelve pounds and was determined to keep it there. He had no limit.

She drank three glasses of ice water, then poured a tall mug full of chicory. She flipped on lights as she climbed the stairs, and eased back into the bed. She flicked the remote controls, and suddenly, there was the President sitting behind his desk looking somehow rather odd in a brown cardigan with no tie. It was an NBC News special report.

"Thomas!" She slapped him on his shoulder. No movement. "Thomas! Wake up!" She pressed a button and the volume roared. The President said good morning.

"Thomas!" She leaned toward the television. Callahan kicked at the sheets and sat up, rubbing his eyes and trying to focus. She handed him the coffee.

The President had tragic news. His eyes were tired and he looked sad, but the rich baritone exuded confidence. He had notes but didn't use them. He looked deep into the camera, and explained to the American people the shocking events of last night.

"What the hell," Callahan mumbled. After announcing the deaths, the President launched into a flowery obituary for Abraham Rosenberg. A towering legend, he called him. It was a strain, but the President kept a straight face while lauding the distinguished career of one of the most hated men in America.

Callahan gaped at the television. Darby stared at it. "That's very touching," she said. She was frozen on the end of the bed. He had been briefed by the FBI and CIA, he explained, and they were assuming the killings were related. He had ordered an immediate, thorough investigation, and those responsible would be brought to justice.

Callahan sat upright and covered himself with the sheets. He blinked his eyes and combed his wild hair with his fingers. "Rosenberg? Murdered?" he mumbled, glaring at the screen. His foggy head had cleared immediately, and the pain was there but he couldn't feel it.

"Check out the sweater," Darby said, sipping the coffee, staring at the orange face with heavy makeup and the brilliant silver hair plastered carefully in place. He was a wonderfully handsome man with a soothing voice; thus he had succeeded greatly in politics. The wrinkles in his forehead squeezed together, and he was even sadder now as he talked of his close friend Justice Glenn Jensen.

"The Montrose Theatre, at midnight," Callahan repeated.

"Where is it?" she asked. Callahan had finished law school at Georgetown.

"Not sure. But I think it's in the gay section."

"Was he gay?"

"I've heard rumors. Evidently." They were both sitting on the end of the bed with the sheets over their legs. The President was ordering a week of national mourning. Flags at half-staff. Federal of-

fices closed tomorrow. Funeral arrangements were incomplete. He rambled for a
few more minutes, still deeply saddened,
even shocked, very human, but nonethe-
less the President and clearly in charge. He
signed off with his patented grandfather's
smile of complete trust and wisdom and re-
assurance.

An NBC reporter on the White House
lawn appeared and filled in the gaps. The
police were mute, but there appeared to be
no suspects at the moment, and no leads.
Yes, both justices had been under the protection of the FBI, which had no comment.
Yes, the Montrose was a place frequented
by homosexuals. Yes, there had been many
threats against both men, especially Rosenberg. And there could be many suspects before it was all over.

Callahan turned off the set and walked
to the french doors, where the early air was
growing thicker. "No suspects," he mumbled.

"I can think of at least twenty," Darby
said.

"Yeah, but why the combination? Rosenberg is easy, but why Jensen? Why not Mc-
Dowell or Yount, both of whom are consis-
tently more liberal than Jensen? It doesn't

make sense." Callahan sat in a wicker chair by the doors and fluffed his hair.

"I'll get you some more coffee," Darby said.

"No, no. I'm awake."

"How's your head?"

"Fine, if I could've slept for three more hours. I think I'll cancel class. I'm not in the mood."

"Great."

"Damn, I can't believe this. That fool has two nominations. That means eight of the nine will be Republican choices."

"They have to be confirmed first."

"We won't recognize the Constitution in ten years. This is sick."

"That's why they were killed, Thomas. Someone or some group wants a different Court, one with an absolute conservative majority. The election is next year. Rosenberg is, or was, ninety-one. Manning is eighty-four. Yount is early eighties. They could die soon, or live ten more years. A Democrat may be elected President. Why take a chance? Kill them now, a year before the election. Makes perfect sense, if one was so inclined."

"But why Jensen?"

"He was an embarrassment. And, obviously, he was an easier target."

"Yes, but he was basically a moderate with an occasional leftward impulse. And he was nominated by a Republican."

"You want a Bloody Mary?"

"Good idea. In a minute. I'm trying to think."

Darby reclined on the bed, sipped the coffee, and watched the sunlight filter across the balcony. "Think of it, Thomas. The timing is beautiful. Reelection, nominations, politics, all that. But think of the violence and the radicals, the zealots, the pro-lifers and gay haters, the Aryans and Nazis, think of all the groups capable of killing, and all the threats against the Court, and the timing is perfect for an unknown, inconspicuous group to knock them off. It's morbid, but the timing is great."

"And who is such a group?"

"Who knows?"

"The Underground Army?"

"They're not exactly inconspicuous. They killed Judge Fernandez in Texas."

"Don't they use bombs?"

"Yeah, experts with plastic explosives."

"Scratch them."

"I'm not scratching anybody right now."
Darby stood and retied the robe. "Come
on. I'll fix you a Bloody Mary."

"Only if you drink with me."

"Thomas, you're a professor. You can
cancel your classes if you want to. I am a
student and—"

"I understand the relationship."

"I cannot cut any more classes."

"I'll flunk you in con law if you don't cut
classes and get drunk with me. I've got a
book of Rosenberg opinions. Let's read
them, sip Bloody Marys, then wine, then
whatever. I miss him already."

"I have Federal Procedure at nine, and I
can't miss it."

"I intend to call the dean and have all
classes canceled. Then will you drink with
me?"

"No. Come on, Thomas." He followed
her down the stairs to the kitchen and the
coffee and the liquor.

SIX

WITHOUT REMOVING the receiver from his shoulder, Fletcher Coal punched another button on the phone on the desk in the Oval Office. Three lines were blinking, holding. He paced slowly in front of the desk and listened while scanning a two-page report from Horton at Justice. He ignored the President, who was crouched in front of the windows, gripping his putter with gloved hands, staring fiercely first at the yellow ball, then slowly across the blue carpet to the brass putting cup ten feet away. Coal growled something into the receiver. His words were unheard by the President, who lightly tapped the ball and watched it roll precisely into the cup. The cup clicked, cleared itself, and the ball rolled three feet to the side. The President inched forward in his socks to the next ball, and breathed downward at it. It was an orange one. He tapped it just so, and it rolled straight into the cup. Eight in a row. Twenty-seven out of thirty.

"That was Chief Runyan," Coal said, slamming the receiver down. "He's quite upset. He wanted to meet with you this afternoon."

"Tell him to take a number."

"I told him to be here at ten tomorrow morning. You have the Cabinet at ten-thirty, and National Security at eleven-thirty."

Without looking up, the President gripped the putter and studied the next ball. "I can't wait. What about the polls?" He swung carefully and followed the ball.

"I just talked to Nellson. He ran two, beginning at noon. The computer is digesting it now, but he thinks the approval rating will be somewhere around fifty-two or fifty-three."

The golfer looked up briefly and smiled, then returned to his game. "What was it last week?"

"Forty-four. It was the cardigan without the tie. Just like I said."

"I thought it was forty-five," he said as

he tapped a yellow one and watched it roll perfectly into the cup.

"You're right. Forty-five."

"That's the highest in—"

"Eleven months. We haven't been above fifty since Flight 402 in November of last year. This is a wonderful crisis, Chief. The people are shocked, yet many of them are happy Rosenberg is gone. And you're the man in the middle. Just wonderful." Coal punched a blinking button and picked up the receiver. He slammed it down without a word. He straightened his tie and buttoned his jacket.

"It's five-thirty, Chief. Voyles and Gminski are waiting."

He putted and watched the ball. It was an inch to the right, and he grimaced. "Let them wait. Let's do a press conference at nine in the morning. I'll take Voyles with me, but I'll keep his mouth shut. Make him stand behind me. I'll give some more details and answer a few questions. Networks'll carry it live, don't you think?"

"Of course. Good idea. I'll get it started."

He picked off his gloves and threw them in a corner. "Show them in." He carefully leaned his putter against the wall and slid into his Bally loafers. As usual, he had changed clothes six times since breakfast, and now wore a glen plaid double-breasted suit with a red and navy polka-dot tie. Office attire. The jacket hung on a rack by the door. He sat at his desk and scowled at some papers. He nodded at Voyles and Gminski, but neither stood nor offered to shake hands. They sat across the desk, and Coal took his usual standing position like a sentry who couldn't wait to fire. The President pinched the bridge of his nose as if the stress of the day had delivered a migraine.

"It's been a long day, Mr. President," Bob Gminski said to break the ice. Voyles looked at the windows.

Coal nodded, and the President said, "Yes, Bob. A very long day. And I have a bunch of Ethiopians invited for dinner tonight, so let's be brief. Let's start with you, Bob. Who killed them?"

"I do not know, Mr. President. But I assure you we had nothing to do with it."

"Do you promise me, Bob?" He was almost prayerful.

Gminski raised his right hand with the palm facing the desk. "I swear. On my mother's grave, I swear."

Coal nodded smugly as if he believed

74

him, and as if his approval meant everything.

The President glared at Voyles, whose
stocky figure filled the chair and was still
draped with a bulky trench coat. The Director chewed his gum slowly and sneered
at the President.

"Ballistics? Autopsies?"

"Got 'em," Voyles said as he opened his
briefcase.

"Just tell me. I'll read it later."

"The gun was small-caliber, probably a
.22. Point-blank range for Rosenberg and
his nurse, powder burns indicate. Hard to
tell for Ferguson, but the shots were fired
from no farther than twelve inches away.
We didn't see the shooting, you understand? Three bullets into each head. They
picked two out of Rosenberg; found another in his pillow. Looks like he and the
nurse were asleep. Same type slugs, same
gun, same gunman, evidently. Complete
autopsy summaries are being prepared,
but there were no surprises. Causes of
deaths are quite obvious."

"Fingerprints?"

"None. We're still looking, but it was a
very clean job. Appears as if he left nothing
but the slugs and the bodies."

"How'd he get into the house?"

"No apparent signs of entry. Ferguson searched the place when Rosenberg arrived around four. Routine procedure. He filed his written report two hours later, and it says he inspected two bedrooms, a bath, and three closets upstairs, and each room downstairs, and of course found nothing. Says he checked all windows and doors. Pursuant to Rosenberg's instructions, our agents were outside, and they estimate Ferguson's four o'clock inspection took from three to four minutes. I suspect the killer was waiting and hiding when the Justice returned and Ferguson walked through."

"Why?" Coal insisted.

Voyles' red eyes watched the President and ignored his hatchet man. "This man is obviously very talented. He killed a Supreme Court Justice—maybe two—and left virtually no trail. A professional assassin, I would guess. Entry would not be a problem for him. Eluding a cursory inspection by Ferguson would be no problem for him. He's probably very patient. He wouldn't risk an entry when the house was occupied and cops around. I think he entered sometime in the afternoon and simply waited, probably in a closet upstairs, or perhaps in the attic. We found two small pieces of attic insulation on the floor under the retractable stairs; suggests they had recently been used."

"Really doesn't matter where he was hiding," the President said. "He wasn't discovered."

"That's correct. We were not allowed to inspect the house, you understand?"

"I understand he's dead. What about Jensen?"

"He's dead too. Broken neck, strangled with a piece of yellow nylon rope that can be found in any hardware store. The medical examiners doubt the broken neck killed him. They're reasonably confident the rope did. No fingerprints. No witnesses. This is not the sort of place where witnesses come rushing forward, so I don't expect to find any. Time of death was around twelve-thirty this morning. The killings were two hours apart."

The President scribbled notes. "When did Jensen leave his apartment?"

"Don't know. We're relegated to the parking lot, remember. We followed him home around 6 P.M., then watched the building for seven hours until we found out he'd been strangled in a queer joint.

We were following his demands, of course. He sneaked out of the building in a friend's car. Found it two blocks from the joint."

Coal took two steps forward with his hands clasped rigidly behind him. "Director, do you think one assassin did both jobs?"

"Who in hell knows. The bodies are still warm. Give us a break. There's precious little evidence right now. With no witnesses, no prints, no screwups, it'll take time to piece this thing together. Could be the same man, I don't know. It's too early."

"Surely you have a gut feeling," the President said.

Voyles paused and glanced at the windows. "Could be the same guy, but he must be superman. Probably two or three, but regardless, they had to have a lot of help. Someone fed them a lot of information."

"Such as?"

"Such as how often Jensen goes to the movies, where does he sit, what time does he get there, does he go by himself, does he meet a friend. Information we didn't have, obviously. Take Rosenberg. Someone had to know his little house had no security system, that our boys were kept outside, that

Ferguson arrived at ten and left at six and had to sit in the backyard, that—"

"You knew all this," the President interrupted.

"Of course we did. But I assure you we didn't share it with anyone." The President shot a quick conspiratorial glance at Coal, who was scratching his chin, deep in thought.

Voyles shifted his rather wide rear and gave Gminski a smile, as if to say, "Let's play along with them."

"You're suggesting a conspiracy," Coal said intelligently with deep eyebrows.

"I'm not suggesting a damned thing. I am proclaiming to you, Mr. Coal, and to you, Mr. President, that, yes, in fact, a large number of people conspired to kill them. There may be only one or two killers, but they had a lot of help. It was too quick and clean and well organized."

Coal seemed satisfied. He stood straight and again clasped his hands behind him.

"Then who are the conspirators?" the President asked. "Who are your suspects?"

Voyles breathed deeply and seemed to settle in his chair. He closed the briefcase and laid it at his feet. "We don't have a prime suspect, at the moment, just a few good possibilities. And this must be kept very quiet."

Coal sprang a step closer. "Of course it's confidential," he snapped. "You're in the Oval Office."

"And I've been here many times before. In fact, I was here when you were running around in dirty diapers, Mr. Coal. Things have a way of leaking out."

"I think you've had leaks yourself," Coal said.

The President raised his hand. "It's confidential, Denton. You have my word." Coal retreated a step.

Voyles watched the President. "Court opened Monday, as you know, and the maniacs have been in town for a few days. For the past two weeks, we've been monitoring various movements. We know of at least eleven members of the Underground Army who've been in the D.C. area for a week. We questioned a couple today, and released them. We know the group has the capability, and the desire. It's our strongest possibility, for now. Could change tomorrow."

Coal was not impressed. The Underground Army was on everyone's list.

"I've heard of them," the President said stupidly.

"Oh yes. They're becoming quite popular. We believe they killed a trial judge in Texas. Can't prove it, though. They're very proficient with explosives. We suspect them in at least a hundred bombings of abortion clinics, ACLU offices, porno houses, gay clubs, all over the country. They're just the people who would hate Rosenberg and Jensen."

"Other suspects?" Coal asked.

"There's an Aryan group called White Resistance that we've been watching for two years. It operates out of Idaho and Oregon. The leader gave a speech in West Virginia last week, and has been in the area for a few days. He was spotted Monday in the demonstration outside the Supreme Court. We'll try to talk to him tomorrow."

"But are these people professional assassins?" Coal asked.

"They don't advertise, you understand. I doubt if any group performed the actual killings. They just hired the assassins and provided the legwork."

"So who're the assassins?" the President asked.

"We may never know, frankly."

The President stood and stretched his legs. Another hard day at the office. He smiled down at Voyles across the desk. "You have a difficult task." It was the grandfather's voice, filled with warmth and understanding. "I don't envy you. If possible, I would like a two-page typewritten double-spaced report by 5 P.M. each day, seven days a week, on the progress of the investigation. If something breaks, I expect you to call me immediately."

Voyles nodded but did not speak.

"I'm having a press conference in the morning at nine. I would like for you to be here."

Voyles nodded but did not speak. Seconds passed and no one spoke. Voyles stood noisily and tied the strap around the trench coat. "Oh well, we'll be going. You've got the Ethiopians and all." He handed the ballistics and autopsy reports to Coal, knowing the President would never read them.

"Thanks for coming, gentlemen," the President said warmly. Coal closed the door behind them, and the President grabbed the putter. "I'm not eating with the Ethiopians," he said, staring at the carpet and a yellow ball.

"I know it. I've already sent your apologies. This is a great hour of crisis, Mr. President, and you are expected to be here in this office surrounded by your advisers, hard at work."

He putted, and the ball rolled perfectly into the cup. "I want to talk to Horton. These nominations must be perfect."

"He's sent a short list of ten. Looks pretty good."

"I want young conservative white men opposed to abortion, pornography, queers, gun control, racial quotas, all that crap." He missed a putt, and kicked off his loafers. "I want judges who hate dope and criminals and are enthusiastic about the death penalty. Understand?"

Coal was on the phone, punching numbers and nodding at his boss. He would select the nominees, then convince the President.

K. O. LEWIS sat with the Director in the back of the quiet limousine as it left the White House and crawled through rush-hour traffic. Voyles had nothing to say. So far, in the early hours of the tragedy, the press had been brutal. The buzzards were circling. No less than three congressional subcommittees had already announced hearings and investigations into the deaths. And the bodies were still warm. The politicians were giddy and wrestling for the spotlight. One outrageous statement fueled another. Senator Larkin from Ohio hated Voyles, and Voyles hated Senator Larkin from Ohio, and the senator had called a press conference three hours earlier and announced his subcommittee would immediately begin investigating the FBI's protection of the two dead justices. But Larkin had a girlfriend, a rather young one, and the FBI had some photographs, and Voyles was confident the investigation could be delayed.

"How's the President?" Lewis finally asked.

"Which one?"

"Not Coal. The other one."

"Swell. Just swell. He's awfully tore up about Rosenberg, though."

"I bet."

They rode in silence in the direction of the Hoover Building. It would be a long night.

"We've got a new suspect," Lewis finally said.

"Do tell."

"A man named Nelson Muncie."

Voyles slowly shook his head. "Never heard of him."

"Neither have I. It's a long story."

"Gimme the short version."

"Muncie is a very wealthy industrialist from Florida. Sixteen years ago his niece was raped and murdered by an Afro-American named Buck Tyrone. The little girl was twelve. Very, very brutal rape and murder. I'll spare you the details. Muncie has no children, and idolized his niece. Tyrone was tried in Orlando, and given the death penalty. He was guarded heavily because there were a bunch of threats. Some Jewish lawyers in a big New York firm filed all sorts of appeals, and in 1984 the case arrives at the Supreme Court. You guessed it: Rosenberg falls in love with Tyrone and concocts this ridiculous Fifth Amendment self-incrimination argument to exclude a confession the punk gave a week after he was arrested. An eight-page confession that he, Tyrone, wrote himself. No confession, no case. Rosenberg writes a convoluted five-to-four opinion overturning the conviction. An extremely controversial decision. Tyrone goes free. Then, two years later he disappears and has not been seen since. Rumor has it Muncie paid to have Tyrone castrated, mutilated, and fed to the sharks. Just a rumor, say the Florida authorities. Then in 1989, Tyrone's main lawyer on the case, man named Kaplan, is gunned down by an apparent mugger outside his apartment in Manhattan. What a coincidence."

"Who tipped you?"

"Florida called two hours ago. They're convinced Muncie paid a bunch of money to eliminate both Tyrone and his lawyer. They just can't prove it. They've got a reluctant, unidentified informant who says he knows Muncie and feeds them a little info. He says Muncie has been talking for years about eliminating Rosenberg. They think he went a little over the edge when his niece was murdered."

"How much money has he got?"

"Enough. Millions. No one is sure. He's very secretive. Florida is convinced he's capable."

"Let's check it out. Sounds interesting."

"I'll get on it tonight. Are you sure you want three hundred agents on this case?"

Voyles lit a cigar and cracked his window. "Yeah, maybe four hundred. We need to crack this baby before the press eats us alive."

"It won't be easy. Except for the slugs and the rope, these guys left nothing."

Voyles blew smoke out the window. "I know. It's almost too clean."

SEVEN

THE CHIEF slouched behind his desk with a loosened tie and a haggard look. Around the room, three of his brethren and a half-dozen clerks sat and talked in subdued tones. The shock and fatigue were evident. Jason Kline, Rosenberg's senior clerk, looked especially hard-hit. He sat on a small sofa and stared blankly at the floor while Justice Archibald Manning, now the senior Justice, talked of protocol and funerals. Jensen's mother wanted a small, private Episcopal service Friday in Providence. Rosenberg's son, a lawyer, had delivered to Runyan a list of instructions the Justice had prepared after his second stroke in which he wanted to be cremated after a nonmilitary ceremony and his ashes dropped over the Sioux Indian Reservation in South Dakota. Though Rosenberg was Jewish, he had abandoned the religion and claimed to be agnostic. He wanted to be buried with the Indians. Runyan thought that was appropriate, but did not say so. In the outer office, six FBI agents sipped coffee and whispered nervously. There had been more threats during the day, several coming within hours of the President's early morning address. It was dark now, almost time to escort the remaining justices home. Each had four agents as bodyguards.

Justice Andrew McDowell, at sixty-one now the youngest member of the Court, stood in the window, smoking his pipe and watching traffic. If Jensen had a friend on the Court, it was McDowell. Fletcher Coal had informed Runyan that the President would not only attend Jensen's service but wanted to deliver a eulogy. No one in the inner office wanted the President to say a word. The Chief had asked McDowell to prepare a few words. A shy man who avoided speeches, McDowell twirled his bow tie and tried to picture his friend in the balcony with a rope around his neck. It was too awful to think about. A Justice of the Supreme Court, one of his distinguished brethren, one of the nine, hiding in such a place watching those movies and being exposed in such a ghastly manner. What a tragic embarrassment. He thought of himself standing before the crowd in the church and looking at Jensen's mother and family, and knowing that every thought would be on the Montrose Theatre. They would ask each other in whispered voices, "Did you know he was gay?" McDowell, for one, did not know, nor did he suspect. Nor did he want to say anything at the funeral.

Justice Ben Thurow, age sixty-eight, was not as concerned about burying the dead as he was about catching the killers. He had been a federal prosecutor in Minnesota, and his theory grouped the suspects into two classes: those acting out of hatred and revenge, and those seeking to affect future decisions. He had instructed his clerks to begin the research.

Thurow was pacing around the room. "We have twenty-seven clerks and seven justices," he said to the group but to no one in particular. "It's obvious we won't get much work done for the next couple of weeks, and all close decisions must wait until we have a full bench. That could take months. I suggest we put our clerks to work trying to solve the killings."

"We're not police," Manning said patiently.

"Can we at least wait until after the burials before we start playing Dick Tracy?" McDowell said without turning from the window.

Thurow ignored them, as usual. "I'll direct the research. Loan me your clerks for two weeks, and I think we can put together a short list of solid suspects."

"The FBI is very capable, Ben," the Chief said. "They haven't asked for our help."

"I'd rather not discuss the FBI," Thurow said. "We can mope around here in official mourning for two weeks, or we can go to work and find these bastards."

"What makes you so sure you can solve this?" Manning asked.

"I'm not sure I can, but I think it's worth a try. Our brethren were murdered for a reason, and that reason is directly related to a case or an issue already decided or now pending before this Court. If it's retribution, then our task is almost impossible. Hell, everybody hates us for one reason or another. But if it's not revenge or hatred, then perhaps someone wanted a different Court for a future decision. That's what's intriguing. Who would kill Abe and Glenn because of how they might vote on a case this year, next year, or five years from now? I want the clerks to pull up every case now pending in the eleven circuits below."

Justice McDowell shook his head. "Come on, Ben. That's over five thousand cases, a small fraction of which will eventually end up here. It's a wild-goose chase."

Manning was equally unimpressed. "Listen, fellas. I served with Abe Rosenberg for thirty-one years, and I often thought of shooting him myself. But I loved him like a brother. His liberal ideas were accepted in the sixties and seventies, but grew old in the eighties, and are now resented in the nineties. He became a symbol for everything that's wrong in this country. He has been killed, I believe, by one of these radical right-wing hate groups, and we can research cases till hell freezes over and not find anything. It's retribution, Ben. Pure and simple."

"And Glenn?" Thurow asked.

"Evidently our friend had some strange proclivities. Word must have spread, and he was an easy target for such groups. They hate homosexuals, Ben."

Ben was still pacing, still ignoring. "They

hate all of us, and if they killed out of hatred the cops'll catch them. Maybe. But
what if they killed to manipulate this
Court? What if some group seized this moment of unrest and violence to eliminate
two of us, and thus realign the Court? I
think it's very possible."

The Chief cleared his throat. "And I
think we'll do nothing until after they are
buried, or scattered. I'm not saying no,
Ben, just wait a few days. Let the dust settle. The rest of us are still in shock."

Thurow excused himself and left the
room. His bodyguards followed him down
the hall.

Justice Manning stood with his cane and
addressed the Chief. "I will not make it to
Providence. I hate flying, and I hate funerals. I'll be having one myself before long,
and I do not enjoy the reminder. I'll send
my sympathies to the family. When you see
them, please apologize for me. I'm a very
old man." He left with a clerk.

"I think Justice Thurow has a point,"
said Jason Kline. "We at least need to review the pending cases and those likely to
arrive here from the lower circuits. It's a
long shot, but we may stumble across something."

"I agree," said the Chief. "It's just a bit premature, don't you think?"

"Yes, but I'd like to get started anyway."

"No. Wait till Monday, and I'll assign you to Thurow."

Kline shrugged and excused himself. Two clerks followed him to Rosenberg's office, where they sat in the darkness and sipped the last of Abe's brandy.

IN A CLUTTERED STUDY CARREL on the fifth level of the law library, between the racks of thick, seldom-used law books, Darby Shaw scanned a printout of the Supreme Court's docket. She had been through it twice, and though it was loaded with controversy, she found nothing that interested her. *Dumond* was causing riots. There was a child pornography case from New Jersey, a sodomy case from Kentucky, a dozen death penalty appeals, a dozen assorted civil rights cases, and the usual array of tax, zoning, Indian, and antitrust cases. From the computer she had pulled summaries of each, then reviewed them twice. She compiled a neat list of possible suspects, but they would be obvious to everyone. The list was now in the garbage.

Callahan was certain it was the Aryans or

the Nazis or the Klan; some easily identifiable collection of domestic terrorists; some radical band of vigilantes. It had to be right-wingers; that much was obvious, he felt. Darby was not so sure. The hate groups were too obvious. They had made too many threats, thrown too many rocks, held too many parades, made too many speeches. They needed Rosenberg alive because he was such an irresistible target for their hatred. Rosenberg kept them in business. She thought it was somebody much more sinister.

He was sitting in a bar on Canal Street, drunk by now, waiting on her though she had not promised to join him. She had checked on him at lunch, and found him on the balcony upstairs, drunk and reading his book of Rosenberg opinions. He had decided to cancel con law for a week; said he might not be able to teach it anymore now that his hero was dead. She told him to sober up, and she left.

A few minutes after ten, she walked to the computer room on the fourth level of the library and sat before a monitor. The room was empty. She pecked away at the keyboard, found what she wanted, and soon the printer was spewing forth page after page of appeals pending in the eleven federal appellate courts around the country. An hour later, the printer stopped, and she now possessed a six-inch-thick summary of the eleven dockets. She hauled it back to her study carrel and placed it in the center of the cluttered desk. It was after eleven, and the fifth level was deserted. A narrow window gave an uninspiring view of a parking lot and trees below.

She kicked off her shoes again and inspected the red paint on the toes. She sipped a warm Fresca and stared blankly at the parking lot. The first assumption was easy—the killings were done by the same group for the same reasons. If not, then the search was hopeless. The second assumption was difficult—the motive was not hatred or revenge, but rather manipulation. There was a case or an issue out there on its way to the Supreme Court, and someone wanted different justices. The third assumption was a bit easier—the case or issue involved a great deal of money.

The answer would not be found in the printout sitting before her. She flipped through it until midnight, and left when the library closed.

EIGHT

AT NOON THURSDAY a secretary
carried a large sack decorated with
grease spots and filled with deli sandwiches
and onion rings into a humid conference
room on the fifth floor of the Hoover
Building. In the center of the square room,
a mahogany table with twenty chairs along
each side was surrounded with the top FBI
people from across the country. All ties
were loosened and sleeves rolled up. A thin
cloud of blue smoke hung around the
cheap government chandelier five feet
above the table.

Director Voyles was talking. Tired and
angry, he puffed on his fourth cigar of the
morning and walked slowly in front of the
screen at his end of the table. Half the men
were listening. The other half had pulled
reports from the pile in the center of the

table and read about the autopsies, the lab report on the nylon rope, Nelson Muncie, and a few other quickly researched subjects. The reports were quite thin.

Listening carefully and reading intently was Special Agent Eric East, only a ten-year man but a brilliant investigator. Six hours earlier Voyles had picked him to lead the investigation. The rest of the team had been selected throughout the morning, and this was the organizational meeting.

East was listening and hearing what he already knew. The investigation could take weeks, probably months. Other than the slugs, nine of them, the rope, and the steel rod used in the tourniquet, there was no evidence. The neighbors in Georgetown had seen nothing; no exceptionally suspicious characters at the Montrose. No prints. No fibers. Nothing. It takes remarkable talent to kill so cleanly, and it takes a lot of money to hire such talent. Voyles was pessimistic about finding the gunmen. They must concentrate on whoever hired them.

Voyles was talking and puffing. "There's a memo on the table regarding one Nelson Muncie, a millionaire from Jacksonville, Florida, who's allegedly made threats against Rosenberg. The Florida authorities are convinced Muncie paid a bunch of money to have the rapist and his lawyer killed. The memo covers it. Two of our men talked with Muncie's lawyer this morning, and were met with great hostility. Muncie is out of the country, according to his lawyer, and of course he has no idea when he will return. I've assigned twenty men to investigate him."

Voyles relit his cigar and looked at a sheet of paper on the table. "Number four is a group called White Resistance, a small group of middle-aged commandos we've been watching for about three years. You've got a memo. Pretty weak suspect, really. They'd rather throw firebombs and burn crosses. Not a lot of finesse. And, most importantly, not much money. I doubt seriously if they could hire guns as slick as these. But I've assigned twenty men anyway."

East unwrapped a heavy sandwich, sniffed it, but decided to leave it alone. The onion rings were cold. His appetite had vanished. He listened and made notes. Number six on the list was a bit unusual. A psycho named Clinton Lane had declared war on homosexuals. His only son had moved from their family farm in Iowa to San Francisco to enjoy the gay life, but had quickly died of AIDS. Lane cracked up, and burned the Gay Coalition office in Des Moines. Caught and sentenced to four years, he escaped in 1989 and had not been found. According to the memo, he had set up an extensive coke-smuggling operation and made millions. And he used the money in his own little private war against gays and lesbians. The FBI had been trying to catch him for five years, but it was believed he operated out of Mexico. For years he had written hate mail to the Congress, the Supreme Court, the President. Voyles was not impressed with Lane as a suspect. He was a nut who was way out in left field, but no stone would go unturned. He assigned only six agents.

The list had ten names. Between six and twenty of the best special agents were assigned to each suspect. A leader was chosen for each unit. They were to report twice daily to East, who would meet each morning and each afternoon with the Director. A hundred or so more agents would scour the streets and countryside for clues.

Voyles talked of secrecy. The press would follow like bloodhounds, so the investigation must be extremely confidential. Only he, the Director, would speak to the press, and he would have precious little to say.

He sat down, and K. O. Lewis delivered a rambling monologue about the funerals, and security, and a request from Chief Runyan to assist in the investigation.

Eric East sipped cold coffee, and stared at the list.

IN THIRTY-FOUR YEARS, Abraham Rosenberg wrote no fewer than twelve hundred opinions. His production was a constant source of amazement to constitutional scholars. He occasionally ignored the dull antitrust cases and tax appeals, but if the issue showed the barest hint of real controversy, he waded in with both fists. He wrote majority opinions, concurrences to majorities, concurrences to dissents, and many, many dissents. Often he dissented alone. Every hot issue in thirty-four years had received an opinion of some sort from Rosenberg. The scholars and critics loved him. They published books and essays and critiques about him and his work. Darby found five separate hardback compilations of his opinions, with editorial notes and annotations. One book contained nothing but his great dissents.

She skipped class Thursday and secluded herself in the study carrel on the fifth level of the library. The computer printouts were scattered neatly on the floor. The Rosenberg books were open and marked and stacked on top of each other.

There was a reason for the killings. Revenge and hatred would be acceptable for Rosenberg alone. But add Jensen to the equation, and revenge and hatred made less sense. Sure he was hateable, but he had not aroused passions like Yount or even Manning.

She found no books of critical thought on the writings of Justice Glenn Jensen. In six years, he had authored only twenty-eight majority opinions, the lowest production on the Court. He had written a few dissents, and joined a few concurrences, but he was a painfully slow worker. At times his writing was clear and lucid, at times disjointed and pathetic.

She studied Jensen's opinions. His ideology swung radically from year to year. He was generally consistent in his protection of the rights of criminal defendants, but there were enough exceptions to astound any scholar. In seven attempts, he had voted with the Indians five times. He had written three majority opinions strongly protective of the environment. He was near perfect in support of tax protestors.

But there were no clues. Jensen was too erratic to take seriously. Compared to the other eight, he was harmless.

She finished another warm Fresca, and put away for the moment her notes on Jensen. Her watch was hidden in a drawer. She had no idea what time it was. Callahan had sobered up and wanted a late dinner at Mr. B's in the Quarter. She needed to call him.

DICK MABRY, the current speechwriter and word wizard, sat in a chair beside the President's desk and watched as Fletcher Coal and the President read the third draft of a proposed eulogy for Justice Jensen. Coal had rejected the first two, and Mabry was still uncertain about what they wanted. Coal would suggest one thing. The President wanted something else. Earlier in the day, Coal had called and said to forget the eulogy because the President would not attend the funeral. Then the President had called, and asked him to prepare a few words because Jensen was a friend and even though he was a queer he was still a friend.

Mabry knew Jensen was not a friend, but he was a freshly assassinated justice who would enjoy a highly visible funeral.

Then Coal had called and said they weren't sure if the President was going but work up something just in case. Mabry's office was in the Old Executive Office Building next door to the White House, and during the day small bets had been placed on whether the President would attend the funeral of a known homosexual. The office odds were three to one that he would not.

"Much better, Dick," Coal said, folding the paper.

"I like it too," the President said. Mabry had noticed that the President usually waited for Coal to express approval or displeasure over his words.

"I can try again," Mabry said, standing.

"No, no," Coal insisted. "This has the right touch. Very poignant. I like it."

He walked Mabry to the door and closed it behind him.

"What do you think?" the President asked.

"Let's call it off. I'm getting bad vibes.

Publicity would be great, but you'd be speaking these beautiful words over a body found in a gay porno house. Too risky."

"Yeah. I think you're—"

"This is our crisis, Chief. The ratings continue to improve, and I just don't want to take a chance."

"Should we send someone?"

"Of course. What about the Vice President?"

"Where is he?"

"Flying in from Guatemala. He'll be in tonight." Coal suddenly smiled to himself. "This is great VP stuff, you know. A gay funeral."

The President chuckled. "Perfect."

Coal stopped smiling and began pacing in front of the desk. "Slight problem. Rosenberg's service is Saturday, only eight blocks from here."

"I'd rather go to hell for a day."

"I know. But your absence would be very conspicuous."

"I could check into Walter Reed with back spasms. It worked before."

"No, Chief. Reelection is next year. You must stay away from hospitals."

The President slapped both hands on his desk and stood. "Dammit, Fletcher! I can't go to his service because I can't keep from smiling. He was hated by ninety percent of the American people. They'll love me if I don't go."

"Protocol, Chief. Good taste. You'll be burned by the press if you don't go. Look, it won't hurt, okay. You don't have to say a word. Just ease in and out, look real sad, and allow the cameras to get a good look. Won't take an hour."

The President was gripping his putter and crouching over an orange ball. "Then I'll have to go to Jensen's."

"Exactly. But forget the eulogy."

He putted. "I met him only twice, you know."

"I know. Let's quietly attend both services, say nothing, then disappear."

He putted again. "I think you're right."

NINE

THOMAS CALLAHAN slept late and alone. He had gone to bed early, and sober, and alone. For the third day in a row he had canceled classes. It was Friday, and Rosenberg's service was tomorrow, and out of respect for his idol, he would not teach con law until the man was properly put to rest.

He fixed coffee and sat on the balcony in his robe. The temperature was in the sixties, the first cold snap of the fall, and Dauphine Street below bustled with brisk energy. He nodded to the old woman without a name on the balcony across the street. Bourbon was a block away and the tourists were already out with their little maps and cameras. Dawn went unnoticed in the Quarter, but by ten the narrow streets were busy with delivery trucks and cabs.

On these late mornings, and they were many in number, Callahan cherished his freedom. He was twenty years out of law school, and most of his contemporaries were strapped into seventy-hour weeks in pressurized law factories. He had lasted two years in private practice. A behemoth in D.C. with two hundred lawyers hired him fresh out of Georgetown and stuck him in a cubbyhole office writing briefs for the first six months. Then he was placed on an assembly line answering interrogatories about IUDs twelve hours a day, and expected to bill sixteen. He was told that if he could cram the next twenty years into the next ten, he just might make partner at the weary age of thirty-five.

Callahan wanted to live past fifty, so he retired from the boredom of private law. He earned a master's in law, and became a professor. He slept late, worked five hours a day, wrote an occasional article, and for the most part enjoyed himself immensely. With no family to support, his salary of seventy thousand a year was more than sufficient to pay for his two-story bungalow, his Porsche, and his liquor. If death came early, it would be from whiskey and not work.

He had sacrificed. Many of his pals from law school were partners in the big firms with fancy letterheads and half-million-dollar earnings. They rubbed shoulders with CEOs from IBM and Texaco and State Farm. They power-schmoozed with senators. They had offices in Tokyo and London. But he did not envy them.

One of his best friends from law school was Gavin Verheek, another dropout from private practice who had gone to work for the government. He first worked in the civil rights division at Justice, then transferred to the FBI. He was now special counsel to the Director. Callahan was due in Washington Monday for a conference of con law professors. He and Verheek planned to eat and get drunk Monday night.

He needed to call and confirm their eating and drinking, and to pick his brain. He dialed the number from memory. The call was routed then rerouted, and after five minutes of asking for Gavin Verheek, the man was on the phone.

"Make it quick," Verheek said.

"So nice to hear your voice," Callahan said.

"How are you, Thomas?"

"It's ten-thirty. I'm not dressed. I'm sitting here in the French Quarter sipping coffee and watching pedestrians on Dauphine. What're you doing?"

"What a life. Here it's eleven-thirty, and I haven't left the office since they found the bodies Wednesday morning."

"I'm just sick, Gavin. He'll nominate two Nazis."

"Well, of course, in my position, I cannot comment on such matters. But I suspect you're correct."

"Suspect my ass. You've already seen his short list of nominees, haven't you, Gavin? You guys are already doing background checks, aren't you? Come on, Gavin, you can tell me. Who's on the list? I'll never tell."

"Neither will I, Thomas. But I promise this—your name is not among the few."

"I'm wounded."

"How's the girl?"

"Which one?"

"Come on, Thomas. The girl?"

"She's beautiful and brilliant and soft and gentle—"

"Keep going."

"Who killed them, Gavin? I have a right

to know. I'm a taxpayer and I have a right to know who killed them."

"What's her name again?"

"Darby. Who killed them, and why?"

"You could always pick names, Thomas. I remember women you turned down because you didn't like the names. Gorgeous, hot women, but with flat names. Darby. Has a nice erotic touch to it. What a name. When do I meet her?"

"I don't know."

"Has she moved in?"

"None of your damned business. Gavin, listen to me. Who did it?"

"Don't you read the papers? We have no suspects. None. *Nada.*"

"Surely you have a motive."

"Mucho motives. Lots of hatred out there, Thomas. Weird combination, wouldn't you say? Jensen's hard to figure. The Director has ordered us to research pending cases and recent decisions and voting patterns and all that crap."

"That's great, Gavin. Every con law scholar in the country is now playing detective and trying to solve the murders."

"And you're not?"

"No. I threw a binge when I heard the news, but I'm sober now. The girl, how-

ever, has buried herself in the same research you're doing. She's ignoring me."

"Darby. What a name. Where's she
from?"

"Denver. Are we on for Monday?"

"Maybe. Voyles wants us to work around
the clock until the computers tell us who
did it. I plan to work you in, though."

"Thanks. I'll expect a full report, Gavin.
Not just the gossip."

"Thomas, Thomas. Always fishing for information. And I, as usual, have none to
give you."

"You'll get drunk and tell all, Gavin. You
always do."

"Why don't you bring Darby? How old is
she? Nineteen?"

"Twenty-four, and she's not invited.
Maybe later."

"Maybe. Gotta run, pal. I meet with the
Director in thirty minutes. The tension is
so thick around here you can smell it."

Callahan punched the number for the
law school library and asked if Darby Shaw
had been seen. She had not.

DARBY PARKED in the near-empty lot of
the federal building in Lafayette, and entered the clerk's office on the first floor. It

was noon Friday, court was not in session, and the hallways were deserted. She stopped at the counter and looked through an open window, and waited. A deputy clerk, late for lunch and with an attitude, walked to the window. "Can I help you?" she asked in the tone of a lowly civil servant who wanted to do anything but help.

Darby slid a strip of paper through the window. "I would like to see this file." The clerk took a quick glance at the name of the case, and looked at Darby. "Why?" she asked.

"I don't have to explain. It's public record, isn't it?"

"Semipublic."

Darby took the strip of paper and folded it. "Are you familiar with the Freedom of Information Act?"

"Are you a lawyer?"

"I don't have to be a lawyer to look at this file."

The clerk opened a drawer in the counter, and took out a key ring. She nodded, pointing with her forehead. "Follow me."

The sign on the door said JURY ROOM, but inside there were no tables or chairs, only

113

file cabinets and boxes lining the walls. Darby looked around the room.

The clerk pointed to a wall. "That's it, on this wall. The rest of the room is other junk. This first file cabinet has all the pleadings and correspondence. The rest is discovery, exhibits, and the trial."

"When was the trial?"

"Last summer. It went on for two months."

"Where's the appeal?"

"Not perfected yet. I think the deadline is November 1. Are you a reporter or something?"

"No."

"Good. As you obviously know, these are indeed public records. But the trial judge has placed certain restrictions. First, I must have your name and the precise hours you visited this room. Second, nothing can be taken from this room. Third, nothing in this file can be copied until the appeal is perfected. Fourth, anything you touch in here must be put back exactly where you found it. Judge's orders."

Darby stared at the wall of file cabinets. "Why can't I make copies?"

"Ask His Honor, okay? Now, what's your name?"

"Darby Shaw."

The clerk scribbled the information on a clipboard hanging near the door. "How long will you be?"

"I don't know. Three or four hours."

"We close at five. Find me at the office when you leave." She closed the door with a smirk. Darby opened a drawer full of pleadings, and began flipping through files and taking notes. The lawsuit was seven years old, with one plaintiff and thirty-eight wealthy corporate defendants who had collectively hired and fired no less than fifteen law firms from all over the country. Big firms, many with hundreds of lawyers in dozens of offices.

Seven years of expensive legal warfare, and the outcome was far from certain. Bitter litigation. The trial verdict was only a temporary victory for the defendants. The verdict had been purchased or in some other way illegally obtained, claimed the plaintiff in its motions for a new trial. Boxes of motions. Accusations and counteraccusations. Requests for sanctions and fines flowing rapidly to and from both sides. Pages and pages of affidavits detailing lies and abuses by the lawyers and their clients. One lawyer was dead.

115

Another had tried suicide, according to a classmate of Darby's who had worked on the fringes of the case during the trial. Her friend had been employed in a summer clerkship with a big firm in Houston, and was kept in the dark but heard a little.

Darby unfolded a chair and stared at the file cabinets. It would take five hours just to find everything.

THE PUBLICITY had not been good for the Montrose. Most of its customers wore dark sunglasses after dark, and tended to enter and exit rather quickly. And now that a U.S. Supreme Court Justice had been found in the balcony, the place was famous and the curious drove by at all hours pointing and taking pictures. Most of the regulars went elsewhere. The bravest darted in when the traffic was light.

He looked just like a regular when he darted in and paid his money inside the door without looking at the cashier. Baseball cap, black sunglasses, jeans, neat hair, leather jacket. He was well disguised, but not because he was a homosexual and ashamed to be hanging around such places.

It was midnight. He climbed the stairs to

the balcony, smiling at the thought of Jensen wearing the tourniquet. The door was locked. He took a seat in the center section on the floor, away from anyone else.

He had never watched queer movies before, and after this night he had no plans to watch another one. This was his third such smut house in the past ninety minutes. He kept the sunglasses on and tried to avoid the screen. But it was difficult, and this irritated him.

There were five other people in the theater. Four rows up and to his right were two lovebirds, kissing and playing. Oh, for a baseball bat and he could put them out of their misery. Or a nice little piece of yellow ski rope.

He suffered for twenty minutes, and was about to reach in his pocket when a hand touched his shoulder. A gentle hand. He played it cool.

"Could I sit by you?" came the rather deep and manly voice from just over his shoulder.

"No, and you can remove your hand."

The hand moved. Seconds passed, and it was obvious there would be no more requests. Then he was gone.

This was torture for a man violently opposed to pornography. He wanted to vomit. He glanced behind him, then reached carefully into the leather jacket and removed a black box, six inches by five and three inches thick. He laid it on the floor between his legs. With a scalpel, he made a careful incision in the cushion of the seat next to him, then, while glancing around, inserted the black box into the cushion. There were springs in this one, a real antique, and he delicately twisted the box from one side to the other until it was in place with the switch and the tube barely visible through the incision.

He took a deep breath. Although the device had been built by a true professional, a legendary genius at miniature explosives, it was not pleasant carrying the damned thing around in a coat pocket, just centimeters from his heart and most other vital organs. And he wasn't particularly comfortable sitting next to it now.

This was his third plant of the night, and he had one more, at another movie house where they showed old-fashioned heterosexual pornography. He was almost looking forward to it, and this irritated him.

He looked at the two lovers, who were oblivious to the movie and growing more

118

excited by the minute, and wished they could be sitting right there when the little black box began silently spewing forth its gas, and then thirty seconds later when the fireball would flash-fry every object between the screen and the popcorn machine. He would like that.

But his was a nonviolent group, opposed to the indiscriminate killing of innocent and/or insignificant people. They had killed a few necessary victims. Their specialty, however, was the demolition of structures used by the enemy. They picked easy targets: unarmed abortion clinics, unprotected ACLU offices, unsuspecting smut houses. They were having a field day. Not one single arrest in eighteen months.

It was twelve-forty, time to leave and hurry four blocks to his car for another black box, then six blocks over to the Pussycat Cinema, which closed at one-thirty. The Pussycat was either eighteen or nineteen on the list, he couldn't remember which, but he was certain that in exactly three hours and twenty minutes the dirty movie business in D.C. would take a helluva blow. Twenty-two of these little joints were supposed to receive black boxes tonight, and at 4 A.M. they were all supposed to be closed and deserted, and demolished. Three all-nighters were scratched from the list, because his was a nonviolent group.

He adjusted his sunglasses and took one last look at the cushion next to him. Judging from the cups and popcorn on the floor, the place got swept once a week. No one would notice the switch and tube barely visible between the ragged threads. He cautiously flipped the switch, and left the Montrose.

TEN

ERIC EAST had never met the President, nor been in the White House. And he'd never met Fletcher Coal, but he knew he wouldn't like him.

He followed Director Voyles and K. O. Lewis into the Oval Office at seven Saturday morning. There were no smiles or handshakes. East was introduced by Voyles. The President nodded from behind the desk but did not stand. Coal was reading something.

Twenty porno houses had been torched in the D.C. area, and many were still smoldering. They had seen the smoke above the city from the back of the limo. At a dump called Angels a janitor had been badly burned and was not expected to live.

An hour ago they had received word that an anonymous caller to a radio station had

claimed responsibility for the Underground Army, and he promised more of
the same in celebration of the death of Rosenberg.

The President spoke first. He looked
tired, East thought. It was such an early
hour for him. "How many places got
bombed?"

"Twenty here," Voyles answered. "Seventeen in Baltimore and around fifteen in
Atlanta. It appears as though the assault
was carefully coordinated because all the
explosions happened at precisely 4 A.M."

Coal looked up from his memo. "Director, do you believe it's the Underground
Army?"

"As of now they're the only ones claiming responsibility. It looks like some of
their work. Could be." Voyles did not look
at Coal when he spoke to him.

"So when do you start making arrests?"
the President asked.

"At the precise moment we obtain probable cause, Mr. President. That's the law,
you understand."

"I understand this outfit is your top suspect in the killings of Rosenberg and Jensen, and that you're certain it killed a federal trial judge in Texas, and it most likely

bombed at least fifty-two smut houses last night. I don't understand why they're bombing and killing with immunity. Hell, Director, we're under siege."

Voyles' neck turned red, but he said nothing. He just looked away while the President glared at him. K. O. Lewis cleared his throat. "Mr. President, if I may, we are not convinced the Underground Army was involved with the deaths of Rosenberg and Jensen. In fact, we have no evidence linking them. They are only one of a dozen suspects. As I've said before, the killings were remarkably clean, well organized, and very professional. Extremely professional."

Coal stepped forward. "What you're trying to say, Mr. Lewis, is that you have no idea who killed them, and you may never know."

"No, that's not what I'm saying. We'll find them, but it will take time."

"How much time?" asked the President. It was an obvious, sophomoric question with no good answer. East immediately disliked the President for asking it.

"Months," Lewis said.

"How many months?"

"Many months."

The President rolled his eyes and shook his head, then with great disgust stood and walked to the window. He spoke to the window. "I can't believe there's no relation between what happened last night and the dead judges. I don't know. Maybe I'm just paranoid."

Voyles shot a quick smirk at Lewis. Paranoid, insecure, clueless, dumb, out of touch. Voyles could think of many others.

The President continued, still pondering the window. "I just get nervous when assassins are loose around here and bombs are going off. Who can blame me? We haven't killed a President in over thirty years."

"Oh, I think you're safe, Mr. President," Voyles said with a trace of amusement. "The Secret Service has things under control."

"Great. Then why do I feel as though I'm in Beirut?" He was almost mumbling into the window.

Coal sensed the awkwardness and picked up a thick memo from the desk. He held it and spoke to Voyles, much like a professor lecturing to his class.

"This is the short list of potential nominees to the Supreme Court. There are eight names, each with a biography. It was prepared by Justice. We started with twenty names, then the President, Attorney General Horton, and myself cut it to eight, none of whom have any idea they are being considered."

Voyles still looked away. The President slowly returned to his desk, and picked up his copy of the memo. Coal continued.

"Some of these people are controversial, and if they are ultimately nominated we'll have a small war getting them approved by the Senate. We'd prefer not to start fighting now. This must be kept confidential."

Voyles suddenly turned and glared at Coal. "You're an idiot, Coal! We've done this before, and I can assure you when we start checking on these people the cat's out of the bag. You want a thorough background investigation, and yet you expect everyone contacted to keep quiet. It doesn't work that way, son."

Coal stepped closer to Voyles. His eyes were glowing. "You bust your ass to make sure these names are kept out of the papers until they're nominated. You make it work, Director. You plug the leaks and keep it out of the papers, understand."

Voyles was on his feet, pointing at Coal. "Listen, asshole, you want them checked out, you do it yourself. Don't start giving me a bunch of boy scout orders."

Lewis stood between them, and the President stood behind his desk, and for a second or two nothing was said. Coal placed his memo on the desk and retreated a few steps, looking away. The President was now the peacemaker. "Sit down, Denton. Sit down."

Voyles returned to his seat while staring at Coal. The President smiled at Lewis and everyone took a seat. "We're all under a lot of pressure," the President said warmly.

Lewis spoke calmly. "We'll perform the routine investigations on your names, Mr. President, and it will be done in the strictest of confidence. You know, however, that we cannot control every person we talk to."

"Yes, Mr. Lewis, I know that. But I want extra caution. These men are young and will shape and reshape the Constitution long after I'm dead. They're staunchly conservative, and the press will eat them alive. They must be free from warts and skeletons in the closet. No dope smokers, or illegitimate children, or DUIs, or radical student activity, or divorces. Understand? No surprises."

"Yes, Mr. President. But we cannot guarantee total secrecy in our investigations."

"Just try, okay."

"Yes, sir." Lewis handed the memo to Eric East.

"Is that all?" Voyles asked.

The President glanced at Coal, who was ignoring them all and standing before the window. "Yes, Denton, that's all. I'd like to have these names checked out in ten days. I want to move fast on this."

Voyles was standing. "You'll have it in ten days."

CALLAHAN WAS IRRITATED when he knocked on the door to Darby's apartment. He was quite perturbed and had a lot on his mind, a lot that he wanted to say, but he knew better than to start a fight because there was something he wanted much worse than to blow off a little steam. She had avoided him for four days now while she played detective and barricaded herself in the law library. She had skipped classes and failed to return his calls, and in general neglected him during his hour of crisis. But he knew when she opened the door he would smile and forget about being neglected.

He held a liter of wine and a real pizza from Mama Rosa's. It was after ten, Saturday night. He knocked again, and looked up and down the street at the neat duplexes and bungalows. The chain rattled from inside, and he instantly smiled. The neglect vanished.

"Who is it?" she asked through the chain.

"Thomas Callahan, remember? I'm at your door begging you to let me in so we can play and be friends again."

The door opened and Callahan stepped in. She took the wine and pecked him on the cheek. "Are we still buddies?" he asked.

"Yes, Thomas. I've been busy." He followed her through the cluttered den to the kitchen. A computer and an assortment of thick books covered the table.

"I called. Why didn't you call me back?"

"I've been out," she said, opening a drawer and removing a corkscrew.

"You've got a machine. I've been talking to it."

"Are you trying to fight, Thomas?"

He looked at her bare legs. "No! I swear I'm not mad. I promise. Please forgive me if I appear to be upset."

"Stop it."

"When can we go to bed?"

"Are you sleepy?"

"Anything but. Come on, Darby, it's been three nights."

"Five. What kind of pizza?" She removed the cork and poured two glasses. Callahan watched every move.

"Oh, it's one of those Saturday night specials where they throw on everything headed for the garbage. Shrimp tails, eggs, crawfish heads. Cheap wine too. I'm a little low on cash, and I'm leaving town tomorrow so I have to watch what I spend, and since I'm leaving I thought I'd just come on over and get laid tonight so I wouldn't be tempted by some contagious woman in D.C. What do you think?"

Darby was opening the pizza box. "Looks like sausage and peppers."

"Can I still get laid?"

"Maybe later. Drink your wine and let's chat. We haven't had a long talk in a while."

"I have. I've been talking to your machine all week."

He took his wineglass and the bottle and followed her closely to the den, where she turned on the stereo. They relaxed on the sofa.

"Let's get drunk," he said.

"You're so romantic."

"I've got some romance for you."

"You've been drunk for a week."

"No I haven't. Eighty percent of a week. It's your fault for avoiding me."

"What's wrong with you, Thomas?"

"I've got the shakes. I'm all keyed up and I need companionship to knock the edge off. Whatta you say?"

"Let's get half drunk." She sipped her wine and draped her legs across his lap. He held his breath as if in pain.

"What time is your flight?" she asked.

He was gulping now. "One-thirty. Nonstop to National. I'm supposed to register at five, and there's a dinner at eight. After that I may be forced to roam the streets looking for love."

She smiled. "Okay, okay. We'll do it in a minute. But let's talk first."

Callahan breathed a sigh of relief. "I can talk for ten minutes, then I'll just collapse."

"What's up for Monday?"

"The usual eight hours of airhead debate on the future of the Fifth Amendment, then a committee will draft a proposed conference report that no one will approve. More debate Tuesday, another report, perhaps an altercation or two, then we adjourn with nothing accomplished and go home. I'll be in late Tuesday evening, and I'd like a date at a very nice restaurant, after which we can go back to my place for an intellectual discussion and animal sex. Where's the pizza?"

"In there. I'll get it."

He was stroking her legs. "Don't move. I'm not the least bit hungry."

"Why do you go to these conferences?"

"I'm a member, and I'm a professor, and we're just sort of expected to roam the country attending meetings with other educated idiots and adopting reports nobody reads. If I didn't go, the dean would think I was not contributing to the academic environment."

She refilled the wineglasses. "You're uptight, Thomas."

"I know. It's been a rough week. I hate the thought of a bunch of Neanderthals rewriting the Constitution. We'll live in a police state in ten years. I can't do anything about it, so I'll probably resort to alcohol."

Darby sipped slowly and watched him. The music was soft and the lights low. "I'm getting a buzz," she said.

"That's about right for you. A glass and a

half and you're history. If you were Irish you could drink all night."

"My father was half Scottish."

"Not good enough." Callahan crossed his feet on the coffee table and relaxed. He gently rubbed her ankles. "Can I paint your toes?"

She said nothing. He had a fetish for her toes, and insisted on doing the nails with bright red polish at least twice a month. They'd seen it in *Bull Durham,* and though he wasn't as neat and sober as Kevin Costner, she had grown to enjoy the intimacy of it.

"No toes tonight?" he asked.

"Maybe later. You look tired."

"I'm relaxing, but I'm filled with virile male electricity, and you will not put me off by telling me I look tired."

"Have some more wine."

Callahan had more wine, and sank deeper in the sofa. "So, Ms. Shaw, who done it?"

"Professionals. Haven't you read the papers?"

"Of course. But who's behind the professionals?"

"I don't know. After last night, the unanimous choice seems to be the Underground Army."

"But you're not convinced."

"No. There have been no arrests. I'm not convinced."

"And you've got some obscure suspect unknown to the rest of the country."

"I had one, but now I'm not so sure. I spent three days tracking it down, even summarized it all real nice and neat in my little computer, and printed out a thin rough draft of a brief which I have now discarded."

Callahan stared at her. "You're telling me you skipped classes for three days, ignored me, worked around the clock playing Sherlock Holmes, and now you're throwing it away."

"It's over there on the table."

"I can't believe this. While I sulked around in loneliness all week, I knew it was for a worthy cause. I knew my suffering was for the good of the country because you would peel away the onion and tell me tonight or perhaps tomorrow who done it."

"It can't be done, at least not with legal research. There's no pattern, no common thread in the murders. I almost burned up the computers at the law school."

"Ha! I told you so. You forget, dear, that I am a genius at constitutional law, and I knew immediately that Rosenberg and Jensen had nothing in common but black robes and death threats. The Nazis or Aryans or Kluxers or Mafia or some other group killed them because Rosenberg was Rosenberg, and because Jensen was the easiest target and somewhat of an embarrassment."

"Well, why don't you call the FBI and share your insights with them? I'm sure they're sitting by the phone."

"Don't be angry. I'm sorry. Please forgive me."

"You're an ass, Thomas."

"Yes, but you love me, don't you?"

"I don't know."

"Can we still go to bed? You promised."

"We'll see."

Callahan placed his glass on the table, and attacked her. "Look, baby. I'll read your brief, okay. And then we'll talk about it, okay. But I'm not thinking clearly right now, and I won't be able to continue until you take my weak and trembling hand and lead me to your bed."

"Forget my little brief."

"Please, dammit, Darby, please."

She grabbed his neck and pulled him to her. They kissed long and hard, a wet, almost violent kiss.

ELEVEN

THE COP stuck his thumb on the button next to the name of Gray Grantham, and held it down for twenty seconds. Then a brief pause. Then another twenty seconds. Pause. Twenty seconds. Pause. Twenty seconds. He thought this was funny because Grantham was a night owl and had probably slept less than three or four hours, and now all this incessant buzzing echoing throughout his hallway. He pushed again and looked at his patrol car parked illegally on the curb under the streetlight. It was almost dawn, Sunday, and the street was empty. Twenty seconds. Pause. Twenty seconds.

Maybe Grantham was dead. Or maybe he was comatose from booze and a late night on the town. Maybe he had someone's woman up there and had no plans to answer the door. Pause. Twenty seconds.

The mike crackled. "Who is it!"

"Police!" answered the cop, who was black and emphasized the *po* in *police* just for the fun of it.

"What do you want?" Grantham demanded.

"Maybe I gotta warrant." The cop was near laughter.

Grantham's voice softened, and he sounded wounded. "Is this Cleve?"

"It is."

"What time is it, Cleve?"

"Almost five-thirty."

"It must be good."

"Don't know. Sarge didn't say, you know. He just said to wake you up 'cause he wanted to talk."

"Why does he always want to talk before the sun comes up?"

"Stupid question, Grantham."

A slight pause. "Yeah, I guess so. I presume he wants to talk right now."

"No. You got thirty minutes. He said be there at six."

"Where?"

"There's a little coffee shop on Fourteenth near the Trinidad Playground. It's dark and safe, and Sarge likes it."

"Where does he find these places?"

"You know, for a reporter you can ask the dumbest questions. The name of the place is Glenda's, and I suggest you get going or you'll be late."

"Will you be there?"

"I'll drop in, just to make sure you're okay."

"I thought you said it was safe."

"It is safe, for that part of town. Can you find it?"

"Yeah. I'll be there as soon as I can."

"Have a nice day, Grantham."

SARGE WAS OLD, very black, with a head full of brilliant white hair that sprang out in all directions. He wore thick sunglasses whenever he was awake, and most of his coworkers in the West Wing of the White House thought he was half blind. He held his head sideways and smiled like Ray Charles. He sometimes bumped into door facings and desks as he unloaded trash cans and dusted furniture. He walked slowly and gingerly as if counting his steps. He worked patiently, always with a smile, always with a kind word for anyone willing to give him one. For the most part he was ignored and dismissed as just another friendly, old, partially disabled black janitor.

Sarge could see around corners. His territory was the West Wing, where he had been cleaning for thirty years now. Cleaning and listening. Cleaning and seeing. He picked up after some terribly important people who were often too busy to watch their words, especially in the presence of poor old Sarge.

He knew which doors stayed open, and which walls were thin, and which air vents carried sound. He could disappear in an instant, then reappear in a shadow where the terribly important people could not see him.

He kept most of it to himself. But from time to time, he fell heir to a juicy bit of information that could be pieced together with another one, and Sarge would make the judgment call that it should be repeated. He was very careful. He had three years until retirement, and he took no chances.

No one ever suspected Sarge of leaking stories to the press. There were usually enough big mouths within any White

House to lay blame on each other. It was hilarious, really. Sarge would talk to Grantham at the *Post,* then wait excitedly for the story, then listen to the wailing in the basement when the heads rolled.

He was an impeccable source, and he talked only to Grantham. His son Cleve, the cop, arranged the meetings, always at odd hours at dark and inconspicuous places. Sarge wore his sunglasses. Grantham wore the same with a hat or cap of some sort. Cleve usually sat with them and watched the crowd.

Grantham arrived at Glenda's a few minutes after six, and walked to a booth in the rear. There were three other customers. Glenda herself was frying eggs on a grill near the register. Cleve sat on a stool watching her.

They shook hands. A cup of coffee had been poured for Grantham.

"Sorry I'm late," he said.

"No problem, my friend. Good to see you." Sarge had a raspy voice that was difficult to suppress with a whisper. No one was listening.

Grantham gulped coffee. "Busy week at the White House."

"You could say that. Lot of excitement. Lot of happiness."

"You don't say." Grantham could not take notes at these meetings. It would be too obvious, Sarge said when he laid the ground rules.

"Yes. The President and his boys were elated with the news of Justice Rosenberg. This made them very happy."

"What about Justice Jensen?"

"Well, as you noticed, the President attended the memorial service, but did not speak. He had planned to give a eulogy, but backed out because he would have been saying nice things about a gay fella."

"Who wrote the eulogy?"

"The speechwriters. Mainly Mabry. Worked on it all day Thursday, then he backed out."

"He also went to Rosenberg's service."

"Yes, he did. But he didn't want to. Said he'd rather go to hell for a day. But in the end, he chickened out and went anyway. He's quite happy Rosenberg was murdered. There was almost a festive mood around the place Wednesday. Fate has dealt him a wonderful hand. He now gets to restructure the Court, and he's very excited about this."

Grantham listened hard. Sarge continued.

"There's a short list of nominees. The original had twenty or so names, then it was cut to eight."

"Who did the cutting?"

"Who do you think? The President and Fletcher Coal. They're terrified of leaks at this point. Evidently the list is nothing but young conservative judges, most of whom are obscure."

"Any names?"

"Just two. A certain man named Pryce from Idaho, and one named MacLawrence from Vermont. That's all I know about names. I think they are both federal judges. Nothing more on this."

"What about the investigation?"

"I haven't heard much, but as usual I'll keep my ears open. There doesn't appear to be much going on."

"Anything else?"

"No. When will you run it?"

"In the morning."

"It'll be fun."

"Thanks, Sarge."

The sun was up now and the café was noisier. Cleve strolled over and sat next to his father. "You guys about finished?"

"We are," Sarge said.

Cleve glanced around. "I think we need to leave. Grantham goes first, I'll follow, then Pop here can stay as long as he wants."

"Mighty nice of you," Sarge said.

"Thanks, fellas," Grantham said as he headed for the door.

TWELVE

VERHEEK WAS LATE as usual. In the twenty-three-year history of their friendship, he had never been on time, and it was never a matter of being only a few minutes late. He had no concept of time and wasn't bothered with it. He wore a watch but never looked at it. Late for Verheek meant at least an hour, sometimes two, especially when the person kept waiting was a friend who expected him to be late and would forgive him.

So Callahan sat for an hour in the bar, which suited him just fine. After eight hours of scholarly debate, he despised the Constitution and those who taught it. He needed Chivas in his veins, and after two doubles on the rocks he was feeling better. He watched himself in the mirror behind the rows of liquor, and in the distance over

144

his shoulder he watched and waited for Gavin Verheek. Small wonder his friend couldn't cut it in private practice, where life depended upon the clock.

When the third double was served, an hour and eleven minutes after 7 P.M., Verheek strolled to the bar and ordered a Moosehead.

"Sorry I'm late," he said as they shook hands. "I knew you'd appreciate the extra time alone with your Chivas."

"You look tired," Callahan said as he inspected him. Old and tired. Verheek was aging badly and gaining weight. His forehead had grown an inch since their last visit, and his pale skin highlighted the heavy circles under his eyes. "How much do you weigh?"

"None of your business," he said, gulping the beer. "Where's our table?"

"It's reserved for eight-thirty. I figured you would be at least ninety minutes late."

"Then I'm early."

"You could say that. Did you come from work?"

"I live at work now. The Director wants no less than a hundred hours a week until something breaks. I told my wife I'd be home for Christmas."

"How is she?"

"Fine. A very patient lady. We get along much better when I live at the office." She was wife number three in seventeen years.

"I'd like to meet her."

"No, you wouldn't. I married the first two for sex and they enjoyed it so much they shared it with others. I married this one for money and she's not much to look at. You wouldn't be impressed." He emptied the bottle. "I doubt if I can hang on until she dies."

"How old is she?"

"Don't ask. I really love her, you know. Honest. But after two years I now realize we have nothing in common but an acute awareness of the stock market." He looked at the bartender. "Another beer, please."

Callahan chuckled and sipped his drink. "How much is she worth?"

"Not nearly as much as I thought. I'm not sure really. Somewhere around five million, I think. She cleaned out husbands one and two, and I think she was attracted to me for the challenge of marrying just an average joe. That, and the sex is great, she said. They all say that, you know."

"You always picked losers, Gavin, even in

law school. You're attracted to neurotic and depressed women."

"And they're attracted to me." He turned the bottle up and drained half of it. "Why do we always eat in this place?"

"I don't know. It's sort of traditional. It brings back fond memories of law school."

"We hated law school, Thomas. Everyone hates law school. Everyone hates lawyers."

"You're in a fine mood."

"Sorry. I've slept six hours since they found the bodies. The Director screams at me at least five times a day. I scream at everybody under me. It's one big brawl over there."

"Drink up, big boy. Our table's ready. Let's drink and eat and talk, and try to enjoy these few hours together."

"I love you more than my wife, Thomas. Do you know that?"

"That's not saying much."

"You're right."

They followed the maître d' to a small table in the corner, the same table they always requested. Callahan ordered another round, and explained they would be in no hurry to eat.

"Did you see that damned thing in the *Post?*" Verheek asked.

"I saw it. Who leaked it?"

"Who knows. The Director got the short list Saturday morning, hand-delivered by the President himself, with rather explicit demands about secrecy. He showed the list to no one over the weekend, then this morning the story hit with the names of Pryce and MacLawrence. Voyles went berserk when he saw it, and a few minutes later the President called. He rushed to the White House and they had a huge cuss fight. Voyles tried to attack Fletcher Coal, and had to be restrained by K. O. Lewis. Very nasty."

Callahan hung on every word. "This is pretty good."

"Yeah. I'm telling you this part because later, after a few more drinks, you'll expect me to tell you who else is on the list and I won't do it. I'm trying to be a friend, Thomas."

"Keep going."

"Anyway, there's no way the leak came from us. Impossible. It had to come from the White House. The place is full of people who hate Coal, and it's leaking like rusty pipes."

"Coal probably leaked it."

"Maybe so. He's a sleazy bastard, and one theory has him leaking Pryce and MacLawrence to scare everyone, then later announcing two nominees who appear more moderate. It sounds like something he would do."

"I've never heard of Pryce and MacLawrence."

"Join the club. They're both very young, early forties, with precious little experience on the bench. We haven't checked them out, but they appear to be radically conservative."

"And the rest of the list?"

"That was quick. Two beers down, and you've already popped the question."

The drinks arrived. "I want some of those mushrooms stuffed with crabmeat," Verheek told the waiter. "Just to munch on. I'm starving."

Callahan handed over his empty glass. "Bring me an order too."

"Don't ask again, Thomas. You may have to carry me out of here in three hours, but I'll never tell. You know that. Let's say that Pryce and MacLawrence seem to be reflective of the entire list."

"All unknowns?"

"Basically, yes."

Callahan sipped the Scotch slowly and shook his head. Verheek removed his jacket and loosened his tie. "Let's talk about women."

"No."

"How old is she?"

"Twenty-four, but very mature."

"You could be her father."

"I may be. Who knows."

"Where's she from?"

"Denver. I told you that."

"I love Western girls. They're so independent and unpretentious and they tend to wear Levis and have long legs. I may marry one. Does she have money?"

"No. Her father was killed in a plane crash four years ago and her mother got a nice settlement."

"Then she has money."

"She's comfortable."

"I'll bet she is. Do you have a photo?"

"No. She's not a grandchild or a poodle."

"Why didn't you bring a picture?"

"I'll get her to send you one. Why is this so amusing to you?"

"It's hilarious. The great Thomas Callahan, he of the disposable women, has fallen hard."

"I have not."

"It must be a record. What, nine, ten months now? You've actually maintained a steady relationship for almost a year, haven't you?"

"Eight months and three weeks, but don't tell anyone, Gavin. It's not easy for me."

"Your secret's safe. Just give me all the details. How tall is she?"

"Five-eight, hundred and twelve pounds, long legs, tight Levis, independent, unpretentious, your typical Western girl."

"I must find one for myself. Are you gonna marry her?"

"Of course not! Finish your drink."

"Are you, like, monogamous now?"

"Are you?"

"Hell no. Never have been. But we're not talking about me, Thomas, we're talking about Peter Pan here, Cool Hand Callahan, the man with the monthly version of the world's most gorgeous woman. Tell me, Thomas, and don't lie to your best friend, just look me in the eyes and tell me if you have succumbed to a state of monogamy."

Verheek was leaning halfway across the table, watching and grinning stupidly.

"Not so loud," Callahan said, looking around.

"Answer me."

"Give me the other names on the list, and I'll tell you."

Verheek withdrew. "Nice try. I think the answer is yes. I think you're in love with this gal, but too cowardly to admit it. I think she's got your number, pal."

"Okay, she does. Do you feel better?"

"Yeah, much better. When can I meet her?"

"When can I meet your wife?"

"You're confused, Thomas. There's a basic difference here. You don't want to meet my wife, but I do want to meet Darby. You see. I assure you they are very dissimilar."

Callahan smiled and sipped. Verheek relaxed and crossed his legs in the aisle. He tilted the green bottle to his lips.

"You're wired, buddy," Callahan said.

"I'm sorry. I'm drinking as fast as I can."

The mushrooms were served in simmering skillets. Verheek stuffed two in his mouth and chewed furiously. Callahan watched. The Chivas had knocked off the hunger pains, and he would wait a few minutes. He preferred alcohol over food anyway.

Four Arabs noisily filled a table next to them, yakking and jabbering in their language. All four ordered Jack Daniel's.

"Who killed them, Gavin?"

He chewed for a minute, then swallowed hard. "If I knew, I wouldn't tell. But I swear I do not know. It's baffling. The killers vanished without a trace. It was meticulously planned and perfectly executed. Not a clue."

"Why the combination?"

He stuffed another in his mouth. "Quite simple. It's so simple, it's easy to overlook. They were such natural targets. Rosenberg had no security system in his townhouse. Any decent cat burglar could come and go. And poor Jensen was hanging around those places at midnight. They were exposed. At the exact moment each died, the other seven Supremes had FBI agents in their homes. That's why they were selected. They were stupid."

"Then who selected them?"

"Someone with a lot of money. The killers were professionals, and they were probably out of the country within hours. We figure there were three, maybe more. The mess at Rosenberg's could have been done by just one. We figure there were at least two working on Jensen. One or more looking out while the guy with the rope did his thing. Even though it was a dirty little place, it was open to the public, and quite risky. But they were good, very good."

"I've read a lone assassin theory."

"Forget it. It's impossible for one man to kill both of them. Impossible."

"How much would these killers charge?"

"Millions. And it took a bunch of money to plan it all."

"And you have no idea?"

"Look, Thomas, I'm not involved in the investigation, so you'll have to ask those guys. I'm sure they know a helluva lot more than I do. I'm just a lowly government lawyer."

"Yeah, who just happens to be on a first-name basis with the Chief Justice."

"He calls occasionally. This is boring. Let's get back to women. I hate lawyer talk."

"Have you talked to him lately?"

"Picking, Thomas, always picking. Yes, we chatted briefly this morning. He's got all twenty-seven law clerks scouring the federal dockets high and low looking for clues. It's fruitless, and I told him so. Every case that reaches the Supreme Court has at least two parties, and each party involved would certainly benefit if one or two or three justices would disappear and be replaced by one or two or three more sympathetic to its cause. There are thousands of appeals that could eventually end up here, and you can't just pick one and say 'This is it! This is the one that got 'em killed.' It's silly."

"What did he say?"

"Of course he agreed with my brilliant analysis. I think he called after he read the *Post* story to see if he could squeeze something out of me. Can you believe the nerve?"

The waiter hovered over them with a hurried look.

Verheek glanced at the menu, closed it, and handed it to him. "Grilled swordfish, blue cheese, no vegetable."

"I'll eat the mushrooms," Callahan said. The waiter disappeared.

Callahan reached into his coat pocket and removed a thick envelope. He laid it on the table next to the empty Moosehead. "Take a look at this when you get a chance."

"What is it?"

"It's sort of a brief."

"I hate briefs, Thomas. In fact, I hate the law, and the lawyers, and with the exception of you, I hate law professors."

"Darby wrote it."

"I'll read it tonight. What's it about?"

"I think I told you. She is very bright and intelligent, and a very aggressive student. She writes better than most. Her passion, other than me of course, is constitutional law."

"Poor thing."

"She took off four days last week, totally ignored me and the rest of the world, and came up with her own theory, which she has now discarded. But read it anyway. It's fascinating."

"Who's the suspect?"

The Arabs erupted in screaming laughter, slapping each other and spilling whiskey. They watched them for a minute until they died down.

"Don't you hate a bunch of drunks?" Verheek said.

"It's sickening."

Verheek stuffed the envelope into his coat on the back of his chair. "What's her theory?"

"It's a bit unusual. But read it. I mean, it can't hurt, can it? You guys need the help."

"I'll read it only because she wrote it. How is she in bed?"

"How's your wife in bed?"

"Rich. In the shower, in the kitchen, at the grocery. She's rich in everything she does."

"It can't last."

"She'll file by the end of the year. Maybe I'll get the townhouse and some change."

"No prenuptial agreement?"

"Yes, there is, but I'm a lawyer, remember. It's got more loopholes than a tax reform act. A buddy of mine prepared it. Don't you love the law?"

"Let's talk about something else."

"Women?"

"I've got an idea. You want to meet the girl, right?"

"We're talking about Darby?"

"Yes. Darby."

"I'd love to meet her."

"We're going to St. Thomas during Thanksgiving. Why don't you meet us there?"

"Do I have to bring my wife?"

"No. She's not invited."

"Will she run around in a little string job

on the beach? Sort of put on a show for us?"

"Probably."

"Wow. I can't believe this."

"You can get a condo next to us, and we'll have a ball."

"Beautiful, beautiful. Just beautiful."

THIRTEEN

THE PHONE RANG four times, the answering machine clicked on, the recorded voice echoed through the apartment, the beep, then no message. It rang again four times, same routine, and no message. A minute later it rang again, and Gray Grantham grabbed it from bed. He sat on a pillow, trying to focus.

"Who is it?" he asked in pain. There was no light coming through the window.

The voice on the other end was low and timid. "Is this Gray Grantham with the *Washington Post?*"

"It is. Who's calling?"

Slowly, "I can't give you my name."

The fog lifted and he focused on the clock. It was five-forty. "Okay, forget the name. Why are you calling?"

"I saw your story yesterday about the White House and the nominees."

"That's good." You and a million others. "Why are you calling me at this obscene hour?"

"I'm sorry. I'm on my way to work and stopped at a pay phone. I can't call from home or the office."

The voice was clear, articulate, and appeared to be intelligent. "What kind of office?"

"I'm an attorney."

Great. Washington was home for half a million lawyers. "Private or government?"

A slight hesitation. "Uh, I'd rather not say."

"Okay. Look, I'd rather be sleeping. Why, exactly, did you call?"

"I may know something about Rosenberg and Jensen."

Grantham sat on the edge of the bed. "Such as—"

A much longer pause. "Are you recording this?"

"No. Should I?"

"I don't know. I'm really very scared and confused, Mr. Grantham. I prefer not to record this. Maybe the next call, okay?"

"Whatever you want. I'm listening."

"Can this call be traced?"

"Possibly, I guess. But you're at a pay phone, right? What difference does it make?"

"I don't know. I'm just scared."

"It's okay. I swear I'm not recording and I swear I won't trace it. Now, what's on your mind?"

"Well, I think I may know who killed them."

Grantham was standing. "That's some pretty valuable knowledge."

"It could get me killed. Do you think they're following me?"

"Who? Who would be following you?"

"I don't know." The voice trailed off, as if he was looking over his shoulder.

Grantham was pacing by the bed. "Relax. Why don't you tell me your name, okay. I swear it's confidential."

"Garcia."

"That's not a real name, is it?"

"Of course not, but it's the best I can do."

"Okay, Garcia. Talk to me."

"I'm not certain, okay. But I think I stumbled across something at the office that I was not supposed to see."

"Do you have a copy of it?"

"Maybe."

"Look, Garcia. You called me, right. Do you want to talk or not?"

"I'm not sure. What will you do if I tell you something?"

"Check it out thoroughly. If we're gonna accuse someone of the assassinations of two Supreme Court Justices, believe me, the story will be handled delicately."

There was a very long silence. Grantham froze by the rocker and waited. "Garcia. Are you there?"

"Yeah. Can we talk later?"

"Of course. We can talk now."

"I need to think about this. I haven't eaten or slept in a week, and I'm not thinking rationally. I might call you later."

"Okay, okay. That's fine. You can call me at work at—"

"No. I won't call you at work. Sorry I woke you."

He hung up. Grantham looked at the row of numbers on his phone and punched seven digits, waited, then six more, then four more. He scribbled a number on a pad by the phone, and hung up. The pay phone was on Fifteenth Street in Pentagon City.

□   □   □   □

GAVIN VERHEEK slept four hours and woke up drunk. When he arrived at the Hoover Building an hour later, the alcohol was fading and the pain was settling in. He cursed himself and he cursed Callahan, who no doubt would sleep until noon and wake up fresh and alive and ready for the flight to New Orleans. They had left the restaurant when it closed at midnight, then hit a few bars and joked about catching a skin flick or two, but since their favorite movie house had been bombed they couldn't. So they just drank until three or four.

He had a meeting with Director Voyles at eleven, and it was imperative to appear sober and alert. It would be impossible. He told his secretary to close the door, and explained to her that he had caught a nasty virus, maybe the flu, and he was to be left alone at his desk unless it was awfully damned important. She studied his eyes and seemed to sniff more than usual. The smell of beer does not always evaporate with sleep.

She left and closed the door behind her. He locked it. To make things equal, he called Callahan's room, but no one answered.

What a life. His best friend earned almost as much as he did, but worked thirty hours in a busy week, and had his pick of pliant young things twenty years his junior. Then he remembered their grand plans for the week in St. Thomas, and the thought of Darby strolling along the beach. He would go, even if it caused a divorce.

A wave of nausea rippled through his chest and up his esophagus, and he quickly lay still on the floor. Cheap government carpet. He breathed deeply, and the pounding started at the top of his head. The plaster ceiling was not spinning, and this was encouraging. After three minutes, it was evident he would not vomit, at least not now.

His briefcase was within reach, and he carefully slid it next to him. He found the envelope inside with the morning paper. He opened it, unfolded the brief, and held it with both hands six inches above his face.

It was thirteen letter-sized pages of computer paper, all double-spaced with wide margins. He could handle it. Notes were scribbled in the margins by hand and whole sections were marked through. The words FIRST DRAFT were handwritten with a felt pen across the top. Her name, address, and phone number were typed on the cover sheet.

He would skim it for a few minutes while he was on the floor, then hopefully he would feel like sitting at the desk and going through the motions of being an important government lawyer. He thought of Voyles, and the pounding intensified.

She wrote well, in the standard, scholarly legal fashion of long sentences filled with large words. But she was clear. She avoided the double-talk and legal lingo most students strive so desperately for. She would never make it as an attorney employed by the United States Government.

Gavin had never heard of her suspect, and was certain it was not on anyone's list. Technically, it was not a brief, but more of a story about a lawsuit in Louisiana. She told the facts succinctly, and made them interesting. Fascinating, really. He was not skimming.

The facts took four pages, then she filled the next three with brief histories of the parties. It dragged a bit here, but he kept reading. He was hooked. On page eight, the brief or whatever it was summarized the trial. On nine, it mentioned the appeal, and the final three pages laid an implausible trail to the removal of Rosenberg and Jensen from the Court. Callahan said she had already discarded this theory, and she appeared to lose steam at the end.

But it was highly readable. For a moment he had forgotten his current state of pain, and read thirteen pages of a law student's brief while lying on the floor on dirty carpet with a million things to do.

There was a soft knock at the door. He slowly sat up, gingerly stood, and walked to the door. "Yes."

It was the secretary. "I hate to bother. But the Director wants you in his office in ten minutes."

Verheek opened the door. "What?"

"Yes sir. Ten minutes."

He rubbed his eyes and breathed rapidly. "What for?"

"I get demoted for asking those questions, sir."

"Do you have any mouthwash?"

"Well, yes, I believe so. Do you want it?"

"I wouldn't have asked if I didn't want it. Bring it to me. Do you have any gum?"

"Gum?"

"Chewing gum."

"Yes sir. Do you want it too?"

"Just bring me the mouthwash and gum,

and some aspirin if you have it." He walked to his desk and sat down, holding his head in his hands and rubbing his temples. He heard her banging drawers, and then she was before him with the goods.

"Thanks. I'm sorry I snapped." He pointed at the brief in a chair by the door. "Send that brief to Eric East, he's on the fourth floor. Write a note from me. Tell him to look it over when he has a minute."

She left with the brief.

FLETCHER COAL opened the door to the Oval Office, and spoke gravely to K. O. Lewis and Eric East. The President was in Puerto Rico viewing hurricane damage, and Director Voyles now refused to meet with Coal alone. He sent his underlings.

Coal waved them to a sofa, and he sat across the coffee table. His coat was buttoned and his tie was perfect. He never relaxed. East had heard tales about his habits. He worked twenty hours a day, seven days a week, drank nothing but water, and ate most meals from a vending machine in the basement. He could read like a computer, and spent hours each day reviewing memos, reports, correspondence, and mountains of pending legislation. He had perfect recall. For a week now they had brought daily reports of their investigation to this office, and handed them to Coal, who devoured the material and memorized it for the next meeting. If they misstated something, he would terrorize them. He was hated, but it was impossible not to respect him. He was smarter than them, and he worked harder. And he knew it.

He was smug in the emptiness of the Oval Office. His boss was away performing for the cameras, but the real power had stayed behind to run the country.

K. O. Lewis placed a four-inch stack of the latest on the table.

"Anything new?" Coal asked.

"Maybe. The French authorities were routinely reviewing footage taken by the security cameras at the Paris airport, and they thought they recognized a face. They checked it against two other cameras in the concourse, different angles, then reported to Interpol. The face is disguised, but Interpol believes it is Khamel, the terrorist. I'm sure you've heard of—"

"I have."

"They've studied the footage at length, and are almost certain he exited a plane that arrived nonstop from Dulles last

Wednesday, about ten hours after Jensen was found."

"The Concorde?"

"No, United. Based on the time and the locations of the cameras, they have ways of determining the gates and flights."

"And Interpol contacted the CIA?"

"Yes. They talked to Gminski around one this afternoon."

Coal's face registered nothing. "How certain are they?"

"Eighty percent. He's a master of disguise, and it would be a bit unusual for him to travel in such a manner. So there's room for doubt. We've got photos and a summary for the President's review. Frankly, I've studied the pictures, and I can't tell anything. But Interpol knows him."

"He hasn't been willingly photographed in years, has he?"

"Not that we know of. And rumor has it he goes under the knife and gets a new face every two or three years."

Coal pondered this for a second. "Okay. What if it's Khamel, and what if he was involved in the killings? What does it mean?"

"It means we'll never find him. There are at least nine countries, including Israel, actively stalking him right now. It means he was paid a bunch of money by someone to use his talents here. We've said all along the killer or killers were professionals who were gone before the bodies were cold."

"So it means little."

"You could say that."

"Fine. What else do you have?"

Lewis glanced at Eric East. "Well, we have the usual daily summary."

"They've been rather dry as of late."

"Yes, they have. We have three hundred and eighty agents working twelve hours a day. Yesterday they interviewed one hundred and sixty people in thirty states. We have—"

Coal held up his hand. "Save it. I'll read the summary. It seems safe to say there is nothing new."

"Maybe a small new wrinkle." Lewis looked at Eric East, who was holding a copy of the brief.

"What is it?" Coal asked.

East shifted uncomfortably. The brief had been passed upward all day until Voyles read it and liked it. He viewed it as a long shot, unworthy of serious attention, but the brief mentioned the President, and he loved the idea of making Coal and his boss sweat. He instructed Lewis and East to deliver the brief to Coal, and to treat it as an important theory the Bureau was taking seriously. For the first time in a week, Voyles had smiled when he talked of the idiots in the Oval Office reading this little brief and running for cover. Play it up, Voyles said. Tell them we intend to pursue with twenty agents.

"It's a theory that has surfaced in the last twenty-four hours, and Director Voyles is quite intrigued by it. He's afraid it could be damaging to the President."

Coal was stone-faced, never flinching. "How's that?"

East placed the brief on the table. "It's all here in this report."

Coal glanced at it, then studied East. "Fine. I'll read it later. Is that all?"

Lewis stood and buttoned his jacket. "Yes, we'll be going."

Coal followed them to the door.

THERE WAS NO FANFARE when Air Force One landed at Andrews a few minutes after ten. The Queen was off raising money, and no friends or family greeted the President as he bounced off the plane and darted into his limousine. Coal was waiting. The President sunk low in the seat. "I didn't expect you," he said.

"I'm sorry. We need to talk." The limo sped away toward the White House.

"It's late and I'm tired."

"How was the hurricane?"

"Impressive. It blew away a million shacks and cardboard huts, and now we'll rush down with a couple of billion and build new homes and power plants. They need a good hurricane every five years."

"I've got the disaster declaration ready."

"Okay. What's so important?"

Coal handed over a copy of what was now known as the pelican brief.

"I don't want to read," said the President. "Just tell me about it."

"Voyles and his motley crew have stumbled across a suspect that no one has mentioned until now. A most obscure, unlikely suspect. An eager-beaver law student at Tulane wrote this damned thing, and it somehow made its way to Voyles, who read it and decided it had merit. Keep in mind, they are desperate for suspects. The theory is so farfetched it's incredible, and on its face it doesn't worry me. But Voyles worries me. He's decided he must pursue with enthusiasm, and the press is watching every move he makes. There could be leaks."

"We can't control his investigation."

"We can manipulate it. Gminski is waiting at the White House, and—"

"Gminski!"

"Relax, Chief. I personally handed him a copy of this three hours ago, and swore him to secrecy. He may be incompetent, but he can keep a secret. I trust him much more than Voyles."

"I don't trust either one of them."

Coal liked to hear this. He wanted the President to trust no one but him. "I think you should ask the CIA to immediately investigate this. I would like to know everything before Voyles starts digging. Neither will find anything, but if we know more than Voyles, you can convince him to back off. It makes sense, Chief."

The President was frustrated. "It's domestic. CIA has no business snooping around. It's probably illegal."

"It is illegal, technically. But Gminski will do it for you, and he can do it quickly, secretly, and more thoroughly than the FBI."

"It's illegal."

"It's been done before, Chief, many times."

The President watched the traffic. His eyes were puffy and red, but not from fatigue. He had slept three hours on the plane. But he'd spent the day looking sad and concerned for the cameras, and it was hard to snap out of it.

He took the brief and tossed it on the empty seat next to him. "Is it someone we know?"

"Yes."

FOURTEEN

BECAUSE IT IS A CITY of the night, New Orleans wakes slowly. It's quiet until well after dawn, then shakes the cobwebs and eases into the morning. There's no early rush except on the corridors to and from the suburbs, and the busy streets downtown. This is the same for all cities. But in the French Quarter, the soul of New Orleans, the smell of last night's whiskey and jambalaya and blackened redfish lingers not far above the empty streets until the sun can be seen. An hour or two later, it is replaced with the aroma of French Market coffee and beignets, and around this time the sidewalks reluctantly show signs of life.

Darby curled herself in a chair on the small balcony, sipping coffee and waiting on the sun. Callahan was a few feet away, through the open french doors, still wrapped in sheets and dead to the world. There was a trace of a breeze, but the humidity would return by noon. She pulled his robe closer around her neck, and inhaled the richness of his cologne. She thought of her father, and his baggy cotton button-downs he allowed her to wear when she was a teenager. She would roll the sleeves tightly to her elbows and let the tails hang to her knees, then walk the malls with her friends, secure in her belief that no one was cooler. Her father was her friend. By the time she finished high school, she had the run of his closet, as long as things were washed and neatly pressed and put back on the hangers. She could still smell the Grey Flannel he splashed on his face every day.

If he was living, he would be four years older than Thomas Callahan. Her mother had remarried and moved to Boise. Darby had a brother in Germany. The three seldom talked. Her father had been the glue in a fractious family, and his death had scattered them.

Twenty other people died in the plane crash, and before the funeral arrangements were complete the lawyers were calling. It was her first real exposure to the

176

legal world, and it was not pleasant. The family attorney was a real estate type who knew nothing about litigation. A slick ambulance chaser got next to her brother, and he persuaded the family to sue quickly. His name was Herschel, and for two years the family suffered as Herschel stalled and lied and bungled the case. They settled a week before trial for half a million, after Herschel's cut, and Darby got a hundred thousand.

She decided to be a lawyer. If a clown like Herschel could do it and make big bucks while wreaking havoc on society, then she certainly could do it for a nobler purpose. She thought of Herschel often. When she passed the bar exam, her first lawsuit would be filed against him for malpractice. She wanted to work for an environmental firm. Finding a job, she knew, would not be a problem.

The hundred thousand was intact. Her mother's new husband was a paper company executive who was a little older and a lot wealthier, and shortly after their marriage she divided her portion of the settlement between Darby and her brother. She said the money reminded her of her deceased husband, and the gesture was symbolic. Though she still loved their father, she had a new life in a new city with a new husband who would retire in five years with money to burn. Darby had been confused by the symbolic gesture, but appreciated it and took the money.

The hundred thousand had doubled. She placed most of it in mutual funds, but only in those without holdings in chemical and petroleum companies. She drove an Accord and lived modestly. Her wardrobe was basic law school, purchased from factory outlet stores. She and Callahan enjoyed the better restaurants in town, and never ate at the same place twice. It was always Dutch treat.

He cared little for money, and never pressed her for information. She had more than the typical law student, but Tulane had its share of rich kids.

They dated for a month before they went to bed. She laid the ground rules, and he anxiously agreed to them. There would be no other women. They would be very discreet. And he had to stop drinking so much.

He stuck to the first two, but the drinking continued. His father, grandfather, and brothers were heavy drinkers, and it was sort of expected of him. But for the first time in his life, Thomas Callahan was in love, madly in love, and he knew the point at which the Scotch was interfering with his woman. He was careful. With the exception of last week and the personal trauma of losing Rosenberg, he never drank before 5 P.M. When they were together, he abandoned the Chivas when he'd had enough and thought it might affect his performance.

It was amusing to watch a forty-five-year-old man fall for the first time. He struggled to maintain a level of coolness, but in their private little moments he was as silly as a sophomore.

She kissed him on the cheek, and covered him with a quilt. Her clothes were placed neatly on a chair. She locked the front door quietly behind her. The sun was up now, peeking through the buildings across Dauphine. The sidewalk was empty.

She had a class in three hours, then Callahan and con law at eleven. There was a mock court appellate brief due in a week. Her casenote for law review was gathering dust. She was behind in classwork for two courses. It was time to be a student again.

She had wasted four days playing detective, and she cursed herself for it.

The Accord was around the corner and down a half a block.

THEY WATCHED HER, and it was enjoyable. Tight jeans, baggy sweater, long legs, sunglasses to hide the eyes with no makeup. They watched her close the door and walk quickly along Royale, then disappear around the corner. The hair was shoulder-length and appeared to be dark red.

It was her.

HE CARRIED HIS LUNCH in a little brown paper bag, and found an empty park bench with his back to New Hampshire. He hated Dupont Circle, with its bums, druggies, perverts, aging hippies, and black-leather punks with red spiked hair and vicious tongues. Across the fountain, a well-dressed man with a loudspeaker was assembling his group of animal rights activists for a march to the White House. The leather people jeered and cursed them, but four mounted policemen were close enough to prevent trouble.

He looked at his watch and peeled a ba-

nana. Noon, and he preferred to eat elsewhere. The meeting would be brief. He
watched the cursing and jeering, and saw
his contact emerge through the crowd.
Their eyes met, a nod, and he was sitting
on the bench next to him. His name was
Booker, from Langley. They met here occasionally, when the lines of communica-
tion became tangled or blurred and their
bosses needed to hear real words that no
one else would hear.

Booker had no lunch. He began shelling
roasted peanuts and throwing the hulls under the circular bench. "How's Mr.
Voyles?"

"Mean as hell. The usual."

He threw peanuts in his mouth. "Gminski was in the White House until midnight
last night," Booker said.

There was no response to this. Voyles
knew it.

Booker continued. "They've panicked
over there. This little pelican thing has
scared them. We've read it too, you know,
and we're almost certain you guys are not
impressed, but for some reason Coal is terrified of it and he's got the President upset.
We sort of figure you guys are just having a
little fun with Coal and his boss, and since

the brief mentions the President and has that photo in it, we figure it's sort of fun for you guys. Know what I mean?"

He took an inch off the banana, and said nothing.

The animal lovers moved away in ragged formation as the leather lovers hissed at them.

"Anyway, it's none of our business, and should be none of our business except the President now wants us to secretly investigate the pelican brief before you guys can get to it. He's convinced we'll find nothing, and he wants to know there's nothing to it so he can convince Voyles to back off."

"There's nothing to it."

Booker watched a drunk urinate in the fountain. The cops were riding off into the sun. "Then Voyles is having a little fun, right?"

"We are pursuing all leads."

"No real suspects, though?"

"No." The banana was history. "Why are they so worried about us investigating this little thing?"

Booker crunched on a small peanut still in the hull. "Well, to them it's quite simple. They are livid over the revelation of Pryce and MacLawrence as nominees, and of course it's all your fault. They distrust Voyles immensely. And if you guys start digging into the pelican brief, they're terrified the press will find out and the President will take a beating. Reelection is next year, blah, blah, blah."

"What did Gminski tell the President?"

"That he had no desire to interfere with an FBI investigation, that we had better things to do, and that it would be illegal as hell. But since the President was begging so hard and Coal was threatening so much, we'd do it anyway. And here I am talking to you."

"Voyles appreciates it."

"We're gonna start digging today, but the whole thing is absurd. We'll go through the motions, stay out of the way, and in a week or so tell the President the whole theory is a shot in the dark."

He folded down the top of his brown bag, and stood. "Good. I'll report to Voyles. Thanks." He walked toward Connecticut, away from the leather punks, and was gone.

THE MONITOR was on a cluttered table in the center of the newsroom, and Gray Grantham glared at it amid the hum and roar of the gathering and reporting. The words were not coming, and he sat and glared. The phone rang. He punched his button, and grabbed the receiver without leaving the monitor. "Gray Grantham."

"It's Garcia."

He forgot the monitor. "Yeah, so what's up?"

"I have two questions. First, do you record these calls, and second, can you trace them?"

"No and yes. We don't record until we ask permission, and we can trace but we don't. I thought you said you would not call me at work."

"Do you want me to hang up?"

"No. It's fine. I'd rather talk at 3 P.M. at the office than 6 A.M. in bed."

"Sorry. I'm just scared, that's all. I'll talk to you as long as I can trust you, but if you ever lie to me, Mr. Grantham, I'll quit talking."

"It's a deal. When do you start talking?"

"I can't talk now. I'm at a pay phone downtown, and I'm in a hurry."

"You said you had a copy of something."

"No, I said I might have a copy of something. We'll see."

"Okay. So when might you call again?"

"Do I have to make an appointment?"

"No. But I'm in and out a lot."

"I'll call during lunch tomorrow."

"I'll be waiting right here."

Garcia was gone. Grantham punched seven digits, then six, then four. He wrote the number, then flipped through the yellow pages until he found Pay Phones Inc. The Vendor Location listed the number on Pennsylvania Avenue near the Justice Department.

FIFTEEN

THE ARGUMENT started with dessert, a portion of the meal Callahan preferred to drink. She was nice enough when she clicked off the drinks he'd already consumed with dinner: two double Scotches while they waited on a table, one more before they ordered, and with the fish two bottles of wine, of which she'd had two glasses. He was drinking too fast and getting sloppy, and by the time she finished rattling off this accounting he was angry. He ordered Drambuie for dessert, because it was his favorite, and because it was suddenly a matter of principle. He gulped it and ordered another, and she was furious.

Darby spooned her coffee and ignored him. Mouton's was packed, and she just wanted to leave without a scene and get to her apartment alone.

The argument turned nasty on the sidewalk as they walked away from the restaurant. He pulled the keys to the Porsche from his pocket, and she said he was too drunk to drive. Give her the keys. He gripped them and staggered on in the direction of the parking lot, three blocks away. She said she would walk. Have a nice one, he said. She followed a few steps behind, embarrassed at the stumbling figure in front of her. She pleaded with him. His blood level was at least point-two-zero. He was a law professor, dammit. He would kill someone. He staggered faster, coming perilously close to the curb, then weaving away. He yelled over his shoulder, something about driving better drunk than she could sober. She fell behind. She'd taken a ride before when he was like this, and she knew what a drunk could do in a Porsche.

He crossed the street blindly, hands stuck deep in his pockets as if out for a casual stroll in the late night. He misjudged the curb, hit it with the toes instead of the sole, and went sprawling and bouncing and cursing along the sidewalk. He scrambled up quickly before she could reach him. Leave me alone, dammit, he told her. Just give me the keys, she begged, or I'm walking. He shoved her away. Have a nice one, he said with a laugh. She'd never seen him this drunk. He'd never touched her in anger, drunk or not.

Next to the parking lot was a greasy little dive with neon beer signs covering the windows. She looked inside the open door for help, but thought, how stupid. It was filled with drunks.

She yelled at him as he approached the Porsche. "Thomas! Please! Let me drive!" She was on the sidewalk and would go no farther.

He stumbled on, waving her off, mumbling to himself. He unlocked the door, squeezed downward, and disappeared between the other cars. The engine started and roared as he gunned it.

Darby leaned on the side of the building a few feet from the parking lot's exit. She looked at the street, and almost hoped for a cop. She would rather have him arrested than dead.

It was too far to walk. She would watch him drive away, then call a cab, then ignore him for a week. At least a week. Have a nice one, she repeated to herself. He gunned it again and squealed tires.

The explosion knocked her to the side-

188

walk. She landed on all fours, face down, stunned for a second, then immediately aware of the heat and the tiny pieces of fiery debris falling in the street. She gaped in horror at the parking lot. The Porsche flipped in a perfect violent somersault and landed upside down. The tires and wheels and doors and fenders slung free. The car was a brilliant fireball, roaring away with flames instantly devouring it.

Darby started toward it, screaming for him. Debris fell around her and the heat slowed her. She stopped thirty feet away, screaming with hands over her mouth.

Then a second explosion flipped it again and drove her away. She tripped, and her head fell hard on the bumper of another car. The pavement was hot to her face, and that was the last she remembered for a moment.

The dive emptied and the drunks were everywhere. They stood along the sidewalk and stared. A couple tried to advance, but the heat reddened their faces and kept them away. Thick, heavy smoke billowed from the fireball, and within seconds two other cars were on fire. There were shouts and voices in panic.

"Whose car is it!"

"Call 911!"

"Is anybody in it!"

"Call 911!"

They dragged her by the elbows back to the sidewalk, to the center of the crowd. She was repeating the name Thomas. A cold cloth came from the dive and was placed on her forehead.

The crowd thickened and the street was busy. Sirens, she heard sirens as she came around. There was a knot on the back of her head, and a coldness on her face. Her mouth was dry. "Thomas. Thomas," she repeated.

"It's okay, it's okay," said a black face just above her. He was carefully holding her head and patting her arm. Other faces stared downward. They all nodded in agreement. "It's okay."

The sirens were screaming now. She gently removed the cloth, and her eyes focused. There were red and blue lights flashing from the street. The sirens were deafening. She sat up. They leaned her against the building beneath the neon beer signs. They eased away, watching her carefully.

"You all right, miss?" asked the black man.

She couldn't answer. Didn't try to. Her head was broken. "Where is Thomas?" she asked, looking at the crack in the sidewalk.

They looked at each other. The first fire truck screamed to a halt twenty feet away, and the crowd parted. Firemen jumped and scrambled in all directions.

"Where is Thomas?" she repeated.

"Miss, who is Thomas?" asked the black man.

"Thomas Callahan," she said softly, as if everyone knew him.

"Was he in that car?"

She nodded, then closed her eyes. The sirens wailed and died, and in between she heard the shouts of anxious men, and the popping of the fire. She could smell the burning.

The second and third fire trucks came blaring in from different directions. A cop shoved his way through the crowd. "Police. Outta the way. Police." He pushed and shoved until he found her. He fell to his knees and waved a badge under her nose. "Ma'am, Sergeant Rupert, NOPD."

Darby heard this but thought nothing of it. He was in her face, this Rupert with bushy hair, a baseball cap, black and gold Saints jacket. She stared blankly at him.

"Is that your car, ma'am? Someone said it was your car."

She shook her head. No.

Rupert was grabbing her elbows and pulling up. He was talking to her, asking if she was all right, and at the same time pulling her up and it hurt like hell. The head was fractured, split, busted, and she was in shock but what did this moron care. She was on her feet. The knees wouldn't lock, and she was limp. He kept asking if she was all right. The black man looked at Rupert as if he was crazy.

There, the legs worked now, and she and Rupert were walking through the crowd, behind a fire truck, around another one to an unmarked cop car. She lowered her head and refused to look at the parking lot. Rupert chatted incessantly. Something about an ambulance. He opened the front door and gingerly placed her in the passenger's seat.

Another cop squatted in the door and started asking questions. He wore jeans and cowboy boots with pointed toes. Darby leaned forward and placed her head in her hands. "I think I need help," she said.

"Sure, lady. Help's on the way. Just a coupla questions. What's your name?"

"Darby Shaw. I think I'm in shock. I'm very dizzy, and I think I need to throw up."

"The ambulance is on the way. Is that your car over there?"

"No."

Another cop car, one with decals and words and lights, squealed to a stop in front of Rupert's. Rupert disappeared for a moment. The cowboy cop suddenly closed her door, and she was all alone in the car. She leaned forward and vomited between her legs. She started crying. She was cold. She slowly laid her head on the driver's seat, and curled into a knot. Silence. Then darkness.

SOMEONE WAS KNOCKING on the window above her. She opened her eyes, and the man wore a uniform and a hat with a badge on it. The door was locked.

"Open the door, lady!" he yelled.

She sat up and opened the door. "Are you drunk, lady?"

The head was pounding. "No," she said desperately.

He opened the door wider. "Is this your car?"

She rubbed her eyes. She had to think.

"Lady, is this your car?"

"No!" She glared at him. "No. It's Rupert's."

"Okay. Who the hell is Rupert?"

There was one fire truck left and most of the crowd was gone. This man in the door was obviously a cop. "Sergeant Rupert. One of you guys," she said.

This made him mad. "Get outta the car, lady."

Gladly. Darby crawled out on the passenger's side, and stood on the sidewalk. In the distance, a solitary fireman hosed down the burnt frame of the Porsche.

Another cop in a uniform joined him and they met her on the sidewalk.

The first cop asked, "What's your name?"

"Darby Shaw."

"Why were you passed out in the car?"

She looked at the car. "I don't know. I got hurt and Rupert put me in the car. Where's Rupert?"

The cops looked at each other. "Who the hell's Rupert?" the first cop asked.

This made her mad and the anger cleared away the cobwebs.

"Rupert said he was a cop."

The second cop asked, "How'd you get hurt?"

Darby glared at him. She pointed to the parking lot across the street. "I was supposed to be in that car over there. But I wasn't, so I'm here, listening to your stupid questions. Where's Rupert?"

They looked blankly at each other. The first cop said, "Stay here," and he walked across the street to another cop car where a man in a suit was talking to a small group. They whispered, then the first cop and the man in the suit walked back to the sidewalk where Darby waited. The man in the suit said, "I'm Lieutenant Olson, New Orleans PD. Did you know the man in the car?" He pointed to the parking lot.

The knees went weak, and she bit her lip. She nodded.

"What's his name?"

"Thomas Callahan."

Olson looked at the first cop. "That's what the computer said. Now, who's this Rupert?"

Darby screamed, "He said he was a cop!"

Olson looked sympathetic. "I'm sorry. There's no cop named Rupert."

She was sobbing loudly. Olson helped her to the hood of Rupert's car, and held her shoulders while the crying subsided and she fought to regain control.

"Check the plates," Olson told the second cop, who quickly scribbled down the tag number from Rupert's car and called it in.

Olson gently held both her shoulders with his hands and looked at her eyes. "Were you with Callahan?"

She nodded, still crying but much quieter. Olson glanced at the first cop.

"How did you get in this car?" Olson asked slowly and softly.

She wiped her eyes with her finger and stared at Olson. "This guy Rupert, who said he was a cop, came and got me from over there, and brought me over here. He put me in the car, and this other cop with cowboy boots starting asking questions. Another cop car pulled up, and they left. Then I guess I passed out. I don't know. I would like to see a doctor."

"Get my car," Olson said to the first cop.

The second cop was back with a puzzled look. "The computer has no record of this tag number. Must be fake tags."

Olson took her arm and led her to his car. He spoke quickly to the two cops. "I'm taking her to Charity. Wrap this up and meet me there. Impound the car. We'll check it later."

She sat in Olson's car listening to the radio squawk and staring at the parking lot. Four cars had burned. The Porsche was upside down in the center, nothing but a crumpled frame. A handful of firemen and other emergency types milled about. A cop was stringing yellow crime-scene tape around the lot.

She touched the knot on the back of her head. No blood. Tears dripped off her chin.

Olson slammed his door, and they eased through the parked cars and headed for St. Charles. He had the blue lights on, but no sirens.

"Do you feel like talking?" he asked.

They were on St. Charles. "I guess," she said. "He's dead, isn't he?"

"Yes, Darby. I'm sorry. I take it he was the only one in the car."

"Yes."

"How'd you get hurt?"

He gave her a handkerchief, and she wiped her eyes. "I fell or something. There were two explosions, and I think the second one knocked me down. I don't remember everything. Please, tell me who Rupert is."

"I have no idea. I don't know a cop named Rupert, and there was no cop here with cowboy boots."

She thought about this for a block and a half.

"What did Callahan do for a living?"

"A law professor at Tulane. I'm a student there."

"Who would want to kill him?"

She stared at the traffic lights and shook her head. "You're certain it was intentional?"

"No doubt about it. It was a very powerful explosive. We found a piece of a foot stuck in a chain-link fence eighty feet away. I'm sorry, okay. He was murdered."

"Maybe someone got the wrong car."

"That's always possible. We'll check out everything. I take it you were supposed to be in the car with him."

She tried to speak, but could not hold the tears. She buried her face in the handkerchief.

He parked between two ambulances near the emergency entrance at Charity, and left the blue lights on. He helped her quickly inside to a dirty room where fifty people sat in various degrees of pain and discomfort. She found a seat by the water fountain. Olson talked to the lady behind the window, and he raised his voice but Darby couldn't understand him. A small boy with a bloody towel around his foot cried in his mother's lap. A young black girl was about to give birth. There was not a doctor or nurse in sight. No one was in a hurry.

Olson crouched in front of her. "It'll be a few minutes. Sit tight. I'm gonna move the car, and I'll be back in a minute. Do you feel like talking?"

"Yeah, sure."

He was gone. She checked again for blood, and found none. The double doors opened wide, and two angry nurses came after the girl in labor. They sort of dragged her away, back through the doors and down the hall.

Darby waited, then followed. With the red eyes and handkerchief, she looked like some child's mother. The hall was a zoo with nurses and orderlies and the wounded yelling and moving about. She turned a corner and saw an EXIT sign. Through the door, into another hall, much quieter, another door, and she was on a loading dock. There were lights in the alley. Don't run. Be strong. It's okay. No one's watching. She was on the street, walking briskly. The cool air cleared her eyes. She refused to cry.

Olson would take his time, and when he returned he would figure they had called her name and she was back there getting worked on. He would wait. And wait.

She turned corners, and saw Rampart. The Quarter was just ahead. She could get lost there. There were people on Royal, tourist types strolling along. She felt safer. She entered the Holiday Inn, paid with plastic, and got a room on the fifth floor. After the door was bolted and chained, she curled up on the bed with all the lights on.

MRS. VERHEEK rolled her plump but rich ass away from the center of the bed, and grabbed the phone. "It's for you, Gavin!" she yelled into the bathroom. Gavin emerged with shaving cream on half his face, and took the receiver from his wife, who burrowed deep into the bed. Like a hog rutting in mud, he thought.

"Hello," he snapped.

It was a female voice he'd never heard

before. "This is Darby Shaw. Do you know who I am?"

He smiled instantly, and for a second thought of the string bikini on St. Thomas. "Well, yes. I believe we have a mutual friend."

"Did you read the little theory I wrote?"

"Ah, yes. The pelican brief, as we refer to it."

"And who is we?"

Verheek sat in a chair by the night table. This was no social call. "Why are you calling, Darby?"

"I need some answers, Mr. Verheek. I'm scared to death."

"It's Gavin, okay?"

"Gavin. Where is the brief now?"

"Here and there. What's wrong?"

"I'll tell you in a minute. Just tell me what you did with the brief."

"Well, I read it, then sent it to another division, and it was seen by some folks within the Bureau, then shown to Director Voyles, who sort of liked it."

"Has it been seen outside the FBI?"

"I can't answer that, Darby."

"Then I won't tell you what's happened to Thomas."

Verheek pondered this for a long minute. She waited patiently. "Okay. Yes, it's been seen outside the FBI. By whom and by how many, I don't know."

"He's dead, Gavin. He was murdered around ten last night. Someone planted a car bomb for both of us. I got lucky, but now they're after me."

Verheek was hovering over the phone, scribbling notes. "Are you hurt?"

"Physically, I'm okay."

"Where are you?"

"New Orleans."

"Are you certain, Darby? I mean, I know you're certain, but, dammit, who would want to kill him?"

"I met a couple of them."

"How'd you—"

"It's a long story. Who saw the brief, Gavin? Thomas gave it to you Monday night. It's been passed around, and forty-eight hours later he's dead. And I'm supposed to be dead with him. It fell into the wrong hands, wouldn't you say?"

"Are you safe?"

"Who the hell knows?"

"Where are you staying? What's your phone number?"

"Not so fast, Gavin. I'm moving real slow

right now. I'm at a pay phone, so no cute stuff."

"Come on, Darby! Give me a break! Thomas Callahan was my best friend. You've got to come in."

"And what might that mean?"

"Look, Darby, give me fifteen minutes, and we'll have a dozen agents pick you up. I'll catch a flight and be there before noon. You can't stay on the streets."

"Why, Gavin? Who's after me? Talk to me, Gavin."

"I'll talk to you when I get there."

"I don't know. Thomas is dead because he talked to you. I'm not that anxious to meet you right now."

"Darby, look, I don't know who or why, but I assure you you're in a very dangerous situation. We can protect you."

"Maybe later."

He breathed deeply and sat on the edge of the bed. "You can trust me, Darby."

"Okay, I trust you. But what about those other people? This is heavy, Gavin. My little brief has someone awfully upset, wouldn't you say?"

"Did he suffer?"

She hesitated. "I don't think so." The voice was cracking.

"Will you call me in two hours? At the office. I'll give you an inside number."

"Give me the number, and I'll think about it."

"Please, Darby. I'll go straight to the Director when I get there. Call me at eight, your time."

"Give me the number."

THE BOMB EXPLODED too late to make the Thursday morning edition of the *Times-Picayune*. Darby flipped through it hurriedly in the hotel room. Nothing. She watched the television, and there it was. A live shot of the burned-out Porsche, still sitting amid the debris in the parking lot, secluded nicely with yellow tape running everywhere. The police were treating it as a homicide. No suspects. No comment. Then the name of Thomas Callahan, age forty-five, a prominent professor of law at Tulane. The dean was suddenly there with a microphone in his face, talking about Professor Callahan and the shock of it all.

The shock of it all, the fatigue, the fear, the pain, and Darby buried her head in the pillow. She hated crying, and this would be the last of it for a while. Mourning would only get her killed.

SIXTEEN

EVEN THOUGH it was a wonderful crisis, with the ratings up and Rosenberg dead, with his image clean and polished and America feeling good about itself because he was in command, with the Democrats running for cover and reelection next year in the bag, he was sick of this crisis and its relentless predawn meetings. He was sick of F. Denton Voyles and his smugness and arrogance, and his squatty little figure sitting on the other side of his desk in a wrinkled trench coat looking out a window while he addressed the President of the United States. He would be here in a minute for another meeting before breakfast, another tense encounter in which Voyles would tell only a portion of what he knew.

He was sick of being in the dark, and fed only what bits and crumbs Voyles chose to throw his way. Gminski would throw him a few, and somehow in the midst of all this crumb scattering and gathering he was supposed to get enough and be satisfied. He knew nothing compared to them. At least he had Coal to plow through their paper and memorize it all, and keep them honest.

He was sick of Coal, too. Sick of his perfectness and sleeplessness. Sick of his brilliance. Sick of his penchant for beginning each day when the sun was somewhere over the Atlantic, and planning every damned minute of every damned hour until it was over the Pacific. Then he, Coal, would load up a box of the day's junk, take it home, read it, decipher it, store it, then come in a few hours later blazing away with all the painfully boring mishmash he had just devoured. When Coal was tired, he slept five hours a night, but normal was three or four. He left his office in the West Wing at eleven each night, read all the way home in the back of his limo, then about the time the limo cooled off Coal was waiting on it for the return ride to the White House. He considered it a sin to arrive at his desk after 5 A.M. And if he could work a hundred and twenty hours a week, then everyone else should be able to do at least eighty. He demanded eighty. After three years, no one in this Administration could remember all the people fired by Fletcher Coal for not working eighty hours a week. Happened at least three times a month.

Coal was happiest on mornings when the tension was thick and a nasty meeting was planned. In the past week this thing with Voyles had kept him smiling. He was standing beside the desk, going through the mail while the President scanned the *Post* and two secretaries scurried about.

The President glanced at him. Perfect black suit, white shirt, red silk tie, a bit too much grease on the hair above the ears. He was sick of him, but he'd get over it when the crisis passed and he could get back to golf and Coal could sweat the details. He told himself he had that kind of energy and stamina when he was only thirty-seven, but he knew better.

Coal snapped his fingers, glared at the secretaries, and they happily ran from the Oval Office.

"And he said he wouldn't come if I was here. That's hilarious." Coal was clearly amused.

"I don't think he likes you," the President said.

"He loves people he can run over."

"I guess I need to be sweet to him."

"Lay it on thick, Chief. He has to back off. This theory is so weak it's comical, but in his hands it could be dangerous."

"What about the law student?"

"We're checking. She appears harmless."

The President stood and stretched. Coal shuffled papers. A secretary on the intercom announced the arrival of Voyles.

"I'll be going," Coal said. He would listen and watch from around the corner. At his insistence, three closed-circuit cameras were installed in the Oval Office. The monitors were in a small, locked room in the West Wing. He had the only key. Sarge knew of the room, but had not bothered to enter. Yet. The cameras were invisible and supposedly a big secret.

The President felt better knowing Coal would at least be watching. He met Voyles at the door with a warm handshake and guided him to the sofa for a warm, friendly little chat. Voyles was not impressed. He knew Coal would be listening. And watching.

But in the spirit of the moment, Voyles

removed his trench coat and laid it properly on a chair. He did not want coffee.

The President crossed his legs. He was wearing the brown cardigan. The grandfather.

"Denton," he said gravely. "I want to apologize for Fletcher Coal. He doesn't have much finesse."

Voyles nodded slightly. You stupid bastard. There are enough wires in this office to electrocute half the bureaucrats in D.C. Coal was somewhere in the basement hearing about his lack of finesse. "He can be an ass, can't he?" Voyles grunted.

"Yes, he can. I have to really watch him. He's very bright and drives hard, but he tends to overdo it at times."

"He's a son of a bitch, and I'll say it to his face." Voyles glanced at an air vent above the portrait of Thomas Jefferson where a camera watched it all below.

"Yes, well, I'll keep him out of your way until this thing is over."

"You do that."

The President slowly sipped from his coffee and pondered what to say next. Voyles was not known for his conversation.

"I need a favor."

Voyles stared with rigid and unblinking eyes. "Yes, sir."

"I need the scoop on this pelican thing. It's a wild idea, but, hell, it mentions me, sort of. How serious are you taking it?"

Oh, this was funny. Voyles fought off a smile. It was working. Mr. President and Mr. Coal were sweating the pelican brief. They had received it late Tuesday, worried with it all day Wednesday, and now in the waking hours of Thursday were on their knees begging about something one notch above a practical joke.

"We're investigating, Mr. President." It was a lie, but how could he know? "We are pursuing all leads, all suspects. I wouldn't have sent it over if I wasn't serious." The wrinkles squeezed together on the tanned forehead, and Voyles wanted to laugh.

"What have you learned?"

"Not much, but we just started. We got it less than forty-eight hours ago, and I assigned fourteen agents in New Orleans to start digging. It's all routine." The lies sounded so good he could almost hear Coal choking.

Fourteen! It hit him in the gut so hard he sat up straight and placed the coffee on a table. Fourteen Fibbies out there flashing badges, asking questions, and it was just a matter of time before this thing got out. "Fourteen, you say. Sounds like it's pretty serious."

Voyles was unyielding. "We're very serious, Mr. President. They've been dead a week, and the trail's growing colder. We're tracking leads as fast as we can. My men are working around the clock."

"I understand all that, but how serious is this pelican theory?"

Damn, this was fun. The brief had yet to be sent to New Orleans. In fact, New Orleans had not been contacted. He had instructed Eric East to mail a copy to that office with orders to quietly ask a few questions. It was a dead end, just like a hundred others they were chasing.

"I doubt if there's anything to it, Mr. President, but we've got to check it out."

The wrinkles relaxed and there was a touch of a smile. "I don't have to tell you, Denton, how much this nonsense could hurt if the press found out."

"We don't consult the press when we investigate."

"I know. Let's not get into that. I just wish you would back off this thing. I mean, what the hell, it's absurd, and I could really get burned. Know what I'm saying?"

Voyles was brutal. "Are you asking me to ignore a suspect, Mr. President?"

Coal leaned toward the screen. No, I'm telling you to forget this pelican brief! He almost said it out loud. He could make it real plain for Voyles. He could spell it out, then slap the dumpy little wretch if he got smart. But he was hiding in a locked room, away from the action. And, for the moment, he knew he was where he belonged.

The President shifted and recrossed his legs at the knees. "Come on, Denton, you know what I'm saying. There are bigger fish in the pond. The press is watching this investigation, just dying to find out who's a suspect. You know how they are. I don't have to tell you that I have no friends with the press. Even my own press secretary dislikes me. Ha, ha, ha. Forget about it for a while. Back off and chase the real suspects. This thing is a joke, but it could embarrass the hell out of me."

Denton looked hard at him. Relentless.

The President shifted again. "What about this Khamel thing? Sounds pretty good, huh?"

"Could be."

"Yeah. Since we're talking numbers, how many men have you assigned to Khamel?"

Voyles said, "Fifteen," and almost laughed. The President's mouth fell open. The hottest suspect in the game gets fifteen, and this damned pelican thing gets fourteen.

Coal smiled and shook his head. Voyles had been caught in his own lies. On the bottom of page four of the Wednesday report, Eric East and K. O. Lewis gave the number at thirty, not fifteen. Relax, Chief, Coal whispered to the screen. He's playing with you.

The President was anything but relaxed. "Good god, Denton. Why only fifteen? I thought this was a significant break."

"Maybe a few more than that. I'm running this investigation, Mr. President."

"I know. And you're doing a fine job. I'm not meddling. I just wish you'd consider spending your time elsewhere. That's all. When I read the pelican brief I almost vomited. If the press saw it and started digging, I'd be crucified."

"So you're asking me to back off?"

The President leaned forward and stared fiercely at Voyles. "I'm not asking, Denton. I'm telling you to leave it alone. Ignore it for a couple of weeks. Spend your time elsewhere. If it flares up again, take another look. I'm still the boss around here, remember?"

Voyles relented and managed a tiny smile. "I'll make you a deal. Your hatchet man Coal has done a number on me with the press. They've eaten my lunch over the security we provided to Rosenberg and Jensen."

The President nodded solemnly.

"You get that pit bull off my ass, keep him away from me, and I'll forget the pelican theory."

"I don't make deals."

Voyles sneered but kept his cool. "Good. I'll send fifty agents to New Orleans tomorrow. And fifty the next day. We'll be flashing badges all over town and doing our damnedest to attract attention."

The President jumped to his feet and walked to the windows overlooking the Rose Garden. Voyles sat motionless and waited.

"All right, all right. It's a deal. I can control Fletcher Coal."

Voyles stood and walked slowly to the desk. "I don't trust him, and if I smell him one more time during this investigation, the deal's off and we investigate the pelican brief with all the weight I can muster."

The President held up his hands and smiled warmly. "It's a deal."

Voyles was smiling and the President was smiling, and in the closet near the Cabinet Room Fletcher Coal was smiling at a screen. Hatchet man, pit bull. He loved it. Those were the words that created legends.

He turned off the screens and locked the door behind him. They would talk another ten minutes about the background checks on the short list, and he would listen in his office where he had audio but no video. He had a staff meeting at nine. A firing at ten. And he had some typing to do. With most memos, he simply dictated into the machine and handed the tape to a secretary. But occasionally, Coal found it necessary to resort to the phantom memo. These were always widely circulated in the West Wing, and always controversial as hell, and usually dripped to the press. Because they came from no one, they could be found lying on almost every desk. Coal would scream and accuse. He had fired people for phantom memos, all of which came from his typewriter.

It was four single-spaced paragraphs on

one page, and it summarized what he knew about Khamel and his recent flight out of Washington. And there were vague links to the Libyans and Palestinians. Coal admired it. How long before it would be in the *Post* or the *Times?* He made little bets with himself about which paper would get it first.

THE DIRECTOR was at the White House, and from there would fly to New York and return tomorrow. Gavin camped outside the office of K. O. Lewis until there was a small opening. He was in.

Lewis was irritated, but always the gentleman. "You look scared."

"I've just lost my best friend."

Lewis waited for more.

"His name was Thomas Callahan. He's the guy from Tulane who brought me the pelican brief, and it got passed around, then sent to the White House and who knows where else, and now he's dead. Blown to bits by a car bomb last night in New Orleans. Murdered, K.O."

"I'm sorry."

"It's not a matter of being sorry. Evidently the bomb was intended for Callahan and the student who wrote it, a girl by the name of Darby Shaw."

216

"I saw her name on the brief."

"That's right. They've been dating, and were supposed to be in the car together when it exploded. But she survived, and I get this call this morning at five, and it's her. Scared to death."

Lewis listened, but was already dismissing it. "You're not certain it was a bomb."

"She said it was a bomb, okay. It went BOOM! and blew the hell out of everything, okay. I'm certain he's dead."

"And you think there's a connection between his death and the brief?"

Gavin was a lawyer, untrained in the art of investigation, and he did not wish to appear gullible. "There could be. I think so, yes. Don't you?"

"Doesn't matter, Gavin. I just got off the phone with the Director. Pelican's off our list. I'm not sure it was ever on, but we're spending no more time on it."

"But my friend's been killed with a car bomb."

"I'm sorry. I'm sure the authorities down there are investigating."

"Listen to me, K.O. I'm asking for a favor."

"Listen to me, Gavin. I don't have any

favors. We're chasing enough rabbits right now, and if the Director says stop, then we stop. You're free to talk to him. I wouldn't advise it."

"Maybe I'm not handling this right. I thought you would listen to me, and at least act interested."

Lewis was walking around the desk. "Gavin, you look bad. Take the day off."

"No. I'll go to my office, wait an hour, and come back in here and do this again. Can we try it again in an hour?"

"No. Voyles was explicit."

"So was the girl, K.O. He was murdered, and now she's hiding somewhere in New Orleans afraid of her shadow, calling us for help, and we're too busy."

"I'm sorry."

"No, you're not. It's my fault. I should've thrown the damned thing in the garbage."

"It served a valuable purpose, Gavin." Lewis placed his hand on his shoulder as if his time was up and he was tired of this drivel. Gavin jerked away and headed for the door.

"Yeah, it gave you guys something to play with. I should've burned it."

"It's too good to burn, Gavin."

"I'm not giving up. I'll be back in an

hour, and we'll do this again. This didn't go right." Verheek slammed the door behind him.

SHE ENTERED Rubinstein Brothers from Canal Street, and got lost between the racks of men's shirts. No one followed her in. She quickly picked out a navy parka, men's small, a genderless pair of aviator sunglasses, and a British driving cap that was also a men's small but fit. She paid for it with plastic. As the clerk ran the card through, she picked the tags off, and put the parka on. It was baggy, like something she would wear to class. She stuffed her hair under the hooded collar. The clerk watched discreetly. She exited on Magazine Street, and got lost in the crowd.

Back on Canal. A busload of tourists swarmed into the Sheraton, and she joined them. She went to the wall of phones, found the number, and called Mrs. Chen, her neighbor in the duplex next door. Had she seen or heard anyone? Very early, there was a knock on the door. It was still dark, and woke them. She didn't see anyone, just heard the knock. Her car was still on the street. Everything okay? Yes, all's fine. Thanks.

She watched the tourists and punched the inside number for Gavin Verheek. Inside meant a minor hassle only, and after three minutes of refusing to give her name and repeating his, she had him.

"Where are you?" he asked.

"Let me explain something. For the moment, I will not tell you or anyone else where I am. So don't ask."

"All right. I guess you're making the rules."

"Thank you. What did Mr. Voyles say?"

"Mr. Voyles was at the White House and unavailable. I'll try to talk to him later today."

"That's pretty weak, Gavin. You've been at the office for almost four hours, and you have nothing. I expected more."

"Be patient, Darby."

"Patience will get me killed. They're after me, aren't they, Gavin?"

"I don't know."

"What would you do if you knew you were supposed to be dead, and the people trying to kill you have had assassinated two Supreme Court Justices, and knocked off a simple law professor, and they have billions of dollars which they obviously don't mind using to kill with? What would you do, Gavin?"

"Go to the FBI."

"Thomas went to the FBI, and he's dead."

"Thanks, Darby. That's not fair."

"I'm not worried about fairness or feelings. I'm more concerned with staying alive until noon."

"Don't go to your apartment."

"I'm not stupid. They've already been there. And I'm sure they're watching his apartment."

"Where's his family?"

"His parents live in Naples, Florida. I guess the university will contact them. I don't know. He has a brother in Mobile, and I thought of calling him and trying to explain all this."

She saw a face. He walked among the tourists at the registration desk. He held a folded newspaper and tried to appear at home, just another guest, but his walk was a bit hesitant and his eyes were searching. The face was long and thin with round glasses and a shiny forehead.

"Gavin, listen to me. Write this down. I see a man I've seen before, not long ago. An hour maybe. Six feet two or three, thin, thirty years old, glasses, receding hair, dark in color. He's gone. He's gone."

"Who the hell is it?"

"We haven't met, dammit!"

"Did he see you? Where the hell are you?"

"In a hotel lobby. I don't know if he saw me. I'm gone."

"Darby! Listen to me. Whatever you do, keep in touch with me, okay?"

"I'll try."

The rest room was around the corner. She went to the last stall, locked the door behind her, and stayed there for an hour.

SEVENTEEN

THE PHOTOGRAPHER'S NAME was Croft, and he'd worked for the *Post* for seven years until his third drug conviction sent him away for nine months. Upon parole, he declared himself to be a free-lance artist, and advertised as such in the yellow pages. The phone seldom rang. He did a little of this work; this slithering around shooting people who did not know they were targets. Many of his clients were divorce lawyers who needed dirt for trial. After two years of free-lancing, he had picked up a few tricks and now considered himself a halfass private investigator. He charged forty bucks an hour when he could get it.

Another client was Gray Grantham, an old friend from his newspaper days who called when he needed dirt. Grantham was a serious, ethical reporter with just a touch of sleaze, and when he needed a dirty trick, he called. He liked Grantham because he was honest about his sleaziness. The rest were so pious.

He was in Grantham's Volvo because it had a phone. It was noon, and he was smoking his lunch, wondering if the smell would linger with all the windows down. He did his best work half-stoned. When you stare at motels for a living, you need to be stoned.

There was a nice breeze coming in from the passenger's side, blowing the smell onto Pennsylvania. He was parked illegally, smoking dope, and not really concerned. He had less than an ounce on him, and his probation officer smoked it too, so what the hell.

The phone booth was a block and a half ahead, on the sidewalk but away from the street. With his telephoto lens, he could almost read the phone book hanging from the rack. Piece of cake. A large woman was inside, filling the booth and talking with her hands. Croft took a drag and watched the mirror for cops. This was a tow-away zone. Traffic was heavy on Pennsylvania.

At twenty after twelve, the woman fought her way out of the booth, and from nowhere a young man with a nice suit appeared and closed the door. Croft got his Nikon and rested the lens on the steering wheel. It was cool and sunny, and the sidewalk bustled with lunch traffic. The shoulders and heads moved quickly by. A gap. Click. A gap. Click. The subject was punching numbers and glancing around. This was their man.

He talked for thirty seconds, and the car phone rang three times and stopped. It was the signal from Grantham at the *Post*. This was their man, and he was talking. Croft fired away. Get all you can get, Grantham had said. A gap. Click. Click. Heads and shoulders. A gap. Click. Click. His eyes darted around as he talked, but he kept his back to the street. Full face. Click. Croft burned a roll of thirty-six in two minutes, then grabbed another Nikon. He screwed on the lens, and waited for a mob to pass.

He took the last drag and thumped it into the street. This was so easy. Oh sure, it took talent to capture the image in a studio, but this street work was much more fun. There was something felonious about stealing a face with a hidden camera.

The subject was a man of few words. He hung up, looked around, opened the door, looked around, and started toward Croft. Click, click, click. Full face, full figure, walking faster, getting closer, beautiful, beautiful. Croft worked feverishly, then at the last moment laid the Nikon in the seat and looked at Pennsylvania as their man walked by and disappeared in a group of secretaries.

What a fool. When you're on the run, never use the same pay phone twice.

GARCIA WAS SHADOW BOXING. He had a wife and child, he said, and he was scared. There was a career ahead with plenty of money, and if he paid his dues and kept his mouth shut he would be a wealthy man. But he wanted to talk. He rambled on about how he wanted to talk, had something to say and all, but just couldn't make the decision. He didn't trust anyone.

Grantham didn't push. He let him ramble long enough for Croft to do his number. Garcia would eventually spill his guts. He wanted to so badly. He had called three times now, and was growing comfortable with his new friend Grantham, who'd played this game many times and knew how it worked. The first step was to relax and build trust, to treat them with warmth and respect, to talk about right and wrong and moralities. Then they would talk.

The pictures were beautiful. Croft was not his first choice. He was usually so bombed you could tell it in the photography. But Croft was sleazy and discreet, with a working knowledge of journalism, and he happened to be available on short notice. He had picked twelve and blown them to five by seven, and they were outstanding. Right profile. Left profile. Full face into the phone. Full face looking at the camera. Full figure less than twenty feet away. Piece of cake, Croft said.

Garcia was under thirty, a very nice-looking, clean-cut lawyer. Dark, short hair. Dark eyes. Maybe Hispanic, but the skin was not dark. The clothes were expensive. Navy suit, probably wool. No stripes or patterns. Basic white spread collar with a silk tie. Basic black or burgundy wing tips with a sparkling shine. The absence of a brief-case was puzzling. But then, it was lunch, and he probably ran from the office to make the call, then back to the office. The Justice Department was a block away.

Grantham studied the pictures and kept an eye on the door. Sarge was never late. It was dark and the club was filling up. Grantham's was the only white face within three blocks.

Of the tens of thousands of government lawyers in D.C., he had seen a few who knew how to dress, but not many. Especially the younger ones. They started at forty a year and clothes were not important. Clothes were important to Garcia, and he was too young and well dressed to be a government lawyer.

So he was a private one, in a firm for about three or four years now and hitting somewhere around eighty grand. Great. That narrowed it down to fifty thousand lawyers and no doubt expanding by the moment.

The door opened and a cop walked in. Through the smoke and haze, he could tell it was Cleve. This was a respectable joint with no dice or whores, so the presence of a cop was not alarming. He sat in the booth across from Grantham.

"Did you pick this place?" Grantham asked.

"Yeah. You like it?"

"Let's put it like this. We're trying to be inconspicuous, right? I'm here picking up secrets from a White House employee.

Pretty heavy stuff. Now tell me, Cleve, do I look inconspicuous sitting here in all my whiteness?"

"I hate to tell you this, Grantham, but you're not nearly as famous as you think. You see those dudes at the bar." They looked at the bar lined with construction workers. "I'd give you my paycheck if any dude there has ever read the *Washington Post,* heard of Gray Grantham, or gives a damn what happens at the White House."

"Okay, okay. Where's Sarge?"

"Sarge is not feeling well. He gave me a message for you."

Wouldn't work. He could use Sarge as an unnamed source, but not Sarge's son or anyone else Sarge talked to. "What's wrong with him?"

"Old age. He didn't want to talk tonight, but it's urgent, he says."

Grantham listened and waited.

"I've got an envelope in my car, all licked and sealed real tight. Sarge got real blunt when he gave it to me, and told me not to open it. Just take it to Mr. Grantham. I think it's important."

"Let's go."

They made their way through the crowd to the door. The patrol car was parked illegally at the curb. Cleve opened the passenger door, and pulled the envelope from the glove box. "He got this in the West Wing."

Grantham stuffed it in his pocket. Sarge was not one to lift things, and in the course of their relationship he had never produced a document.

"Thanks, Cleve."

"He wouldn't tell me what it is—told me I'll just have to wait and read it in the paper."

"Tell Sarge I love him."

"I'm sure that'll give him a thrill."

The patrol car drove away, and Grantham hurried to his Volvo, now filled with the stench of burnt grass. He locked the door, turned on the dome light, and ripped open the envelope. It was clearly an internal White House memo, and it was about an assassin named Khamel.

HE WAS FLYING across town. Out of Brightwood, onto Sixteenth and south toward central Washington. It was almost seven-thirty, and if he could put it together in an hour, it would make the Late City edition, the largest of half a dozen editions that began rolling off the presses at ten-thirty. Thank god for the little yuppie car phone he had been embarrassed to buy. He called Smith Keen, the assistant managing editor/investigations, who was still in the newsroom on the fifth floor. He called a friend at the foreign desk, and asked him to pull everything on Khamel.

He was suspicious of the memo. The words were too sensitive to put on paper, then sling around the office like the latest policy on coffee or bottled water or vacations. Someone, probably Fletcher Coal, wanted the world to know that Khamel had emerged as a suspect, and that he was an Arab of all things, and had close ties to Libya and Iran and Iraq, countries led by fiery idiots who hated America. Someone in the White House of Fools wanted the story on the front page.

But it was a helluva story and it was front-page news. He and Smith Keen had it finished by nine. They found two old pictures of a man widely believed to be Khamel, but so dissimilar they appeared to be of different people. Keen said run both of them. The file on Khamel was thin. Much rumor and legend, but little meat. Grantham mentioned the Pope, the British diplomat, the German banker, and the ambush of the Israeli soldiers. And now, according to a confidential source at the White House, a most reliable and trusted source, Khamel was a suspect in the killings of Justices Rosenberg and Jensen.

TWENTY-FOUR HOURS after hitting the street, she was still alive. If she could make it to morning, she could start another day with new ideas about what to do and where to go. For now, she was tired. She was in a room on the fifteenth floor of the Marriott, with the door bolted, lights on, and the mighty can of Mace lying on the bedspread. Her thick, dark red hair was now in a paper sack in the closet. The last time she cut her hair she was three years old, and her mother whipped her tail.

It took two painful hours with dull scissors to cut it off yet leave some semblance of style. She would keep it under a cap or hat until who knows when. It took another two hours to color it black. She could've bleached it and gone blonde, but that would be obvious. She assumed she was dealing with professionals, and for some unfathomable reason she determined at the drugstore that they might expect her to do this and become a blonde. And what the hell. The stuff came in a bottle, and if she woke up tomorrow with a wild hair she could go blonde. The chameleon strategy. Change colors every day and drive 'em crazy. Clairol had at least eighty-five shades.

She was dead tired but afraid of sleep. She had not seen her friend from the Sheraton during the day, but the more she moved around the more the faces looked the same. He was out there, she knew. And he had friends. If they could assassinate Rosenberg and Jensen, and knock off Thomas Callahan, she would be easy.

She couldn't go near her car, and she didn't want to rent one. Rentals leave records. And they were probably watching. She could fly, but they were stalking the airports. Take a bus, but she'd never bought a ticket or seen the inside of a Greyhound.

And after they realized she had disappeared, they would expect her to run. She was just an amateur, a little college girl brokenhearted after watching her man blown to bits and fried. She would make a mad dash somewhere, get out of the city, and they would pick her off.

She rather liked the city at this moment. It had a million hotel rooms, almost as many alleys and dives and bars, and it always had crowds of people strolling along Bourbon, Chartres, Dauphine, and Royal. She knew it well, especially the Quarter, where life was within walking distance. She would move from hotel to hotel for a few days, until when? She didn't know when. She didn't know why. Moving just seemed intelligent under the circumstances. She would stay off the streets in the mornings, and try to sleep then. She would change clothes and hats and sunglasses. She would start smoking, and keep one in her face. She would move until she got tired of moving, then she might leave. It was okay to be scared. She had to keep thinking. She would survive.

She thought of calling the cops, but not now. They took names and kept records, and they could be dangerous. She thought of calling Thomas' brother in Mobile, but there wasn't a single thing the poor man could do to help her at this moment. She thought of calling the dean, but how could she explain the brief, Gavin Verheek, the FBI, the car bomb, Rosenberg and Jensen, and her on the run and make it sound believable. Forget the dean. She didn't like him anyway. She thought of calling a couple of friends from law school, but people talk, and people listen, and they could be out there listening to the people talking about poor Callahan. She wanted to talk to Alice Stark, her best friend. Alice was worried, and Alice would go to the cops and tell them her friend Darby Shaw was missing. She would call Alice tomorrow.

She dialed room service, and ordered a Mexican salad and a bottle of red wine. She would drink all of it, then sit in a chair with the Mace and watch the door until she fell asleep.

EIGHTEEN

GMINSKI'S LIMO made a wild U-turn on Canal as if it owned the street, and came to a sudden stop in front of the Sheraton. Both rear doors flew open. Gminski was out first, followed quickly by three aides who scurried after him with bags and briefcases.

It was almost 2 A.M., and the Director was obviously in a hurry. He did not stop at the front desk, but went straight for the elevators. The aides ran behind him and held the elevator door for him, and no one spoke as they rode up six floors.

Three of his agents were waiting in a corner room. One of them opened the door, and Gminski barged through it without any sort of greeting. The aides threw the bags on one bed. The Director yanked off his jacket and threw it in a chair.

"Where is she?" he snapped at an agent by the name of Hooten. The one named Swank opened the curtains, and Gminski walked to the window.

Swank was pointing to the Marriott, across the street and down a block. "She's on the fifteenth floor, third room from the street, lights are still on."

Gminski stared at the Marriott. "You're certain?"

"Yes. We saw her go in, and she paid with a credit card."

"Poor kid," Gminski said as he walked away from the window. "Where was she last night?"

"Holiday Inn on Royal. Paid with a credit card."

"Have you seen anyone following her?" the Director asked.

"No."

"I need some water," he said to an aide, who jumped toward the ice bucket and rattled cubes.

Gminski sat on the edge of the bed, laced his fingers together, and cracked every possible knuckle. "What do you think?" he asked Hooten, the oldest of the three agents.

"They're chasing her. They're looking

237

under rocks. She's using credit cards. She'll be dead in forty-eight hours."

"She's not completely stupid," Swank inserted. "She cut her hair and colored it black. She's moving around. It's apparent she has no plans to leave the city any time soon. I'll give her seventy-two hours before they find her."

Gminski sipped his water. "This means her little brief is directly on point. And it means our friend is now a very desperate man. Where is he?"

Hooten answered quickly. "We have no idea."

"We have to find him."

"He hasn't been seen in three weeks."

Gminski set the glass on the desk, and picked up a room key. "So what do you think?" he asked Hooten.

"Do we bring her in?" Hooten asked.

"It won't be easy," Swank said. "She may have a gun. Someone could get hurt."

"She's a scared kid," Gminski said. "She's also a civilian, not a member. We can't go around snatching civilians off the sidewalk."

"Then she won't last long," Swank said.

"How do you take her?" Gminski asked.

"There are ways," Hooten answered.

"Catch her on the street. Go to her room. I could be inside her room in less than ten minutes if I left right now. It's not that difficult. She's not a pro."

Gminski paced slowly around the room and everyone watched him. He glanced at his watch. "I'm not inclined to take her. Let's sleep four hours, and meet here at six-thirty. Sleep on it. If you can convince me to snatch her, then I'll say do it. Okay?"

They nodded obediently.

THE WINE WORKED. She dozed in the chair, then made it to the bed and slept hard. The phone was ringing. The bedspread was hanging to the floor, and her feet were on the pillows. The phone was ringing. The eyelids were glued together. The mind was numb and lost in dreams, but somewhere in the deep recesses something worked and told her the phone was ringing.

The eyes opened but saw little. The sun was up, the lights were on, and she stared at the phone. No, she did not ask for a wake-up call. She thought about this for a second, then she was certain. No wake-up call. She sat on the edge of the bed and listened to it ring. Five times, ten, fifteen, twenty. It would not stop. Could be a wrong number, but they would stop after twenty rings.

It was not a wrong number. The cobwebs began to clear, and she moved closer to the phone. With the exception of the registration clerk and maybe his boss, and perhaps room service, not a single living soul knew she was in this room. She had ordered food, but made no other calls.

It stopped ringing. Good, wrong number. She walked to the bathroom, and it was ringing again. She counted. After the fourteenth ring, she lifted the receiver. "Hello."

"Darby, it's Gavin Verheek. Are you okay?"

She sat on the bed. "How'd you get the number?"

"We have ways. Listen, have—"

"Wait, Gavin. Wait a minute. Let me think. The credit card, right?"

"Yes. The credit card. The paper trail. It's the FBI, Darby. We have ways. It's not that difficult."

"Then they could do it too."

"I suppose. Stay in the small joints and pay with cash."

There was a thick knot in her stomach,

and she stretched on the bed. Just like that. Not difficult. The paper trail. She could be dead. Killed along the paper trail.

"Darby, are you there?"

"Yes." She looked at the door to make sure it was chained. "Yes, I'm here."

"Are you safe?"

"I thought so."

"We've got some information. There will be a memorial service tomorrow at three on campus, with burial afterward in the city. I've talked to his brother, and the family wants me to serve as a pallbearer. I'll be there tonight. I think we should meet."

"Why should we meet?"

"You've got to trust me, Darby. Your life is in danger right now, and you need to listen to me."

"What're you guys up to?"

There was a pause. "What do you mean?"

"What did Director Voyles say?"

"I haven't talked to him."

"I thought you were his attorney, so to speak. What's the matter, Gavin?"

"We're taking no action at this time."

"And what might that mean, Gavin? Talk to me."

"That's why we need to meet. I don't want to do this over the phone."

"The phone is working fine, and it's all you're going to get right now. So let's have it, Gavin."

"Why won't you trust me?" He was wounded.

"I'm hanging up, okay. I don't like this. If you guys know where I am, then someone could be out there in the hallway waiting."

"Nonsense, Darby. You've got to use your head. I've had your room number for an hour, and done nothing but call. We're on your side, I swear."

She thought about this. It made sense, but they had found her so easily. "I'm listening. You haven't talked to the Director, but the FBI's taking no action. Why not?"

"I'm not sure. He made the decision yesterday to back off the pelican brief, and gave instructions to leave it alone. That's all I can tell you."

"That's not very much. Does he know about Thomas? Does he know that I'm supposed to be dead because I wrote it and forty-eight hours after Thomas gave it to you, his old buddy from law school, they, whoever in hell they are, tried to kill both of us? Does he know all this, Gavin?"

"I don't think so."

"That means no, doesn't it?"

"Yes. It means no."

"Okay, listen to me. Do you think he was killed because of the brief?"

"Probably."

"That means yes, doesn't it?"

"Yes."

"Thanks. If Thomas was murdered because of the brief, then we know who killed him. And if we know who killed Thomas, then we know who killed Rosenberg and Jensen. Right?"

Verheek hesitated.

"Just say yes, dammit!" Darby snapped.

"I'll say probably."

"Fine. *Probably* means yes for a lawyer. I know it's the best you can do. It's a very strong *probably,* yet you're telling me the FBI is backing off my little suspect."

"Settle down, Darby. Let's meet tonight and talk about it. I could save your life."

She carefully laid the receiver under a pillow, and walked to the bathroom. She brushed her teeth and what was left of her hair, then threw the toiletries and change of clothes into a new canvas bag. She put on the parka, cap, and sunglasses, and quietly closed the door behind her. The hall was empty. She walked up two flights to the seventeenth, then took the elevator to the tenth, then casually walked down ten flights to the lobby. The door from the stairway opened near the rest rooms, and she was quickly inside the women's. The lobby appeared to be deserted. She went to a stall, locked the door, and waited for a while.

FRIDAY MORNING in the Quarter. The air was cool and clean without the lingering smell of food and sin. Eight A.M.—too early for people. She walked a few blocks to clear her head and plan the day. On Dumaine near Jackson Square she found a coffee shop she'd seen before. It was nearly empty and had a pay phone in the back. She poured her own thick coffee, and set it on a table near the phone. She could talk here.

Verheek was on the phone in less than a minute. "I'm listening," he said.

"Where will you stay tonight?" she asked, watching the front door.

"Hilton, by the river."

"I know where it is. I'll call late tonight

244

or early in the morning. Don't track me again. I'm into cash now. No plastic."

"That's smart, Darby. Keep moving."

"I may be dead by the time you get here."

"No, you won't. Can you find a *Washington Post* down there?"

"Maybe. Why?"

"Get one quick. This morning's. Nice little story about Rosenberg and Jensen and perhaps who done it."

"I can't wait. I'll call later."

The first newsstand did not have the *Post*. She zigzagged toward Canal, covering her tracks, watching her rear, down St. Ann, along the antique shops on Royal, through the seedy bars on both sides of Bienville, and finally to the French Market along Decatur and North Peters. She was quick but nonchalant. She walked with an air of business, her eyes darting in all directions behind the shades. If they were back there somewhere in the shadows watching and keeping up, they were good.

She bought a *Post* and a *Times-Picayune* from a sidewalk vendor, and found a table in a deserted corner of Café du Monde.

Front page. Citing a confidential source, the story dwelt on the legend of Khamel and his sudden involvement in the killings. In his younger days, it said, he had killed for his beliefs, but now he just did it for money. Lots of money, speculated a retired intelligence expert who allowed himself to be quoted but certainly not identified. The photos were blurred and indistinct, but ominous beside each other. They could not be of the same person. But then, said the expert, he was unidentifiable and had not been photographed in over a decade.

A waiter finally made it by, and she ordered coffee and a plain bagel. The expert said many thought he was dead. Interpol believed he had killed as recently as six months ago. The expert doubted he would travel by commercial air. The FBI had him at the top of their list.

She opened the New Orleans paper slowly. Thomas did not make page one, but his picture was on page two with a long story. The cops were treating it as a homicide, but there wasn't much to go on. A white female had been seen in the area shortly before the explosion. The law school was in shock, according to the dean. The cops said little. Services were tomorrow on campus. A horrible mistake had been made, the dean said. If it was murder, then someone had obviously killed the wrong person.

Her eyes were wet, and suddenly she was afraid again. Maybe it was simply a mistake. It was a violent city with crazy people, and maybe someone got their wires crossed and the wrong car was chosen. Maybe there was no one out there stalking her.

She put the sunglasses on and looked at his photo. They had pulled it from the law school annual, and there was that smirk he habitually wore when he was the professor. He was clean shaven, and so handsome.

GRANTHAM'S KHAMEL STORY electrified Washington Friday morning. It mentioned neither the memo nor the White House, so the hottest game in town was speculating about the source.

The game was especially hot in the Hoover Building. In the office of the Director, Eric East and K. O. Lewis paced nervously about while Voyles talked to the President for the third time in two hours. Voyles was cussing, not directly at the President, but all around him. He cussed Coal, and when the President cussed back, Voyles suggested they set up the polygraph, strap in everyone on his staff, beginning with Coal, and just see where the damned leaks were coming from. Yes, hell yes, he, Voyles, would take the test, and so would everyone who worked in the Hoover Building. And they cussed back and forth. Voyles was red and sweating, and the fact that he was yelling into the telephone and the President was on the other end receiving all this mattered not a bit. He knew Coal was listening somewhere.

Evidently, the President gained control of the conversation and launched into a long-winded sermon of some sort. Voyles wiped his forehead with a handkerchief, sat in his ancient leather swivel, and began controlled breathing to lower the pressure and pulse. He had survived one heart attack and was due for another, and had told K. O. Lewis many times that Fletcher Coal and his idiot boss would eventually kill him. But he'd said that about the last three Presidents. He pinched the fat wrinkles on his forehead and sunk lower into the chair. "We can do that, Mr. President." He was almost pleasant now. He was a man of swift and radical mood swings, and suddenly before their eyes he was courteous. A real charmer. "Thank you, Mr. President. I'll be there tomorrow."

He hung up gently, and spoke with his eyes closed. "He wants us to place that *Post* reporter under surveillance. Says we've done it before, so will we do it again? I told him we would."

"What type of surveillance?" asked K.O.

"Let's just follow him in the city. Around the clock with two men. See where he goes at night, who he sleeps with. He's single, isn't he?"

"Divorced seven years ago," Lewis answered.

"Make damned sure we don't get caught. Do it with plainclothes, and switch 'em up every three days."

"Does he really believe the leaks are coming from us?"

"No, I don't think so. If we were leaking, why would he want us to trail the reporter? I think he knows it's his own people. And he wants to catch them."

"It's a small favor," Lewis added helpfully.

"Yeah. Just don't get caught, okay?"

THE OFFICE of L. Matthew Barr was tucked away on the third floor of a tacky and decaying office building on M Street in Georgetown. There were no signs on the doors. An armed guard in a coat and tie turned people away at the elevator. The carpet was worn and the furniture was old. Dust covered it, and it was apparent the Unit spent no money on housekeeping.

Barr ran the Unit, which was an unofficial, hidden, little division of the Committee to Reelect the President. CRP had a vast suite of plush offices across the river in Rosslyn. It had windows that opened and secretaries who smiled and maids that cleaned every night. But not this dump.

Fletcher Coal stepped off the elevator and nodded at the security guard, who nodded back without making another move. They were old acquaintances. He made his way through the small maze of dingy offices in the direction of Barr's. Coal took pride in being honest with himself, and he honestly did not fear any man in Washington, maybe with the possible exception of Matthew Barr. Sometimes he feared him, sometimes not, but he always admired him.

Barr was an ex-Marine, ex-CIA, ex-spy with two felony convictions for security scams from which he earned millions and buried the money. He had served a few months in one of the country clubs, but no real time. Coal had personally recruited Barr to head the Unit, which officially did not exist. It had an annual budget of four million, all cash from various slush funds, and Barr supervised a small band of highly trained thugs who quietly did the work of the Unit.

Barr's door was always locked. He opened it and Coal entered. The meeting would be brief, as usual.

"Let me guess," Barr started. "You want to find the leak."

"In a way, yes. I want you to follow this reporter, Grantham, around the clock and see who he's talking to. He's getting some awfully good stuff, and I'm afraid it's coming from us."

"You're leaking like cardboard."

"We've got some problems, but the Khamel story was a plant. Did it myself."

Barr smiled at this. "I thought so. It seemed too clean and pat."

"Did you ever run across Khamel?"

"No. Ten years ago we were sure he was dead. He likes it that way. He has no ego, so he'll never get caught. He can live in a paper shack in São Paulo for six months, eating roots and rats, then fly off to Rome to murder a diplomat, then off to Singapore for a few months. He doesn't read his press clippings."

"How old is he?"

"Why are you interested?"

"I'm fascinated. I think I know who hired him to kill Rosenberg and Jensen."

"Oh, really. Can you share this bit of gossip?"

"No. Not yet."

"He's between forty and forty-five, which is not that old, but he killed a Lebanese general when he was fifteen. So he's had a long career. This is all legend, you understand. He can kill with either hand, either foot, a car key, a pencil, whatever. He's an expert marksman with all weapons. Speaks twelve languages. You've heard all this, haven't you?"

"Yeah, but it's fun."

"Okay. He's believed to be the most proficient and expensive assassin in the world. In his early years he was just another terrorist, but he was much too talented for simple bomb throwing. So he became an assassin for hire. He's a bit older now, and kills just for money."

"How much money?"

"Good question. He's probably in the ten-to-twenty-million-a-job range, and there's not but one other guy I know of in that league. One theory believes he shares it with other terrorist groups. No one knows, really. Let me guess, you want me to find Khamel and bring him back alive."

"You leave Khamel alone. I sort of like the work he did here."

"He's very talented."

"I want you to follow Gray Grantham and find out who he's talking to."

"Any ideas?"

"A couple. There's a man by the name of Milton Hardy who works as a janitor in the West Wing." Coal threw an envelope on the desk. "He's been around for a long time, appears to be half blind, but I think he sees and hears a lot. Follow him for a week or two. Everyone calls him Sarge. Make plans to take him out."

"This is great, Coal. We're spending all this money to track blind Negroes."

"Just do as I say. Make it three weeks." Coal stood and headed for the door.

"So you know who hired the killer?" Barr said.

"We're getting close."

"The Unit is more than anxious to help."

"I'm sure."

NINETEEN

MRS. CHEN owned the duplex, and had been renting the other half to female law students for fifteen years. She was picky but private, and lived and let live as long as all was quiet. It was six blocks from campus.

It was dark when she answered the door. The person on the porch was an attractive young lady with short dark hair and a nervous smile. Very nervous.

Mrs. Chen frowned at her until she spoke.

"I'm Alice Stark, a friend of Darby's. May I come in?" She glanced over her shoulder. The street was quiet and still. Mrs. Chen lived alone with the doors and windows locked tightly, but she was a pretty girl with an innocent smile, and if she was a friend

254

of Darby's, then she could be trusted. She opened the door, and Alice was inside.

"Something's wrong," Mrs. Chen said.

"Yes. Darby is in a bit of trouble, but we can't talk about it. Did she call this afternoon?"

"Yes. She said a young woman would look through her apartment."

Alice breathed deeply and tried to appear calm. "It'll just take a minute. She said there was a door through a wall somewhere. I prefer not to use the front or rear doors." Mrs. Chen frowned and her eyes asked, Why not? but she said nothing.

"Has anyone been in the apartment in the last two days?" Alice asked. She followed Mrs. Chen down a narrow hallway.

"I've seen no one. There was a knock early yesterday before the sun, but I didn't look." She moved a table away from a door, pushed a key around, and opened it.

Alice stepped in front of her. "She wanted me to go in alone, okay?" Mrs. Chen wanted to check it out, but she nodded and closed the door behind Alice. It opened into a tiny hallway that was suddenly dark. To the left was the den, and a light switch that couldn't be used. Alice froze in the darkness. The apartment was black and hot with a thick smell of old garbage. She'd expected to be alone, but she was a second-year law student, dammit!, not some hotshot private detective.

Get a grip. She fumbled through a large purse and found a pencil-thin flashlight. There were three of them in there. Just in case. In case of what? She didn't know. Darby had been quite specific. No lights could be seen through the windows. They could be watching.

Who in hell are they? Alice wanted to know. Darby didn't know, said she would explain it later but first the apartment had to be examined.

Alice had been in the apartment a dozen times in the past year, but she'd been allowed to enter through the front door with a full array of lights and other conveniences. She had been in all the rooms, and felt confident she could feel around in the darkness. The confidence was gone. Vanished. Replaced with trembling fear.

Get a grip. You're all alone. They wouldn't camp out here with a nosy woman next door. If they had indeed been here, it was only for a brief visit.

After staring at the end of it, she determined that the flashlight worked. It glowed with all the energy of a fading match. She pointed it at the floor, and saw a faint round circle the size of a small orange. The circle was shaking.

She tiptoed around a corner in the direction of the den. Darby said there was a small lamp on the bookshelves next to the television, and that the light was always on. She used it as a nightlight, and it was supposed to cast a faint glow across the den to the kitchen. Either Darby lied, or the bulb was gone, or someone had unscrewed it. It didn't matter, really, at this point, because the den and kitchen were pitch-black.

She was on the rug in the center of the den, inching toward the kitchen table where there was supposed to be a computer. She kicked the edge of the coffee table, and the flashlight quit. She shook it. Nothing. She found number two in the purse.

The odor was heavier in the kitchen. The computer was on the table along with an assortment of empty files and casebooks. She examined the mainframe with her dinky little light. The power switch was on the front. She pushed it, and the monochrome screen slowly warmed up. It emitted a greenish light that covered the table but did not escape the kitchen.

Alice sat down in front of the keyboard and began pecking. She found Menu, then List, then Files. The Directory covered the screen. She studied it closely. There were supposed to be somewhere around forty entries, but she saw no more than ten. Most of the hard-drive memory was gone. She turned on the laser printer, and within seconds the Directory was on paper. She tore it off and stuffed it in the purse.

She stood with her flashlight and inspected the clutter around the computer. Darby estimated the number of floppy disks at twenty, but they were all gone. Not a single floppy. The casebooks were for con law and civil procedure, and so dull and generic no one would want them. The red expandable files were stacked neatly together, but empty.

It was a clean, patient job. He or they had spent a couple of hours erasing and gathering, then left with no more than one briefcase or bag of goods.

In the den by the television, Alice peeked out the side window. The red Accord was still there, not four feet from the window. It looked fine.

She twisted the bulb in the nightlight, and quickly flicked the switch on, then off. Worked perfectly. She unscrewed it just as he or they had left it.

Her eyes had focused; she could see the outlines of doors and furniture. She turned the computer off, and eased through the den to the hall.

Mrs. Chen was waiting exactly where she'd left her. "Okay?" she asked.

"Everything's fine," Alice said. "Just watch it real close. I'll call you in a day or two to see if anyone has been by. And please, don't tell anyone I was here."

Mrs. Chen listened intently as she moved the table in front of the door. "What about her car?"

"It'll be fine. Just watch it."

"Is she all right?"

They were in the den, almost to the front door. "She's gonna be fine. I think she'll be back in a few days. Thank you, Mrs. Chen."

Mrs. Chen closed the door, bolted it, and watched from the small window. The lady was on the sidewalk, then gone in the darkness.

Alice walked three blocks to her car.

□   □   □   □

FRIDAY NIGHT in the Quarter! Tulane played in the Dome tomorrow, then the Saints on Sunday, and the rowdies were out by the thousands, parking everywhere, blocking streets, roaming in noisy mobs, drinking from go cups, crowding bars, just having a delightful time raising hell and enjoying themselves. The Inner Quarter was gridlocked by nine.

Alice parked on Poydras, far away from where she wanted to park, and was an hour late when she arrived at the crowded oyster bar on St. Peter, deep in the Quarter. There were no tables. They were packed three deep at the bar. She retreated to a corner with a cigarette machine, and surveyed the people. Most were students in town for the game.

A waiter walked directly to her. "Are you looking for another female?" he asked.

She hesitated. "Well, yes."

He pointed beyond the bar. "Around the corner, first room on the right, there's some small tables. I think your friend is there."

Darby was in a tiny booth, crouched over a beer bottle, with sunglasses and a hat. Alice squeezed her hand. "It's good to see you." She studied the hairdo, and was amused by it. Darby removed the sunglasses. The eyes were red and tired.

"I didn't know who else to call."

Alice listened with a blank face, unable to think of something appropriate and unable to take her eyes off the hair. "Who did the hair?" she asked.

"Nice, huh. It's sort of the punk look, which I think is making a comeback and will certainly impress folks when I start interviewing for a job."

"Why?"

"Someone tried to kill me, Alice. My name's on a list that some very nasty people are holding. I think they're following me."

"Kill? Did you say 'kill'? Who would want to kill you, Darby?"

"I'm not sure. What about my apartment?"

Alice stopped looking at the hair, and handed her the printout of the Directory. Darby studied it. It was real. This was not a dream or a mistake. The bomb had found the right car. Rupert and the cowboy had had their hands on her. The face she had seen was looking for her. They had gone to her apartment and erased what they wanted to erase. They were out there.

"What about floppies?"

"None. Not a single one. The expandable files on the kitchen table were placed together real neat and are real empty. Everything else appears to be in order. They unscrewed the bulb in the nightlight, so there's total darkness. I checked it. Works fine. These are very patient people."

"What about Mrs. Chen?"

"She's seen nothing."

Darby stuffed the printout into a pocket. "Look, Alice, suddenly I'm very scared. You don't need to be seen with me. Maybe this was not a good idea."

"Who are these people?"

"I don't know. They killed Thomas, and they tried to kill me. I got lucky, and now they're after me."

"But why, Darby?"

"You don't want to know, and I'm not going to tell. The more you know, the more danger you're in. Trust me, Alice. I can't tell you what I know."

"But I won't tell. I swear."

"What if they make you tell?"

Alice glanced around as if all was fine. She studied her friend. They had been close since freshman orientation. They had studied hours together, shared notes, sweated exams, teamed up for mock trials, gossiped about men. Alice was hopefully the only student who knew about Darby and Callahan. "I want to help, Darby. I'm not afraid."

Darby had not touched the beer. She slowly spun the bottle. "Well, I'm terrified. I was there when he died, Alice. The ground shook. He was blown to pieces and I was supposed to be with him. It was intended for me."

"Then go to the cops."

"Not yet. Maybe later. I'm afraid to. Thomas went to the FBI, and two days later we were supposed to be dead."

"So the FBI is after you?"

"I don't think so. They started talking, and someone was listening very closely, and it found the wrong ears."

"Talked about what! Come on, Darby. It's me. Your best friend. Stop playing games."

Darby took the first tiny swallow from the bottle. Eye contact was avoided. She stared at the table. "Please, Alice. Allow me to wait. There's no sense telling you something that could get you killed." A long pause. "If you want to help, go to the memorial service tomorrow. Watch everything. Spread the word that I called you from Denver where I'm staying with an aunt with a name you don't know, and that I've dropped out this semester but I'll be back in the spring. Make sure that rumor gets started. I think some people will be listening carefully."

"Okay. The paper mentioned a white female near the scene when he was killed, as if she might be a suspect or something."

"Or something. I was there and I was supposed to be a victim. I'm reading the papers with a magnifying glass. The cops are clueless."

"Okay, Darby. You're smarter than I am. You're smarter than every person I've ever met. So what now?"

"First, go out the back door. There's a white door at the end of the hall where the rest rooms are. It goes into a storage room, then to the kitchen, then out the back door. Don't stop. The alley leads to Royal. Catch a cab and ride back to your car. Watch your rear."

"Are you serious?"

"Look at this hair, Alice. Would I mutilate myself like this if I was playing games?"

"Okay, okay. Then what?"

"Go to the service tomorrow, start the rumor, and I'll call you within two days."

"Where are you staying?"

"Here and there. I move around a lot."

Alice stood and pecked her on the cheek. Then she was gone.

FOR TWO HOURS, Verheek stomped the floor, picking up magazines, tossing them around, ordering room service, unpacking, stomping. Then for the next two hours, he sat on the bed, sipping a hot beer and staring at the phone. He would do this until midnight, he told himself, and then, well, then what?

She said she would call.

He could save her life if she would only call.

At midnight, he threw another magazine and left the room. An agent in the New Orleans office had helped a little, and given him a couple of law school hangouts close to campus. He would go there and mix and mingle, drink a beer, and listen. The students were in town for the game. She wouldn't be there, and it wouldn't matter because he'd never seen her. But maybe he would hear something, and he could drop a name, leave a card, make a friend who knew her or maybe knew someone who knew her. A long shot, but a helluva lot more productive than staring at the phone.

He found a seat at the bar in a joint called Barrister's, three blocks from campus. It had a nice little varsity look to it with football schedules and pinups on the walls. The crowd was rowdy and under thirty.

The bartender looked like a student. After two beers, the crowd thinned and the bar was half empty. There would be another wave in a moment.

Verheek ordered number three. It was one-thirty. "Are you a law student?" he asked the bartender.

"Afraid so."

"It's not that bad, is it?"

He was wiping around the peanuts. "I've had more fun."

Verheek longed for the bartenders who served his beer in law school. Those guys knew the art of conversation. Never met a stranger. Talk about anything.

"I'm a lawyer," Verheek said in desperation.

Oh, hey, wow, this guy's a lawyer. How rare. Someone special. The kid walked off.

Little son of a bitch. I hope you flunk out. Verheek grabbed his bottle and turned to face the tables. He felt like a grandfather amid the children. Though he hated law school and the memories of it, there had been some long Friday nights in the bars of Georgetown with his pal Callahan. Those were good memories.

"So what kind of law?" The bartender was back. Gavin turned to the bar, and smiled.

"Special counsel, FBI."

He was still wiping. "So you're in Washington?"

"Yeah, in town for the game Sunday. I'm a Redskins freak." He hated the Redskins and every other organized football team. Don't get the kid started on football. "Where do you go to school?"

"Here. Tulane. I'll finish in May."

"Then where?"

"Probably Cincinnati for a clerkship for a year or two."

"You must be a good student."

He shrugged it off. "You need a beer?"

"No. Did you have Thomas Callahan?"

"Sure. You know him?"

"I was in law school with him at Georgetown." Verheek pulled a card from his pocket and handed it to the kid. "I'm Gavin Verheek." The kid looked at it, then politely laid it next to the ice. The bar was quiet and the kid was tired of chitchat.

"Do you know a student by the name of Darby Shaw?"

The kid glanced at the tables. "No. I haven't met her, but I know who she is. I think she's second year." A long, rather suspicious pause. "Why?"

"We need to talk to her." We, as in FBI. Not simply he, as in Gavin Verheek. The "we" part sounded much graver. "Does she hang out in here?"

"I've seen her a few times. She's hard to miss."

"I've heard." Gavin looked at the tables. "Do you think these guys might know her?"

"Doubt it. They're all first year. Can't you tell? They're over there arguing property rights and search and seizure."

Yeah, those were the days. Gavin pulled a dozen cards from his pocket and laid them on the bar. "I'll be at the Hilton for a few days. If you see her, or hear anything, drop one of these."

"Sure. There was a cop in last night asking questions. You don't think she was involved in his death?"

"No, not at all. We just need to talk to her."

"I'll keep my eyes open."

Verheek paid for the beer, thanked the kid again, and was on the sidewalk. He walked three blocks to the Half Shell. It was almost two. He was dead tired, half drunk, and a band cranked up the second he walked through the door. The place was dark, packed, and fifty fraternity joes with their sorority sues were immediately dancing on tables. He weaved through the uprising and found safety in the back near the bar. They were three deep, shoulder to shoulder, and no one moved. He clawed his way forward, got a beer to be cool, and realized again he was by far the oldest one there. He retreated to a dark but crowded corner. It was hopeless. He couldn't hear himself think, let alone carry on a conversation.

He watched the bartenders: all young, all students. The oldest looked late twenties, and he rang up check after check as if he was closing out. His moves were hurried, as if it was time to go. Gavin studied every move.

He quickly untied his apron, flung it in a corner, ducked under the bar, and was gone. Gavin elbowed through the mob, and caught him as he stepped through the kitchen door. He had an FBI business card ready. "I'm sorry. I'm with the FBI." He stuck the card in his face. "Your name is?"

The kid froze, and looked wildly at Verheek. "Uh, Fountain. Jeff Fountain."

"Fine, Jeff. Look, nothing's wrong, okay? Just a couple of questions." The kitchen had shut down hours ago, and they were alone. "Just take a second."

"Well, okay. What's up?"

"You're a law student, right?" Please say yes. His friend said most of the bartenders here were law students.

"Yes. At Loyola."

Loyola! Where the hell! "Yeah, well, that's what I thought. You've heard about Professor Callahan at Tulane. Funeral's to-morrow."

"Sure. It's all over the papers. Most of my friends go to Tulane."

"Do you know a second-year student there by the name of Darby Shaw? Very at-tractive female."

Fountain smiled. "Yeah, she dated a

friend of mine last year. She's in here occasionally."

"How long ago?"

"It's been a month or two. What's wrong?"

"We need to talk to her." He handed Fountain a stack of cards. "Hang on to these. I'll be at the Hilton for a few days. If you see her around, or if you hear anything, drop one of these."

"What might I hear?"

"Something about Callahan. We need to see her real bad, okay?"

"Sure." He stuck the cards in a pocket.

Verheek thanked him and returned to the revelry. He inched through the mob, listening to the attempts at conversation. A fresh mob was entering, and he wrestled his way out the door. He was too old for this.

Six blocks away, he parked illegally in front of a fraternity house next to the campus. His last stop for the night would be a dark little pool hall, which, at the moment, was not crowded. He paid for beer at the bar, and surveyed the place. There were four pool tables and the action was light. A young man in a T-shirt walked to the bar and ordered another beer. The shirt was

271

green and gray with the words TULANE LAW
SCHOOL stamped across the front with what
appeared to be an inmate identification
number under the words.

Verheek spoke without hesitating. "You a
law student?"

The young man glanced at him while
pulling money from his jeans. "Afraid so."

"Did you know Thomas Callahan?"

"Who are you?"

"FBI. Callahan was a friend of mine."

The student sipped the beer and was
suspicious. "I was in his con law class."

Bingo! So was Darby. Verheek tried to
appear uninterested. "Do you know Darby
Shaw?"

"Why do you want to know?"

"We need to talk to her. That's all."

"Who is we?" The student was even
more suspicious. He took a step closer to
Gavin as if he wanted some hard answers.

"FBI," Verheek said nonchalantly.

"You got a badge or something?"

"Sure," he said as he pulled a card from
his pocket. The student read it carefully,
then handed it back. "You're a lawyer, not
an agent."

This was a very valid point, and the lawyer knew he would lose his job if his boss

knew he was asking questions and in general impersonating an agent. "Yes, I'm a lawyer. Callahan and I were in law school together."

"Then why do you want to see Darby Shaw?"

The bartender had eased closer and was eavesdropping.

"Do you know her?"

"I don't know," the student said, and it was obvious he did in fact know her but was not about to talk. "Is she in trouble?"

"No. You know her, don't you?"

"Maybe. Maybe not."

"Look, what's your name?"

"Show me a badge, and I'll tell you my name."

Gavin took a long drink from the bottle and smiled at the bartender. "I need to see her, okay. It's very important. I'll be at the Hilton for a few days. If you see her, ask her to call." He offered the card to the student, who looked at it and walked away.

AT THREE, he unlocked the door to his room, and checked the phone. No messages. Wherever Darby was, she still had not called. Assuming, of course, she was still alive.

TWENTY

GARCIA CALLED for the last time. Grantham took the call before dawn Saturday, less than two hours before they were to meet for the first time. He was backing out, he said. The time was not right. If the story broke, then some very powerful lawyers and their very rich clients would fall hard, and these people were not accustomed to falling, and they would take people with them. And Garcia might get hurt. He had a wife and little daughter. He had a job that he could endure because the money was great. Why take chances? He had done nothing wrong. His conscience was clear.

"Then why do you keep calling me?" Grantham asked.

"I think I know why they were killed.

274

I'm not certain, but I've got a good idea. I saw something, okay."

"We've had this conversation for a week now, Garcia. You saw something, or you have something. And it's all useless unless you show it to me." Grantham opened a file and took out the five by sevens of the man on the phone. "You're driven by a sense of morality, Garcia. That's why you want to talk."

"Yeah, but there's a chance they know that I know. They've been treating me funny, as if they want to ask if I saw it. But they can't ask because they're not sure."

"These are the guys in your firm?"

"Yeah. No. Wait. How'd you know I was in a firm? I haven't told you that."

"It's easy. You go to work too early to be a government lawyer. You're in one of those two-hundred-lawyer firms where they expect the associates and junior partners to work a hundred hours a week. The first time you called me you said you were on the way to the office, and it was something like 5 A.M."

"Well, well, what else do you know?"

"Not much. We're playing games, Garcia. If you're not willing to talk, then hang up and leave me alone. I'm losing sleep."

275

"Sweet dreams." Garcia hung up. Grantham stared at the receiver.

THREE TIMES in the past eight years he had unlisted his phone number. He lived by the phone, and his biggest stories came out of nowhere over the phone. But after or during each big one, there had been a thousand insignificant ones from sources who felt compelled to call at all hours of the night with their hot little morsels. He was known as a reporter who would face a firing squad before revealing a source, so they called and called and called. He'd get sick of it, and get a new, unlisted number. Then hit a dry spell. Then rush to get back in the D.C. directory.

He was there now. Gray S. Grantham. The only one in the book. They could get him at work twelve hours a day, but it was so much more secretive and private to call him at home, especially at odd hours when he was trying to sleep.

He fumed over Garcia for thirty minutes, then fell asleep. He was in a rhythm and dead to the world when it rang again. He found it in the darkness. "Hello."

It was not Garcia. It was a female. "Is this Gray Grantham with the *Washington Post?*"

"It is. And who are you?"

"Are you still on the story about Rosenberg and Jensen?"

He sat in the darkness and stared at the clock. Five-thirty. "It's a big story. We've got a lot of people on it, but, yes, I'm investigating."

"Have you heard of the pelican brief?"

He breathed deeply and tried to think. "The pelican brief. No. What is it?"

"It's a harmless little theory about who killed them. It was taken to Washington last Sunday by a man named Thomas Callahan, a professor of law at Tulane. He gave it to a friend with the FBI, and it was passed around. Things snowballed, and Callahan was killed in a car bombing Wednesday night in New Orleans."

The lamp was on and he was scribbling. "Where are you calling from?"

"New Orleans. A pay phone, so don't bother."

"How do you know all this?"

"I wrote the brief."

He was wide awake now, wild-eyed and breathing rapidly. "Okay. If you wrote it, tell me about it."

"I don't want to do it that way, because

even if you had a copy you couldn't run the story."

"Try me."

"You couldn't. It'll take some thorough verification."

"Okay. We've got the Klan, the terrorist Khamel, the Underground Army, the Aryans, the—"

"Nope. None of the above. They're a bit obvious. The brief is about an obscure suspect."

He was pacing at the foot of the bed, holding the phone. "Why can't you tell me who it is?"

"Maybe later. You seem to have these magical sources. Let's see what you find."

"Callahan will be easy to check out. That's one phone call. Give me twenty-four hours."

"I'll try to call Monday morning. If we're gonna do business, Mr. Grantham, you must show me something. The next time I call, tell me something I don't know."

She was at a pay phone in the dark. "Are you in danger?" he asked.

"I think so. But I'm okay for now."

She sounded young, mid-twenties, maybe. She wrote a brief. She knew the law professor. "Are you a lawyer?"

"No, and don't spend your time digging after me. You've got work to do, Mr. Grantham, or I'll go elsewhere."

"Fine. You need a name."

"I've got one."

"I mean a code name."

"You mean like spies and all. Gee, this could be fun."

"Either that or give me your real name."

"Nice try. Just call me Pelican."

HIS PARENTS were good Irish Catholics, but he had sort of quit many years ago. They were a handsome couple, dignified in mourning, well tanned and dressed. He had seldom mentioned them. They walked hand-in-hand with the rest of the family into Rogers Chapel. His brother from Mobile was shorter and looked much older. Thomas said he had a drinking problem.

For half an hour, students and faculty had streamed into the small chapel. The game was tonight and there was a nice crowd on campus. A television van was parked in the street. A cameraman kept a respectable distance and shot the front of the chapel. A campus policeman watched him carefully and kept him in place.

It was odd seeing these law students with

dresses and heels and coats and ties. In a dark room on the third floor of Newcomb Hall, the Pelican sat with her face to the window and watched the students mill about and speak softly and finish their cigarettes. Under her chair were four newspapers, already read and discarded. She'd been there for two hours, reading by sunlight and waiting on the service. There was no other place to be. She was certain the bad guys were lurking in the bushes around the chapel, but she was learning patience. She had come early, would stay late, and move in the shadows. If they found her, maybe they would do it quick and it would be over.

She gripped a wadded paper towel and dried her eyes. It was okay to cry now, but this was the last one. The people were all inside, and the television van left. The paper said it was a memorial service with private burial later. There was no casket inside.

She had selected this moment to run, to rent a car and drive to Baton Rouge, then jump on the first plane headed to any place except New Orleans. She would get out of the country, perhaps Montreal or Calgary. She would hide there for a year and hope the crime would be solved and the bad guys put away.

But it was a dream. The quickest route to justice ran smack through her. She knew more than anyone. The Fibbies had circled close, then backed off, and were now chasing who knows who. Verheek had gotten nowhere, and he was close to the Director. She would have to piece it together. Her little brief had killed Thomas, and now they were after her. She knew the identity of the man behind the murders of Rosenberg and Jensen and Callahan, and this knowledge made her rather unique.

Suddenly, she leaned forward. The tears dried on her cheeks. There he was! The thin man with the narrow face! He was wearing a coat and tie and looked properly mournful as he walked quickly to the chapel. It was him! The man she'd last seen in the lobby of the Sheraton on, when was it, Thursday morning. She'd been talking to Verheek when he strolled suspiciously through.

He stopped at the door, jerked his head nervously around—he was a klutz, really, a giveaway. He stared for a second at three cars parked innocently on the street, less than fifty yards away. He opened the door, and was in the chapel. Beautiful. The bastards killed him, and now they joined his family and friends for last respects.

Her nose touched the window. The cars were too far away, but she was certain there was a man in one watching for her. Surely they knew she was not so dumb and so heartbroken as to show up and mourn her lover. They knew that. She had eluded them for two and a half days. The tears were gone.

Ten minutes later, the thin man came out by himself, lit a cigarette, and strolled with hands stuck deep in his pockets toward the three cars. He was sad. What a guy.

He walked in front of the cars but did not stop. When he was out of sight, a door opened and a man in a green Tulane sweatshirt emerged from the middle car. He walked down the street after the thin one. He was not thin. He was short, thick, and powerful. A regular stump.

He disappeared down the sidewalk behind the thin man, behind the chapel. Darby poised on the edge of the folding chair. Within a minute, they emerged on the sidewalk from behind the building. They were together now, whispering, but for only a moment because the thin man peeled off and disappeared down the street. Stump walked quickly to his car and got in. He just sat there, waiting for the service to break up and get one last look at the crowd on the off chance that she was in fact stupid enough to show up.

It had taken less than ten minutes for the thin man to sneak inside, scan the crowd of, say, two hundred people, and determine she was not there. Perhaps he was looking for the red hair. Or bleached blond. No, it made more sense for them to have people already in there, sitting around prayerfully and looking sad, looking for her or anyone who might resemble her. They could nod or shake or wink at the thin man.

This place was crawling with them.

HAVANA was a perfect sanctuary. It mattered not if ten or a hundred countries had bounties on his throat. Fidel was an admirer and occasional client. They drank together, shared women, and smoked cigars. He had the run of the place: a nice little apartment on Calle de Torre in the old section, a car with a driver, a banker who was a wizard at blitzing money around the world, any size boat he wanted, a military plane if needed, and plenty of young women. He spoke the language and his skin was not pale. He loved the place.

He had once agreed to kill Fidel, but couldn't do it. He was in place and two hours away from the murder, but just wouldn't pull it off. There was too much admiration. It was back in the days when he did not always kill for money. He pulled a double cross, and confessed to Fidel. They faked an ambush, and word spread that the great Khamel had been gunned down in the streets of Havana.

Never again would he travel by commercial air. The photographs in Paris were embarrassing for such a professional. He was losing his touch; getting careless in the twilight of his career. Got his picture on the front pages in America. How shameful. His client was not pleased.

The boat was a forty-foot schooner with two crew members and a young woman, all Cubans. She was below in the cabin. He had finished with her a few minutes before they saw the lights of Biloxi. He was all business now, inspecting his raft, packing his bag, saying nothing. The crew members crouched on the deck and stayed away from him.

At exactly nine, they lowered the raft onto the water. He dropped his bag into it, and was gone. They heard the trolling motor as he disappeared into the blackness of the Sound. They were to remain anchored until dawn, then haul it back to Havana. They held perfect papers declaring them to be Americans, in the event they were discovered and someone began asking questions.

He eased patiently through the still water, dodging buoy lights and the sight of an occasional small craft. He held perfect papers too, and three weapons in the bag.

It had been years since he struck twice in one month. After he was allegedly gunned down in Cuba, there had been a five-year drought. Patience was his forte. He averaged one a year.

And this little victim would go unnoticed. No one would suspect him. It was such a small job, but his client was adamant and he happened to be in the neighborhood, and the money was right, so here he was in another six-foot rubber raft cruising toward a beach, hoping like hell his pal Luke would be there dressed not as a farmer, but a fisherman this time.

This would be the last for a long time, maybe forever. He had more money than he could ever spend or give away. And he had started making small mistakes.

He saw the pier in the distance, and moved away from it. He had thirty minutes to waste. He followed the shoreline for a quarter of a mile, then headed for it. Two hundred yards out, he turned off the trolling motor, unhitched it, and dropped it into the water. He lay low in the raft, worked a plastic oar when necessary, and gently guided himself to a dark spot behind a row of cheap brick buildings thirty feet ashore. He stood in two feet of water and ripped holes in the raft with a small pocketknife. It sank and disappeared. The beach was deserted.

Luke was alone at the end of the pier. It was exactly eleven, and he was in place with a rod and reel. He wore a white cap, and the bill moved slowly back and forth as he scanned the water in search of the raft. He checked his watch.

Suddenly a man was beside him, appearing from nowhere like an angel. "Luke?" the man said.

This was not the code. Luke was startled. He had a gun in the tackle box at his feet, but there was no way. "Sam?" he asked. Maybe he had missed something. Maybe Khamel couldn't find the pier from the raft.

"Yes, Luke, it's me. Sorry about the deviation. Trouble with the raft."

Luke's heart settled and he breathed relief.

"Where's the vehicle?" Khamel asked.

Luke glanced at him ever so quickly. Yes, it was Khamel, and he was staring at the ocean behind dark glasses.

Luke nodded at a building. "Red Pontiac next to the liquor store."

"How far to New Orleans?"

"Half an hour," Luke said as he reeled in nothing.

Khamel stepped back, and hit him twice at the base of the neck. Once with each hand. The vertebrae burst and snapped the spinal cord. Luke fell hard and moaned once. Khamel watched him die, then found the keys in a pocket. He kicked the corpse off into the water.

EDWIN SNELLER or whatever his name was did not open the door, but quietly slid the key under it. Khamel picked it up, and opened the door to the next room. He walked in, and moved quickly to the bed where he placed his bag, then to the window where the curtains were open and the river was in the distance. He pulled the curtains together, and studied the lights of the French Quarter below.

He walked to the phone and punched Sneller's number.

"Tell me about her," Khamel said softly to the floor.

"There are two photos in the briefcase."

Khamel opened it and removed the photos. "I've got them."

"They're numbered, one and two. One we got from the law school yearbook. It's about a year old, and the most current we have. It's a blowup from a tiny picture, so we lost a lot of detail. The other photo is two years old. We lifted it from a yearbook at Arizona State."

Khamel held both pictures. "A beautiful woman."

"Yes. Quite beautiful. All that lovely hair is gone, though. Thursday night she paid for a hotel room with a credit card. We barely missed her Friday morning. We found long strands of hair on the floor and a small sample of something we now know to be black hair color. Very black."

"What a shame."

"We haven't seen her since Wednesday night. She's proven to be elusive: credit card for a room Wednesday, credit card at another hotel Thursday, then nothing from last night. She withdrew five thousand in cash from her checking account Friday afternoon, so the trail has become cold."

"Maybe she's gone."

"Could be, but I don't think so. Someone was in her apartment last night. We've got the place wired, and we were late by two minutes."

"Moving sort of slow, aren't you?"

"It's a big town. We've camped out at the airport and train station. We're watching her mother's house in Idaho. No sign. I think she's still here."

"Where would she be?"

"Moving around, changing hotels, using pay phones, staying away from the usual places. The New Orleans police are looking for her. They talked to her after the bomb Wednesday, then lost her. We're looking, they're looking, she'll turn up."

"What happened with the bomb?"

"Very simple. She didn't get in the car."

"Who made the bomb?"

Sneller hesitated. "Can't say."

Khamel smiled slightly as he took some street maps from the briefcase. "Tell me about the maps."

"Oh, just a few points of interest around town. Her place, his place, the law school, the hotels she's been to, the bomb site, a few little bars she enjoys as a student."

"She's stayed in the Quarter so far."

"She's smart. There are a million places to hide."

Khamel picked up the most recent photo, and sat on the other bed. He liked this face. Even with short dark hair, it would be an intriguing face. He could kill it, but it would not be pleasant.

"It's a shame, isn't it?" he said, almost to himself.

"Yes. It's a shame."

TWENTY-ONE

GAVIN VERHEEK had been a tired old man when he arrived in New Orleans, and after two nights of barhopping he was drained and weakened. He had hit the first bar not long after the burial, and for seven hours had sipped beer with the young and restless while talking of torts and contracts and Wall Street firms and other things he despised. He knew he shouldn't tell strangers he was FBI. He wasn't FBI. There was no badge.

He prowled five or six bars Saturday night. Tulane lost again, and after the game the bars filled with rowdies. Things got hopeless, and he quit at midnight.

He was sleeping hard with his shoes on when the phone rang. He lunged for it. "Hello! Hello!"

"Gavin?" she asked.

"Darby! Is this you?"

"Who else?"

"Why haven't you called before now?"

"Please, don't start asking a bunch of stupid questions. I'm at a pay phone, so no funny stuff."

"Come on, Darby. I swear you can trust me."

"Okay, I trust you. Now what?"

He looked at his watch, and began untying his shoelaces. "Well, you tell me. What's next? How long do you plan to hide in New Orleans?"

"How do you know I'm in New Orleans?"

He paused for a second.

"I'm in New Orleans," she said. "And I assume you want me to meet with you, and become close friends, then come in, as you say, and trust you guys to protect me forever."

"That's correct. You'll be dead in a matter of days if you don't."

"Get right to the point, don't you?"

"Yes. You're playing games and you don't know what you're doing."

"Who's after me, Gavin?"

"Could be a number of people."

"Who are they?"

"I don't know."

"Now you're playing games, Gavin. How can I trust you if you won't talk to me?"

"Okay. I think it's safe to say your little brief hit someone in the gut. You guessed right, the wrong people learned of the brief, and now Thomas is dead. And they'll kill you the instant they find you."

"We know who killed Rosenberg and Jensen, don't we, Gavin?"

"I think we do."

"Then why doesn't the FBI do something?"

"We may be in the midst of a cover-up."

"Bless you for saying that. Bless you."

"I could lose my job."

"Who would I tell, Gavin? Who's covering up what?"

"I'm not sure. We were very interested in the brief until the White House pressed hard, now we've dismissed it."

"I can understand that. Why do they think they can kill me and it will be kept quiet?"

"I can't answer that. Maybe they think you know more."

"Can I tell you something? Moments after the bomb, while Thomas was in the car burning and I was semiconscious, a cop named Rupert took me to his car and put me inside. Another cop with cowboy boots and jeans started asking me questions. I was sick and in shock. They disappeared, Rupert and his cowboy, and they never returned. They were not cops, Gavin. They watched the bomb, and went to plan B when I wasn't in the car. I didn't know it, but I was probably a minute or two away from a bullet in the head."

Verheek listened with his eyes closed. "What happened to them?"

"Not sure. I think they got scared when the real cops swarmed on the scene. They vanished. I was in their car, Gavin. They had me."

"You have to come in, Darby. Listen to me."

"Do you remember our phone chat Thursday morning when I suddenly saw a face that looked familiar and I described it to you?"

"Of course."

"That face was at the memorial service yesterday, along with some friends."

"Where were you?"

"Watching. He walked in a few minutes late, stayed ten minutes, then sneaked out and met with Stump."

"Stump?"

"Yes, he's one of the gang. Stump, Rupert, Cowboy, and the Thin Man. Great characters. I'm sure there are others, but I haven't met them yet."

"The next meeting will be the last, Darby. You have about forty-eight hours to live."

"We'll see. How long will you be in town?"

"A few days. I'd planned to stay until I found you."

"Here I am. I may call you tomorrow."

Verheek breathed deeply. "Okay, Darby. Whatever you say. Just be careful."

She hung up. He threw the phone across the room, and cursed it.

TWO BLOCKS AWAY and fifteen floors up, Khamel stared at the television and mumbled rapidly to himself. It was a movie about people in a big city. They spoke English, his third language, and he repeated every word in his best generic American tongue. He did this for hours. He had absorbed the language while hiding in Belfast, and in the past twenty years had watched thousands of American movies. His favorite was *Three Days of the Condor*. He watched it four times before he figured out who was killing whom and why. He could have killed Redford.

He repeated every word out loud. He had been told his English could pass for that of an American, but one slip, one tiny mistake, and she would be gone.

THE VOLVO was parked in a lot a block and a half from its owner, who paid one hundred dollars a month for the space and for what he thought was security. They eased through the gate that was supposed to be locked.

It was a 1986 GL without a security system, and within seconds the driver's door was open. One sat on the trunk and lit a cigarette. It was almost 4 A.M. Sunday.

The other one opened a small tool case he kept in his pocket, and went to work on the yuppie car phone that Grantham had been embarrassed to buy. The dome light was enough, and he worked quickly. Easy work. With the receiver open, he installed a tiny transmitter and glued it in place. A minute later, he eased out of the car and squatted at the rear bumper. The one with the cigarette handed him a small black cube, which he stuck under the car to a grille and behind the gas tank. It was a magnetized transmitter, and it would send signals for six days before it died and needed replacing.

They were gone in less than seven minutes. Monday, as soon as he was spotted entering the *Post* building on Fifteenth, they would enter his apartment and fix his phones.

TWENTY-TWO

HER SECOND NIGHT in the bed and breakfast was better than the first. She slept until mid-morning. Maybe she was used to it now. She stared at the curtains over the tiny window and determined that there had been no nightmares, no movements in the dark with guns and knives emerging and attacking. It was a thick, heavy sleep, and she studied the curtains for a long time while the brain woke up.

She tried to be disciplined about her thinking. This was her fourth day as the Pelican, and to see number five she would have to think like a fastidious killer. It was day number four of the rest of her life. She was supposed to be dead.

But after the eyes opened, and she realized she was indeed alive and safe, and the door wasn't squeaking and the floor wasn't cracking, and there was no gunman lurking in the closet, her first thought was always of Thomas. The shock of his death was fading, and she found it easier to put aside the sound of the explosion and the roar of the fire. She knew he had been blown to pieces and killed instantly. She knew he did not suffer.

So she thought of other things, like the feel of him next to her, and his whispering and snickering when they were in bed and the sex was over and he wanted to cuddle. He was a cuddler, and he wanted to play and kiss and caress after the lovemaking. And giggle. He loved her madly, had fallen hard, and for the first time in his life could be silly with a woman. Many times in the middle of his lectures, she had thought of his cooing and snickering, and bit her lip to keep from smiling.

She loved him too. And it hurt so badly. She wanted to stay in bed and cry for a week. The day after her father's funeral, a psychiatrist had explained that the soul needs a brief, very intense period of grieving, then it moves to the next phase. But it must have the pain; it must suffer without restraint before it can properly move on. She took his advice, and grieved without courage for two weeks, then got tired of it and moved to the next stage. It worked.

But it wasn't working with Thomas. She couldn't scream and throw things the way she wanted. Rupert and Thin Man and the rest of the boys were denying her a healthy mourning.

After a few minutes of Thomas, she thought of them next. Where would they be today? Where could she go without being seen? After two nights in this place, should she find another room? Yes, she would do that. After dark. She would call and reserve a room at another tiny guest house. Where were they staying? Were they patrolling the streets hoping to simply bump into her? Did they know where she was at this moment? No. She would be dead. Did they know she was now a blonde?

The hair got her out of bed. She walked to the mirror over the desk, and looked at herself. It was even shorter now, and very white. Not a bad job. She had worked on it for three hours last night. If she lived another two days, she would cut some more and go back to black. If she lived another week, she might be bald.

A hunger pain hit, and for a second she

thought about food. She was not eating, and this would have to change. It was almost ten. Oddly, this bed and breakfast didn't cook on Sunday mornings. She would venture out to find food and a Sunday *Post,* and to see if they could catch her now that she was a butch blonde.

She showered quickly, and the hair took less than a minute. No makeup. She put on a new pair of Army fatigues and a new flight jacket, and she was ready for battle. The eyes were covered with aviator shades.

Although she had made a few entrances, she had not exited a building through the front door in four days. She crept through the dark kitchen, unlocked the rear door, and stepped into the alley behind the little inn. It was cool enough to wear the flight jacket without being suspicious. Silly, she thought. In the French Quarter, she could wear the hide and head of a polar bear and not appear suspicious. She walked briskly through the alley with her hands deep in the fatigues and her eyes darting behind the shades.

He saw her when she stepped onto the sidewalk next to Burgundy Street. The hair under the cap was different, but she was still five-eight and she couldn't change that. The legs were still long and she walked a certain way, and after four days he could pick her out of a crowd regardless of the face and hair. The cowboy boots—snakeskin with pointed toes—hit the sidewalk and started following.

She was a smart girl, turning every corner, changing streets every block, walking quickly but not too fast. He figured she was headed for Jackson Square, where there was a crowd on Sundays and she thought she could disappear. She could stroll about with the tourists and the locals, maybe eat a bite, enjoy the sun, pick up a paper.

Darby casually lit a cigarette and puffed as she walked. She could not inhale. She tried three days ago, and got dizzy. Such a nasty habit. How ironic it would be if she lived through all this only to die from lung cancer. Please, let her die of cancer.

He was sitting at a table in a crowded sidewalk café at the corner of St. Peter and Chartres, and he was less than ten feet away when she saw him. A split second later, he saw her, and she probably would have made it if she hadn't hesitated for a step and swallowed hard when she saw him. He saw her, and probably would have been only suspicious, but the slight hesitation and the curious look gave her away. She kept walking, but faster now.

It was Stump. He was on his feet and weaving through the tables when she lost sight of him. At ground level, he was anything but chubby. He seemed quick and muscular. She lost him for a second on Chartres as she ducked between the arches of St. Louis Cathedral. The church was open, and she thought maybe she should get inside, as if it would be a sanctuary and he would not kill her there. Yes, he would kill her there, or on the street, or in a crowd. Anywhere he caught her. He was back there, and Darby wanted to know how fast he was coming. Was he just walking real fast and trying to play it cool? Was he sort of jogging? Or was he barreling down the sidewalk preparing to make a flying tackle as soon as he caught sight of her? She kept moving.

She hung a left on St. Ann, crossed the street, and was almost to Royal when she took a quick glance behind her. He was coming. He was on the other side of the street, but very much in pursuit.

The nervous look over the shoulder

nailed her. It was a dead giveaway, and he was into a jog now.

Get to Bourbon Street, she decided. Kickoff was four hours away, and the Saints fans were out in force celebrating before the game because there would be little to celebrate afterward. She turned on Royal and ran hard for a few steps, then slowed to a fast walk. He turned on Royal and was trotting. He was poised to break and run hard at any second. Darby moved to the center of the street where a group of football rowdies were moving around, killing time. She turned left on Dumaine, and started running. Bourbon was ahead and there were people everywhere.

She could hear him now. No sense looking anymore. He was back there, running and gaining. When she turned onto Bourbon, Mr. Stump was fifty feet behind her, and the race was over. She saw her angels as they made a noisy exit from a bar. Three large, overweight young men dressed in a wild assortment of black and gold Saints garb stepped into the middle of the street just as Darby ran to them.

"Help!" she screamed wildly and pointed at Stump. "Help me! That man is after me! He's trying to rape me!"

Well, hell, now, sex in the streets of New Orleans is not at all uncommon, but they'd be damned if this girl was going to be abused.

"Please help me!" she screamed pitifully. Suddenly, the street was silent. Everyone froze, including Stump, who stopped for a step or two, then rushed forward. The three Saints stepped in front of him with folded arms and glowing eyes. It was over in seconds. Stump used both hands at once: a right to the throat of the first one, and a vicious blow to the mouth of the second. They squealed and fell hard. Number three was not about to run. His two buddies were hurt and this upset him. He would have been a piece of cake for Stump, but number one fell on Stump's right foot and this threw him off. As he yanked his foot away, Mr. Benjamin Chop of Thibodaux, Louisiana, number three, kicked him squarely in the crotch, and Stump was history. As Darby eased back into the crowd, she heard him cry in pain.

While he was falling, Mr. Chop kicked him in the ribs. Number two, with blood all over his face, charged wild-eyed into Stump, and the massacre was on. He curled around his hands, which were curled around his severely damaged testicles, and they kicked him and cursed him without mercy until someone yelled, "Cops," and this saved his life. Mr. Chop and number two helped number one to his feet, and the Saints were last seen darting into a bar. Stump made it to his feet, and crawled away like a dog hit by a Mack truck but still alive and determined to die at home.

She hid in a dark corner of a pub on Decatur, drinking coffee then a beer, coffee then a beer. Her hands shook and her stomach flipped. The po'boys smelled delicious, but she could not eat. After three beers in three hours, she ordered a plate of boiled shrimp and switched to spring water.

The alcohol had calmed her, and the shrimp settled her. She was safe in here, she thought, so why not watch the game and just sit here, maybe, until it closed.

The pub was packed at kickoff. They watched the wide screen above the bar, and got drunk. She was a Saints fan now. She hoped her three buddies were okay and enjoying the game. The crowd yelled and cursed the Redskins.

Darby stayed in her little corner until the game was long over, then slid into the darkness.

AT SOME POINT in the fourth quarter, with the Saints down by four field goals, Edwin Sneller hung up the phone and turned off the television. He stretched his legs, then returned to the phone and called Khamel next door.

"Listen to my English," the assassin said. "Tell me if you hear a trace of an accent."

"Okay. She's here," Sneller said. "One of our men saw her this morning at Jackson Square. He followed her for three blocks, then lost her."

"How did he lose her?"

"Doesn't matter, does it? She got away, but she's here. Her hair is very short and almost white."

"White?"

Sneller hated to repeat himself, especially to this mongrel.

"He said it was not blond but white, and she was wearing green Army pants and a brown bomber jacket. Somehow she recognized him, and took off."

"How would she recognize him? Has she seen him before?"

These idiot questions. It was hard to believe he was considered Superman. "I can't answer that."

"How's my English?"

"Perfect. There's a small card under your door. You need to see it."

Khamel laid the phone on a pillow and walked to the door. In a second he was back on the phone. "Who is this?"

"The name is Verheek. Dutch, but he's an American. Works for the FBI in Washington. Evidently, he and Callahan were friends. They finished law school together at Georgetown, and Verheek was an honorary pallbearer at the memorial service yesterday. Last night he was hanging out in a bar not far from the campus, and was asking questions about the girl. Two hours ago, one of our men was in the same bar posing as an FBI agent, and he struck up a conversation with the bartender, who turns out to be a law student who knows the girl. They watched football and talked for a while, then the kid produced the card. Look on the back. He's in room 1909 at the Hilton."

"That's a five-minute walk." The street maps were scattered on one bed.

"Yes. We've made a few phone calls to Washington. He's not an agent, just a lawyer. He knew Callahan, and he might know the girl. It's obvious he's trying to find her."

"She would talk to him, wouldn't she?"

"Probably."

"How's my English?"

"Perfect."

KHAMEL WAITED AN HOUR and left the hotel. With the coat and tie, he was just an average joe strolling along Canal at dusk headed for the river. He carried a large gym bag and smoked a cigarette, and five minutes later entered the lobby of the Hilton. He worked his way through the crowd of fans returning from the Dome. The elevator stopped on the twentieth floor, and he walked one flight down to the nineteenth.

There was no answer at 1909. If the door had opened with the chain locked, he would have apologized and explained he had the wrong room. If the door had opened without the chain and with a face in the crack, he would have kicked it sharply and been inside. But it did not open.

His new pal Verheek was probably hanging around a bar, passing out cards, begging kids to talk to him about Darby Shaw. What a nut.

He knocked again, and while he waited he slid a six-inch plastic ruler between the door and the facing, and worked it gently until the bolt clicked. Locks were minor nuisances for Khamel. Without a key, he could open a locked car and start the engine in less than thirty seconds.

Inside, he locked the door behind him, and placed his bag on the bed. Like a surgeon, he picked the gloves from a pocket and pulled them tightly over his fingers. He laid a .22 and silencer on the table.

The phone was quick work. He plugged the recorder into the jack under the bed, where it could sit for weeks before it was noticed. He called the weather station twice to test the recorder. Perfect.

His new pal Verheek was a slob. Most of the clothes in the room were dirty and simply thrown in the direction of the suitcase sitting on a table. He had not unpacked. A cheap garment bag hung in the closet with one solitary shirt.

Khamel covered his tracks and settled

low in the closet. He was a patient man, and he could wait for hours. He held the .22 just in case this clown happened to barge into the closet and he had to kill him with bullets. If not, he would just listen.

TWENTY-THREE

GAVIN QUIT THE BARS SUNDAY. He was getting nowhere. She had called him, and she was not hanging around those places, so what the hell. He was drinking too much and eating too much, and he was tired of New Orleans. He already had a flight booked for late Monday afternoon, and if she didn't call again he was finished playing detective.

He couldn't find her, and it wasn't his fault. Cabdrivers got lost in this city. Voyles would be screaming by noon. He had done his best.

He was stretched on the bed in nothing but boxer shorts, flipping through a magazine and ignoring the television. It was almost eleven. He would wait on her until twelve, then try to sleep.

It rang at exactly eleven. He pushed a

312

button and remotely killed the television. "Hello."

It was her. "It's me, Gavin."

"So you're alive."

"Barely."

He sat on the edge of the bed. "What's happened?"

"They saw me today, and one of their goons, my friend Stump, chased me through the Quarter. You haven't met Stump, but he's the one who watched you and everyone else walk into the chapel."

"But you got away."

"Yeah. A small miracle, but I got away."

"What happened to Stump?"

"He was mortally wounded. He's probably lying in a bed somewhere wearing an ice pack in his shorts. He was just a few steps from me when he picked a fight with the wrong guys. I'm scared, Gavin."

"Did he follow you from somewhere?"

"No. We just sort of met on the street."

Verheek paused a second. Her voice was shaking, but under control. She was losing her cool. "Look, Darby. I've got a flight out of here tomorrow afternoon. I have this little job and my boss expects me to be at the office. So I can't hang around New Orleans for the next month hoping you don't get killed and hoping you come to your senses and trust me. I'm leaving tomorrow, and I think you need to go with me."

"Go where?"

"To Washington. To my house. To some-place other than where you are."

"What happens then?"

"Well, you get to live, for one thing. I'll plead with the Director, and I promise you'll be safe. We'll do something, dammit. Anything beats this."

"What makes you think we can just fly out of here?"

"Because we'll have three FBI agents surrounding you. Because I'm not a complete dumbass. Look, Darby, tell me where you want to meet right now, and within fifteen minutes I'll come get you with three agents. These guys have guns, and they're not afraid of your little Stump and his pals. We'll get you out of the city tonight, and take you to Washington tomorrow. I promise you'll personally meet my boss, the Honorable F. Denton Voyles, tomorrow, and we'll go from there."

"I thought the FBI was not involved."

"It's not involved, but it may be."

"Then where do the three agents come from?"

"I've got friends."

She thought for a moment, and her voice was suddenly stronger. "Behind your hotel is a place called Riverwalk. It's a shopping area with restaurants and—"

"I spent two hours there this afternoon."

"Good. On the second level is a clothing store called Frenchmen's Bend."

"I saw it."

"At precisely noon tomorrow, I want you to stand by the entrance, and wait for five minutes."

"Come on, Darby. You won't be alive at noon tomorrow. Enough of this cat and mouse."

"Just do as I say, Gavin. We've never met, so I have no idea what you look like. Wear a black shirt of some type and a red baseball cap."

"Where might I find such articles?"

"Just get them."

"Okay, okay, I'll have them. I guess you want me to pick my nose with a shovel or something. This is silly."

"I'm not in a silly mood, and if you don't shut up we'll call it off."

"It's your neck."

"Please, Gavin."

"I'm sorry. I'll do whatever you say. That's a very busy spot to be."

"Yes, it is. I just feel safer in a crowd. Stand by the door for five minutes or so, and hold a folded newspaper. I'll be watching. After five minutes, walk inside the store, and go to the right rear corner where there's a rack of safari jackets. Browse around a bit, and I'll find you."

"And what might you be wearing?"

"Don't worry about me."

"Fine. Then what do we do?"

"You and I, and only you and I, will leave the city. I don't want anyone else to know of this. Do you understand?"

"No, I don't understand. I can arrange security."

"No, Gavin. I'm the boss, okay. No one else. Forget your three agent friends. Agreed?"

"Agreed. How do you propose we leave the city?"

"I've got a plan for that too."

"I don't like any of your plans, Darby. These thugs are breathing down your neck, and now you're getting me in the middle of it. This is not what I wanted. It's much safer to do it my way. Safer for you, safer for me."

"But you'll be there at noon, won't you?"

He stood by the bed and spoke with his eyes closed. "Yes. I'll be there. I just hope you make it."

"How tall are you?"

"Five-ten."

"How much do you weigh?"

"I was afraid of this. I usually lie, you know. Two hundred, but I plan to lose it. I swear."

"I'll see you tomorrow, Gavin."

"I hope I see you, dear."

She was gone. He hung up. "Son of a bitch!" he yelled to the walls. "Son of a bitch!" He walked along the end of the bed a few times, then to the bathroom, where he closed the door and turned on the shower.

He cussed her in the shower for ten minutes, then stepped out, and dried himself. It was more like two hundred and fifteen pounds, and all of it was situated badly on the five-nine frame. It was painful to look at. Here he was, about to meet this gorgeous woman who suddenly trusted him with her life, and what a slob he was.

He opened the door. The room was dark. Dark? He had left on the lights. What the hell? He headed for the switch next to the dresser.

The first blow crushed his larynx. It was a perfect blow that came from the side, somewhere near the wall. He grunted painfully and fell to one knee, which made the second blow so easy, like an ax on a fat log. It hit like a rock at the base of the skull, and Gavin was dead.

Khamel flipped on a light, and looked at the pitiful nude figure frozen on the floor. He was not one to admire his work. He didn't want carpet burns, so he lifted the pudgy corpse onto his shoulders and laid it across the bed. Working quickly without any wasted motion, Khamel turned on the television and raised it to full volume, unzipped his bag, removed a cheap .25 caliber automatic, and placed it precisely on the right temple of the late Gavin Verheek. He covered the gun and the head with two pillows, and pulled the trigger. Now the critical part: he took one pillow and placed it under the head, threw the other one on the floor, and carefully curled the fingers of the right hand around the pistol, leaving it twelve inches from the head.

He took the recorder from under the bed, and ran the telephone wire directly into the wall. He punched a button, listened, and there she was. He turned off the television.

Every job was different. He had once stalked his prey for three weeks in Mexico City, then caught him in bed with two prostitutes. It was a dumb mistake, and during his career he had been assisted by numerous dumb mistakes by the opposition. This guy was a dumb mistake, a stupid lawyer pilfering around running his mouth, passing out cards with his room number on the back. He had stuck his nose into the world of big-league killing, and look at him now.

With a little luck, the cops would look around the room for a few minutes and declare it to be another suicide. They would go through the motions and ask themselves a couple of questions they could not answer, but there were always some of those. Because he was an important FBI lawyer, an autopsy would be done in a day or so, and probably by Tuesday an examiner would suddenly discover it was not a suicide.

By Tuesday, the girl would be dead and he would be in Managua.

TWENTY-FOUR

HIS USUAL, official sources at the White House denied any knowledge of the pelican brief. Sarge had never heard of it. Long-shot phone calls to the FBI produced nothing. A friend at Justice denied ever hearing about it. He dug all weekend, and had nothing to show for it. The story about Callahan was verified when he found a copy of the New Orleans paper. When her call came in at the newsroom Monday, he had nothing fresh to tell her. But at least she called.

The Pelican said she was at a pay phone, so don't bother.

"I'm still digging," he said. "If there's such a brief in town, it's being closely protected."

"I assure you it's there, and I understand why it's being protected."

"I'm sure you can tell me more."

"Lots more. The brief almost got me killed yesterday, so I may be ready to talk sooner than I thought. I need to spill my guts while I'm still alive."

"Who's trying to kill you?"

"Same people who killed Rosenberg and Jensen, and Thomas Callahan."

"Do you know their names?"

"No, but I've seen at least four of them since Wednesday. They're here in New Orleans, snooping around, hoping I'll do something stupid and they can kill me."

"How many people know about the pelican brief?"

"Good question. Callahan took it to the FBI, and I think from there it went to the White House where it evidently caused quite a fuss, and from there who knows. Two days after he handed it to the FBI, Callahan was dead. I, of course, was supposed to have been killed with him."

"Were you with him?"

"I was close, but not close enough."

"So you're the unidentified female on the scene?"

"That's how the paper described me."

"Then the police have your name?"

"My name is Darby Shaw. I am a second-year law student at Tulane. Thomas Callahan was my professor and lover. I wrote the brief, gave it to him, and you know the rest. Are you getting all this?"

Grantham scribbled furiously. "Yes. I'm listening."

"I'm rather tired of the French Quarter, and I plan to leave today. I'll call you from somewhere tomorrow. Do you have access to presidential campaign disclosure forms?"

"It's public record."

"I know that. But how quickly can you get the information?"

"What information?"

"A list of all major contributors to the President's last election."

"That's not difficult. I can have it by this afternoon."

"Do that, and I'll call you in the morning."

"Okay. Do you have a copy of the brief?"

She hesitated. "No, but it's memorized."

"And you know who's doing the killing?"

"Yes, and as soon as I tell you, they'll put your name on the hit list."

"Tell me now."

"Let's take it slow. I'll call you tomorrow."

Grantham listened hard, then hung up. He took his notepad and zigzagged through the maze of desks and people to the glass office of his editor, Smith Keen. Keen was a hale and hearty type with an open-door policy that ensured chaos in his office. He was finishing a phone chat when Grantham barged in and closed the door.

"That door stays open," Keen said sharply.

"We have to talk, Smith."

"We'll talk with the door open. Open the damned door."

"I'll open it in just a second." Grantham spoke with both palms facing the editor. Yes, it was serious. "Let's talk."

"Okay. What is it?"

"It's big, Smith."

"I know it's big. You shut the damned door, so I know it's big."

"I just finished my second phone conversation with a young lady by the name of Darby Shaw, and she knows who killed Rosenberg and Jensen."

Keen sat slowly and glared at Grantham. "Yes, son, that's big. But how do you know? How does she know? What can you prove?"

"I don't have a story yet, Smith, but she's

talking to me. Read this." Grantham handed over a copy of the newspaper account of Callahan's death. Keen read it slowly.

"Okay. Who's Callahan?"

"One week ago today, he handed a little paper known as the pelican brief to the FBI here in town. Evidently, the brief implicates an obscure person in the killings. The brief gets passed around, then sent to the White House, then beyond that no one knows. Two days later, Callahan cranks his Porsche for the last time. Darby Shaw claims to be the unidentified female mentioned there. She was with Callahan, and was supposed to die with him."

"Why was she supposed to die?"

"She wrote the brief, Smith. Or she claims she did."

Keen sank deeper into his seat and placed his feet on the desk. He studied the photo of Callahan. "Where's the brief?"

"I don't know."

"What's in it?"

"Don't know that either."

"Then we don't have anything, do we?"

"Not yet. But what if she tells me everything that's in it?"

"And when will she do this?"

Grantham hesitated. "Soon, I think. Real soon."

Keen shook his head and threw the copy on the desk. "If we had the brief, we'd have a helluva story, Gray, but we couldn't run it. There's gotta be some heavy, painful, flawless, and accurate verification before we can run it."

"But I've got the green light?"

"Yeah, but you keep me posted every hour. Don't write a word until we talk."

Grantham smiled and opened the door.

THIS WAS NOT forty-bucks-an-hour work. Not even thirty, or twenty. Croft knew he'd be lucky to squeeze fifteen out of Grantham for this needle-in-the-haystack Mickey Mouse crap. If he'd had other work, he'd have told Grantham to find someone else, or better yet, do it himself.

But things had been slow, and he could do a lot worse than fifteen bucks an hour. He finished a joint in the last stall, flushed it, and opened the door. He stuck the dark sunglasses over his ears, and entered the hallway that led to the atrium where four escalators carried a thousand lawyers up to their little rooms, where they would spend the day bitching and threatening by the hour. He had Garcia's face memorized. He was even dreaming of this kid with the bright face and good looks, the slim physique draped with an expensive suit. He would know him if he saw him.

He stood by a pillar, holding a newspaper and trying to watch everyone from behind the dark shades. Lawyers everywhere, scurrying upward with their smug little faces and carrying their smug little attaché cases. Man, how he hated lawyers. Why did they all dress alike? Dark suits. Dark shoes. Dark faces. An occasional nonconformist with a daring little bow tie. Where did they all come from? Shortly after his arrest with the drugs, the first lawyers had been a group of angry mouthpieces hired by the *Post*. Then he hired his own, an overpriced moron who couldn't find the courtroom. Then, the prosecutor was of course a lawyer. Lawyers, lawyers.

Two hours in the morning, two hours at lunch, two hours during the evening, and then Grantham would have another building for him to patrol. Ninety bucks a day was cheap, and he would give this up as soon as he got a better deal. He told Grantham this was hopeless, just shooting in the dark. Grantham agreed, but said to keep

shooting. It's all they could do. He said
Garcia was scared and wouldn't call anymore. They had to find him.

In his pocket he had two photos just in
case, and from the directory he had made a
list of the firms in the building. It was a
long list. The building had twelve floors
filled mainly with firms filled with nothing
but these fancy little esquires. He was in a
den of snakes.

By nine-thirty the rush was over, and
some of the faces looked familiar coming
back down the escalators, headed no doubt
for the courtrooms and agencies and com-
missions. Croft eased through the revolving doors, and wiped his feet on the sidewalk.

FOUR BLOCKS AWAY, Fletcher Coal
paced in front of the President's desk and
listened intently to the phone in his ear. He
frowned, then closed his eyes, then glared
at the President as if to say, "Bad news,
Chief. Really bad news." The President
held a letter and peered at Coal over his
reading glasses. Coal's pacing back and
forth like Der Führer really irritated him,
and he made a mental note to say something about it.

Coal slammed the phone down.

"Don't slam the damned phones!" the President said.

Coal was unfazed. "Sorry. That was Zikman. Gray Grantham called thirty minutes ago, and asked if he had any knowledge of the pelican brief."

"Wonderful. Fabulous. How'd he get a copy of it?"

Coal was still pacing. "Zikman knows nothing about it, so his ignorance was genuine."

"His ignorance is always genuine. He's the dumbest ass on my staff, Fletcher, and I want him gone."

"Whatever." Coal sat in a chair across the desk and folded his hands in a little steeple in front of his chin. He was very deep in thought, and the President tried to ignore him. They thought for a moment.

"Voyles leaked it?" the President finally said.

"Maybe, if it was leaked. Grantham is known for bluffing. We can't be certain he's seen the brief. Maybe he heard about it, and he's fishing."

"Maybe, my ass. What if they run some crazy story about that damned thing? What then?" The President slapped his desk and bolted to his feet. "What then, Fletcher? That paper hates me!" He moped to the windows.

"They can't run it without another source, and there can't be another source because there's no truth to it. It's a wild idea that's gone much further than it deserves."

The President sulked for a while and stared through the glass. "How did Grantham find out about it?"

Coal stood and began pacing, but much slower now. He was still painfully in thought. "Who knows. No one here knows about it but you and I. They brought one copy, and it's locked away in my office. I personally Xeroxed it once, and gave it to Gminski. I swore him to secrecy."

The President sneered at the windows.

Coal continued. "Okay, you're right. There could be a thousand copies out there by now. But it's harmless, unless of course our friend actually did these dirty deeds, then—"

"Then my ass is cooked."

"Yes, I would say our asses are cooked."

"How much money did we take?"

"Millions, directly and indirectly." And legally and illegally, but the President knew little of these transactions and Coal chose to stay quiet.

The President walked slowly to the sofa. "Why don't you call Grantham? Pick his brain. See what he knows. If he's bluffing, it'll be obvious. What do you think?"

"I don't know."

"You've talked to him before, haven't you? Everyone knows Grantham."

Coal was now pacing behind the sofa. "Yeah, I've talked to him. But if I suddenly call out of nowhere, he'll be suspicious."

"Yeah, I guess you're right." The President paced on one end of the sofa, and Coal on the other.

"What's the downside?" the President finally asked.

"Our friend could be involved. You asked Voyles to back off our friend. Our friend could be exposed by the press. Voyles covers his tail and says you told him to chase other suspects and ignore our friend. The *Post* goes berserk with another cover-up smear. And we can forget reelection."

"Anything else?"

Coal thought for a second. "Yeah, this is all completely off the wall. The brief is fantasy. Grantham will find nothing, and I'm late for a staff meeting." He walked to the door. "I've got a squash game for lunch. Be back at one."

The President watched the door close, and breathed easier. He had eighteen holes planned for the afternoon, so forget the pelican thing. If Coal wasn't worried, neither was he.

He punched numbers on his phone, waited patiently, and finally had Bob Gminski on the line. The director of the CIA was a terrible golfer, one of the few the President could humiliate, and he invited him to play this afternoon. Certainly, said Gminski, a man with a thousand things to do but, well, it was the President so he would be delighted to join him.

"By the way, Bob, what about this pelican thing in New Orleans?"

Gminski cleared his throat and tried to sound relaxed. "Well, Chief, I told Fletcher Coal Friday that it was very imaginative and a fine work of fiction. I think its author should forget about law school and pursue a career as a novelist. Ha, ha, ha."

"Great, Bob. Nothing to it then."

"We're digging."

"See you at three." The President hung up, and went straight for his putter.

TWENTY-FIVE

RIVERWALK RUNS for a quarter of a mile along the water, and is always crowded. It is packed with two hundred shops and cafés and restaurants on several levels, most under the same roof, and several with doors leading onto a boardwalk next to the river. It's at the foot of Poydras Street, a stone's throw from the Quarter.

She arrived at eleven, and sipped espresso in the rear of a tiny bistro while trying to read the paper and appear calm. Frenchmen's Bend was one level down and around a corner. She was nervous, and the espresso didn't help.

She had a list in her pocket of things to do, specific steps at specific moments, even words and sentences she had memorized in the event things went terribly wrong and Verheek got out of control. She had slept two hours, and spent the rest of the time with a legal pad diagraming and charting. If she died, it would not be from a lack of preparation.

She could not trust Gavin Verheek. He was employed by a law enforcement agency that at times operated by its own rules. He took orders from a man with a history of paranoia and dirty tricks. His boss reported to a President in charge of an Administration run by fools. The President had rich, sleazy friends who gave him lots of money.

But at this moment, dear, there was no one else to trust. After five days and two near misses, she was throwing in the towel. New Orleans had lost its allure. She needed help, and if she had to trust cops, the Fibbies were as clean as any.

Eleven forty-five. She paid for the espresso, waited for a crowd of shoppers, and fell in behind them. There were a dozen people browsing in Frenchmen's Bend as she walked past the entrance where her friend should be in about ten minutes. She eased into a bookstore two doors down. There were at least three stores in the vicinity from which she could shop and hide and watch the front door of

Frenchmen's Bend. She chose the bookstore because the clerks weren't pushy and
killing time was expected of the customers.
She looked at the magazines first, then with
three minutes to go she stepped between
two rows of cookbooks and watched for
Gavin.

Thomas said he was never on time. An
hour late was early for him, but she would
give him fifteen minutes and she'd be
gone.

She expected him at precisely noon, and
there he was. Black sweatshirt, red baseball
cap, folded newspaper. He was a bit thin-
ner than she expected, but he could lose a
few pounds. Her heart pounded away. Be
cool, she said. Just be cool, dammit.

She held a cookbook to her eyes and
peered over it. He had gray hair and dark
skin. The eyes were hidden behind sunglasses. He fidgeted and looked irritated,
the way he sounded on the phone. He
passed the newspaper from hand to hand,
shifted his weight from foot to foot, and
glanced around nervously.

He was okay. She liked the way he
looked. He had a vulnerable, nonprofes-
sional manner about him that said he was
scared too.

After five minutes, he walked through the door as he was told, and went to the right rear of the store.

KHAMEL HAD BEEN TRAINED to welcome death. He had been close to it many times, but never afraid of it. And after thirty years of expecting it, nothing, absolutely nothing, made him tense. He got somewhat excited about sex, but that was it. The fidgeting was an act. The jittery little movements were contrived. He'd survived face-offs with men almost as talented as he, and he could certainly handle this little rendezvous with a desperate child. He picked through the safari jackets and tried to appear nervous.

He had a handkerchief in his pocket, because he suddenly had caught a cold so his voice was a bit thick and scratchy. He had listened to the recording a hundred times, and he was confident he had the inflection and rhythm and slight upper Midwest accent. But Verheek was a bit more nasal; thus, the handkerchief for the cold.

It was difficult to allow anyone to approach from the rear, but he knew he must. He did not see her. She was behind him but very close when she said, "Gavin."

He jerked quickly around. She was holding a white Panama hat and speaking to it. "Darby," he said, pulling the handkerchief out for a fake sneeze. Her hair was a gold color and shorter than his. He sneezed and coughed. "Let's get out of here," he said. "I don't like this idea."

Darby didn't like it either. It was Monday and her classmates were going about their business of clawing through law school, and here she was camouflaged to the max and playing cloak and dagger with this man who could get her killed. "Just do as I say, okay. Where'd you get the cold?"

He sneezed into the handkerchief and talked as low as possible. It sounded painful. "Last night. I left the air on too low. Let's get out of here."

"Follow me." They left the store. Darby took his hand, and they walked quickly down a flight of stairs leading to the boardwalk.

"Have you seen them?" he asked.

"No. Not yet. But I'm sure they're around."

"Where the hell are we going?" The voice was scratchy.

They were on the boardwalk, almost jogging, talking without looking at each other. "Just come with me."

"You're going too fast, Darby. We look suspicious. Slow down. Look, this is crazy. Let me make a phone call, and we'll be safe and secure. I can have three agents here in ten minutes." He was sounding good. This was working. They were holding hands, running for their lives.

"Nope." She slowed. The boardwalk was crowded, and a line had formed beside the *Bayou Queen,* a paddle wheeler. They stopped at the end of the line.

"What the hell is this?" he asked.

"Do you bitch about everything?" she almost whispered.

"Yes. Especially stupid things, and this is very stupid. Are we getting on this boat?"

"Yes."

"Why?" he sneezed again, then coughed out of control. He could take her out now with one hand, but there were people everywhere. People in front, people behind. He took great pride in his cleanliness, and this would be a dirty place to do it. Get on the boat, play along for a few more minutes, see what happens. He would get her on the upper deck, kill her, dump her in the river, then start yelling. Another terrible drowning accident. That might work. If not, he'd be patient. She'd be dead in an hour. Gavin was a bitch, so keep bitching.

"Because I've got a car a mile upriver at a park where we'll stop in thirty minutes," she explained in a low voice. "We get off the boat, into the car, and we haul ass."

The line was moving now. "I don't like boats. They make me seasick. This is dangerous, Darby." He coughed and looked around like a man pursued.

"Relax, Gavin. It's gonna work."

Khamel tugged at his pants. They were thirty-six inches in the waist and covered eight layers of briefs and gym shorts. The sweatshirt was extra large, and instead of weighing one-fifty, he could pass for one-ninety. Whatever. It seemed to be working.

They were almost to the steps of the *Bayou Queen*. "I don't like this," he mumbled loud enough for her to hear.

"Just shut up," she said.

The man with the gun ran to the end of the line and elbowed his way through the people with their bags and cameras. The tourists were packed tightly together as if a ride on the riverboat was the greatest trip in the world. He had killed before, but never in such a public place as this. The back of her head was visible through the crowd. He shoved his way desperately through the line. A few cursed him, but he couldn't care less. The gun was in a pocket, but as he neared the girl he yanked it out and kept it by his right leg. She was almost to the steps, almost on the boat. He shoved harder and knocked people out of the way. They protested angrily until they saw the gun, then they began yelling. She was holding hands with the man, who was talking nonstop. She was about to step up onto the boat when he knocked the last person out of the way and quickly stuck the gun into the base of the skull just below the red baseball cap. He fired once, and people screamed and fell to the ground.

Gavin fell hard into the steps. Darby screamed and backed away in horror. Her ears were ringing from the shot, and voices were yelling and people were pointing. The man with the gun was running hard toward a row of shops and a crowd of people. A heavy man with a camera was yelling at him, and Darby watched for a second as he disappeared. Maybe she'd seen him before, but she couldn't think now. She was yelling and couldn't stop.

"He's got a gun!" a woman near the boat

yelled, and the crowd backed away from Gavin, who was on all fours with a small pistol in his right hand. He rocked pitifully back and forth like an infant trying to crawl. Blood streamed from his chin and puddled under his face. His head hung almost to the boards. His eyes were closed. He moved forward just a few inches, his knees now in the dark red puddle.

The crowd backed farther away, horrified at the sight of this wounded man fighting death. He teetered and wobbled forward again, headed nowhere but wanting to move, to live. He started yelling; loud painful moans in a language Darby did not recognize.

The blood was pouring, gushing from the nose and chin. He was wailing in that unknown tongue. Two crew members from the boat hovered on the steps, watching but afraid to move. The pistol concerned them.

A woman was crying, then another. Darby inched farther back. "He's Egyptian," a small, dark woman said. That news meant nothing to the crowd, now mesmerized.

He rocked forward and lunged to the edge of the boardwalk. The gun dropped into the water. He collapsed on his stomach with his head hanging over and dripping into the river. Shouts came from the rear, and two policemen rushed to him.

A hundred people now inched forward to see the dead man. Darby shuffled backward, then left the scene. The cops would have questions, and since she had no answers, she preferred not to talk. She was weak and needed to sit for a while, and think. There was an oyster bar inside Riverwalk. It was crowded for lunch, and she found the rest rooms in the back. She locked the door and sat on a toilet.

SHORTLY AFTER DARK, she left Riverwalk. The Westin Hotel is two blocks away, and she hoped maybe she could make it there without being gunned down on the sidewalk. Her clothes were different and hidden under a new black trench coat. The sunglasses and hat were also new. She was tired of spending good money on disposable clothes. She was tired of a lot of things.

She made it to the Westin in one piece. There were no rooms, and she sat in the well-lit lounge for an hour drinking coffee. It was time to run, but she couldn't get careless. She had to think.

Maybe she was thinking too damned much. Maybe they now thought of her as a thinker, and planned accordingly.

She left the Westin, and walked to Poydras, where she flagged a cab. An elderly black man sat low behind the wheel.

"I need to go to Baton Rouge," she said.

"Lord, honey, that's a heckuva ride."

"How much?" she asked quickly.

He thought a second. "A hundred and fifty."

She crawled in the backseat and threw two bills over the seat. "There's two hundred. Get there as fast as you can, and watch your rear. We may be followed."

He turned off the meter and stuffed the money in his shirt pocket. Darby lay down in the backseat and closed her eyes. This was not an intelligent move, but playing the percentages was getting nowhere. The old man was a fast driver, and within minutes they were on the expressway.

The ringing in her ears had stopped, but she still heard the gunshot and saw him on all fours, rocking back and forth, trying to live just a moment longer. Thomas had once referred to him as Dutch Verheek, but said the nickname was dropped after law school when they became serious about their careers. Dutch Verheek was not an Egyptian.

She had caught just a glimpse of his killer as he was running away. There was something familiar about him. He had glanced to his right just once as he was running, and something clicked. But she was screaming and hysterical, and it was a blur.

Everything blurred. Halfway to Baton Rouge, she fell into a deep sleep.

TWENTY-SIX

DIRECTOR VOYLES stood behind his executive swivel chair. His jacket was off, and most of the buttons on his tired and wrinkled shirt were unfastened. It was 9 P.M., and judging from the shirt he had been at the office at least fifteen hours. And he hadn't thought of leaving.

He listened to the receiver, mumbled a few instructions, and hung it up. K. O. Lewis sat across the desk. The door was open; the lights were on; no one had left. The mood was somber with small huddles of soft whispers.

"That was Eric East," Voyles said, sitting gently into the chair. "He's been there about two hours, and they just finished the autopsy. He watched it, his first. Single bullet to the right temple, but death came sooner from a single blow at C-2 and C-3.

344

The vertebrae were shattered into tiny chips and pieces. No powder burns on his hand. Another blow severely bruised his larynx, but did not cause death. He was nude. Estimate of between ten and eleven last night."

"Who found him?" Lewis asked.

"Maids checked in around eleven this morning. Will you deliver the news to his wife?"

"Yea, sure," K.O. said. "When's the body coming back?"

"East said they'll release it in a couple of hours, and it should be here by 2 A.M. Tell her we'll do whatever she wants. Tell her I'm sending a hundred agents in tomorrow to blanket the city. Tell her we'll find the killer, etc., etc."

"Any evidence?"

"Probably not. East said they've had the hotel room since 3 P.M., and it appears to be a clean job. No forced entry. No signs of resistance. Nothing that would be of any help, but it's a bit early." Voyles rubbed his red eyes, and thought for a while.

"How could he go down for a simple funeral, and end up dead?" Lewis asked.

"He was snooping around on this pelican thing. One of our agents, guy named

Carlton, told East that Gavin was trying to find the girl, and that the girl had called him, and that he might need some help bringing her in. Carlton talked to him a few times, and gave him the names of a few student hangouts in the city. That was all, so he says. Carlton says that he, Carlton, was a bit worried about Gavin throwing his FBI weight around. Said he thought he was sort of a klutz."

"Has anyone seen the girl?"

"She's probably dead. I've instructed New Orleans to find her, if possible."

"Her little brief is getting folks killed right and left. When do we take it seriously?"

Voyles nodded at the door, and Lewis got up and closed it. The Director was standing again, cracking his knuckles and thinking aloud. "We have to cover our asses. I think we should assign at least two hundred agents to pelican, but try like hell to keep it quiet. There's something there, K.O., something really nasty. But at the same time, I promised the President we would back off. He personally asked me to back off the pelican brief, remember, and I said we would, in part because we thought it was a joke." Voyles managed a tight

346

smile. "Well, I taped our little conversation when he asked me to back off. I figure he and Coal tape everything within a half mile of the White House, so why can't I? I had my best body mike, and I've listened to the tape. Clear as a bell."

"I'm not following."

"Simple. We go in and investigate like mad. If this is it, we crack the case, get the indictments, and everyone's happy. But it'll be a bitch to do in a hurry. Meanwhile, idiot and Coal over there know nothing about the investigation. If the press gets wind of it, and if the pelican brief is on target, then I'll make damned sure the country knows the President asked us to back off because it's one of his pals."

Lewis was smiling. "It'll kill him."

"Yes! Coal will hemorrhage, and the President will never recover. The election is next year, K.O."

"I like it, Denton, but we have to solve this thing."

Denton walked slowly behind his chair, and slid out of his shoes. He was even shorter now. "We'll look under every stone, K.O., but it won't be easy. If it's Mattiece, then we've got a very wealthy man in a very elaborate plot to use very talented killers to take out two justices. These people don't talk, and they don't leave trails. Look at our friend Gavin. We'll spend two thousand hours digging around that hotel, and I'll bet you there won't be a shred of useful evidence. Just like Rosenberg and Jensen."

"And Callahan."

"And Callahan. And probably the girl, if we ever find her body."

"I'm somewhat responsible, Denton. Gavin came to me Thursday morning after he learned of Callahan, and I didn't listen. I knew he was going down there, but I just didn't listen."

"Look, I'm sorry he's dead. He was a fine lawyer and he was loyal to me. I value that. I trusted Gavin. But he got himself killed because he stepped out of bounds. He had no business playing cop and trying to find the girl."

Lewis stood and stretched. "I'd better go see Mrs. Verheek. How much do I tell her?"

"Let's say it looks like a burglary, cops ain't sure down there, still investigating, we'll know more tomorrow, etc. Tell her I'm devastated, and we'll do whatever she wants."

COAL'S LIMO stopped abruptly at the curb so an ambulance could scream by. The limo was wandering aimlessly through the city, a ritual not unusual when Coal and Matthew Barr met to talk about really dirty business. They sat deep in the back of it, sipping drinks. Coal was indulging in a spring water. Barr had a sixteen-ounce Bud purchased from a convenience store.

They ignored the ambulance.

"I must know what Grantham knows," Coal was saying. "Today he called Zikman, Zikman's aide Trandell, Nelson DeVan, one of my many former assistants who's now with the Committee to Reelect. And these are just the ones I know of. All in one day. He's hot on this pelican brief."

"You think he's seen it?" The limo was moving again.

"No. Not at all. If he knew what was in it, he wouldn't be fishing for it. But dammit, he knows about it."

"He's good. I've watched him for years. He seems to move in the shadows and keeps in touch with an odd network of sources. He's written some crazy stuff, but it's usually accurate as hell."

"That's what worries me. He's tenacious, and he smells blood with this story."

Barr sipped from the can. "Of course, it would be asking too much if I wanted to know what was in the brief."

"Don't ask. It's so damned confidential it's frightening."

"Then how does Grantham know about it?"

"Perfect question. And that's what I want to know. How'd he find out, and how much does he know? Where are his sources?"

"We got his car phone, but we haven't been inside the apartment yet."

"Why not?"

"We almost got caught this morning by his cleaning lady. We'll try again tomorrow."

"Don't get caught, Barr. Remember Watergate."

"They were morons, Fletcher. We, on the other hand, are quite talented."

"That's right. So tell me, can you and your quite talented associates bug Grantham's phone at the *Post?*"

Barr turned and frowned at Coal. "Have you lost your mind? Impossible. That place is busy at all hours. They have security guards. The works."

"It could be done."

"Then do it, Coal. If you know so damned much, you do it."

"Start thinking about ways to do it, okay. Just give it some thought."

"Okay. I've thought about it. It's impossible."

Coal was amused by this thought, and his amusement irritated Barr. The limo eased into downtown.

"Tap his apartment," Coal instructed. "I want a report twice a day on all his calls." The limo stopped, and Barr climbed out.

TWENTY-SEVEN

BREAKFAST at Dupont Circle. It was quite chilly, but at least the addicts and transvestites were still unconscious somewhere in their sick little worlds. A few winos lay about like driftwood. But the sun was up and he felt safe, and anyway he was still an FBI agent with a shoulder harness and a piece under his arm. Who was he to fear? He hadn't used it in fifteen years, and he seldom left the office, but he'd love to yank it out and blast away.

His name was Trope, a very special assistant to Mr. Voyles. He was so special that no one except he and Mr. Voyles knew about these secret little chats with Booker from Langley. He sat on a circular bench with his back to New Hampshire, and unpacked a store-bought breakfast of banana and muffin. He checked his watch. Booker

352

was never late. Trope always arrived first, then Booker five minutes later, and they always talked quickly and Trope left first, then Booker. They were both office boys now, far into their twilights but very close to their bosses, who from time to time grew weary of trying to figure out what the hell the other was doing, or perhaps just needed to know something quick.

His real name was Trope, and he wondered if Booker was a real name. Probably not. Booker was from Langley, and they were so paranoid even the pencil pushers probably had fakes. He took an inch off the banana. Hell, the secretaries over there probably had three or four names.

Booker strolled near the fountain with a tall white cup of coffee. He glanced around, then sat down next to his friend. Voyles wanted this meeting, so Trope would speak first.

"We lost a man in New Orleans," he said.

Booker cuddled the hot cup and sipped. "He got himself killed."

"Yeah, but he's still dead. Were you there?"

"Yes, but we didn't know he was there. We were close, but watching others. What was he doing?"

Trope unwrapped the cold muffin. "We don't know. Went down for the funeral, tried to find the girl, found someone else, and here we are." He took a long bite and the banana was finished. Now to the muffin. "It was a clean job, wasn't it?"

Booker shrugged. What did the FBI know about killing people? "It was okay. Pretty weak effort at suicide, from what we hear." He sipped the hot coffee.

"Where's the girl?" Trope asked.

"We lost her at O'Hare. Maybe she's in Manhattan, but we're not certain. We're looking."

"And they're looking." Trope sipped cold coffee.

"I'm sure they are."

They watched a wino stagger from his bench and fall. His head hit first with a thud, but he probably felt nothing. He rolled over and his forehead was bleeding.

Booker checked his watch. These meetings were extremely brief. "What are Mr. Voyles' plans?"

"Oh, he's going in. He sent fifty troops last night, with more today. He doesn't like losing people, especially someone he knows."

"What about the White House?"

"Not going to tell them, and maybe they won't find out. What do they know?"

"They know Mattiece."

Trope managed a slight smile at this thought. "Where is Mr. Mattiece?"

"Who knows. In the past three years, he's been seen little in this country. He owns at least a half-dozen homes in as many countries, and he's got jets and boats, so who knows."

Trope finished the muffin and stuffed the wrapper in the sack. "The brief nailed him, didn't it?"

"It's beautiful. And if he'd played it cool, the brief would have been ignored. But he goes berserk, starts killing people, and the more he kills the more credibility the brief has."

Trope glanced at his watch. Too long already, but this was good stuff. "Voyles says we may need your help."

Booker nodded. "Done. But this will be a very difficult matter. First, the probable gunman is dead. Second, the probable bagman is very elusive. There was an elaborate conspiracy, but the conspirators are gone. We'll try to find Mattiece."

"And the girl?"

"Yes. We'll try."

"What's she thinking?"

"How to stay alive."

"Can't you bring her in?" Trope asked.

"No. We don't know where she is, and we can't just snatch innocent civilians off the streets. She doesn't trust anyone right now."

Trope stood with his coffee and sack. "I can't blame her." He was gone.

GRANTHAM HELD a cloudy fax photo sent to him from Phoenix. She was a junior at Arizona State, a very attractive twenty-year-old coed. She was listed as a biology major from Denver. He had called twenty Shaws in Denver before he stopped. The second fax was sent by an AP stringer in New Orleans. It was a copy of her freshman photo at Tulane. The hair was longer. Somewhere in the middle of the yearbook, the stringer had found a photo of Darby Shaw drinking a Diet Coke at a law school picnic. She wore a baggy sweater with faded jeans that fit just right, and it was obvious the photo was placed in the yearbook by a great admirer of Darby's. It looked like something out of *Vogue*. She was laughing at something or someone at the picnic. The teeth were perfect and the face was warm. He had tacked this one onto the small corkboard beside his news desk.

There was a fourth fax, a photo of Thomas Callahan, just for the record.

He placed his feet on the desk. It was almost nine-thirty, Tuesday. The newsroom hummed and rocked like a well-organized riot. He'd made eighty phone calls in the last twenty-four hours, and had nothing to show but the four photos and a stack of campaign finance forms. He was getting nowhere, and, really, why bother? She was about to tell all.

He skimmed the *Post,* and saw the strange story about one Gavin Verheek and his demise. The phone rang. It was Darby.

"Seen the *Post?*" she asked.

"I write the *Post,* remember."

She was not in the mood for small talk. "The story about the FBI lawyer murdered in New Orleans, have you seen it?"

"I'm just reading it. Does it mean something to you?"

"You could say that. Listen carefully, Grantham. Callahan gave the brief to Verheek, who was his best friend. Friday, Verheek came to New Orleans for the funeral. I talked to him by phone over the weekend. He wanted to help me, but I was scared. We agreed to meet yesterday at noon. Verheek was murdered in his room around eleven Sunday night. Got all that?"

"Yeah, I got it."

"Verheek didn't show for our meeting. He was, of course, dead by then. I got scared, and left the city. I'm in New York."

"Okay." Grantham wrote furiously. "Who killed Verheek?"

"I do not know. There's a lot more to the story. I've read the *Post* and the *New York Times* from front to back, and I've seen nothing about another killing in New Orleans. It happened to a man I was talking to and I thought was Verheek. It's a long story."

"Sounds like it. When do I get this long story?"

"When can you come to New York?"

"I can be there by noon."

"That's a little quick. Let's plan on tomorrow. I'll call you at this time tomorrow with instructions. You must be careful, Grantham."

He admired the jeans and the smile on the corkboard. "It's Gray, okay? Not Grantham."

"Whatever. There are some powerful people afraid of what I know. If I tell you, it could kill you. I've seen the bodies, okay, Gray? I've heard bombs and gunshots. I saw a man's brains yesterday, and I have no idea who he was or why he was killed, except that he knew about the pelican brief. I thought he was my friend. I trusted him with my life, and he was shot in the head in front of fifty people. As I watched him die, it occurred to me that perhaps he was not my friend. I read the paper this morning, and I realize he was definitely not my friend."

"Who killed him?"

"We'll talk about it when you get here."

"Okay, Darby."

"There's one small point to cover. I'll tell you everything I know, but you can never use my name. I've already written enough to get at least three people killed, and I'm quite confident I'll be next. But I don't want to ask for more trouble. I shall always be unidentified, okay, Gray?"

"It's a deal."

"I'm putting a lot of trust in you, and I'm not sure why. If I ever doubt you, I'll disappear."

"You have my word, Darby. I swear."

"I think you're making a mistake. This is

not your average investigative job. This one could get you killed."

"By the same people who killed Rosenberg and Jensen?"

"Yes."

"Do you know who killed Rosenberg and Jensen?"

"I know who paid for the killings. I know his name. I know his business. I know his politics."

"And you'll tell me tomorrow?"

"If I'm still alive." There was a long pause as both thought of something appropriate.

"Perhaps we should talk immediately," he said.

"Perhaps. But I'll call you in the morning."

Grantham hung up, and for a moment admired the slightly blurred photo of this very beautiful law student who was convinced she was about to die. For a second he succumbed to thoughts of chivalry and gallantry and rescue. She was in her early twenties, liked older men, according to the photo of Callahan, and suddenly she trusted him to the exclusion of all others. He would make it work. And he would protect her.

THE MOTORCADE moved quietly out of downtown. He was due for a speech at College Park in an hour, and he relaxed in his limo with his jacket off, reading the words Mabry had put together. He shook his head and wrote in the margins. On a normal day, this would be a pleasant drive out of the city to a beautiful campus for a light little speech, but it wasn't working out. Coal was seated next to him in the limo.

The Chief of Staff routinely avoided these trips. He treasured the moments the President was out of the White House and he had the run of the place. But they needed to talk.

"I'm tired of Mabry's speeches," the President said in frustration. "They're all sounding the same. I swear I gave this one last week at the Rotary convention."

"He's the best we've got, but I'm exploring," Coal said without looking up from his memo. He'd read the speech, and it wasn't that bad. But Mabry had been writing for six months, and the ideas were stale and Coal wanted to fire him anyway.

The President glanced at Coal's memo. "What's that?"

"The short list."

"Who's left?"

"Siler-Spence, Watson, and Calderon." Coal flipped a page.

"That's just great, Fletcher. A woman, a black, and a Cuban. Whatever happened to white men? I thought I said I wanted young white men. Young, tough, conservative judges with impeccable credentials and years to live. Didn't I say that?"

Coal kept reading. "They have to be confirmed, Chief."

"We'll get 'em confirmed. I'll twist arms until they break, but they'll be confirmed. Do you realize that nine of every ten white men in this country voted for me?"

"Eighty-four percent."

"Right. So what's wrong with white men?"

"This is not exactly patronage."

"The hell it's not. It's patronage pure and simple. I reward my friends, and I punish my enemies. That's how you survive in politics. You dance with the ones that brought you. I can't believe you want a female and a black. You're getting soft, Fletcher."

Coal flipped another page. He'd heard this before. "I'm more concerned with re-election," he said quietly.

"And I'm not? I've appointed so many Asians and Hispanics and women and blacks you'd think I was a Democrat. Hell, Fletcher, what's wrong with white people? Look, there must be a hundred good, qualified, conservative judges out there, right? Why can't you find just two, only two, who look and think like I do?"

"You got ninety percent of the Cuban vote."

The President tossed the speech in a seat and picked up the morning's *Post*. "Okay, let's go with Calderon. How old is he?"

"Fifty-one. Married, eight kids, Catholic, poor background, worked his way through Yale, very solid. Very conservative. No warts or skeletons, except he was treated for alcoholism twenty years ago. He's been sober since. A teetotaler."

"Has he ever smoked dope?"

"He denies it."

"I like him." The President was reading the front page.

"So do I. Justice and FBI have checked his underwear, and he's very clean. Now, do you want Siler-Spence or Watson?"

"What kind of name is Siler-Spence? I mean, what's wrong with these women who use hyphens? What if her name was

Skowinski, and she married a guy named Levondowski? Would her little liberated soul insist she go through life as F. Gwendolyn Skowinski-Levondowski? Give me a break. I'll never appoint a woman with a hyphen."

"You already have."

"Who?"

"Kay Jones-Roddy, ambassador to Brazil."

"Then call her home and fire her."

Coal managed a slight grin and placed the memo on the seat. He watched the traffic through his window. They would decide on number two later. Calderon was in the bag, and he wanted Linda Siler-Spence, so he would keep pushing the black and force the President to the woman. Basic manipulation.

"I think we should wait another two weeks before announcing them," he said.

"Whatever," the President mumbled as he read a story on page one. He would announce them when he got ready, regardless of Coal's timetable. He was not yet convinced they should be announced together.

"Judge Watson is a very conservative black judge with a reputation for toughness. He would be ideal."

"I don't know," the President mumbled as he read about Gavin Verheek.

Coal had seen the story on page two. Verheek was found dead in a room at the Hilton in New Orleans under strange circumstances. According to the story, official FBI was in the dark and had nothing to say about why Verheek was in New Orleans. Voyles was deeply saddened. Fine, loyal employee, etc.

The President flipped through the paper. "Our friend Grantham has been quiet."

"He's digging. I think he's heard of the brief, but just can't get a handle on it. He's called everyone in town, but doesn't know what to ask. He's chasing rabbits."

"Well, I played golf with Gminski yesterday," the President said smugly. "And he assures me everything's under control. We had a real heart-to-heart talk over eighteen holes. He's a horrible golfer, couldn't stay out of the sand and water. It was funny, really."

Coal had never touched a golf club, and hated the idle chatter about handicaps and such. "Do you think Voyles is investigating down there?"

"No. He gave me his word he would not.

Not that I trust him, but Gminski didn't mention Voyles."

"How much do you trust Gminski?" Coal asked with a quick glance and frown at the President.

"None. But if he knew something about the pelican brief, I think he would tell me. . . ." The President's words trailed off, and he knew he sounded naive.

Coal grunted his disbelief.

They crossed the Anacostia River and were in Prince Georges County. The President picked up the speech and looked out his window. Two weeks after the killings, and the ratings were still above fifty percent. The Democrats had no visible candidate out there making noise. He was strong and getting stronger. Americans were tired of dope and crime, and noisy minorities getting all the attention, and liberal idiots interpreting the Constitution in favor of criminals and radicals. This was his moment. Two nominations to the Supreme Court at the same time. It would be his legacy.

He smiled to himself. What a wonderful tragedy.

TWENTY-EIGHT

THE TAXI stopped abruptly at the corner of Fifth and Fifty-second, and Gray, doing exactly what he was told, paid quickly and jumped out with his bag. The car behind was honking and flipping birds, and he thought how nice it was to be back in New York City.

It was almost 5 P.M., and the pedestrians were thick on Fifth, and he figured that was precisely what she wanted. She had been specific. Take this flight from National to La Guardia. Take a cab to the Vista Hotel in the World Trade Center. Go to the bar, have a drink, maybe two, watch your rear, then after an hour catch a cab to the corner of Fifth and Fifty-second. Move quickly, wear sunglasses, and watch for everything because if he was being followed he could get them killed.

She made him write it all down. It was a bit silly, a bit of overkill, but she had a voice he couldn't argue with. Didn't want to, really. She was lucky to be alive, she said, and she would take no more chances. And if he wanted to talk to her, then he would do exactly as he was told.

He wrote it down. He fought the crowd and walked as fast as possible up Fifth to Fifty-ninth to the Plaza, up the steps and through its lobby, then out onto Central Park South. No one could follow him. And if she was this cautious, no one could follow her.

The sidewalk was packed along Central Park South, and as he neared Sixth Avenue he walked even faster. He was keyed up, and regardless of how restrained he tried to be, he was terribly excited about meeting her. On the phone she had been cool and methodical, but with a trace of fear and uncertainty. She was just a law student, she said, and she didn't know what she was doing, and she would probably be dead in a week if not sooner, but anyway this was the way the game would be played. Always assume you're being followed, she said. She had survived seven days of being chased by bloodhounds, so please do as she said.

She said to duck into the St. Moritz at the corner of Sixth, and he did. She had reserved a room for him under the name of Warren Clark. He paid cash for the room, and rode the elevator to the ninth floor. He was to wait. Just sit and wait, she'd said.

He stood in the window for an hour and watched Central Park grow dark. The phone rang.

"Mr. Clark?" a female asked.

"Uh, yes."

"It's me. Did you arrive alone?"

"Yes. Where are you?"

"Six floors up. Take the elevator to the eighteenth, then walk down to the fifteenth. Room 1520."

"Okay. Now?"

"Yes. I'm waiting."

He brushed his teeth again, checked his hair, and ten minutes later was standing before room 1520. He felt like a sophomore on his first date. He hadn't had butterflies this bad since high school football.

But he was Gray Grantham of the *Washington Post,* and this was just another story and she was just another woman, so grab the reins, buddy.

He knocked, and waited. "Who is it?"

"Grantham," he said to the door.

The bolt clicked, and she opened the door slowly. The hair was gone, but she smiled, and there was the cover girl. She shook his hand firmly. "Come in."

She closed and bolted the door behind him. "Would you care for a drink?" she asked.

"Sure, what do you have?"

"Water, with ice."

"Sounds great."

She walked into a small sitting room where the television was on with no sound. "In here," she said. He set his bag on the table, and took a seat on the sofa. She was standing at the bar, and for a quick second he admired the jeans. No shoes. Extra-large sweatshirt with the collar to one side where a bra strap peeked through.

She handed him the water, and sat in a chair by the door.

"Thanks," he said.

"Have you eaten?" she asked.

"You didn't tell me to."

She chuckled at this. "Forgive me. I've been through a lot. Let's order room service."

He nodded and smiled at her. "Sure. Anything you want is fine with me."

"I'd love a greasy cheeseburger with fries and a cold beer."

"Perfect."

She picked up the phone and ordered the food. Grantham walked to the window and watched the lights crawling along Fifth Avenue.

"I'm twenty-four. How old are you?" She was on the sofa now, sipping ice water.

He took the chair nearest to her. "Thirty-eight. Married once. Divorced seven years and three months ago. No children. Live alone with a cat. Why'd you pick the St. Moritz?"

"Rooms were available, and I convinced them it was important to pay with cash and present no identification. Do you like it?"

"It's fine. Sort of past its prime."

"This is not exactly a vacation."

"It's fine. How long do you think we might be here?"

She watched him carefully. He'd published a book six years earlier on HUD scandals, and though it didn't sell she'd found a copy in a public library in New Orleans. He looked six years older than the photo on the dust jacket, but he was aging nicely with a touch of gray over the ears.

"I don't know how long you'll stay," she

said. "My plans are subject to change by the minute. I may see a face on the street and fly to New Zealand."

"When did you leave New Orleans?"

"Monday night. I took a cab to Baton Rouge, and that would have been easy to follow. I flew to Chicago, where I bought four tickets to four different cities, including Boise, where my mother lives. I jumped on the plane to La Guardia at the last moment. I don't think anyone followed."

"You're safe."

"Maybe for the moment. We'll both be hunted when this story is published. Assuming it's published."

Gray rattled his ice and studied her. "Depends on what you tell me. And it depends on how much can be verified from other sources."

"The verification is up to you. I'll tell you what I know, and from there you're on your own."

"Okay. When do we start talking?"

"After dinner. I'd rather do it on a full stomach. You're in no hurry, are you?"

"Of course not. I've got all night, and all day tomorrow, and the next day and the next. I mean, you're talking about the biggest story in twenty years, so I'll hang around as long as you'll talk to me."

Darby smiled and looked away. Exactly a week ago, she and Thomas were waiting for dinner in the bar at Mouton's. He was wearing a black silk blazer, denim shirt, red paisley tie and heavily starched khakis. Shoes, but no socks. The shirt was unbuttoned and the tie was loose. They had talked about the Virgin Islands and Thanksgiving and Gavin Verheek while they waited on a table. He was drinking fast, and that was not unusual. He got drunk later, and it saved her life.

She had lived a year in the past seven days, and she was having a real conversation with a live person who did not wish her dead. She crossed her feet on the coffee table. It was not uncomfortable having him here in her room. She relaxed. His face said, "Trust me." And why not? Whom else could she trust?

"What are you thinking about?" he asked.

"It's been a long week. Seven days ago I was just another law student busting my tail to get to the top. Now look at me."

He was looking at her. Trying to be cool, not like a gawking sophomore, but he was

373

looking. The hair was dark and very short, and quite stylish, but he liked the long version in yesterday's fax.

"Tell me about Thomas Callahan," he said.

"Why?"

"I don't know. He's part of the story, isn't he?"

"Yeah. I'll get to it later."

"Fine. Your mother lives in Boise?"

"Yes, but she knows nothing. Where's your mother?"

"Short Hills, New Jersey," he answered with a smile. He crunched on an ice cube and waited for her. She was thinking.

"What do you like about New York?" she asked.

"The airport. It's the quickest way out."

"Thomas and I were here in the summer. It's hotter than New Orleans."

Suddenly, Grantham realized she was not just a hot little coed, but a widow in mourning. The poor lady was suffering. She had not been checking out his hair or his clothes or his eyes. She was in pain. Dammit!

"I'm very sorry about Thomas," he said. "I won't ask about him again."

She smiled but said nothing.

There was a loud knock. Darby jerked her feet off the table, and glared at the door. Then she breathed deeply. It was the food.

"I'll get it," Gray said. "Just relax."

TWENTY-NINE

FOR CENTURIES, a quiet but mammoth battle of nature raged without interference along the coastline of what would become Louisiana. It was a battle for territory. No humans were involved until recent years. From the south, the ocean pushed inland with its tides and winds and floods. From the north, the Mississippi River hauled down an inexhaustible supply of freshwater and sediment, and fed the marshes with the soil they needed to vegetate and thrive. The saltwater from the Gulf eroded the coastline and burned the freshwater marshes by killing the grasses that held them together. The river responded by draining half the continent and depositing its soil in lower Louisiana. It slowly built a long succession of sedimentary deltas, each of which in turn eventu-

376

ally blocked the river's path and forced it to change course yet again. The lush wetlands were built by the deltas.

It was an epic struggle of give-and-take, with the forces of nature firmly in control. With the constant replenishment from the mighty river, the deltas not only held their own against the Gulf, but expanded.

The marshlands were a marvel of natural evolution. Using the rich sediment as food, they grew into a green paradise of cypress and oak and dense patches of pickerelweed and bulrush and cattails. The water was filled with crawfish, shrimp, oysters, red snappers, flounder, pompano, bream, crabs, and alligators. The coastal plain was a sanctuary for wildlife. Hundreds of species of migratory birds came to roost.

The wetlands were vast and limitless, rich and abundant.

Then oil was discovered there in 1930, and the rape was on. The oil companies dredged ten thousand miles of canals to get to the riches. They crisscrossed the fragile delta with a slashing array of neat little ditches. They sliced the marshes to ribbons.

They drilled, found oil, then dredged like maniacs to get to it. Their canals were perfect conduits for the Gulf and its saltwater, which ate away at the marshes.

Since oil was found, tens of thousands of acres of wetlands have been devoured by the ocean. Sixty square miles of Louisiana vanishes every year. Every fourteen minutes, another acre disappears under water.

IN 1979, AN OIL COMPANY punched a hole deep in Terrebonne Parish and hit oil. It was a routine day on just another rig, but it was not a routine hit. There was a lot of oil. They drilled again an eighth of a mile away, and hit another big one. They backed off a mile, drilled, and hit an even bigger one. Three miles away, they struck gold again.

The oil company capped the wells and pondered the situation, which had all the markings of a major new field.

The oil company was owned by Victor Mattiece, a Cajun from Lafayette who'd made and lost several fortunes drilling for oil in south Louisiana. In 1979, he happened to be wealthy, and more importantly, he had access to other people's money. He was quickly convinced he had just tapped a major reserve. He began buying land around the capped wells.

Secrets are crucial but hard to keep in the oilfields. And Mattiece knew if he threw around too much money, there would soon be a mad rush of drilling around his new gold mine. A man of infinite patience and planning, he looked at the big picture and said no to the quick buck. He decided he would have it all. He huddled with his lawyers and other advisers, and devised a plan to methodically buy the surrounding land under a myriad of corporate names. They formed new companies, used some of his old ones, purchased all or portions of struggling firms, and went about the business of acquiring acreage.

Those in the business knew Mattiece, and knew he had money and could get more. Mattiece knew they knew, so he quietly unleashed two dozen faceless entities upon the landowners of Terrebonne Parish. It worked without a major hitch.

The plan was to consolidate territory, then dredge yet another channel through the hapless and beleaguered marshlands so that the men and their equipment could get to the rigs and the oil could be brought out with haste. The canal would be thirty-five miles long and twice as wide as the others. There would be a lot of traffic.

Because Mattiece had money, he was a popular man with the politicians and bureaucrats. He played their game skillfully. He sprinkled money around where needed. He loved politics, but hated publicity. He was paranoid and reclusive.

As the land acquisition sailed smoothly along, Mattiece suddenly found himself short of cash. The industry turned downward in the early eighties, and his other rigs stopped pumping. He needed big money, and he wanted partners adept at putting it up and remaining silent about it. So he stayed away from Texas. He went overseas and found some Arabs who studied his maps and believed his estimate of a mammoth reserve of crude and natural gas. They bought a piece of the action, and Mattiece had plenty of cash again.

He did the sprinkling act, and obtained official permission to gouge his way through the delicate marshes and cypress swamps. The pieces were falling majestically into place, and Victor Mattiece could smell a billion dollars. Maybe two or three.

Then an odd thing happened. A lawsuit was filed to stop the dredging and drilling. The plaintiff was an obscure environmental outfit known simply as Green Fund.

The lawsuit was unexpected because for fifty years Louisiana had allowed itself to be devoured and polluted by oil companies and people like Victor Mattiece. It had been a trade-off. The oil business employed many and paid well. The oil and gas taxes collected in Baton Rouge paid the salaries of state employees. The small bayou villages had been turned into boomtowns. The politicians from the governors down took the oil money and played along. All was well, and so what if some of the marshlands suffered.

Green Fund filed the lawsuit in the U.S. District Court in Lafayette. A federal judge halted the project pending a trial on all issues.

Mattiece went over the edge. He spent weeks with his lawyers plotting and scheming. He would spare no expense to win. Do whatever it took, he instructed them. Break any rule, violate any ethic, hire any expert, commission any study, cut any throat, spend any amount of money. Just win the damned lawsuit.

Never one to be seen, he assumed an even lower profile. He moved to the Bahamas and operated from an armed fortress at Lyford Cay. He flew to New Orleans once a week to meet with the lawyers, then returned to the island.

Though invisible now, he made certain his political contributions increased. His jackpot was still safe beneath Terrebonne Parish, and he would one day extract it, but one never knows when one will be forced to call in favors.

BY THE TIME the Green Fund lawyers, both of them, had waded in ankle deep, they had identified over thirty separate defendants. Some owned land. Some did exploring. Others laid pipe. Others drilled. The joint ventures and limited partnerships and corporate associations were an impenetrable maze.

The defendants and their legions of high-priced lawyers answered with a vengeance. They filed a thick motion asking the judge to dismiss the lawsuit as frivolous. Denied. They asked him to allow the drilling to continue while they waited on a trial. Denied. They squealed with pain and explained in another heavy motion how much money was already tied up in exploration, drilling, etc. Denied again. They filed motions by the truckload, and when they were all denied and it was evident there would one day be a trial by jury, the oil lawyers dug in and played dirty.

Luckily for Green Fund's lawsuit, the heart of the new oil reserve was near a ring of marshes that had been for years a natural refuge for waterfowl. Ospreys, egrets, pelicans, ducks, cranes, geese, and many others migrated to it. Though Louisiana has not always been kind to its land, it has shown a bit more sympathy for its animals. Since the verdict would one day be rendered by a jury of average and hopefully ordinary people, the Green Fund lawyers played heavy on the birds.

The pelican became the hero. After thirty years of insidious contamination by DDT and other pesticides, the Louisiana brown pelican perched on the brink of extinction. Almost too late, it was classified as an endangered species, and afforded a higher class of protection. Green Fund seized the majestic bird, and enlisted a half-dozen experts from around the country to testify on its behalf.

With a hundred lawyers involved, the lawsuit moved slowly. At times it went nowhere, which suited Green Fund just fine. The rigs were idle.

Seven years after Mattiece first buzzed

over Terrebonne Bay in his jet helicopter and followed the swamplands along the route his precious canal would take, the pelican suit went to trial in Lake Charles. It was a bitter trial that lasted ten weeks. Green Fund sought money damages for the havoc already inflicted, and it wanted a permanent injunction against further drilling.

The oil companies brought in a fancy litigator from Houston to talk to the jury. He wore elephant-skin boots and a Stetson, and could talk like a Cajun when necessary. He was stout medicine, especially when compared to the Green Fund lawyers, both of whom had beards and very intense faces.

Green Fund lost the trial, and it was not altogether unexpected. The oil companies spent millions, and it's difficult to whip a bear with a switch. David pulled it off, but the best bet is always on Goliath. The jurors were not impressed with the dire warnings about pollution and the frailness of wetland ecology. Oil meant money, and folks needed jobs.

The judge kept the injunction in place for two reasons. First, he thought Green Fund had proven its point about the pelican, a federally protected species. And it was apparent to all that Green Fund would appeal, so the matter was far from over.

The dust settled for a while, and Mattiece had a small victory. But he knew there would be other days in other courtrooms. He was a man of infinite patience and planning.

THIRTY

THE TAPE RECORDER was in the center of the small table with four empty beer bottles around.

He made notes as he talked. "Who told you about the lawsuit?"

"A guy named John Del Greco. He's a law student at Tulane, a year ahead of me. He clerked last summer for a big firm in Houston, and the firm was on the periphery of the hostilities. He was not close to the trial, but the rumors and gossip were heavy."

"And all the firms were from New Orleans and Houston?"

"Yes, the principal litigation firms. But these companies are from a dozen different cities, so of course they brought their local counsel with them. There were lawyers from Dallas, Chicago, and several other cities. It was a circus."

"What's the status of the lawsuit?"

"From the trial level, it will be appealed to the Fifth Circuit Court of Appeals. That appeal has not been perfected, but should be in a month or so."

"Where's the Fifth Circuit?"

"New Orleans. About twenty-four months after it arrives there, a three-judge panel will hear and decide. The losing party will undoubtedly request a rehearing by the full panel, and this will take another three or four months. There are enough defects in the verdict to insure either a reversal or a remand."

"What's a remand?"

"The appellate court can do any of three things. Affirm the verdict, reverse the verdict, or find enough error to send the whole thing back for a new trial. If it goes back, it's been remanded. They can also affirm part, reverse part, remand part, sort of scramble things up."

Gray shook his head in frustration as he scribbled away. "Why would anyone want to be a lawyer?"

"I've asked myself that a few times in the past week."

"Any idea what the Fifth Circuit might do?"

"None. They haven't even seen it yet. The plaintiffs are alleging a multitude of procedural sins by the defendants, and given the nature of the conspiracy, a lot of it's probably true. It could be reversed."

"Then what happens?"

"The fun starts. If either side is unhappy with the Fifth Circuit, they can appeal to the Supreme Court."

"Surprise, surprise."

"Each year the Supreme Court receives thousands of appeals, but is very selective about what it takes. Because of the money and pressure and issues involved, this one has a decent chance of being heard."

"From today, how long would it take for the case to be decided by the Supreme Court?"

"Anywhere from three to five years."

"Rosenberg would have died from natural causes."

"Yes, but there could be a Democrat in the White House when he died from natural causes. So take him out now when you can sort of predict his replacement."

"Makes sense."

"Oh, it's beautiful. If you're Victor Mattiece, and you've only got fifty million or so, and you want to be a billionaire, and you don't mind killing a couple of Supremes, then now is the time."

"But what if the Supreme Court refused to hear the case?"

"He's in good shape if the Fifth Circuit affirms the trial verdict. But if it reverses, and the Supreme Court denies cert, he's got problems. My guess is that he would go back to square one, stir up some new litigation, and try it all again. There's too much money involved to lick his wounds and go home. When he took care of Rosenberg and Jensen, one has to assume he committed himself to a cause."

"Where was he during the trial?"

"Completely invisible. Keep in mind, it is not public knowledge that he's the ringleader of the litigation. By the time the trial started, there were thirty-eight corporate defendants. No individuals were named, just corporations. Of the thirty-eight, seven are traded publicly, and he owns no more than twenty percent of any one. These are just small firms traded over the counter. The other thirty-one are privately held, and I couldn't get much information. But I did learn that many of these private companies are owned by each other, and some are even owned by the public corporations. It's almost impenetrable."

"But he's in control."

"Yes. I suspect he owns or controls eighty percent of the project. I checked out four of the private companies, and three are chartered offshore. Two in the Bahamas, and one in the Caymans. Del Greco heard that Mattiece operates from behind offshore banks and companies."

"Do you remember the seven public companies?"

"Most of them. They, of course, were footnoted in the brief, a copy of which I do not have. But I've rewritten most of it in longhand."

"Can I see it?"

"You can have it. But it's lethal."

"I'll read it later. Tell me about the photograph."

"Mattiece is from a small town near Lafayette, and in his younger years was a big money man for politicians in south Louisiana. He was a shadowy type back then, always in the background giving money. He spent big bucks on Democrats locally and Republicans nationally, and over the years he was wined and dined by big shots from

Washington. He has never sought publicity, but his kind of money is hard to hide, especially when it's being handed out to politicians. Seven years ago, when the President was the Vice President, he was in New Orleans for a Republican fundraiser. All the heavy hitters were there, including Mattiece. It was ten thousand dollars a plate, so the press tried to get in. Somehow a photographer snapped a picture of Mattiece shaking hands with the VP. The New Orleans paper ran it the next day. It's a wonderful picture. They're grinning at each other like best friends."

"It'll be easy to get."

"I stuck it on the last page of the brief, just for the fun of it. This is fun, isn't it?"

"I'm having a ball."

"Mattiece dropped out of sight a few years ago, and is now believed to live in several places. He's very eccentric. Del Greco said most people believe he's demented."

The recorder beeped, and Gray changed tapes. Darby stood and stretched her long legs. He watched her as he fumbled with the recorder. Two other tapes were already used and marked.

"Are you tired?" he asked.

"I haven't been sleeping well. How many more questions?"

"How much more do you know?"

"We've covered the basics. There are some gaps we can fill in the morning."

Gray turned off the recorder and stood. She was at the window, stretching and yawning. He relaxed on the sofa.

"What happened to the hair?" he asked.

Darby sat in a chair and pulled her feet under her. Red toenails. Her chin rested on her knees. "I left it in a hotel in New Orleans. How did you know about it?"

"I saw a photograph."

"From where?"

"Three photos, actually. Two from the Tulane yearbook, and one from Arizona State."

"Who sent them to you?"

"I have contacts. They were faxed to me, so they weren't that good. But there was this gorgeous hair."

"I wish you hadn't done that."

"Why?"

"Every phone call leaves a trail."

"Come on, Darby. Give me a little credit."

"You were snooping around on me."

"Just a little background. That's all."

"No more, okay? If you want something from me, just ask. If I say no, then leave it alone."

Grantham shrugged and agreed. Forget the hair. On to less sensitive matters. "So who selected Rosenberg and Jensen? Mattiece is not a lawyer."

"Rosenberg is easy. Jensen wrote little on environmental issues, but he was consistent in voting against all types of development. If they shared common ground with any consistency, it was protecting the environment."

"And you think Mattiece figured this out by himself?"

"Of course not. A pretty wicked legal mind presented him with the two names. He has a thousand lawyers."

"And none in D.C.?"

Darby raised her chin and frowned at him. "What did you say?"

"None of his lawyers are in D.C."

"I didn't say that."

"I thought you said the law firms were primarily from New Orleans and Houston and other cities. You didn't mention D.C."

Darby shook her head. "You're assuming too much. I can think of at least two D.C. firms that I ran across. One is White and

Blazevich, a very old, powerful, rich Republican firm with four hundred lawyers."

Gray moved to the edge of the sofa.

"What's the matter?" she asked. He was suddenly wired. He was on his feet walking to the door, then back to the sofa.

"This may fit. This may be it, Darby."

"I'm listening."

"Are you listening?"

"I swear I'm listening."

He was at the window. "Okay, last week I got three phone calls from a lawyer in D.C. named Garcia, but that's not his name. He said he knew something and saw something about Rosenberg and Jensen, and he wanted so badly to tell me what he knew. But he got scared and disappeared."

"There are a million lawyers in D.C."

"Two million. But I know he works in a private firm. He sort of admitted it. He was sincere and very frightened, thought they were following. I asked who they were, and he of course wouldn't say."

"What happened to him?"

"We had a meeting planned for last Saturday morning, and he called early and said forget it. Said he was married and had a good job, and why risk it. He never admitted it, but I think he has a copy of something that he was about to show me."

"He could be your verification."

"What if he works for White and Blazevich? We've suddenly narrowed it to four hundred lawyers."

"The haystack is much smaller."

Grantham darted to his bag, flipped through some papers, and presto! pulled out a five-by-seven black and white. He dropped it in her lap. "This is Mr. Garcia."

Darby studied the picture. It was a man on a busy sidewalk. The face was clear. "I take it he didn't pose for this."

"Not exactly." Grantham was pacing.

"Then how'd you get it?"

"I cannot reveal my sources."

She slid it onto the coffee table, and rubbed her eyes. "You're scaring me, Grantham. This has a sleazy feel to it. Tell me it's not sleazy."

"It's just a little sleazy, okay. The kid was using the same pay phone, and that's a mistake."

"Yes, I know. That's a mistake."

"And I wanted to know what he looked like."

"Did you ask if you could take his photograph?"

"No."

"Then it's sleazy as hell."

"Okay. It's sleazy as hell. But I did it, and there it is, and it could be our link to Mattiece."

"Our link?"

"Yes, our link. I thought you wanted to nail Mattiece."

"Did I say that? I want him to pay, but I'd rather leave him alone. He's made a believer out of me, Gray. I've seen enough blood to last me a long time. You take this ball and run with it."

He didn't hear this. He walked behind her to the window, then back to the bar. "You mentioned two firms. What's the other?"

"Brim, Stearns, and somebody. I didn't get a chance to check them out. It's sort of odd because neither firm is listed as counsel of record for any of the defendants, but both firms, especially White and Blazevich, kept popping up as I went through the file."

"How big is Brim, Stearns, and somebody?"

"I can find out tomorrow."

"As big as White and Blazevich?"

"I doubt it."

"Just guess. How big?"

"Two hundred lawyers."

"Okay. Now we're up to six hundred lawyers in two firms. You're the lawyer, Darby. How can we find Garcia?"

"I'm not a lawyer, and I'm not a private detective. You're the investigative reporter." She didn't like this "we" business.

"Yeah, but I've never been in a law office, except for the divorce."

"Then you're very fortunate."

"How can we find him?"

She was yawning again. They had been talking for almost three hours, and she was exhausted. This could resume in the morning. "I don't know how to find him, and I really haven't given it much thought. I'll sleep on it, and explain it to you in the morning."

Grantham was suddenly calm. She stood and walked to the bar for a glass of water.

"I'll get my things," he said, picking up the tapes.

"Would you do me a favor?" she asked.

"Maybe."

She paused and looked at the sofa. "Would you mind sleeping on the sofa tonight? I mean, I haven't slept well in a long time, and I need the rest. It would, well, it would be nice if I knew you were in here."

He swallowed hard, and looked at the sofa. They both looked at the sofa. It was a five-footer at most, and did not appear to be the least bit comfortable.

"Sure," he said, smiling at her. "I understand."

"I'm spooked, okay?"

"I understand."

"It's nice to have someone like you around." She smiled demurely, and Gray melted.

"I don't mind," he said. "No problem."

"Thanks."

"Lock the door, get in the bed, and sleep well. I'll be right here, and everything's all right."

"Thanks." She nodded and smiled again, then closed the door to her bedroom. He listened, and she did not lock it.

He sat on the sofa in the darkness, watching her door. Some time after midnight, he dozed and slept with his knees not far from his chin.

THIRTY-ONE

HER BOSS was Jackson Feldman, and he was the executive editor, and this was her turf, and she didn't take any crap off anyone but Mr. Feldman. Especially an insolent brat like Gray Grantham, who was standing in front of Mr. Feldman's door, guarding it like a Doberman. She glared at him, and he sneered at her, and this had been going on for ten minutes, ever since they huddled in there and closed the door. Why Grantham was waiting outside, she did not know. But this was her turf.

Her phone rang, and Grantham yelled at her. "No calls!"

Her face was instantly red, and her mouth flew open. She picked up the receiver, listened for a second, then said, "I'm sorry, but Mr. Feldman is in a meeting." She glared at Grantham, who was shaking his head as if to dare her. "Yes, I'll have him call you back as soon as possible." She hung up.

"Thanks!" Grantham said, and this threw her off guard. She was about to say something nasty, but with the "Thanks" her mind went blank. He smiled at her. And it made her even madder.

It was five-thirty, time for her to leave, but Mr. Feldman asked her to stay. He was still smirking at her over there by the door, not ten feet away. She had never liked Gray Grantham. But then, there weren't too many people at the *Post* she did like. A news aide approached and appeared headed for the door when the Doberman stepped in front of him. "Sorry, you can't go in right now," Grantham said.

"And why not?"

"They're in a meeting. Leave it with her." He pointed at the secretary, who despised being pointed at and despised being referred to simply as "her." She had been here for twenty-one years.

The news aide was not easily intimidated. "That's fine. But Mr. Feldman instructed me to have these papers here at precisely five-thirty. It's precisely five-thirty, here I am, and here are the papers."

"Look, we're real proud of you. But you can't go in, understand? Now just leave the papers with that nice lady over there, and the sun will come up tomorrow." Grantham moved squarely in front of the door, and appeared ready for combat if the kid insisted.

"I'll take those," the secretary said. She took them, and the news aide left.

"Thanks!" Grantham said loudly again.

"I find you to be very rude," she snapped.

"I said 'Thanks.'" He tried to look hurt.

"You're a real smartass."

"Thanks!"

The door suddenly opened, and a voice called out, "Grantham."

He smiled at her, and stepped inside. Jackson Feldman was standing behind his desk. The tie was down to the second button and the sleeves were rolled to the elbows. He was six-six, with no fat. At fifty-eight, he ran two marathons a year and worked fifteen hours a day.

Smith Keen was also standing, and holding the four-page outline of a story along with a copy of Darby's handwritten reproduction of the pelican brief. Feldman's copy was lying on the desk. They appeared dazed.

"Close the door," Feldman said to Grantham.

Gray closed the door and sat on the edge of a table. No one spoke.

Feldman rubbed his eyes roughly, then looked at Keen. "Wow," he finally said.

Gray smiled. "You mean that's it. I hand you the biggest story in twenty years, and you are so moved you say 'Wow.' "

"Where's Darby Shaw?" Keen asked.

"I can't tell you. It's part of the deal."

"What deal?" Keen asked.

"I can't tell you that either."

"When did you talk to her?"

"Last night, and again this morning."

"And this was in New York?" Keen asked.

"What difference does it make where we talked? We talked, okay. She talked. I listened. I flew home. I wrote the outline. So what do you think?"

Feldman slowly folded his thin frame and sat deep in his chair. "How much does the White House know?"

"Not sure. Verheek told Darby that it was delivered to the White House one day last week, and at the time the FBI thought it should be pursued. Then for some reason, after the White House had it, the FBI backed off. That's all I know."

"How much did Mattiece give the President three years ago?"

"Millions. Virtually all of it through a myriad of PACs that he controls. This guy is very smart. He's got all kinds of lawyers, and they figure out ways to funnel money here and there. It's probably legal."

The editors were thinking slowly. They were stunned, as if they'd just survived a bomb blast. Grantham was quite proud, and swung his feet under the table like a kid on a pier.

Feldman slowly picked up the papers clipped together and flipped through until he found the photograph of Mattiece and the President. He shook his head.

"It's dynamite, Gray," Keen said. "We just can't run without a bunch of corroboration. Hell, you're talking about the world's greatest job of verifying. This is powerful stuff, son."

"How can you do it?" Feldman asked.

"I've got some ideas."

"I'd like to hear them. You could get yourself killed with this."

Grantham jumped to his feet, and stuck

his hands in his pockets. "First, we'll try to find Garcia."

"We? Who's we?" Keen asked.

"Me, okay. Me. I'll try to find Garcia."

"Is the girl in on this?" Keen asked.

"I can't answer that. It's part of the deal."

"Answer the question," Feldman said. "Look at where we are if she gets killed helping you with the story. It's much too risky. Now where is she and what have you guys got planned?"

"I'm not telling where she is. She's a source, and I always protect my sources. No, she's not helping with the investigation. She's just a source, okay?"

They stared at him in disbelief. They looked at each other, and finally Keen shrugged.

"Do you want some help?" Feldman asked.

"No. She insists on me doing it alone. She's very scared, and you can't blame her."

"I got scared just reading the damned thing," Keen said.

Feldman kicked back in his chair and crossed his feet on the desk. Size fourteens. He smiled for the first time. "You've got to start with Garcia. If he can't be found, then you could dig for months on Mattiece and not put it together. And before you start digging on Mattiece, let's have a long talk. I sort of like you, Grantham, and this is not worth getting killed over."

"I see every word you write, okay?" Keen said.

"And I want a daily report, okay?" Feldman said.

"No problem."

Keen walked to the glass wall and watched the madness in the newsroom. In the course of each day, the chaos came and went a half a dozen times. Things got crazy at five-thirty. The news was being written, and the second story conference was at six-thirty.

Feldman watched from his desk. "This could be the end of the slump," he said to Gray without looking at him. "What's it been, five, six years?"

"Try seven," Keen said.

"I've written some good stories," Gray said defensively.

"Sure," Feldman said, still watching the newsroom. "But you've been hitting doubles and triples. The last grand slam was a long time ago."

"There have been a lot of strikeouts too," Keen added helpfully.

"Happens to all of us," Gray said. "But this grand slam will be in the seventh game of the World Series." He opened the door.

Feldman glared at him. "Don't get hurt, and don't allow her to get hurt. Understand?"

Gray smiled and left the office.

HE WAS ALMOST to Thomas Circle when he saw the blue lights behind him. The cop did not pass, but stayed on his bumper. He was oblivious to both the speed limit and his speedometer. It would be his third ticket in sixteen months.

He parked in a small lot next to an apartment house. It was dark, and the blue lights flashed in his mirrors. He rubbed his temples.

"Step out," the cop demanded from the bumper.

Gray opened the door and did what he was told. The cop was black, and was suddenly smiling. It was Cleve. He pointed to the patrol car. "Get in."

They sat in the car under the blue lights and stared at the Volvo. "Why do you do this to me?" Gray asked.

"We have quotas, Grantham. We have to stop so many white people and harass them. Chief wants to even things out. The white cops pick on innocent poor black folks, so us black cops have to pick on innocent rich white folks."

"I suppose you're gonna handcuff me and beat the hell out of me."

"Only if you ask me to. Sarge can't talk anymore."

"I'm listening."

"He smells something around the place. He's caught a few strange looks, and he's heard a thing or two."

"Such as?"

"Such as they're talking about you, and how much they need to know what you know. He thinks they might be listening."

"Come on, Cleve. Is he serious?"

"He's heard them talk about you and how you're asking questions about the pelican something or other. You've got 'em shook up."

"What has he heard about this pelican thing?"

"Just that you're hot on it, and they're serious about it. These are mean and paranoid people, Gray. Sarge says to be careful where you go and who you talk to."

"And we can't meet anymore?"

"Not for a while. He wants to lay low, and run things through me."

"We'll do that. I need his help, but tell him to be careful. This is very touchy."

"What is this pelican business?"

"I can't say. But tell Sarge it could get him killed."

"Not Sarge. He's smarter than all of them over there."

Gray opened the door and got out. "Thanks, Cleve."

He turned off the blue lights. "I'll be around. I'm working nights for the next six months, so I'll try and keep an eye on you."

"Thanks."

RUPERT PAID for his cinnamon roll and sat on a bar stool overlooking the sidewalk. It was midnight, exactly midnight, and Georgetown was winding down. A few cars sped along M Street, and the remaining pedestrians headed for home. The coffee shop was busy, but not crowded. He sipped black coffee.

He recognized the face on the sidewalk, and moments later the man was sitting on the next bar stool. He was a flunkie of some sort. They had met a few days ago in New Orleans.

"So what's the score?" Rupert asked.

"We can't find her. And that worries us because we got some bad news today."

"And?"

"Well, we heard voices, unconfirmed, that the bad guys have freaked out, and that the number one bad guy wants to start killing everybody. Money is no object, and these voices tell us he'll spend whatever it takes to snuff this thing out. He's sending in big boys with big guns. Of course, they say he's deranged, but he's mean as hell and money can kill a lot of people."

This killing talk did not faze Rupert. "Who's on the list?"

"The girl. And I guess anyone else on the outside who happens to know about that little paper."

"So what's my plan?"

"Hang around. We'll meet here tomorrow night, same time. If we find the girl, it'll be your show."

"How do you plan to find her?"

"We think she's in New York. We have ways."

Rupert pulled off a piece of cinnamon

roll and stuffed it in his mouth. "Where would you be?"

The messenger thought of a dozen places he might go, but, dammit, they were like Paris and Rome and Monte Carlo, places he'd seen and places everyone went to. He couldn't think of that one exotic spot where he would go and hide for the rest of his life. "I don't know. Where would you be?"

"New York City. You can live there for years and never be seen. You speak the language and know the rules. It's the perfect hiding place for an American."

"Yeah, I guess you're right. You think she's there?"

"I don't know. At times she's clever. Then she has bad moments."

The messenger was on his feet. "Tomorrow night," he said.

Rupert waved him off. What a goofy little twerp, he thought. Running around whispering important messages in coffee shops and beer joints. Then running back to his boss and reliving it all in vivid detail.

He threw the coffee cup in the trash and was on the sidewalk.

THIRTY ~ TWO

BRIM, STEARNS, AND KIDLOW had a hundred and ninety lawyers, according to the latest edition of the Martindale-Hubbell Legal Directory. And White and Blazevich had four hundred and twelve, so hopefully Garcia was only one of a possible six hundred and two. But if Mattiece used other D.C. firms, the number would be higher and they didn't have a chance.

As expected, White and Blazevich had no one named Garcia. Darby searched for another Hispanic name, but found none. It was one of those lily-white silk-stocking outfits filled with Ivy Leaguers with long names that ended in numerals. There were a few female names sprinkled about, but only two were partners. Most of the women had joined after 1980. If she lived long enough to finish law school, she would not consider working for a factory like White and Blazevich.

Grantham had suggested she check for Hispanics because Garcia was a bit unusual for an alias. Maybe the guy was Hispanic, and since Garcia is common for them, then maybe he just said it real quick. It didn't work. There were no Hispanics in this firm.

According to the directory, their clients were big and rich. Banks, Fortune 500s, and lots of oil companies. They listed four of the defendants in the lawsuit as clients, but not Mr. Mattiece. There were chemical companies and shipping lines, and White and Blazevich also represented the governments of South Korea, Libya, and Syria. Silly, she thought. Some of our enemies hire our lawyers to lobby our government. But then, you can hire lawyers to do anything.

Brim, Stearns, and Kidlow was a smaller version of White and Blazevich, but, gosh, there were four Hispanic names listed. She wrote them down. Two men and two women. She figured this firm must have been sued for race and sex discrimination. In the past ten years they had hired all kinds of people. The client list was predictable: oil and gas, insurance, banks, government relations. Pretty dull stuff.

She sat in a corner of the Fordham law library for an hour. It was Friday morning, ten in New York and nine in New Orleans, and instead of hiding in a library she'd never seen before, she was supposed to be sitting in Federal Procedure under Alleck, a professor she never liked but now missed sorely. Alice Stark would be sitting next to her. One of her favorite law nerds, D. Ronald Petrie, would be sitting behind her asking for a date and making lewd comments. She missed him too. She missed the quiet mornings on Thomas' balcony, sipping coffee and waiting for the French Quarter to shake its cobwebs and come to life. She missed the smell of cologne on his bathrobe.

She thanked the librarian, and left the building. On Sixty-second, she headed east toward the park. It was a brilliant October morning with a perfect sky and cool wind. A pleasant change from New Orleans, but difficult to appreciate under the circumstances. She wore new Ray-Bans and a muffler up to her chin. The hair was still dark, but she would cut no more. She was determined to walk without looking over her shoulder. They probably weren't back there, but she knew it would be years before she could stroll along a street without a doubt.

The trees in the park were a magnificent display of yellow and orange and red. The leaves fell gently in the breeze. She turned south on Central Park West. She would leave tomorrow, and spend a few days in Washington. If she survived, she would then leave the country, go maybe to the Caribbean. She'd been there twice, and there were a thousand little islands where most people spoke some form of English.

Now was the time to leave the country. They'd lost her trail, and she'd already checked on flights to Nassau and Jamaica. She could be there by dark.

She found a pay phone in the rear of a bagel shop on Sixth, and punched Gray's number at the *Post*. "It's me," she said.

"Well, well. I was afraid you had skipped the country."

"Thinking about it."

"Can you wait a week?"

"Probably. I'll be there tomorrow. What do you know?"

"I'm just gathering junk. I've got copies

414

of the annual statements for the seven public corporations involved in the suit."

"It's lawsuit, not suit. A suit is something you wear."

"How can you ever forgive me? Mattiece is neither an officer nor director of any."

"What else?"

"Just the thousand phone calls routine. I spent three hours yesterday hanging around courthouses looking for Garcia."

"You won't find him at a courthouse, Gray. He's not that kind of lawyer. He's in a corporate firm."

"I take it you have a better idea."

"I've got several ideas."

"Well, then, I'm just sitting here waiting on you."

"I'll call you when I get there."

"Don't call me at home."

She paused for a second. "May I ask why not?"

"There's a chance someone is listening, and maybe following. One of my best sources thinks I've ruffled enough feathers to get myself placed under surveillance."

"Fabulous. And you want me to rush down there and team up with you?"

"We'll be safe, Darby. We just have to be careful."

She gripped the phone and clenched her teeth. "How dare you talk to me about being careful! I've been dodging bombs and bullets for ten days now, and you're smug enough to tell me to be careful. Kiss my ass, Grantham! Maybe I should stay away from you."

There was a pause as she looked around the tiny café. Two men at the nearest table looked at her. She was much too loud. She turned away and breathed deeply.

Grantham spoke slowly. "I'm sorry. I—"

"Forget it. Just forget it."

He waited a moment. "Are you okay?"

"I'm terrific. Never felt better."

"Are you coming to D.C.?"

"I don't know. I'm safe here, and I'll be much safer when I get on a plane and leave the country."

"Sure, but I thought you had this wonderful idea about finding Garcia, then hopefully nailing Mattiece. I thought you were outraged and morally indignant and motivated by revenge. What's happened to you?"

"Well, for one, I have this burning desire to see my twenty-fifth birthday. I'm not selfish, but perhaps I'd like to see my thirtieth too. That would be nice."

"I understand."

"I'm not sure you understand. I think you're more concerned with Pulitzers and glory than my pretty little neck."

"I assure you that's not true. Trust me, Darby. You'll be safe. You've told me the story of your life. You must trust me."

"I'll think about it."

"That's not definite."

"No, it's not. Give me some time."

"Okay."

She hung up, and ordered a bagel. A dozen languages rattled around her as the café was suddenly packed. Run, baby, run, her good sense told her. Take a cab to the airport. Pay cash for a ticket to Miami. Find the nearest flight south, and get on the plane. Let Grantham dig and wish him the best. He was very good, and he'd find a way to break the story. And she would read about it one day while lying on a sun-drenched beach sipping a piña colada and watching the windsurfers.

Stump limped by on the sidewalk. She caught a glimpse of him through the crowd and through the window. Her mouth was suddenly dry and she was dizzy. He didn't look inside. He just ambled by, looking rather lost. She ran through the tables and watched him through the door. He limped slightly to the corner of Sixth and Fifty-eighth and waited for the light. He started to cross Sixth, then changed his mind and crossed Fifty-eighth. A taxi almost smeared him.

He was going nowhere, just strolling along with a slight limp.

CROFT SAW THE KID as he stepped from an elevator into the atrium. He was with another young lawyer, and they didn't have their briefcases so it was obvious they were headed for a late lunch. After five days of watching lawyers, Croft had learned their habits.

The building was on Pennsylvania, and Brim, Stearns, and Kidlow covered floors three through eleven. Garcia left the building with his buddy, and they laughed their way down the sidewalk. Something was very funny. Croft followed as closely as possible. They walked and laughed for five blocks, then, just as he figured, they ducked into a yuppie corporate fern bar for a quick bite.

Croft called Grantham three times before he got him. It was almost two, and the lunch was winding down by now, and if

Grantham wanted to catch the guy, then stay close to the damned phone. Gray slammed it down. They would meet back at the building.

Garcia and his friend walked a bit slower on the return. It was a beautiful day, and it was Friday, and they enjoyed this brief respite from the grind of suing people or whatever they did for two hundred bucks an hour. Croft hid behind his sunshades and kept his distance.

Gray was waiting in the lobby near the elevators. Croft was close behind them as they spun through the revolving door. He pointed quickly to their man. Gray caught the signal and punched the elevator button. It opened and he stepped in just before Garcia and his friend. Croft stayed behind.

Garcia punched number six a split second before Gray punched it too. Gray read the paper and listened as the two lawyers talked football. The kid was no more than twenty-seven or twenty-eight. The voice maybe had a vague familiarity to it, but it had been on the phone and there was nothing distinctive about it. The face was close, but he couldn't study it. The odds said go for it. He looked very similar to the man in the photograph, and he worked for Brim, Stearns, and Kidlow, and one of its countless clients was Mr. Mattiece. He would give it a shot, but be cautious. He was a reporter. It was his job to go barging in with questions.

They left the elevator on six still yakking about the Redskins, and Gray loitered behind them, casually reading the paper. The firm's lobby was rich and opulent, with chandeliers and Oriental rugs, and on one wall thick gold letters with the firm's name. The lawyers stopped at the front desk and picked up their phone messages. Gray strolled purposefully in front of the receptionist, who eyed him carefully.

"May I help you, sir?" she asked in the tone that meant, "What the hell do you want?"

Gray did not miss a step. "I'm in a meeting with Roger Martin." He'd found the name in the phone book, and he'd called from the lobby a minute earlier to make sure lawyer Martin was in today. The building directory listed the firm on floors three through eleven, but did not list all one hundred and ninety lawyers. Using the yellow pages listing, he made a dozen quick calls to find a lawyer on each floor. Roger Martin was the man on the sixth floor.

He frowned at the receptionist. "I've been meeting with him for two hours."

This puzzled her, and she could think of nothing to say. Gray was around the corner and into a hallway. He caught a glimpse of Garcia entering his office four doors down.

The name beside the door was David M. Underwood. Gray did not knock on it. He wanted to strike quickly, and perhaps exit quickly. Mr. Underwood was hanging his jacket on a rack.

"Hi. I'm Gray Grantham with the *Washington Post.* I'm looking for a man named Garcia."

Underwood froze and looked puzzled. "How'd you get in here?" he asked.

The voice was suddenly familiar. "I walked. You are Garcia, aren't you?"

He pointed to a desk plate with his name in gold letters. "David M. Underwood. There's no one on this floor named Garcia. I don't know of a Garcia in this firm."

Gray smiled as if to play along. Underwood was scared. Or irritated.

"How's your daughter?" Gray asked.

Underwood was coming around the

desk, staring and getting very perturbed. "Which one?"

This didn't fit. Garcia had been quite concerned about his daughter, a baby, and if there had been more than one, he would have mentioned it.

"The youngest. And your wife?"

Underwood was now within striking distance, and inching closer. It was obvious he was a man unafraid of physical contact.

"I don't have a wife. I'm divorced." He held up his left fist, and for a split second Gray thought he'd gone wild. Then he saw the four ringless fingers. No wife. No ring. Garcia adored his wife, and there would be a ring. It was now time to leave.

"What do you want?" Underwood demanded.

"I thought Garcia was on this floor," he said, easing away.

"Is your pal Garcia a lawyer?"

"Yes."

Underwood relaxed a bit. "Not in this firm. We have a Perez and a Hernandez, and maybe one other. But I don't know a Garcia."

"Well, it's a big firm," Gray said by the door. "Sorry to bother."

Underwood was following. "Look, Mr.

Grantham, we're not accustomed to reporters barging in around here. I'll call security, and maybe they can help you."

"Won't be necessary. Thanks." Grantham was in the hall and gone. Underwood
reported to security.

Grantham cursed himself in the elevator.
It was empty except for him, and he cursed
out loud. Then he thought of Croft, and
was cursing him when the elevator landed
and opened, and there was Croft in the
lobby near the pay phones. Cool it, he told
himself.

They left the building together. "Didn't
work," Gray said.

"Did you talk to him?"

"Yep. Wrong man."

"Dammit. I knew it was him. It was the
kid in the photos, wasn't it?"

"No. Close but no cigar. Keep trying."

"I'm really tired of this, Grantham.
I've—"

"You're getting paid, aren't you? Do it
for one more week, okay? I can think of
harder work."

Croft stopped on the sidewalk, and Gray
kept walking. "One more week, and I'm
through," Croft yelled to him. Grantham
waved him off.

He unlocked the illegally parked Volvo and sped back to the *Post*. It was not a smart move. It was quite stupid, and he was much too experienced for such a mistake. He would omit it from his daily chat with Jackson Feldman and Smith Keen.

FELDMAN WAS LOOKING for him, another reporter said, and he walked quickly to his office. He smiled sweetly to the secretary, who was poised to attack. Keen and Howard Krauthammer, the managing editor, were waiting with Feldman. Keen closed the door and handed Gray a newspaper. "Have you seen this?"

It was the New Orleans paper, the *Times-Picayune*, and the front-page story was about the deaths of Verheek and Callahan, along with big photos. He read it quickly while they watched him. It talked about their friendship, and their strange deaths just six days apart. And it mentioned Darby Shaw, who had disappeared. But no link to the brief.

"I guess the cat's out of the bag," Feldman said.

"It's nothing but the basics," Gray said. "We could've run this three days ago."

"Why didn't we?" asked Krauthammer.

"There's nothing here. It's two dead bodies, the name of the girl, and a thousand questions, none of which they answered. They've found a cop who'll talk, but he knows nothing beyond the blood and gore."

"But they're digging, Gray," Keen said.

"You want me to stop them?"

"The *Times* has picked it up," Feldman said. "They're running something tomorrow or Sunday. How much can they know?"

"Why ask me? Look, it's possible they have a copy of the brief. Very unlikely, but possible. But they haven't talked to the girl. We've got the girl, okay. She's ours."

"We hope," said Krauthammer.

Feldman rubbed his eyes and stared at the ceiling. "Let's say they have a copy of the brief, and that they know she wrote it, and now she's vanished. They can't verify it right now, but they're not afraid to mention the brief without naming Mattiece. Let's say they know Callahan was her professor, among other things, and that he brought the brief here and gave it to his good friend Verheek. And now they're dead and she's on the run. That's a pretty damned good story, wouldn't you say, Gray?"

"It's a big story," Krauthammer said.

"It's peanuts compared to what's coming," Gray said. "I don't want to run it because it's the tip of the iceberg, and it'll attract every paper in the country. We don't need a thousand reporters bumping into each other."

"I say we run it," Krauthammer said. "If not, the *Times* will beat our ass with it."

"We can't run the story," Gray said.

"Why not?" asked Krauthammer.

"Because I'm not going to write it, and if it's written by someone else here, then we lose the girl. It's that simple. She's debating right now about whether to jump on a plane and leave the country, and one mistake by us and she's gone."

"But she's already spilled her guts," Keen said.

"I gave her my word, okay. I will not write the story until it's pieced together and Mattiece can be named. It's very simple."

"You're using her, aren't you?" Keen asked.

"She's a source. But she's not in the city."

"If the *Times* has the brief, then they know about Mattiece," Feldman said. "And if they know about Mattiece, you can bet they're digging like hell to verify it. What if they beat us?"

Krauthammer grunted in disgust. "We're going to sit on our asses and lose the biggest story I've seen in twenty years. I say we run what we've got. It's just the surface, but it's a helluva story right now."

"No," Gray said. "I won't write it until I have all of it."

"And how long might that take?" Feldman asked.

"A week, maybe."

"We don't have a week," Krauthammer said.

Gray was desperate. "I can find out how much the *Times* knows. Give me forty-eight hours."

"They're running something tomorrow or Sunday," Feldman said again.

"Let 'em run it. I'll bet money it'll be the same story with probably the same mug shots. You guys are assuming a hell of a lot. You're assuming they've got a copy of the brief, but its author doesn't have a copy of it. We don't have a copy of it. Let's wait, and read their little story, then go from there."

The editors studied each other. Krauthammer was frustrated. Keen was anxious. But the boss was Feldman, and he said, "Okay. If they run something in the morning, we'll meet here at noon and look at it."

"Fine," Gray said quickly and reached for the door.

"You'd better move fast, Grantham," Feldman said. "We can't sit on this much longer."

Grantham was gone.

THIRTY-THREE

THE LIMOUSINE moved patiently in the Beltway rush hour. It was dark, and Matthew Barr read with the aid of a reading light in the ceiling. Coal sipped Perrier and watched the traffic. He had the brief memorized, and could have simply explained it to Barr, but he wanted to watch his reaction.

Barr had no reaction until he got to the photograph, then slowly shook his head. He laid it on the seat, and thought about it for a moment. "Very nasty," he said.

Coal grunted.

"How true is it?" Barr asked.

"I'd love to know."

"When did you first see it?"

"Tuesday of last week. It came over from the FBI in one of their daily reports."

"What'd the President say?"

"He was not that happy with it, but there was no cause for alarm. It's just another wild shot in the dark, we thought. He talked to Voyles about it, and Voyles agreed to leave it alone for a while. Now I'm not so sure."

"Did the President ask Voyles to back off?" Barr asked the question slowly.

"Yes."

"That's awfully close to obstruction of justice, assuming of course the brief turns out to be true."

"And what if it's true?"

"Then the President has problems. I've got one conviction for obstruction, so I've been there. It's like mail fraud. It's broad and wide and fairly easy to prove. Were you in on it?"

"What do you think?"

"Then I think you've got problems too."

They rode in silence and watched the traffic. Coal had thought through the obstruction angle, but he wanted Barr's opinion. He wasn't worried about criminal charges. The President had one brief little chat with Voyles, asked him to look elsewhere for the time being, and that was it. Hardly the work of felons. But Coal was terribly concerned with reelection, and a scandal involving a major contributor like Mattiece would be devastating. The thought was sickening—a man the President knew and took millions from paid money to have two Supreme Court Justices knocked off so his pal the President could appoint more reasonable men to the bench so that the oil could be harvested. The Democrats would fall in the streets howling with glee. Every subcommittee in Congress would hold hearings. Every newspaper would run it every day for a year. The Justice Department would be forced to investigate. Coal would be forced to take the blame and resign. Hell, everyone in the White House, except the President, would have to go.

It was a nightmare of horrific proportions.

"We've got to find out if the brief is true," Coal said to the window.

"If people are dying, then it's true. Give me a better reason for killing Callahan and Verheek."

There was no other reason, and Coal knew it. "I want you to do something."

"Find the girl."

"No. She's either dead or hiding in a

cave somewhere. I want you to talk to Mattiece."

"I'm sure he's in the yellow pages."

"You can find him. We need to establish a link that the President knows nothing about. We need to first determine how much of this is true."

"And you think Victor will take me into his confidence and tell me his secrets."

"Yes, eventually. You're not a cop, remember. Assume it's true, and he thinks he's about to be exposed. He's desperate and he's killing people. What if you told him the press had the story and the end was near, and if he is inclined to disappear, then now's the time? You're coming to him from Washington, remember? From the inside. From the President, or so he thinks. He'll listen to you."

"Okay. What if he tells me it's true? What's in it for us?"

"I've got some ideas, all in the category of damage control. The first thing we'll do is immediately appoint two nature lovers to the Court. I mean, wild-eyed radical bird watchers. It would show that down deep we're good little environmentalists. And it would kill Mattiece and his oil field, etc. We could do this in a matter of hours. Almost

432

simultaneously, the President will call in Voyles and the Attorney General and Justice and demand an immediate investigation into Mattiece. We'll leak copies of the brief to every reporter in town, then hunker down and ride out the storm."

Barr was smiling with admiration.

Coal continued. "It won't be pretty, but it's far better than sitting back and hoping the brief is a work of fiction."

"How do you explain that photograph?"

"You can't. It'll hurt for a while, but it was seven years ago, and people go crazy. We'll portray Mattiece as a good citizen back then, but now he's a madman."

"He is a madman."

"Yes, he is. And right now he's like a wounded dog backed in a corner. You must convince him to throw in the towel, and haul ass. I think he'll listen to you. And I think we'll find out from him if it's true."

"So how do I find him?"

"I've got a man working on that. I'll pull some strings, and make a contact. Be ready to go on Sunday."

Barr smiled to the window. He would like to meet Mattiece.

The traffic slowed. Coal slowly sipped his water. "Anything on Grantham?"

"Not really. We're listening and watching, but nothing exciting. He talks to his mother and a couple of gals, but nothing worth reporting. He works a lot. He left town Wednesday and returned Thursday."

"Where did he go?"

"New York. Probably working on some story."

CLEVE WAS SUPPOSED to be at the corner of Rhode Island and Sixth at exactly 10 P.M., but he wasn't. Gray was supposed to race down Rhode Island until Cleve caught him, so that if anyone was indeed following him they would think he was simply a dangerous driver. He raced down Rhode Island, through Sixth at fifty miles per hour, and watched for blue lights. There were none. He looped around, and fifteen minutes later barreled down Rhode Island again. There! He saw blue lights and pulled to the curb.

It was not Cleve. It was a white cop who was very agitated. He jerked Gray's license, examined it, and asked if he'd been drinking. No sir, he said. The cop wrote the ticket, and proudly handed it to Gray, who sat behind the wheel staring at the ticket until he heard voices coming from the rear bumper.

Another cop was on the scene, and they were arguing. It was Cleve, and he wanted the white cop to forget the ticket, but the white cop explained it had already been written and besides the idiot was doing fifty-six miles an hour through the intersection. He's a friend, Cleve said. Then teach him how to drive before he kills somebody, the white cop said as he got in his patrol car and drove away.

Cleve was snickering as he looked in Gray's window. "Sorry about that," he said with a smile.

"It's all your fault."

"Slow it down next time."

Gray threw the ticket on the floorboard. "Let's talk quick. You said Sarge said the boys in the West Wing are talking about me. Right?"

"Right."

"Okay, I need to know from Sarge if they're talking about any other reporters, especially from the *New York Times*. I need to know if they think anybody else is hot on the story."

"Is that all?"

"Yes. I need it quick."

"Slow it down," Cleve said loudly and walked to his car.

DARBY PAID for the room for the next seven days, in part because she wanted a familiar place to return to if necessary, and in part because she wanted to leave some new clothes she had purchased. It was sinful, this running and leaving everything behind. The clothes were nothing fancy, sort of upscale safari law school, but they cost even more in New York, and it would be nice to keep them. She would not take risks over clothes, but she liked the room and she liked the city and she wanted the clothes.

It was time to run again, and she would travel light. She carried a small canvas bag when she darted from the St. Moritz into a waiting cab. It was almost 11 P.M., Friday, and Central Park South was busy. Across the street, a line of horses and carriages waited for customers and brief excursions through the park.

The cab took ten minutes to get to Seventy-second and Broadway, which was the wrong direction, but this entire journey should be hard to follow. She walked thirty feet, and disappeared into the subway. She had studied a map and a book of the system, and she hoped it would be easy. The subway was not appealing because she'd never used it and she'd heard the stories. But this was the Broadway line, the most commonly used train in Manhattan, and it was rumored to be safe, at times. And things weren't so swell above the ground. The subway could hardly be worse.

She waited in the correct spot with a group of drunk but well-dressed teenagers, and the train arrived in a couple of minutes. It wasn't crowded, and she took a seat near the center doors. Stare at the floor and hold the bag, she kept telling herself. She looked at the floor, but from behind the dark shades, she studied the people. It was her lucky night. No street punks with knives. No beggars. No perverts, at least none she could spot. But for a novice, it was nerve-racking anyway.

The drunk kids exited at Times Square, and she got off quickly at the next stop. She had never seen Penn Station, but this was not the time to sightsee. Maybe one day she could return and spend a month and admire the city without watching for Stump and Thin Man and who knows who else who was out there. But not now.

She had five minutes, and found her train as it was boarding. Again, she sat in the rear and watched every passenger. There were no familiar faces. Surely, please, surely, they had not stuck to her on this jagged escape. Once again, her mistake had been credit cards. She had bought four tickets at O'Hare with American Express, and somehow they knew she was in New York. She was certain Stump had not seen her, but he was in the city, and of course he had friends. There could be twenty of them. But then, she was not certain of anything.

The train left six minutes late. It was half empty. She pulled a paperback from the bag and pretended to read it.

Fifteen minutes later, they stopped in Newark, and she got off. She was a lucky girl. There were cabs lined up outside the station, and ten minutes later she was at the airport.

THIRTY·FOUR

I T WAS SATURDAY MORNING, and the Queen was in Florida taking money from the rich, and it was clear and cool outside. He wanted to sleep late, then play golf whenever he woke up. But it was seven, and he was sitting at his desk wearing a tie, listening to Fletcher Coal suggest what they ought to do about this and about that. Richard Horton, the Attorney General, had talked to Coal, and now Coal was alarmed.

Someone opened the door and Horton entered alone. They shook hands and Horton sat across the desk. Coal stood nearby, and this really irritated the President.

Horton was dull but sincere. He was not dumb or slow, he just thought carefully about everything before he acted. He thought about each word before he said it.

He was loyal to the President, and could be trusted for sound judgment.

"We are seriously considering a formal grand jury investigation into the deaths of Rosenberg and Jensen," he announced gravely. "In light of what's happened in New Orleans, we think this should be pursued immediately."

"The FBI is investigating," the President said. "They've got three hundred agents on the case. Why should we get involved?"

"Are they investigating the pelican brief?" Horton asked. He knew the answer. He knew Voyles was in New Orleans at this moment with hundreds of agents. He knew they had talked to hundreds of people, collected a pile of useless evidence. He knew the President had asked Voyles to back off, and he knew Voyles was not telling the President everything.

Horton had never mentioned the pelican brief to the President, and the fact that he even knew about the damned thing was exasperating. How many more knew about it? Probably thousands.

"They are pursuing all leads," Coal said. "They gave us a copy of it almost two weeks ago, so we assume they're pursuing it."

Exactly what Horton expected out of

Coal. "I feel strongly that the Administration should investigate this matter at once." He spoke as though this was all memorized, and this irritated the President.

"Why?" asked the President.

"What if the brief is on target? If we do nothing, and the truth eventually surfaces, the damage will be irreparable."

"Do you honestly believe there's any truth to it?" the President asked.

"It's awfully suspicious. The first two men who saw it are dead, and the person who wrote it has disappeared. It is perfectly logical, if one is so inclined to kill Supreme Court Justices. There are no other compelling suspects. From what I hear, the FBI is baffled. Yes, it needs to be pursued."

Horton's investigations leaked worse than the White House basement, and Coal was terrified of this clown impaneling a grand jury and calling witnesses. Horton was an honorable man, but the Justice Department was filled with lawyers who talked too much.

"Don't you think it's a bit premature?" Coal asked.

"I don't think so."

"Have you seen the papers this morning?" Coal asked.

Horton had glanced at the front page of the *Post,* and read the sports section. It was Saturday, after all. He had heard that Coal read eight newspapers before dawn, so he didn't like this question.

"I've read a couple of them," he said.

"I've looked at several," Coal said modestly. "And there's not a word anywhere about those two dead lawyers or the girl or Mattiece or anything related to the brief. If you start a formal investigation at this point, it'll be front-page news for a month."

"Do you think it will simply go away?" Horton asked Coal.

"It might. For obvious reasons, we hope so."

"I think you're optimistic, Mr. Coal. We don't normally sit back and wait for the press to do our investigating."

Coal grinned and almost laughed at this one. He smiled at the President, who shot him a quick look, and Horton started a slow burn.

"What's wrong with waiting a week?" asked the President.

"Nothing," shot Coal.

Just that quick the decision was made to wait a week, and Horton knew it. "Things

442

could blow up in a week," he said without conviction.

"Wait a week," the President ordered. "We'll meet here next Friday, and go from there. I'm not saying no, Richard, just wait seven days."

Horton shrugged. This was more than he expected. He'd covered his rear. He would go straight to his office and dictate a lengthy memo detailing everything he could remember about this meeting, and his neck would be protected.

Coal stepped forward and handed him a sheet of paper.

"What's this?"

"More names. Do you know them?"

It was the bird-watcher list: four judges who were much too liberal for comfort, but Plan B called for radical environmentalists on the Court.

Horton blinked several times and studied it hard. "You must be kidding."

"Check 'em out," said the President.

"These guys are off-the-wall liberals," Horton mumbled.

"Yes, but they worship the sun and moon, and trees and birds," Coal explained helpfully.

Horton caught on, and suddenly smiled. "I see. Pelican lovers."

"They're almost extinct, you know," the President said.

Coal headed for the door. "I wish they'd been wiped out ten years ago."

SHE HADN'T CALLED by nine when Gray arrived at his desk in the newsroom. He'd read the *Times* and there was nothing in it. He spread the New Orleans paper over the clutter and skimmed it. Nothing. They had reported all they knew. Callahan, Verheek, Darby, and a thousand unanswered questions. He had to assume the *Times* and maybe the *Times-Picayune* in New Orleans had seen the brief or heard about it, and thus knew of Mattiece. And he had to assume they were clawing like cats to verify it. But he had Darby, and they would find Garcia, and if Mattiece could be verified, they would do it.

At the moment, there was no alternative plan. If Garcia was gone or refused to help, they would be forced to explore the dark and murky world of Victor Mattiece. Darby would not last long at that, and he didn't blame her. He was uncertain how long he would last.

Smith Keen appeared with a cup of coffee and sat on the desk. "If the *Times* had it, would they hold off until tomorrow?"

Gray shook his head. "No. If they had more than the *Times-Picayune*, it would've run today."

"Krauthammer wants to run what we've got. He thinks we can name Mattiece."

"I don't follow."

"He's leaning on Feldman. His angle is that we can run the whole story about Callahan and Verheek getting killed over this brief, which happens to name Mattiece who happens to be a friend of the President's, without directly accusing Mattiece. He says we can be extremely cautious and make sure the story says Mattiece is named in the brief, but not named by us. And since the brief is causing all this death, then it has been verified to some extent."

"He wants to hide behind the brief."

"Exactly."

"But it's all speculation until it's confirmed. Krauthammer's losing it. Assume for a second that Mr. Mattiece is in no way involved with this. Completely innocent. We run the story with his name in it, and then what? We look like fools, and we get sued for the next ten years. I'm not writing the story."

"He wants someone else to write it."

"If this paper runs a pelican story not written by me, the girl is gone, okay. I thought I explained that yesterday."

"You did. And Feldman heard you. He's on your side, Gray, and I am too. But if this thing's true, it'll blow up in a matter of days. We all believe that. You know how Krauthammer hates the *Times,* and he's afraid those bastards'll run it."

"They can't run it, Smith. They may have a few more facts than the *Times-Picayune,* but they can't name Mattiece. Look, we'll verify before anyone. And when it's nailed down, I'll write the story with everyone's name along with that cute little picture of Mattiece and his friend in the White House, and the fat lady will sing."

"We? You said it again. You said, 'We'll verify it.' "

"My source and I, okay." Gray opened a drawer and found the photo of Darby and the Diet Coke. He handed it to Keen, who admired it.

"Where is she?" he asked.

"I'm not sure. I think she's on her way here from New York."

"Don't get her killed."

"We're being very cautious." Gray looked over both shoulders and leaned closer. "In fact, Smith, I think I'm being followed. I just wanted you to know."

"Who might they be?"

"It came from a source at the White House. I'm not using my phones."

"I'd better tell Feldman."

"Okay. I don't think it's dangerous, yet."

"He needs to know." Keen jumped to his feet and disappeared.

She called within minutes. "I'm here," she said. "I don't know how many I've brought with me, but I'm here, and alive, for the moment."

"Where are you?"

"Tabard Inn on N Street. I saw an old friend on Sixth Avenue yesterday. Remember Stump, who was grievously wounded on Bourbon Street? Did I tell you that story?"

"Yes."

"Well, he's walking again. A slight limp, but he was wandering around Manhattan yesterday. I don't think he saw me."

"Are you serious! That's scary, Darby."

"It's worse than scary. I left six trails when I left last night, and if I see him in

this city, limping along a sidewalk somewhere, I intend to surrender. I'll walk up
to him and turn myself in."

"I don't know what to say."

"Say as little as possible, because these
people have radar. I'll play private eye for
three days, and I'm out of here. If I live to
see Wednesday morning, I'm on a plane to
Aruba or Trinidad or some place with a
beach. When I die, I want to be on a
beach."

"When do we meet?"

"I'm thinking about that. I want you to
do two things."

"I'm listening."

"Where do you park your car?"

"Close to my apartment."

"Leave it there, and go rent another one.
Nothing fancy, just a generic Ford or something. Pretend someone's watching you
through a rifle scope. Go to the Marbury
Hotel in Georgetown and get a room for
three nights. They'll take cash—I've already checked. Do it under another
name."

Grantham took notes and shook his
head.

"Can you sneak out of your apartment
after dark?" she asked.

"I think so."

"Do it, and take a cab to the Marbury. Have them deliver the rental car to you there. Take two cabs to the Tabard Inn, and walk into the restaurant at exactly nine tonight."

"Okay. Anything else?"

"Bring clothes. Plan to be away from your apartment for at least three days. And plan to stay away from the office."

"Really, Darby, I think the office is safe."

"I'm not in the mood to argue. If you're going to be difficult, Gray, I'll simply disappear. I'm convinced I'll live longer the sooner I get out of the country."

"Yes, ma'am."

"That's a good boy."

"I assume there's a master plan rattling around somewhere in your brain."

"Maybe. We'll talk about it over dinner."

"Is this sort of like a date?"

"Let's eat a bite and call it business."

"Yes, ma'am."

"I'm hanging up now. Be cautious, Gray. They're watching." She was gone.

SHE WAS SITTING at table thirty-seven, in a dark corner of the tiny restaurant when he found her at exactly nine. The first thing he noticed was the dress, and as he walked to the table he knew the legs were under it but he couldn't see them. Maybe later when she stood. He wore a coat and tie, and they were an attractive couple.

He sat close to her in the darkness so they could both watch the small crowd. The Tabard Inn appeared old enough to have served food to Thomas Jefferson. A rowdy crowd of Germans laughed and talked on the patio outside the restaurant. The windows were open and the air was cool, and for one brief moment it was easy to forget why they were hiding.

"Where'd you get the dress?"

"You like it?"

"It's very nice."

"I shopped a little this afternoon. Like most of my recent wardrobe, it's disposable. I'll probably leave it in the room the next time I flee for my life."

The waiter was before them with menus. They ordered drinks. The restaurant was quiet and harmless.

"How'd you get here?" he asked.

"Around the world."

"I'd like to know."

"I took a train to Newark, a plane to Boston, a plane to Detroit, and a plane to Dulles. I was up all night, and twice I forgot where I was."

"How could they follow that?"

"They couldn't. I paid with cash, something I'm running out of."

"How much do you need?"

"I'd like to wire some from my bank in New Orleans."

"We'll do it Monday. I think you're safe, Darby."

"I've thought that before. In fact, I felt very safe when I was getting on the boat with Verheek, except it wasn't Verheek. And I felt very safe in New York. Then Stump waddled down the sidewalk, and I haven't eaten since."

"You look thin."

"Thanks. I guess. Have you eaten here?" She looked at her menu.

He looked at his. "No, but I hear the food is great. You changed your hair again." It was light brown, and there was a trace of mascara and blush. And lipstick.

"It's going to fall out if I keep seeing these people."

The drinks arrived, and they ordered.

"We expect something in the *Times* in the morning." He would not mention the New

Orleans paper because it had pictures of Callahan and Verheek. He assumed she'd seen it.

This didn't seem to interest her. "Such as?" she asked, looking around.

"We're not sure. We hate to get beat by the *Times*. It's an old rivalry."

"I'm not interested in that. I know nothing about journalism, and don't care to learn. I'm here because I have one, and only one, idea about finding Garcia. And if it doesn't work, and quickly, I'm out of here."

"Forgive me. What would you like to talk about?"

"Europe. What's your favorite place in Europe?"

"I hate Europe, and I hate Europeans. I go to Canada and Australia, and New Zealand occasionally. Why do you like Europe?"

"My grandfather was a Scottish immigrant, and I've got a bunch of cousins over there. I've visited twice."

Gray squeezed the lime in his gin and tonic. A party of six entered from the bar and she watched them carefully. When she talked her eyes darted quickly around the room.

"I think you need a couple of drinks to relax," Gray said.

She nodded but said nothing. The six were seated at a nearby table and began speaking in French. It was pleasant to hear.

"Have you ever heard Cajun French?" she asked.

"No."

"It's a dialect that's rapidly disappearing, just like the wetlands. They say it cannot be understood by Frenchmen."

"That's fair. I'm sure the Cajuns can't understand the French."

She took a long drink of white wine. "Did I tell you about Chad Brunet?"

"I don't think so."

"He was a poor Cajun boy from Eunice. His family survived by trapping and fishing in the marshes. He was a very bright kid who attended LSU on a full academic scholarship, then was admitted to law school at Stanford, where he finished with the highest grade point average in the school's history. He was twenty-one when he was admitted to the California bar. He could have worked for any law firm in the country, but he took a job with an environmental defense outfit in San Francisco. He was brilliant, a real legal genius who worked very hard and was soon winning huge lawsuits against oil and chemical companies. At the age of twenty-eight, he was a highly polished courtroom lawyer. He was feared by big oil and other corporate polluters." She took a sip of wine. "He made a lot of money, and established a group to preserve the Louisiana wetlands. He wanted to participate in the pelican case, as it was known, but had too many other trial commitments. He gave Green Fund a lot of money for litigation expenses. Shortly before the trial started in Lafayette, he announced he was coming home to assist the Green Fund lawyers. There were a couple of stories about him in the New Orleans paper."

"What happened to him?"

"He committed suicide."

"What?"

"A week before the trial, they found him in a car with the engine running. A garden hose ran from the exhaust pipe into the front seat. Just another simple suicide from carbon monoxide poisoning."

"Where was the car?"

"In a wooded area along Bayou Lafourche near the town of Galliano. He knew the area well. Some camping gear and fishing equipment were in the trunk. No suicide note. The police investigated, but found nothing suspicious. The case was closed."

"This is incredible."

"He had had some problems with alcohol, and had been treated by an analyst in San Francisco. But the suicide was a surprise."

"Do you think he was murdered?"

"A lot of people do. His death was a big blow to Green Fund. His passion for the wetlands would've been potent in the courtroom."

Gray finished his drink and rattled the ice. She inched closer to him. The waiter appeared, and they ordered.

THIRTY-FIVE

THE LOBBY of the Marbury Hotel was empty at 6 A.M. Sunday when Gray found a copy of the *Times*. It was six inches deep and weighed twelve pounds, and he wondered how much thicker they planned to make it. He raced back to his room on the eighth floor, spread the paper on the bed, and hovered over it as he skimmed intensely. The front page was empty, and this was crucial. If they had the big story, it would of course be there. He feared large photographs of Rosenberg, Jensen, Callahan, Verheek, maybe Darby and Khamel, who knows, maybe they had a nice picture of Mattiece, and all of these would be lined up on the front page like a cast of characters, and the *Times* had beat them again. He had dreamed of this while he had slept, which had not been for long.

456

But there was nothing. And the less he found, the faster he skimmed until he was down to sports and classifieds, and he stopped and sort of danced to the phone. He called Smith Keen, who was awake. "Have you seen it?" he asked.

"Ain't it beautiful," Keen said. "I wonder what happened."

"They don't have it, Smith. They're digging like hell, but they don't have it yet. Who did Feldman talk to?"

"He never says. But it was supposed to be reliable."

Keen was divorced and lived alone in an apartment not far from the Marbury.

"Are you busy?" Gray asked.

"Well, not exactly. It's almost six-thirty on Sunday morning."

"We need to talk. Pick me up outside the Marbury Hotel in fifteen minutes."

"The Marbury Hotel?"

"It's a long story. I'll explain."

"Ah, the girl. You lucky stiff."

"I wish. She's in another hotel."

"Here? In Washington?"

"Yes. Fifteen minutes."

"I'll be there."

Gray nervously sipped coffee from a paper cup and waited in the lobby. She'd made him paranoid, and he half expected thugs to be hiding on the sidewalk with automatic weapons. This frustrated him. He saw Keen's Toyota ease by on M Street, and he walked quickly to it.

"What would you like to see?" Keen said as he drove away from the curb.

"Oh, I don't know. It's a beautiful day. How about Virginia?"

"As you wish. Did you get kicked out of your apartment?"

"Not exactly. I'm following orders from the girl. She thinks like a field marshal, and I'm here because I was told to be here. I must stay until Tuesday, or until she gets jumpy and moves me again. I'm in room eight-thirty-three if you need me, but don't tell anyone."

"I assume you want the *Post* to pay for this," Keen said with a smile.

"I'm not thinking about money right now. The same people who tried to kill her in New Orleans turned up in New York on Friday, or so she thinks. They have amazing talent in pursuit, and she's being painfully cautious."

"Well, if you're being followed by someone, and she's being followed by someone, then perhaps she knows what she's doing."

"Oh, listen, Smith, she knows exactly what she's doing. She's so good it's scary, and she's leaving here Wednesday morning for good. So we've got two days to find Garcia."

"What if Garcia's overrated? What if you find him and he won't talk, or what if he knows nothing? Have you thought about that?"

"I've had nightmares about that. I think he knows something big. There's a document or a piece of paper, something tangible, and he's got it. He referred to it a time or two, and when I pressed him he wouldn't admit it. But the day we were supposed to meet, he planned to show it to me. I'm convinced of that. He's got something, Smith."

"And if he won't show it to you?"

"I'll break his neck."

They crossed the Potomac and cruised by Arlington Cemetery. Keen lit his pipe and cracked a window. "What if you can't find Garcia?"

"Plan B. She's gone and the deal's off. Once she leaves the country, I have permission to do anything with the brief except use her name as a source. The poor girl is convinced she's dead regardless of whether we get the story, but she wants as much protection as possible. I can never use her name, not even as the author of the brief."

"Does she talk much about the brief?"

"Not the actual writing of it. It was a wild idea, she pursued it, and had almost dismissed it when bombs started going off. She's sorry she wrote the damned thing. She and Callahan were really in love, and she's loaded down with a lot of pain and guilt."

"So what's Plan B?"

"We attack the lawyers. Mattiece is too devious and slippery to penetrate without subpoenas and warrants and things we can't dispense, but we know his lawyers. He's represented by two big firms here in town, and we go after them. A lawyer or a group of them carefully analyzed the Supreme Court, and suggested the names of Rosenberg and Jensen. Mattiece wouldn't know who to kill. So his lawyers told him. It's a conspiracy angle."

"But you can't make them talk."

"Not about a client. But if the lawyers are guilty, and we start asking questions, something'll break. We'll need a dozen reporters making a million phone calls to lawyers, paralegals, law clerks, secretaries, copy room clerks, everybody. We assault these bastards."

Keen puffed his pipe and was noncommittal. "Who are the firms?"

"White and Blazevich, and Brim, Stearns, and Kidlow. Check our library on them."

"I've heard of White and Blazevich. It's a big Republican outfit."

Gray nodded and sipped the last of his coffee.

"What if it's another firm?" Keen asked. "What if the firm is not in Washington? What if the conspirators don't break? What if there's only one legal mind at work here and it belongs to a part-time paralegal in Shreveport? What if one of Mattiece's in-house lawyers devised the scheme?"

"Sometimes you irritate the hell out of me. Do you know that?"

"These are valid questions. What if?"

"Then we go to Plan C."

"And what's that?"

"I don't know yet. She hasn't gotten that far."

SHE HAD INSTRUCTED HIM to stay off the streets and to eat in his room. He had a

sandwich and fries in a bag, and was obediently walking to his room on the eighth
floor of the Marbury. An Asian maid was
pushing her cart near his room. He
stopped at his door and pulled the key
from his pocket.

"You forget something, sir?" the maid
asked.

Gray looked at her. "I beg your pardon."

"You forget something?"

"Well, no. Why?"

The maid took a step closer to him. "You
just left, sir, and now you are back."

"I left four hours ago."

She shook her head and took another
step for a closer look. "No sir. A man left
your room ten minutes ago." She hesitated
and studied his face intently. "But, sir, now
I think it was another man."

Gray glanced at the room number on the
door. 833. He stared at the woman. "Are
you certain another man was in this
room?"

"Yes, sir. Just minutes ago."

He panicked. He walked quickly to the
stairs, and ran down eight flights. What
was in the room? Nothing but clothes.
Nothing about Darby. He stopped and
reached into a pocket. The note with the

Tabard Inn address and her phone number was in the pocket. He caught his breath, and eased into the lobby.

He had to find her, and quick.

DARBY FOUND an empty table in the reading room on the second floor of the Edward Bennett Williams Law Library at Georgetown. In her new hobby as a traveling critic of law school libraries, she found Georgetown's to be the nicest so far. It was a separate five-story building across a small courtyard from McDonough Hall, the law school. The library was new, sleek, and modern, but still a law library and quickly filling with Sunday students now thinking of final exams.

She opened volume five of Martindale-Hubbell, and found the section for D.C. firms. White and Blazevich ran for twenty-eight pages. Names, birth dates, birthplaces, schools, professional organizations, distinctions, awards, committees, and publications of four hundred and twelve lawyers, the partners first, then the associates. She took notes on a legal pad.

The firm had eighty-one partners, and the rest were associates. She grouped them by alphabet, and wrote every name on the legal pad. She was just another law student checking out law firms in the relentless chase of employment.

The work was boring and her mind wandered. Thomas had studied here twenty years ago. He'd been a top student and claimed to have spent many hours in the library. He'd written for the law journal, a chore she would be enduring under normal circumstances.

Death was a subject she'd analyzed from different angles in the past ten days. Except for going quietly in one's sleep, she was undecided as to the best approach. A slow, agonizing demise from a disease was a nightmare for the victim and the loved ones, but at least there was time for preparation and farewells. A violent, unexpected death was over in a second and probably best for the deceased. But the shock was numbing for those left behind. There were so many painful questions. Did he suffer? What was his last thought? Why did it happen? And watching the quick death of a loved one was beyond description.

She loved him more because she watched him die, and she told herself to stop hearing the explosion, and stop smelling the smoke, and stop watching him die.

If she survived three more days, she would be in a place where she could lock the door and cry and throw things until the grieving was over. She was determined to make it to that place. She was determined to grieve, and to heal. It was the least she deserved.

She memorized names until she knew more about White and Blazevich than any-one outside the firm. She eased into the darkness and caught a cab to the hotel.

MATTHEW BARR went to New Orleans, where he met with a lawyer who instructed him to fly to a certain hotel in Fort Lauder-dale. The lawyer was vague about what would happen at the hotel, but Barr checked in Sunday night and found a room waiting for him. A note at the desk said he would receive a call in the early a.m.

He called Fletcher Coal at home at ten, and briefed him on the journey so far.

Coal had other things on his mind. "Grantham's gone crazy. He and a guy named Rifkin with the *Times* are making calls everywhere. They could be deadly."

"Have they seen the brief?"

"I don't know if they've seen it, but they've heard of it. Rifkin called one of my aides at home yesterday and asked what he knew about the pelican brief. The aide knew nothing, and got the impression Rifkin knew even less. I don't think he's seen it, but we can't be certain."

"Damn, Fletcher. We can't keep up with a bunch of reporters. Those guys make a hundred phone calls a minute."

"Just two. Grantham and Rifkin. You've already got Grantham wired. Do the same for Rifkin."

"Grantham's wired, but he's using neither the phone in his apartment nor the one in his car. I called Bailey from the airport in New Orleans. Grantham hasn't been home in twenty-four hours, but his car's still there. They called and knocked on his door. He's either dead in the apartment, or he sneaked out last night."

"Maybe he's dead."

"I don't think so. We were following, and so were the Fibbies. I think he got wind of it."

"You must find him."

"He'll turn up. He can't get too far away from the newsroom on the fifth floor."

"I want Rifkin wired too. Call Bailey tonight and get it started, okay?"

"Yes sir," Barr said.

"What do you think Mattiece would do if

he thought Grantham had the story and was about to spread it across the front page of the *Washington Post?*" Coal asked.

Barr stretched on the hotel bed and closed his eyes. Months ago he had made the decision never to cross Fletcher Coal. He was an animal.

"He's not afraid of killing people, is he?" Barr said.

"Do you think you'll see Mattiece tomorrow?"

"I don't know. These guys are very secretive. They speak in hushed tones behind closed doors. They've told me little."

"Why do they want you in Fort Lauderdale?"

"I do not know, but it's much closer to the Bahamas. I think I'm going there tomorrow, or perhaps he's coming here. I just don't know."

"Perhaps you should exaggerate the Grantham angle. Mattiece will snuff out the story."

"I'll think about it."

"Call me in the morning."

SHE STEPPED ON THE NOTE when she opened her door. It said: *Darby, I'm on the patio. It's urgent, Gray.* She took a deep breath and crammed the note in her pocket. She locked the door, and followed the narrow, winding hallways to the lobby, then through the dark sitting room, by the bar, through the restaurant, and onto the patio. He was at a small table, partially hidden by a brick wall.

"Why are you here?" she demanded in a whisper as she sat close to him. He looked tired and worried.

"Where have you been?" he asked.

"That's not as important as why you're here. You're not supposed to come here unless I say so. What's going on?"

He gave her a quick summary of his morning, from the first phone call to Smith Keen to the maid in the hotel. He'd spent the rest of the day darting all over the city in various cabs, almost eighty bucks' worth of cabs, and he waited until dark to sneak into the Tabard Inn. He was certain he had not been followed.

She listened. She watched the restaurant and the entrance to the patio, and heard every word.

"I have no idea how anyone could find my room," he said.

"Did you tell anyone your room number?"

He thought for a second. "Only Smith Keen. But he'd never repeat it."

She was not looking at him. "Where were you when you told him your room number?"

"In his car."

She shook her head slowly. "I distinctly told you not to tell anyone. Didn't I?"

He would not answer.

"It's all fun and games, isn't it, Gray? Just another day at the beach. You're a big stud reporter who's had death threats before, but you're fearless. The bullets will bounce off, won't they? You and I can spend a few days here frolicking around town playing detective so you can win a Pulitzer and get rich and famous, and the bad guys aren't really so bad because, hey, you're Gray Grantham of the *Washington Post* and that makes you a mean son of a bitch."

"Come on, Darby."

"I've tried to impress upon you how dangerous these people are. I've seen what they can do. I know what they'll do to me if they find me. But no, Gray, it's all a game to you. Cops and robbers. Hide-and-seek."

"I'm convinced, okay?"

"Listen, hotshot, you'd better be convinced. One more screwup and we're dead. I'm out of lucky breaks. Do you understand?"

"Yes! I swear I understand."

"Get a room here. Tomorrow night, if we're alive, I'll find you another small hotel."

"What if this place is full?"

"Then you can sleep in my bathroom with the door closed."

She was dead serious. He felt like a first-grader who'd just received his first spanking. They didn't speak for five minutes.

"So how'd they find me?" he finally asked.

"I would assume the phones in your apartment are tapped, and your car is bugged. And I would assume Smith Keen's car is also wired. These people are not amateurs."

THIRTY ⋈ SIX

HE SPENT THE NIGHT in room 14 upstairs, but slept little. The restaurant opened at six, and he sneaked down for coffee, then sneaked back to his room. The inn was quaint and ancient, and had somehow been formed when three old townhouses were connected. Small doors and narrow hallways ran in all directions. The atmosphere was timeless.

It would be a long, tiresome day, but it would all be spent with her, and he looked forward to it. He'd made a mistake, a bad one, but she'd forgiven him. At precisely eight-thirty, he knocked on the door to room 1. She quickly opened it, then closed it behind him.

She was a law student again, with jeans and a flannel shirt. She poured him coffee, and sat at the small table where the phone was surrounded by notes from a legal pad.

"Did you sleep well?" she asked, but only out of courtesy.

"No." He threw a copy of the *Times* on the bed. He'd already scanned it, and it was empty again.

Darby took the phone and punched the number of the Georgetown law school. She looked at him, and listened, then said, "Placement office, please." There was a long pause. "Yes, this is Sandra Jernigan. I'm a partner with White and Blazevich here in town, and we're having a problem with our computers. We're trying to reconstruct some payroll records, and the accountants have asked me to ask you for the names of your students who clerked here last summer. I think there were four of them." She listened for a second. "Jernigan. Sandra Jernigan," she repeated. "I see. How long will it take?" A pause. "And your name is, Joan. Thank you, Joan." Darby covered the receiver and breathed deeply. Gray watched intently, but with an admiring grin.

"Yes, Joan. Seven of them. Our records are a mess. Do you have their addresses and social security numbers? We need it for tax purposes. Sure. How long will it take? Fine. We have an office boy in the area. His name is Snowden, and he'll be there in thirty minutes. Thank you, Joan." Darby hung up and closed her eyes.

"Sandra Jernigan?" he said.

"I'm not good at lying," she said.

"You're wonderful. I guess I'm the office boy."

"You could pass for an office boy. You have an aging law school dropout look about you." And you're sort of cute, she thought to herself.

"I like the flannel shirt."

She took a long drink of cold coffee. "This could be a long day."

"So far, so good. I get the list, and meet you in the library. Right?"

"Yes. The placement office is on the fifth floor of the law school. I'll be in room 336. It's a small conference room on the third floor. You take a cab first. I'll meet you there in fifteen minutes."

"Yes, ma'am." Grantham was out the door. Darby waited five minutes, then left with her canvas bag.

The cab ride was short but slow in the morning traffic. Life on the lam was bad enough, but running and playing detective at the same time was too much. She'd been in the cab five minutes before she thought about being followed. And maybe that was good. Maybe a hard day as an investigative reporter would take her mind off Stump and the other tormentors. She would work today, and tomorrow, and by late Wednesday she would be on a beach.

They would start with the law school at Georgetown. If it was a dead end, they would try the one at George Washington. If there was time, they would try American University. Three strikes, and she was gone.

The cab stopped at McDonough Hall, at the grungy base of Capitol Hill. With her bag and flannel shirt, she was just one of many law students milling about before class. She took the stairs to the third level, and closed the door to the conference room behind her. The room was used for an occasional class and on campus job interviews. She spread her notes on the table, and was just another law student preparing for class.

Within minutes, Gray eased through the door. "Joan's a sweet lady," he said as he placed the list on the table. "Names, addresses, and social security numbers. Ain't that nice."

Darby looked at the list and pulled a phone book from her bag. They found five of the names in the book. She looked at her watch. "It's five minutes after nine. I'll bet no more than half of these are in class at this moment. Some will have later classes. I'll call these five, and see who's at home. You take the two with no phone number, and get their class schedules from the registrar."

Gray looked at his watch. "Let's meet back here in fifteen minutes." He left first, then Darby. She went to the pay phones on the first level outside the classrooms, and dialed the number of James Maylor.

A male voice answered, "Hello."

"Is this Dennis Maylor?" she asked.

"No. I'm James Maylor."

"Sorry." She hung up. His address was ten minutes away. He didn't have a nine o'clock class, and if he had one at ten he would be home for another forty minutes. Maybe.

She called the other four. Two answered and she confirmed, and there was no answer at the other two.

Gray waited impatiently in the registrar's

office on the third floor. A part-time student clerk was trying to find the registrar, who was somewhere in the back. The student informed him that she wasn't sure if they could give out class schedules. Gray said he was certain they could if they wanted to.

The registrar walked suspiciously around a corner. "May I help you?"

"Yes, I'm Gray Grantham with the *Washington Post,* and I'm trying to find two of your students, Laura Kaas and Michael Akers."

"Is there a problem?" she asked nervously.

"Not at all. Just a few questions. Are they in class this morning?" He was smiling, and it was a warm, trusting smile that he flashed usually at older women. It seldom failed him.

"Do you have an ID or something?"

"Certainly." He opened his wallet and slowly waved it at her, much like a cop who knows he's a cop and doesn't care to spell it out.

"Well, I really should talk to the dean, but—"

"Fine. Where's his office?"

"But he's not here. He's out of town."

476

"I just need their class schedules so I can find them. I'm not asking for home addresses or grades or transcripts. Nothing confidential or personal."

She glanced at the part-time student clerk, who sort of shrugged, like "What's the big deal?" "Just a minute," she said, and disappeared around the corner.

Darby was waiting in the small room when he laid the computer printouts on the table. "According to these, Akers and Kaas should be in class right now," he said.

Darby looked at the schedules. "Akers has criminal procedure. Kaas has administrative law; both from nine to ten. I'll try to find them." She showed Gray her notes. "Maylor, Reinhart, and Wilson were at home. I couldn't get Ratliff and Linney."

"Maylor's the closest. I can be there in a few minutes."

"What about a car?" Darby asked.

"I called Hertz. It's supposed to be delivered to the *Post* parking lot in fifteen minutes."

MAYLOR'S APARTMENT was on the third floor of a warehouse converted for students and others on very low budgets.

He answered the door shortly after the first knock. He spoke through the chain.

"Looking for James Maylor," Gray said like an old pal.

"That's me."

"I'm Gray Grantham with the *Washington Post*. I'd like to ask you a couple of very quick questions."

The door was unchained and opened. Gray stepped inside the two-room apartment. A bicycle was parked in the center, and took up most of the space.

"What's up?" Maylor asked. He was intrigued by this, and appeared eager to answer questions.

"I understand you clerked for White and Blazevich last summer."

"That's correct. For three months."

Gray scribbled on his notepad. "What section were you in?"

"International. Mostly grunt work. Nothing glamorous. A lot of research and rough drafting of agreements."

"Who was your supervisor?"

"No single person. There were three associates who kept me busy. The partner above them was Stanley Coopman."

Gray pulled a photograph from his coat

pocket. It was Garcia on the sidewalk. "Do you recognize this face?"

Maylor held the picture and studied it. He shook his head. "I don't think so. Who is he?"

"He's a lawyer, I think with White and Blazevich."

"It's a big firm. I was stuck in the corner of one section. It's over four hundred lawyers, you know."

"Yeah, so I've heard. You're sure you haven't seen him?"

"Positive. They cover twelve floors, most of which I never went on."

Gray placed the photo in his pocket. "Did you meet any other clerks?"

"Oh. Sure. A couple from Georgetown that I already knew, Laura Kaas and Jo-Anne Ratliff. Two guys from George Washington, Patrick Franks and a guy named Vanlandingham; a girl from Harvard named Elizabeth Larson; a girl from Michigan named Amy MacGregor; and a guy from Emory named Moke, but I think they fired him. There are always a lot of clerks in the summer."

"You plan to work there when you finish?"

"I don't know. I'm not sure I'm cut out for the big firms."

Gray smiled and stuck the notepad in his rear pocket. "Look, you've been in the firm. How would I find this guy?"

Maylor pondered this for a second. "I assume you can't go there and start asking around."

"Good assumption."

"And all you've got is the picture?"

"Yep."

"Then I guess you're doing the right thing. One of the clerks will recognize him."

"Thanks."

"Is the guy in trouble?"

"Oh no. He may have witnessed something. It's probably a long shot." Gray opened the door. "Thanks again."

DARBY STUDIED the fall listing of classes on the bulletin board across the lobby from the phones. She wasn't exactly sure what she'd do when the nine o'clock classes were over, but she was trying like hell to think of something. The bulletin board was exactly like the one at Tulane: class listings tacked neatly in a row; notices for assignments; ads for books, bikes, rooms, roommates, and a hundred other necessities stuck haphazardly about; announcements of parties, intramural games, and club meetings. A young woman with a backpack and hiking books stopped nearby and looked at the board. She was undoubtedly a student.

Darby smiled at her. "Excuse me. Would you happen to know Laura Kaas?"

"Sure."

"I need to give her a message. Could you point her out?"

"Is she in class?"

"Yeah, she's in administrative law under Ship, room 207."

They walked and chatted in the direction of Ship's admin law. The lobby was suddenly busy as four classrooms emptied. The hiker pointed to a tall, heavyset girl walking toward them. Darby thanked her, and followed Laura Kaas until the crowd thinned and scattered.

"Excuse me, Laura. Are you Laura Kaas?" The big girl stopped and stared. "Yes."

This was the part she didn't like; the lying. "I'm Sara Jacobs, and I'm working on a story for the *Washington Post*. Can I ask you a few questions?" She selected Laura Kaas first because she did not have a class at ten. Michael Akers did. She would try him at eleven.

"What about?"

"It'll just take a minute. Could we step in here?" Darby was nodding and walking to an empty classroom. Laura followed slowly.

"You clerked for White and Blazevich last summer."

"I did." She spoke slowly, suspiciously.

Sara Jacobs fought to control her nerves. This was awful. "What section?"

"Tax."

"You like tax, huh?" It was a weak effort at small talk.

"I did. Now I hate it."

Darby smiled like this was the funniest thing she'd heard in years. She pulled a photo from her pocket, and handed it to Laura Kaas.

"Do you recognize this man?"

"No."

"I think he's a lawyer with White and Blazevich."

"There are plenty of them."

"Are you certain?"

She handed it back. "Yep. I never left the fifth floor. It would take years to meet everyone, and they come and go so fast. You know how lawyers are."

Laura glanced around, and the conversation was over. "I really appreciate this," Darby said.

"No problem," Laura said on her way out the door.

AT EXACTLY TEN-THIRTY, they met again in room 336. Gray had caught Ellen Reinhart in the driveway as she was leaving for class. She had worked in the litigation section under a partner by the name of Daniel O'Malley, and spent most of the summer in a class action trial in Miami. She was gone for two months, and spent little time in the Washington office. White and Blazevich had offices in four cities, including Tampa. She did not recognize Garcia, and she was in a hurry.

Judith Wilson was not at her apartment, but her roommate said she would return around one.

They scratched off Maylor, Kaas, and Reinhart. They whispered their plans, and split again. Gray left to find Edward Linney, who according to the list had clerked the past two summers at White and Blazevich. He was not in the phone book, but his address was in Wesley Heights, north of Georgetown's main campus.

At ten forty-five, Darby found herself loitering again in front of the bulletin board, hoping for another miracle. Akers was a male, and there were different ways to approach him. She hoped he was where he was supposed to be—in room 201 studying criminal procedure. She eased that way and waited a moment or two until the door opened and fifty law students emptied into the hall. She could never be a reporter. She could never walk up to strangers and start asking a bunch of questions. It was awkward and uncomfortable. But she walked up to a shy-looking young man with sad eyes and thick glasses, and said, "Excuse me. Do you happen to know Michael Akers? I think he's in this class."

The guy smiled. It was nice to be noticed. He pointed at a group of men walking toward the front entrance. "That's him, in the gray sweater."

"Thanks." She left him standing there. The group disassembled as it left the building, and Akers and a friend were on the sidewalk.

"Mr. Akers," she called after him.

They both stopped and turned around,

then smiled as she nervously approached them. "Are you Michael Akers?" she asked.

"That's me. Who are you?"

"My name is Sara Jacobs, and I'm working on a story for the *Washington Post*. Can I speak to you alone?"

"Sure." The friend took the hint and left.

"What about?" Akers asked.

"Did you clerk for White and Blazevich last summer?"

"Yes." Akers was friendly and enjoying this.

"What section?"

"Real estate. Boring as hell, but it was a job. Why do you want to know?"

She handed him the photo. "Do you recognize this man? He works for White and Blazevich."

Akers wanted to recognize him. He wanted to be helpful and have a long conversation with her, but the face did not register.

"Kind of a suspicious picture, isn't it?" he said.

"I guess. Do you know him?"

"No. I've never seen him. It's an awfully big firm. The partners wear name badges to their meetings. Can you believe it? The guys who own the firm don't know each other. There must be a hundred partners."

Eighty-one, to be exact. "Did you have a supervisor?"

"Yeah, a partner named Walter Welch. A real snot. I didn't like the firm, really."

"Do you remember any other clerks?"

"Sure. The place was crawling with summer clerks."

"If I needed their names, could I get back with you?"

"Anytime. This guy in trouble?"

"I don't think so. He may know something."

"I hope they all get disbarred. A bunch of thugs, really. It's a rotten place to work. Everything's political."

"Thanks." She smiled, and turned away. He admired the rear view, and said, "Call me anytime."

"Thanks."

Darby, the investigative reporter, walked next door to the library building, and climbed the stairs to the fifth floor where the *Georgetown Law Journal* had a suite of crowded offices. She'd found the most recent edition of the *Journal* in the library, and noticed that JoAnne Ratliff was an assistant editor. She suspected most law reviews and law journals were much the same. The top students hung out there and prepared their scholarly articles and comments. They were superior to the rest of the students, and were a clannish bunch who appreciated their brilliant minds. They hung out in the law journal suite. It was their second home.

She stepped inside and asked the first person where she might find JoAnne Ratliff. He pointed around a corner. Second door on the right. The second door opened into a cluttered workroom lined with rows of books. Two females were hard at work.

"JoAnne Ratliff," Darby said.

"That's me," an older woman of maybe forty responded.

"Hi. My name is Sara Jacobs, and I'm working on a story for the *Washington Post*. Can I ask you a few quick questions?"

She slowly laid her pen on the table, and frowned at the other woman. Whatever they were doing was terribly important, and this interruption was a real pain in the ass. They were significant law students.

Darby wanted to smirk and say something smart. She was number two in her class, dammit!, so don't act so high and mighty.

"What's the story about?" Ratliff asked.

"Could we speak in private?"

They frowned at each other again.

"I'm very busy," Ratliff said.

So am I, thought Darby. You're checking citations for some meaningless article, and I'm trying to nail the man who killed two Supreme Court Justices.

"I'm sorry," Darby said. "I promise I'll just take a minute."

They stepped into the hall. "I'm very sorry to disturb you, but I'm in sort of a rush."

"And you're a reporter with the *Post?*" It was more of a challenge than a question, and she was forced to lie some more. She told herself she could lie and cheat and steal for two days, then it was off to the Caribbean and Grantham could have it.

"Yes. Did you work for White and Blazevich last summer?"

"I did. Why?"

Quickly, the photo. Ratliff took it and analyzed it.

"Do you recognize him?"

She shook her head slowly. "I don't think so. Who is he?"

This bitch'll make a fine lawyer. So many questions. If she knew who he was, she wouldn't be standing in this tiny hallway acting like a reporter and putting up with this haughty legal eagle.

"He's a lawyer with White and Blazevich," Darby said as sincerely as possible. "I thought you might recognize him."

"Nope." She handed the photo back.

Enough of this. "Well, thanks. Again, sorry to bother."

"No problem," Ratliff said as she disappeared through the door.

SHE JUMPED into the new Hertz Pontiac as it stopped at the corner, and they were off in traffic. She had seen enough of the Georgetown Law School.

"I struck out," Gray said. "Linney wasn't home."

"I talked to Akers and Ratliff, and both said no. That's five of seven who don't recognize Garcia."

"I'm hungry. You want some lunch?"

"That's fine."

"Is it possible to have five clerks work three months in a law firm and not one of them recognize a young associate?"

"Yeah, it's not only possible, it's very

probable. This is a long shot, remember. Four hundred lawyers means a thousand people when you add secretaries, paralegals, law clerks, office clerks, copy room clerks, mail room clerks, all kinds of clerks and support people. The lawyers tend to keep to themselves in their own little sections."

"Physically, are the sections on separate territory?"

"Yes. It's possible for a lawyer in banking on the third floor to go weeks without seeing an acquaintance in litigation on the tenth floor. These are very busy people, remember."

"Do you think we've got the wrong firm?"

"Maybe the wrong firm, maybe the wrong law school."

"The first guy, Maylor, gave me two names of George Washington students who clerked there last summer. Let's get them after lunch." He slowed and parked illegally behind a row of small buildings.

"Where are we?" she asked.

"A block off Mount Vernon Square, downtown. The *Post* is six blocks that way. My bank is four blocks that way. And this little deli is just around the corner."

490

They walked to the deli, which was filling fast with lunch traffic. She waited at a table by the window as he stood in line and ordered club sandwiches. Half the day had flown by, and though she didn't enjoy this line of work, it was nice to stay busy and forget about the shadows. She wouldn't be a reporter, and at the moment a career in law looked doubtful. Not long ago, she'd thought of being a judge after a few years in practice. Forget it. It was much too dangerous.

Gray brought a tray of food and iced tea, and they began eating.

"Is this a typical day for you?" she asked.

"This is what I do for a living. I snoop all day, write the stories late in the afternoon, then dig until late at night."

"How many stories a week?"

"Sometimes three or four, sometimes none. I pick and choose, and there's little supervision. This is a bit different. I haven't run one in ten days."

"What if you can't link Mattiece? What'll you write about the story?"

"Depends on how far I get. We could've run that story about Verheek and Callahan, but why bother. It was a big story, but they had nothing to go with it. It scratched the surface and stopped."

"And you're going for the big bang."

"Hopefully. If we can verify your little brief, then we'll run one helluva story."

"You can see the headlines, can't you?"

"I can. The adrenaline is pumping. This will be the biggest story since—"

"Watergate?"

"No. Watergate was a series of stories that started small and kept getting bigger. Those guys chased leads for months and kept pecking away until the pieces came together. A lot of people knew different parts of the story. This, my dear, is very different. This is a much bigger story, and the truth is known only by a very small group. Watergate was a stupid burglary and a bungled cover-up. These are masterfully planned crimes by very rich and smart people."

"And the cover-up?"

"That comes next. After we link Mattiece to the killings, we run the big story. The cat's out of the bag, and a half a dozen investigations will crank up overnight. This place will be shell-shocked, especially at the news that the President and Mattiece are old friends. As the dust is settling, we go

after the Administration and try to determine who knew what and when."

"But first, Garcia."

"Ah, yes. I know he's out there. He's a
lawyer in this city, and he knows something
very important."

"What if we stumble across him, and he
won't talk?"

"We have ways."

"Such as?"

"Torture, kidnapping, extortion, threats
of all types."

A burly man with a contorted face was
suddenly beside the table. "Hurry up!" he
yelled. "You're talkin' too much!"

"Thanks, Pete," Gray said without looking up. Pete was lost in the crowd, but
could be heard yelling at another table.
Darby dropped her sandwich.

"He owns the place," Gray explained.
"It's part of the ambience."

"How charming. Does it cost extra?"

"Oh no. The food's cheap, so he depends on volume. He refuses to serve coffee because he doesn't want socializing. He
expects us to eat like refugees and get out."

"I'm finished."

Gray looked at his watch. "It's twelve-fif-
teen. We need to be at Judith Wilson's

apartment at one. Do you want to wire the money now?"

"How long will it take?"

"We can start the wire now, and pick the money up later."

"Let's go."

"How much do you want to wire?"

"Fifteen thousand."

JUDITH WILSON lived on the second floor of a decaying old house filled with two-room student apartments. She was not there at one, and they drove around for an hour. Gray became a tour guide. He drove slowly by the Montrose Theatre, still boarded and burned out. He showed her the daily circus at Dupont Circle.

They were parked on the street at two-fifteen when a red Mazda stopped in the narrow driveway. "There she is," Gray said, and got out. Darby stayed in the car.

He caught Judith near the front steps. She was friendly enough. They chatted, he showed her the photo, she looked at it for a few seconds and began shaking her head. Moments later he was in the car.

"Zero for six," he said.

"That leaves Edward Linney, who probably is our best shot because he clerked there two summers."

They found a pay phone at a convenience store three blocks away, and Gray called Linney's number. No answer. He slammed the phone down and got in the car. "He wasn't at home at ten this morning, and he's not at home now."

"Could be in class," Darby said. "We need his schedule. You should've picked it up with the others."

"You didn't suggest it then."

"Who's the detective here? Who's the big-shot investigative reporter with the *Washington Post?* I'm just a lowly ex–law student who's thrilled to be sitting here in the front seat watching you operate."

What about the backseat? he almost said. "Whatever. Where to?"

"Back to the law school," she said. "I'll wait in the car while you march in there and get Linney's class schedule."

"Yes, ma'am."

A DIFFERENT STUDENT was behind the desk in the registrar's office. Gray asked for the class schedule for Edward Linney, and the student went to look for the registrar. Five minutes later, the registrar walked slowly around the corner and glared at him.

He flashed the smile. "Hi, remember me? Gray Grantham with the *Post*. I need another class schedule."

"The dean says no."

"I thought the dean was out of town."

"He is. The assistant dean says no. No more class schedules. You've already gotten me in a lot of trouble."

"I don't understand. I'm not asking for personal records."

"The assistant dean says no."

"Where is the assistant dean?"

"He's busy."

"I'll wait. Where's his office?"

"He'll be busy for a long time."

"I'll wait for a long time."

She dug in and folded her arms. "He will not allow you to have any more class schedules. Our students are entitled to privacy."

"Sure they are. What kind of trouble have I caused?"

"Well, I'll just tell you."

"Please do."

The student clerk eased around the corner and disappeared.

"One of the students you talked to this morning called White and Blazevich, and they called the assistant dean, and the assistant dean called me and said no more class schedules will be given to reporters."

"Why should they care?"

"They care, okay? We've had a long relationship with White and Blazevich. They hire a lot of our students."

Gray tried to look pitiful and helpless. "I'm just trying to find Edward Linney. I swear he's not in trouble. I just need to ask him a few questions."

She smelled victory. She had backed down a reporter from the *Post,* and she was quite proud. So offer him a crumb. "Mr. Linney is no longer enrolled here. That's all I can say."

He backed toward the door, and mumbled, "Thanks."

He was almost to the car when someone called his name. It was the student from the registrar's office.

"Mr. Grantham," he said as he ran to him. "I know Edward. He's sort of dropped out of school for a while. Personal problems."

"Where is he?"

"His parents put him in a private hospital. He's being detoxified."

"Where is it?"

"Silver Spring. A place called Parklane Hospital."

"How long's he been there?"

"About a month."

Grantham shook his hand. "Thanks. I won't tell anyone you told me."

"He's not in trouble, is he?"

"No. I promise."

They stopped at the bank, and Darby left with fifteen thousand in cash. Carrying the money scared her. Linney scared her. White and Blazevich suddenly scared her.

PARKLANE was a detox center for the rich, or for those with expensive insurance. It was a small building, surrounded by trees and sitting alone a half mile off the highway. This might be difficult, they decided.

Gray entered the lobby first, and asked the receptionist for Edward Linney.

"He is a patient here," she said rather officially.

He used his best smile. "Yes. I know he is a patient. They told me at the law school that he was a patient. What room is he in?"

Darby entered the lobby and strolled to the water fountain for a very long drink.

"He's in room 22, but you can't see him."

"They told me at the law school I could see him."

"And who might you be?"

He was so friendly. "Gray Grantham, with the *Washington Post*. They told me at the law school I could ask him a couple of questions."

"I'm sorry they told you that. You see, Mr. Grantham, we run this hospital, and they run their law school."

Darby picked up a magazine and sat on a sofa.

His smile faded considerably, but was still there. "I understand that," he said, still courteous. "Could I see the administrator?"

"Why?"

"Because this is a very important matter, and I must see Mr. Linney this afternoon. If you won't allow it, then I have to talk to your boss. I will not leave here until I speak to the administrator."

She gave him her best go-to-hell look, and backed away from the counter. "Just a moment. You may have a seat."

"Thank you."

She left and Gray turned to Darby. He

pointed to a set of double doors that appeared to lead to the only hallway. She took a deep breath, and walked quickly through them. They opened into a large junction from which three sterile corridors branched out. A brass plate pointed to rooms 18 through 30. It was the center wing of the hospital, and the hall was dark and quiet with thick, industrial carpet and floral wallpaper.

This would get her arrested. She would be tackled by a large security guard or a heavy nurse and taken to a locked room where the cops would rough her up when they arrived, and her sidekick out there would stand and watch helplessly as they led her away in shackles. Her name would be in the paper, the *Post,* and Stump, if he was literate, would see it, and they'd get her.

As she crept along by these closed doors, the beaches and piña coladas seemed unreachable. The door to number 22 was closed and had the names Edward L. Linney and Dr. Wayne McLatchee tacked on it. She knocked.

THE ADMINISTRATOR was more of an ass than the receptionist. But then, he was paid well for it. He explained they had strict policies about visitation. These were very sick and delicate people, his patients, and they had to protect them. And their doctors, who were the finest in their field, were very strict about who could see the patients. Visitation was allowed only on Saturdays and Sundays, and even then only a carefully selected group of people, usually just family and friends, could sit with the patients, and then only for thirty minutes. They had to be very strict.

These were fragile people, and they certainly could not withstand interrogation by a reporter, regardless of how grave the circumstances.

Mr. Grantham asked when Mr. Linney might be discharged. Absolutely confidential, the administrator exclaimed. Probably when the insurance expired, suggested Mr. Grantham, who was talking and stalling and halfway expecting to hear loud and angry voices coming from behind the double doors.

This mention of insurance really agitated the administrator. Mr. Grantham asked if he, the administrator, would ask Mr. Linney if he would answer two questions from

Mr. Grantham, and the whole thing would take less than thirty seconds.

Out of the question, snapped the administrator. They had strict policies.

A VOICE answered softly, and she stepped into the room. The carpet was thicker and the furniture was made from wood. He sat on the bed in a pair of jeans, no shirt, reading a thick novel. She was struck by his good looks.

"Excuse me," she said warmly as she closed the door behind her.

"Come in," he said with a soft smile. It was the first nonmedical face he'd seen in two days. What a beautiful face. He closed the book.

She walked to the end of the bed. "I'm Sara Jacobs, and I'm working on a story for the *Washington Post.*"

"How'd you get in?" he asked, obviously glad she was in.

"Just walked. Did you clerk last summer for White and Blazevich?"

"Yes, and the summer before. They offered me a job when I graduate. If I graduate."

She handed him the photo. "Do you recognize this man?"

He took it and smiled. "Yeah. His name is, uh, wait a minute. He works in the oil and gas section on the ninth floor. What's his name?"

Darby held her breath.

Linney closed his eyes hard and tried to think. He looked at the photo, and said, "Morgan. I think his name is Morgan. Yep."

"His last name is Morgan?"

"That's him. I can't remember his first name. It's something like Charles, but that's not it. I think it starts with a *C*."

"And you're certain he's in oil and gas?" Though she couldn't remember the exact number, she was certain there was more than one Morgan at White and Blazevich.

"Yeah."

"On the ninth floor?"

"Yeah. I worked in the bankruptcy section on the eighth floor, and oil and gas covers half of eight and all of nine."

He handed the photo back.

"When are you getting out?" she asked. It would be rude to run from the room.

"Next week, I hope. What's this guy done?"

"Nothing. We just need to talk to him."

She was backing away from the bed. "I have to run. Thanks. And good luck."

"Yeah. No problem."

She quietly closed the door behind her, and scooted toward the lobby. The voice came from behind her.

"Hey! You! What're you doing?"

Darby turned and faced a tall, black security guard with a gun on his hip. She looked completely guilty.

"What're you doing?" he demanded again as he backed her into the wall.

"Visiting my brother," she said. "And don't yell at me again."

"Who's your brother?"

She nodded at his door. "Room 22."

"You can't visit right now. This is off limits."

"It was important. I'm leaving, okay?"

The door to 22 opened, and Linney looked at them.

"This your sister?" the guard demanded.

Darby pleaded with her eyes.

"Yeah, leave her alone," Linney said. "She's leaving."

She exhaled and smiled at Linney. "Mom will be up this weekend."

"Good," Linney said softly.

The guard backed off, and Darby almost

ran to the double doors. Grantham was preaching to the administrator about the cost of health care. She walked quickly through the doors, into the lobby, and was almost to the front door when the administrator spoke to her.

"Miss! Oh, miss! Can I have your name?"

Darby was out the front door, headed for the car. Grantham shrugged at the administrator, and casually left the building. They jumped in, and sped away.

"Garcia's last name is Morgan. Linney recognized him immediately, but he had trouble with the name. First name starts with a *C*." She was digging through her notes from Martindale-Hubbell. "Said he works in oil and gas on the ninth floor."

Grantham was speeding away from Parklane. "Oil and gas!"

"That's what he said." She found it. "Curtis D. Morgan, oil and gas section, age twenty-nine. There's another Morgan in litigation, but he's a partner and, let's see, he's fifty-one."

"Garcia is Curtis Morgan," Gray said with relief. He looked at his watch. "It's a quarter till four. We'll have to hurry."

"I can't wait."

□ □ □ □

RUPERT PICKED THEM UP as they turned out of Parklane's driveway. The rented Pontiac was flying all over the street. He drove like an idiot just to keep up, then radioed ahead.

THIRTY ~ SEVEN

MATTHEW BARR had never experienced a speedboat before, and after five hours of a bone-jarring voyage through the ocean he was soaked and in pain. His body was numb, and when he saw land he said a prayer, the first in decades. Then he resumed his nonstop cursing of Fletcher Coal.

They docked at a small marina near a city that he believed to be Freeport. The captain had said something about Freeport to the man known as Larry when they left Florida. No other word was spoken during the ordeal. Larry's role in the journey was uncertain. He was at least six-six, with a neck as thick as a utility pole, and he did nothing but watch Barr, which was okay at first but after five hours became quite a nuisance.

They stood awkwardly when the boat stopped. Larry was the first one out, and he motioned for Barr to join him. Another large man was approaching on the pier, and together they escorted Barr to a waiting van. The van was suspiciously short of windows.

At this point, Barr preferred to say goodbye to his new pals, and simply disappear in the direction of Freeport. He'd catch a plane to D.C., and slap Coal the moment he saw his shining forehead. But he had to be cool. They wouldn't dare hurt him.

The van stopped moments later at a small airstrip, and Barr was escorted to a black Lear. He admired it briefly before following Larry up the steps. He was cool and relaxed; just another job. After all, he was at one time one of the best CIA agents in Europe. He was an ex-Marine. He could take care of himself.

He sat by himself in the cabin. The windows were covered, and this annoyed him. But he understood. Mr. Mattiece treasured his privacy, and Barr could certainly respect that. Larry and the other heavyweight were at the front of the cabin, flipping through magazines and completely ignoring him.

Thirty minutes after takeoff, the Lear began its descent, and Larry lumbered toward him.

"Put this on," he demanded as he handed over a thick, cloth blindfold. At this point, a rookie would panic. An amateur would start asking questions. But Barr had been blindfolded before, and while he was having serious doubts about this mission, he calmly took the blindfold and covered his eyes.

THE MAN who removed the blindfold introduced himself as Emil, an assistant to Mr. Mattiece. He was a small, wiry type with dark hair and a thin mustache winding around the lip. He sat in a chair four feet away and lit a cigarette.

"Our people tell us you are legitimate, sort of," he said with a friendly smile. Barr looked around the room. There were no walls, only windows in small panes. The sun was bright and pierced his eyes. A plush garden surrounded a series of fountains and pools outside the room. They were in the rear of a very large house.

"I'm here on behalf of the President," Barr said.

"We believe you." Emil nodded. He was undoubtedly a Cajun.

"May I ask who you are?" Barr said.

"I'm Emil, and that's enough. Mr. Mattiece is not feeling well. Perhaps you should leave your message with me."

"I have orders to speak directly to him."

"Orders from Mr. Coal, I believe." Emil never stopped smiling.

"That's correct."

"I see. Mr. Mattiece prefers not to meet you. He wants you to talk to me."

Barr shook his head. Now, if push came to shove, if things got out of hand, then he would gladly talk to Emil if it was necessary. But for now, he would hold firm.

"I am not authorized to talk to anyone but Mr. Mattiece," Barr said properly.

The smile almost disappeared. Emil pointed beyond the pools and fountains to a large gazebo-shaped building with tall windows from floor to ceiling. Rows of perfectly manicured shrubs and flowers surrounded it. "Mr. Mattiece is in his gazebo. Follow me."

They left the sun room and walked slowly around a wading pool. Barr had a thick knot in his stomach, but he followed his little friend as if this was simply another day at the office. The sound of falling water echoed through the garden. A narrow boardwalk led to the gazebo. They stopped at the door.

"I'm afraid you must remove your shoes," Emil said with a smile. Emil was barefoot. Barr untied his shoes and placed them next to the door.

"Do not step on the towels," Emil said gravely.

The towels?

Emil opened the door for Barr, who stepped in alone. The room was perfectly round, about fifty feet in diameter. There were three chairs and a sofa, all covered with white sheets. Thick cotton towels were on the floor in perfect little trails around the room. The sun shone brightly through skylights. A door opened, and Victor Mattiece emerged from a small room.

Barr froze and gawked at the man. He was thin and gaunt, with long gray hair and a dirty beard. He wore only a pair of white gym shorts, and walked carefully on the towels without looking at Barr.

"Sit over there," he said, pointing at a chair. "Don't step on the towels."

Barr avoided the towels and took his seat. Mattiece turned his back and faced the windows. His skin was leathery and dark bronze. His bare feet were lined with ugly veins. His toenails were long and yellow. He was crazy as hell.

"What do you want?" he asked quietly to the windows.

"The President sent me."

"He did not. Fletcher Coal sent you. I doubt if the President knows you're here."

Maybe he wasn't crazy. He spoke without moving a muscle in his body.

"Fletcher Coal is the President's chief of staff. He sent me."

"I know about Coal. And I know about you. And I know about your little Unit. Now, what do you want?"

"Information."

"Don't play games with me. What do you want?"

"Have you read the pelican brief?" Barr asked.

The frail body did not flinch. "Have you read it?"

"Yes," Barr answered quickly.

"Do you believe it to be truc?"

"Perhaps. That's why I'm here."

"Why is Mr. Coal so concerned about the pelican brief?"

"Because a couple of reporters have

wind of it. And if it's true, then we need to know immediately."

"Who are these reporters?"

"Gray Grantham with the *Washington Post*. He picked it up first, and he knows more than anyone. He's digging hard. Coal thinks he's about to run something."

"We can take care of him, can't we?" Mattiece said to the windows. "Who's the other one?"

"Rifkin with the *Times*."

Mattiece still had not moved an inch. Barr glanced around at the sheets and towels. Yes, he had to be crazy. The place was sanitized and smelled of rubbing alcohol. Maybe he was ill.

"Does Mr. Coal believe it to be true?"

"I don't know. He's very concerned about it. That's why I'm here, Mr. Mattiece. We have to know."

"What if it's true?"

"Then we have problems."

Mattiece finally moved. He shifted his weight to the right leg, and folded his arms across his narrow chest. But his eyes never moved. Sand dunes and sea oats were in the distance, but not the ocean.

"Do you know what I think?" he said quietly.

"What?"

"I think Coal is the problem. He gave the brief to too many people. He handed it to the CIA. He allowed you to see it. This really disturbs me."

Barr could think of no response. It was ludicrous to imply that Coal wanted to distribute the brief. The problem is you, Mattiece. You killed the justices. You panicked and killed Callahan. You're the greedy bastard who was not content with a mere fifty million.

Mattiece turned slowly and looked at Barr. The eyes were dark and red. He looked nothing like the photo with the Vice President, but that was seven years ago. He'd aged twenty years in the last seven, and perhaps gone off the deep end along the way.

"You clowns in Washington are to blame for this," he said, somewhat louder.

Barr could not look at him. "Is it true, Mr. Mattiece? That's all I want to know."

Behind Barr, a door opened without a sound. Larry, in his socks and avoiding the towels, eased forward two steps and stopped.

Mattiece walked on the towels to a glass door, and opened it. He looked outside and spoke softly. "Of course it's true." He walked through the door, and closed it slowly behind him. Barr watched as the idiot shuffled along a sidewalk toward the sand dunes.

What now? he thought. Perhaps Emil would come get him. Perhaps.

Larry inched forward with a rope, and Barr did not hear or feel anything until it was too late. Mattiece did not want blood in his gazebo, so Larry simply broke the neck and choked him until it was over.

THIRTY-EIGHT

THE GAME PLAN called for her to be on this elevator at this point in the search, but she thought enough unexpected events had occurred to warrant a change in the game plan. He thought not. They had engaged in a healthy debate over this elevator ride, and here she was. He was right; this was the quickest route to Curtis Morgan. And she was right; it was a dangerous route to Curtis Morgan. But the other routes could be just as dangerous. The entire game plan was deadly.

She wore her only dress and her only pair of heels. Gray said she looked really nice, but that was to be expected. The elevator stopped on the ninth floor, and when she walked off it there was a pain in her stomach and she could barely breathe.

The receptionist was across a plush

lobby. The name WHITE AND BLAZEVICH covered the wall behind her in thick, brass let-
tering. Her knees were weak, but she made
it to the receptionist, who smiled properly.
It was ten minutes before five.

"May I help you?" she asked. The name-
plate proclaimed her to be Peggy Young.

"Yes," Darby managed, clearing her
throat. "I have a five o'clock appointment
with Curtis Morgan. My name is Dorothy
Blythe."

The receptionist was stunned. Her
mouth fell open, and she stared blankly at
Darby, now Dorothy. She couldn't speak.

Darby's heart stopped. "Is something the
matter?"

"Well, no. I'm sorry. Just a moment."
Peggy Young stood quickly, and disappeared in a rush.

Run! Her heart pounded like a drum.
Run! She tried to control her breathing,
but she was battling hyperventilation. Her
legs were rubbery. Run!

She looked around, trying to be nonchalant as if she was just another client waiting
on her lawyer. Surely they wouldn't gun
her down here in the lobby of a law office.

He came first, followed by the receptionist. He was about fifty with bushy gray hair

and a terrible scowl. "Hi," he said, but only because he had to. "I'm Jarreld Schwabe, a partner here. You say you have an appointment with Curtis Morgan."

Keep it up. "Yes. At five. Is there a problem?"

"And your name is Dorothy Blythe?"

Yeah, but you can call me Dot. "That's what I said. Yes. What's the matter?" She sounded genuinely irritated.

He was inching closer. "When did you make the appointment?"

"I don't know. About two weeks ago. I met Curtis at a party in Georgetown. He told me he was an oil and gas lawyer, and I happen to need one. I called the office here, and made an appointment. Now, will you please tell me what's going on?" She was amazed at how well these words were coming from her dry mouth.

"Why do you need an oil and gas lawyer?"

"I don't think I have to explain myself to you," she said, real bitchy-like.

The elevator opened, and a man in a cheap suit approached quickly to join the conversation. Darby scowled at him. Her legs would give way just any second.

Schwabe was really bearing down. "We

don't have any record of such an appointment."

"Then fire the appointment secretary. Do you welcome all new clients this way?" Oh, she was indignant, but Schwabe did not let up.

"You can't see Curtis Morgan," he said.

"And why not?" she demanded.

"He's dead."

The knees were jelly and about to go. A sharp pain rippled through the stomach. But, she thought quickly, it was okay to looked shocked. He was, after all, supposed to be her new lawyer.

"I'm sorry. Why didn't anyone call me?"

Schwabe was still suspicious. "As I said, we have no record of a Dorothy Blythe."

"What happened to him?" she asked, stunned.

"He was mugged a week ago. Shot by street punks, we believe."

The guy in the cheap suit took a step closer. "Do you have any identification?"

"Who in the hell are you?" she snapped loudly.

"He's security," said Schwabe.

"Security for what?" she demanded, even louder. "Is this a law firm or a prison?"

The partner looked at the man in the cheap suit, and it was obvious neither knew exactly what to do at this point. She was very attractive, and they had upset her, and her story was somewhat believable. They relaxed a little.

"Why don't you leave, Ms. Blythe?" Schwabe said.

"I can't wait!"

The security man reached to assist her. "Here," he said.

She slapped his hand. "Touch me and I'll sue your ass first thing tomorrow morning. Get away from me!"

This shook them a bit. She was mad and lashing out. Perhaps they were being a bit hard.

"I'll see you down," the security man said.

"I know how to leave. I'm amazed you clowns have any clients." She was stepping backward. Her face was red, but not from anger. It was fear. "I've got lawyers in four states, and I've never been treated like this," she yelled at them. She was in the center of the lobby. "I paid a half a million last year in legal fees, and I've got a million to pay next year, but you idiots won't get any of it." The closer she got to the elevator, the louder she yelled. She was a crazy woman. They watched her until the elevator door opened and she was gone.

GRAY PACED along the end of the bed, holding the phone and waiting for Smith Keen. Darby was stretched out on the bed with her eyes closed.

Gray stopped. "Hello, Smith. I need you to check something quick."

"Where are you?" Keen asked.

"A hotel. Look back six or seven days. I need the obituary for Curtis D. Morgan."

"Who's he?"

"Garcia."

"Garcia! What happened to Garcia?"

"He died, obviously. Shot by muggers."

"I remember that. We ran a story last week about a young lawyer who was robbed and shot."

"Probably him. Can you check it for me? I need his wife's name and address if we have it."

"How'd you find him?"

"It's a long story. We'll try to talk to his widow tonight."

"Garcia's dead. This is weird, baby."

"It's more than weird. The kid knew something, and they knocked him off."

"Do you think you're safe?"

"Who knows?"

"Where's the girl?"

"She's with me."

"What if they're watching his house?"

Gray hadn't thought about it. "We'll have to take that chance. I'll call you back in fifteen minutes."

He placed the phone on the floor and sat in an antique rocker. There was a warm beer on the table, and he took a long drink. He watched her. A forearm covered both eyes. She was in jeans and a sweatshirt. The dress was thrown in a corner. The heels had been kicked across the room.

"You okay?" he asked softly.

"Wonderful."

She was a real smartass, and he liked that in a woman. Of course, she was almost a lawyer, and they must teach smartassness in law school. He sipped the beer and admired the jeans. He enjoyed this brief moment of uninterrupted staring without getting caught.

"Are you staring at me?" she asked.

"Yes."

"Sex is the last thing on my mind."

"Then why'd you mention it?"

"Because I can feel you lusting after my red toenails."

"True."

"I've got a headache. A real, genuine, pounding headache."

"You've worked for it. Can I get you something?"

"Yes. A one-way ticket to Jamaica."

"You can leave tonight. I'll take you to the airport right now."

She removed the forearm from her eyes and gently massaged both temples. "I'm sorry I cried."

He finished the beer with a long drink. "You earned the right." She was in tears when she stepped off the elevator. He was waiting like an expectant father, except he had a .38 in his coat pocket—a .38 she knew nothing about.

"So what do you think of investigative reporting?" he asked.

"I'd rather butcher hogs."

"Well, in all honesty, not every day is this eventful. Some days I simply sit at my desk and make hundreds of phone calls to bureaucrats who have no comment."

"Sounds great. Let's do that tomorrow."

He kicked his shoes off and placed his feet on the bed. She closed her eyes and breathed deeply. Minutes passed without a word.

"Do you know that Louisiana is known as the Pelican State?" she asked with her eyes closed.

"No. I didn't know that."

"It's a shame really, because the brown pelicans were virtually wiped out the the early 1960s."

"What happened to them?"

"Pesticides. They eat nothing but fish, and the fish live in river water filled with chlorinated hydrocarbons from pesticides. The rains wash the pesticides from the soil into small streams which eventually empty into rivers which eventually empty into the Mississippi. By the time the pelicans in Louisiana eat the fish, they are loaded with DDT and other chemicals which accumulate in the fatty tissues of the birds. Death is seldom immediate, but in times of stress such as hunger or bad weather, the pelicans and eagles and cormorants are forced to draw upon their reserves, and can literally be poisoned by their own fat. If they don't die, they are usually unable to reproduce. Their eggs are so thin and fragile they crack during incubation. Did you know that?"

"Why would I know that?"

"In the late sixties, Louisiana began transplanting brown pelicans from southern Florida, and over the years the population has slowly increased. But the birds are still very much in danger. Forty years ago there were thousands of them. The cypress swamp that Mattiece wants to destroy is home to only a few dozen pelicans."

Gray pondered these things. She was silent for a long time.

"What day is it?" she asked without opening her eyes.

"Monday."

"I left New Orleans a week ago today. Thomas and Verheek had dinner two weeks ago today. That, of course, was the fateful moment when the pelican brief changed hands."

"Three weeks ago tomorrow, Rosenberg and Jensen were murdered."

"I was an innocent little law student minding my own business and having a wonderful love affair with my professor. I guess those days are gone."

Law school and the professor might be gone, he thought. "What're your plans?"

"I have none. I'm just trying to get out of this damned mess and stay alive. I'll run off somewhere and hide for a few months, maybe a few years. I've got enough money to live for a long time. If and when I reach the point when I'm not looking over my shoulder, I might come back."

"To law school?"

"I don't think so. The law has lost its allure."

"Why'd you want to be a lawyer?"

"Idealism, and money. I thought I could change the world and get paid for it."

"But there are so damned many lawyers already. Why do all these bright students keep flocking to law school?"

"Simple. It's greed. They want BMWs and gold credit cards. If you go to a good law school, finish in the top ten percent, and get a job with a big firm, you'll be earning six figures in a few short years, and it only goes up. It's guaranteed. At the age of thirty-five, you'll be a partner raking in at least two hundred thousand a year. Some earn much more."

"What about the other ninety percent?"

"It's not such a good deal for them. They get the leftovers."

"Most lawyers I know hate it. They'd rather be doing something else."

"But they can't leave it because of the

money. Even a lousy lawyer in a small office can earn a hundred thousand a year after ten years of practice, and he may hate it, but where can he go and match the money?"

"I detest lawyers."

"And I guess you think reporters are adored."

Good point. Gray looked at his watch, then picked up the phone. He dialed Keen's number. Keen read him the obit, and the *Post* story about the senseless street killing of this young lawyer. Gray took notes.

"A couple of other things," Keen said. "Feldman is very concerned about your safety. He expected a briefing in his office today, and he was pissed when he didn't get one. Make sure you report to him before noon tomorrow. Understand?"

"I'll try."

"Do more than try, Gray. We're very nervous over here."

"The *Times* is sucking wind, isn't it?"

"I'm not worried about the *Times* right now. I'm much more concerned about you and the girl."

"We're fine. Everything's lovely. What else have you got?"

"You have three messages in the past two hours from a man named Cleve. Says he's a cop. Do you know him?"

"Yes."

"Well, he wants to talk tonight. Says it's urgent."

"I'll call him later."

"Okay. You guys be careful. We'll be here till late, so check in."

Gray hung up and looked at his notes. It was almost seven. "I'm going to see Mrs. Morgan. I want you to stay here."

She sat between the pillows and crossed her arms on her knees. "I'd rather go."

"What if they're watching the house?" he asked.

"Why would they watch the house? He's dead."

"Maybe they're suspicious now, because a mysterious client appeared today looking for him. Even though he's dead, he's attracting attention."

She thought about this for a minute. "No. I'm going."

"It's too risky, Darby."

"Don't talk to me about risks. I've survived in the minefields for twelve days. This is easy."

528

He waited on her by the door. "By the way, where am I staying tonight?"

"Jefferson Hotel."

"Do you have the phone number?"

"What do you think?"

"Dumb question."

THE PRIVATE JET with Edwin Sneller aboard landed at National in Washington a few minutes after seven. He was delighted to leave New York. He'd spent six days there bouncing off the walls in his suite at the Plaza. For almost a week, his men had checked hotels and watched airports and walked streets, and they knew damned well they were wasting their time, but orders were orders. They were told to stay there until something broke and they could move on. It was silly trying to find the girl in Manhattan, but they had to stay close in case she made a mistake like a phone call or a plastic transaction that could be traced, and suddenly they were needed.

She made no mistakes until two-thirty this afternoon when she needed money and went to the account. They knew this would happen, especially if she planned to leave the country and was afraid to use plastic. At some point, she would need cash, and she'd have to wire it since the bank was in New Orleans and she wasn't. Sneller's client owned eight percent of the bank; not a lot, but a nice little twelve-million-dollar holding that could make things happen. A few minutes after three, he'd received a call from Freeport.

They did not suspect her to be in Washington. She was a smart girl who was running away from trouble, not to it. And they certainly didn't expect her to link up with the reporter. They had no idea, but now it seemed so logical. And it was worse than critical.

Fifteen thousand went from her account to his, and suddenly Sneller was back in business. He had two men with him. Another private jet was en route from Miami. He had asked for a dozen men immediately. It would be a quick job, or no job at all. There was not a second to spare.

Sneller was not hopeful. With Khamel on the team, everything seemed possible. He had killed Rosenberg and Jensen so cleanly, then disappeared without a trace. Now he was dead, shot in the head because of one little innocent female law student.

□ □ □ □

THE MORGAN HOUSE was in a neat sub-
urb in Alexandria. The neighborhood was
young and affluent, with bikes and tricycles
in every yard.

Three cars were parked in the drive.
One had Ohio plates. Gray rang the door-
bell and watched the street. Nothing suspicious.

An older man opened the door slightly.
"Yes," he said softly.

"I'm Gray Grantham with the *Washington
Post,* and this is my assistant, Sara Jacobs."
Darby forced a smile. "We would like to
speak with Mrs. Morgan."

"I don't think so."

"Please. It's very important."

He looked at them carefully. "Wait a
minute." He closed the door and disappeared.

The house had a narrow wooden porch
with a small veranda over it. They were in
the darkness and could not be seen from
the street. A car passed slowly.

He opened the door again. "I'm Tom
Kupcheck, her father, and she doesn't want
to talk."

Gray nodded as if this was understandable. "We won't be five minutes. I promise."

He walked onto the porch and closed the door behind him. "I guess you're hard of hearing. I said she doesn't want to talk."

"I heard you, Mr. Kupcheck. And I respect her privacy, and I know what she's been through."

"Since when do you guys respect anyone's privacy?"

Evidently, Mr. Kupcheck had a short fuse. It was about to blow.

Gray kept calm. Darby backed away. She'd been involved in enough altercations for one day.

"Her husband called me three times before he died. I talked to him on the phone, and I don't believe his death was a random killing by street punks."

"He's dead. My daughter is upset. She doesn't want to talk. Now get the hell out of here."

"Mr. Kupcheck," Darby said warmly. "We have reason to believe your son-in-law was a witness to some highly organized criminal activity."

This calmed him a bit, and he glared at Darby. "Is that so? Well, you can't ask him about it, can you? My daughter knows nothing. She's had a bad day and she's on medication. Now leave."

"Can we see her tomorrow?" Darby asked.

"I doubt it. Call first."

Gray handed him a business card. "If she wants to talk, use the number on the back. I'm staying at a hotel. I'll call around noon tomorrow."

"You do that. For now, just leave. You've already upset her."

"We're sorry," Gray said, as they walked off the porch. Mr. Kupcheck opened the door but watched them as they left. Gray stopped, and turned to him. "Has any other reporter called or stopped by?"

"A bunch of them called the day after he was killed. They wanted all sorts of stuff. Rude people."

"But none in the past few days?"

"No. Now leave."

"Any from the *New York Times?*"

"No." He stepped inside and slammed the door.

They hurried to the car parked four doors down. There was no traffic on the street. Gray zigzagged through the short suburban streets, and crisscrossed his way out of the neighborhood. He watched the mirror until he was convinced they were not being followed.

"End of Garcia," Darby said as they entered 395 and headed for the city.

"Not yet. We'll make one final, dying gasp tomorrow, and maybe she'll talk to us."

"If she knew something, her father would know. And if her father knew, why wouldn't he cooperate? There's nothing there, Gray."

This made perfect sense. They rode in silence for a few minutes. Fatigue was setting in.

"We can be at the airport in fifteen minutes," he said. "I'll drop you off, and you can be out of here in thirty minutes. Take a plane anywhere, just vanish."

"I'll leave tomorrow. I need some rest, and I want to think about where to go. Thanks."

"Do you feel safe?"

"At this moment, yes. But it's subject to change in seconds."

"I'll be glad to sleep in your room tonight. Just like in New York."

"You didn't sleep in my room in New York. You slept on a sofa in the sitting room." She was smiling, and this was a good sign.

He was smiling too. "Okay. I'll sleep in the sitting room tonight."

"I don't have a sitting room."

"Well, well. Then where can I sleep?"

Suddenly, she was not smiling. She bit her lip and her eyes watered. He had pushed too far. It was Callahan again.

"I'm just not ready," she said.

"When might you be ready?"

"Gray, please. Just leave it alone."

She watched the traffic ahead and said nothing. "I'm sorry," he said.

Slowly, she lay down in the seat and placed her head in his lap. He gently rubbed her shoulder, and she clutched his hand. "I'm scared to death," she said quietly.

THIRTY-NINE

HE HAD LEFT HER ROOM around ten, after a bottle of wine and egg rolls. He had called Mason Paypur, the night police reporter for the *Post,* and asked him to check with his sources about the Morgan street killing. It had happened downtown in an area not noted for killings; just a few muggings and beatings.

He was tired and discouraged. And he was unhappy because she would leave tomorrow. The *Post* owed him six weeks of vacation, and he was tempted to leave with her. Mattiece could have his oil. But he was afraid he'd never come back, which wouldn't be the end of his world except for the troublesome fact that she had money and he didn't. They could skip along the beaches and frolic in the sun for about two months on his money, then it would be up to her. And, more importantly, she hadn't invited him to join in her getaway. She was grieving. When she mentioned Thomas Callahan, he could feel the pain.

He was now at the Jefferson Hotel on Sixteenth, pursuant, of course, to her instructions. He called Cleve at home.

"Where are you?" Cleve asked, irritated.

"A hotel. It's a long story. What's up?"

"They put Sarge on medical leave for ninety days."

"What's wrong with him?"

"Nothing. He says they want him out of the place for a while. It's like a bunker over there. Everybody's been told to shut up and speak to no one. They're scared to death. They made Sarge leave at noon today. He thinks you could be in serious danger. He's heard your name a thousand times in the past week. They're obsessed with you and how much you know."

"Who's they?"

"Coal, of course, and his aide Birchfield. They run the West Wing like the Gestapo. Sometimes they include, what's his name, the little squirrel with the bow tie? Domestic affairs?"

"Emmitt Waycross."

"That's him. It's mainly Coal and Birchfield making the threats and plotting strategy."

"What kind of threats?"

"No one in the White House, except for the President, can talk to the press on the record or off without Coal's approval. This includes the press secretary. Coal clears everything."

"That's incredible."

"They're terrified. And Sarge thinks they're dangerous."

"Okay. I'm hiding."

"I stopped by your apartment late last night. I wish you'd tell me when you disappear."

"I'll check in tomorrow night."

"What're you driving?"

"A rented Pontiac with four doors. Very sporty."

"I checked the Volvo this afternoon. It's fine."

"Thanks, Cleve."

"You okay?"

"I think so. Tell Sarge I'm fine."

"Call me tomorrow. I'm worried."

HE SLEPT FOUR HOURS and was awake when the phone rang. It was dark outside, and would remain that way for at least two hours. He stared at the phone, and picked it up on the fifth ring.

"Hello," he said suspiciously.

"Is this Gray Grantham?" It was a very timid female.

"Yes. Who is this?"

"Beverly Morgan. You stopped by last night."

Gray was on his feet, listening hard, wide awake. "Yes. I'm sorry if we upset you."

"No. My father is very protective. And angry. The reporters were awful after Curtis was killed. They called from everywhere. They wanted old pictures of him and new photos of me and the child. They called at all hours. It was terrible, and my father got tired of it. He pushed two of them off the porch."

"I guess we were lucky."

"I hope he didn't offend you." The voice was hollow and detached, yet trying to be strong.

"Not at all."

"He's asleep now, downstairs on the sofa. So we can talk."

"Why aren't you asleep?" he asked.

"I'm taking some pills to make me sleep, and I'm all out of sync. I've been sleeping days and rambling nights." It was obvious she was awake and wanted to talk.

Gray sat on the bed and tried to relax. "I can't imagine the shock of something like this."

"It takes several days for it to become real. At first, the pain is horrible. Just horrible. I couldn't move my body without hurting. I couldn't think because of the shock and disbelief. I went through the motions to get through the funeral, which now seems like a bad dream. Is this boring?"

"Not at all."

"I've got to get off these pills. I sleep so much I don't get to talk to adults. Plus, my father tends to run people off. Are you taping this?"

"No. I'm just listening."

"He was killed a week ago tonight. I thought he was working very late, which was not unusual. They shot him and took his wallet, so the cops couldn't identify him. I saw on the late news where a young lawyer had been murdered downtown, and I knew it was Curtis. Don't ask me how they knew he was a lawyer without knowing his name. It's strange, all the little weird things that go with a murder."

"Why was he working late?"

"He worked eighty hours a week, sometimes more. White and Blazevich is a sweatshop. They try to kill the associates for seven years, and if they can't kill them they make them partners. Curtis hated the place. He was tired of being a lawyer."

"How long was he there?"

"Five years. He was making ninety thousand a year, so he put up with the hassle."

"Did you know he called me?"

"No. My father told me you said that, and I've thought about it all night. What did he say?"

"He never identified himself. He used the code name of Garcia. Don't ask how I learned his identity—it'll take hours. He said he possibly knew something about the assassinations of Justices Rosenberg and Jensen, and he wanted to tell me what he knew."

"Randy Garcia was his best friend in elementary school."

"I got the impression he had seen something at the office, and perhaps someone at the office knew he had seen it. He was very nervous, and always called from pay phones. He thought he was being followed. We had planned to meet early Saturday before last, but he called that morning and said no. He was scared, and said he had to protect his family. Did you know any of this?"

"No. I knew he was under a great deal of stress, but he'd been that way for five years. He never brought the office home with him. He hated the place, really."

"Why'd he hate the place?"

"He worked for a bunch of cutthroats, a bunch of thugs who'd watch you bleed for a buck. They spend tons of money on this marvelous facade of respectability, but they are scum. Curtis was a top student and had his pick of jobs. They were such a great bunch of guys when they recruited him, and complete monsters to work with. Very unethical."

"Why did he stay with the firm?"

"The money kept getting better. He almost left a year ago, but the job offer fell through. He was very unhappy, but he tried to keep it to himself. I think he felt guilty for making such a big mistake. We had a little routine around here. When he came home, I would ask him how his day went. Sometimes this was at ten at night, so I knew it was a bad day. But he always said the day had been profitable; that was the word, profitable. And then we talked about our baby. He didn't want to talk about the office, and I didn't want to hear it."

Well, so much for Garcia. He's dead, and he told his wife nothing. "Who cleaned out his desk?"

"Someone at the office. They brought his stuff Friday, all neatly packaged and taped in three cardboard boxes. You're welcome to go through it."

"No, thanks. I'm sure it's been sanitized. How much life insurance did he have?"

She paused for a second. "You're a smart man, Mr. Grantham. Two weeks ago, he bought a million-dollar term policy with double indemnity for accidental death."

"That's two million dollars."

"Yes sir. I guess you're right. I guess he was suspicious."

"I don't think he was killed by muggers, Mrs. Morgan."

"I can't believe this." She choked a little, but fought it off.

"Have the cops asked you a lot of questions?"

"No. It's just another D.C. mugging that went one step further. No big deal. Happens every day."

The insurance bit was interesting, but

useless. Gray was getting tired of Mrs. Morgan and her unhurried monotone. He was sorry for her, but if she knew nothing, it was time to say good-bye.

"What do you think he knew?" she asked.

This could take hours. "I don't know," Gray answered, glancing at his watch. "He said he knew something about the killings, but that's as far as he would go. I was convinced we would meet somewhere and he would spill his guts and show me something. I was wrong."

"How would he know anything about those dead judges?"

"I don't know. He just called me out of the blue."

"If he had something to show you, what would it be?" she asked.

He was the reporter. He was supposed to ask the questions. "I have no idea. He never hinted."

"Where would he hide such a thing?" The question was sincere, but irritating. Then it hit him. She was going somewhere with this.

"I don't know. Where did he keep his valuable papers?"

"We have a lockbox at the bank for deeds

and wills and stuff. I've always known about the lockbox. He handled all the legal business, Mr. Grantham. I looked at the lockbox last Thursday with my father, and there was nothing unusual in it."

"You didn't expect anything unusual, did you?"

"No. Then Saturday morning, early, it was still dark, I was going through his papers in his desk in the bedroom. We have this antique rolltop desk that he used for his personal correspondence and papers, and I found something a bit unusual."

Gray was on his feet, holding the phone, and staring wildly at the floor. She had called at four in the morning. She had chitchatted for twenty minutes. And she waited until he was ready to hang up to drop the bomb.

"What is it?" he asked as coolly as possible.

"It's a key."

He had a lump in his throat. "A key to what?"

"Another lockbox."

"Which bank?"

"First Columbia. We've never banked there."

"I see. And you knew nothing about this other lockbox?"

"Oh no. Not until Saturday morning. I was puzzled by it, still am, but I found all of our legal papers in the old lockbox, so I had no reason to check this one. I figured I'd run by when I felt like it."

"Would you like me to check it for you?"

"I thought you would say that. What if you find what you're looking for?"

"I don't know what I'm looking for. But what if I find something he left behind, and this something proves to be very, let's say, newsworthy?"

"Use it."

"No conditions?"

"One. If it disparages my husband in any way, you can't use it."

"It's a deal. I swear."

"When do you want the key?"

"Do you have it in your hand?"

"Yes."

"If you'll stand on the front porch, I'll be there in about three seconds."

THE PRIVATE JET from Miami had brought only five men, so Edwin Sneller had only seven to plan with. Seven men, no time, and precious little equipment. He had not slept Monday night. His hotel suite was a mini–command center as they stared at maps through the night, and tried to plan the next twenty-four hours. A few things were certain. Grantham had an apartment, but he was not there. He had a car he was not using. He worked at the *Post,* and it was on Fifteenth Street. White and Blazevich was in a building on Tenth near New York, but she would not return there. Morgan's widow lived in Alexandria. Beyond that, they were searching for two people out of three million.

These were not the type of men you could rustle out of the bunkhouse and send in to fight. They had to be found and hired, and he'd been promised as many as possible by the end of the day.

Sneller was no novice at the killing game, and this was hopeless. This was desperation. The sky was falling. He would do his best under the circumstances, but Edwin Sneller had one foot out the back door.

She was on his mind. She had met Khamel on his terms, and walked away from it. She had dodged bullets and bombs, and evaded the best in the business. He would love to see her, not to kill her, but to congratulate her. A rookie running loose and living to tell about it.

They would concentrate on the *Post* building. It was the one spot he had to come back to.

FORTY

THE DOWNTOWN TRAFFIC was bumper to bumper, and that suited Darby just fine. She was in no hurry. The bank lobby opened at nine-thirty, and some time around seven, over coffee and untouched bagels in her room, he had convinced her that she should be the one to visit the vault. She was not really convinced, but a woman should do it, and there weren't many available. Beverly Morgan told Gray that her bank, First Hamilton, froze their box as soon as they learned of Curtis's death, and that she was allowed only to view the contents and make an inventory. She was also allowed to copy the will, but the original was placed back in the box and secured in the vault. The box would be released only after the tax auditors finished their work.

549

So the immediate question was whether or not First Columbia knew he was dead. The Morgans had never banked there. Beverly had no idea why he chose it. It was a huge bank with a million customers, and they decided that the odds were against it.

Darby was tired of playing the odds. She'd blown a wonderful opportunity last night to get on a plane, and now here she was about to be Beverly Morgan matching wits with First Columbia so she could steal from a dead man. And what was her sidekick going to do? He was going to protect her. He had this gun, which scared her to death and had the same effect on him though he wouldn't admit it, and he planned to play bodyguard by the front door while she pilfered the lockbox.

"What if they know he's dead," she asked, "and I tell them he isn't?"

"Then slap the bitch in the face and run like hell. I'll catch you at the front door. I've got a gun, and we'll blast our way down the sidewalk."

"Come on, Gray. I don't know if I can do this."

"You can do it, okay? Play it cool. Be assertive. Be a smartass. It should come natural."

"Thanks so much. What if they call security on me? I have this sudden phobia of security guards."

"I'll rescue you. I'll come blazing through the lobby like a SWAT team."

"We'll all be killed."

"Relax, Darby. It'll work."

"Why are you so chipper?"

"I smell it. Something's in that lockbox, Darby. And you have to bring it out, kid. It's all riding on you."

"Thanks for easing the pressure."

They were on E Street near Ninth. Gray slowed the car, then parked illegally in a loading zone forty feet from the front entrance of First Columbia. He jumped out. Darby's exit was slower. Together, they walked quickly to the door. It was almost ten. "I'll wait here," he said, pointing to a marble column. "Go do it."

"Go do it," she mumbled as she disappeared inside the revolving door. She was always the one being fed to the lions. The lobby was as big as a football field, with columns and chandeliers and fake Persian rugs.

"Safe deposit boxes?" she asked a young woman behind the information desk. The girl pointed to a corner in the far right.

"Thanks," she said, and strolled toward it. The lines in front of the tellers were four deep to her left, and to her right a hundred busy vice presidents talked on their phones. It was the largest bank in the city, and no one noticed her.

The vault was behind a set of massive bronze doors that were polished enough to appear almost golden, no doubt to give the appearance of infinite safety and invulnerability. The doors were opened slightly to allow a select few in and out. To the left, an important-looking lady of sixty sat behind a desk with the words SAFE DEPOSIT BOXES across its front. Her name was Virginia Baskin.

Virginia Baskin stared at Darby as she approached the desk. There was no smile.

"I need access to a box," Darby said without breathing. She hadn't breathed in the last two and a half minutes.

"The number, please," Ms. Baskin said as she hit the keyboard and turned to the monitor.

"F566."

She punched the number and waited for the words to flash on the screen. She frowned, and moved her face to within inches of it. Run! Darby thought. She frowned harder and scratched her chin. Run, before she picks up the phone and calls the guards. Run, before the alarms go off and my idiot cohort comes blazing through the lobby.

Ms. Baskin withdrew her head from the monitor. "That was rented just two weeks ago," she said almost to herself.

"Yes," Darby said as if she had rented it.

"I assume you're Mrs. Morgan," she said, pecking on the keyboard.

Keep assuming, baby. "Yes, Beverly Anne Morgan."

"And your address?"

"891 Pembroke, Alexandria."

She nodded at the screen as if it could see her and give its approval. She pecked again. "Phone number?"

"703-664-5980."

Ms. Baskin liked this too. So did the computer. "Who rented this box?"

"My husband, Curtis D. Morgan."

"And his social security number?"

Darby casually opened her new, rather large leather shoulder bag, and pulled out her wallet. How many wives memorized their husband's social security number? She opened the wallet. "510-96-8686."

"Very well," Ms. Baskin said properly as

she left the keyboard and reached into her desk. "How long will this take?"

"Just a minute."

She placed a wide card on a small clipboard on the desk, and pointed at it. "Sign here, Mrs. Morgan."

Darby nervously signed on the second slot. Mr. Morgan had made the first entry the day he rented the box.

Ms. Baskin glanced at the signature while Darby held her breath.

"Do you have your key?" she asked.

"Of course," Darby said with a warm smile.

Ms. Baskin took a small box from the drawer, and walked around the desk. "Follow me." They went through the bronze doors. The vault was as big as a branch bank in the suburbs. Designed along the lines of a mausoleum, it was a maze of hallways and small chambers. Two men in uniform walked by. They passed four identical rooms with walls lined with rows of lockboxes. The fifth room held F566, evidently, because Ms. Baskin stepped into it and opened her little black box. Darby looked nervously around and behind her.

Virginia was all business. She walked to F566, which was shoulder-high, and stuck in the key. She rolled her eyes at Darby as if to say, "Your turn, dumbass." Darby yanked the key from a pocket, and inserted it next to the other one. Virginia then turned both keys, and slid the box two inches from its slot. She removed the bank's key.

She pointed to a small booth with a folding wooden door. "Take it in there. When you finish, lock it back in place and come to my desk." She was leaving the room as she spoke.

"Thanks," Darby said. She waited until Virginia was out of sight, then slid the box from the wall. It was not heavy. The front was six inches by twelve, and it was a foot and a half long. The top was open, and inside were two items: a thin, brown legal-sized envelope, and an unmarked video-tape.

She didn't need the booth. She stuffed the envelope and videotape in her shoulder bag, and slid the box back into its slot. She left the room.

Virginia had rounded the corner of her desk when Darby walked behind her. "I'm finished," she said.

"My, that was quick."

Damned right. Things happen fast when

your nerves are popping through your skin. "I found what I needed," she said.

"Very well." Ms. Baskin was suddenly a warm person. "You know, that awful story in the paper last week about that lawyer. You know, the one killed by muggers not far from here. Wasn't his name Curtis Morgan? Seems like it was Curtis Morgan. What a shame."

Oh, you dumb woman. "I didn't see that," Darby said. "I've been out of the country. Thanks."

Her step was a bit quicker the second time through the lobby. The bank was crowded, and there were no security guards in sight. Piece of cake. It was about time she pulled a job without being grabbed.

The gunman was guarding the marble column. The revolving door spun her onto the sidewalk, and she was almost to the car before he caught her. "Get in the car!" she demanded.

"What'd you find!" he demanded.

"Just get outta here." She yanked the door open, and jumped in. He started the car and sped away.

"Talk to me," he said.

"I cleaned out the box," she said. "Is anyone behind us?"

He glanced in the mirror. "How the hell do I know? What is it?"

She opened her purse and pulled out the envelope. She opened it. Gray slammed on the brakes and almost smashed a car in front.

"Watch where you're going!" she yelled.

"Okay! Okay. What's in the envelope!"

"I don't know! I haven't read it yet, and if you get me killed, I'll never read it."

The car was moving again. Gray breathed deeply. "Look, let's stop yelling, okay. Let's be cool."

"Yes. You drive, and I'll be cool."

"Okay. Now. Are we cool?"

"Yes. Just relax. And watch where you're going. Where are you going?"

"I don't know. What's in the envelope?"

She pulled out a document of some sort. She glanced at him, and he was staring at the document. "Watch where we're going."

"Just read the damned thing."

"It makes me carsick. I can't read in the car."

"Dammit! Dammit! Dammit!"

"You're yelling again."

He yanked the wheel to the right and

pulled into another tow-away zone on E Street. Horns honked as he slammed his brakes. He glared at her.

"Thanks," she said, and started reading it aloud.

It was a four-page affidavit, typed real neat and sworn to under oath before a notary public. It was dated Friday, the day before the last phone call to Grantham. Under oath, Curtis Morgan said he worked in the oil and gas section of White and Blazevich, and had since he joined the firm five years earlier. His clients were privately owned oil exploration firms from many countries, but primarily Americans. Since he joined the firm, he had worked for a client who was engaged in a huge lawsuit in south Louisiana. The client was a man named Victor Mattiece, and Mr. Mattiece, whom he'd never met but was well known to the senior partners of White and Blazevich, wanted desperately to win the lawsuit and eventually harvest millions of barrels of oil from the swamplands of Terrebonne Parish, Louisiana. There were also hundreds of millions of cubic yards of natural gas. The partner supervising the case for White and Blazevich was F. Sims Wakefield, who was very close to Victor Mattiece and often visited him in the Bahamas.

They sat in the tow-away zone with the bumper of the Pontiac protruding perilously into the right lane, and were oblivious to the cars swerving around it. She read slowly, and he sat with his eyes closed.

Continuing, the lawsuit was very important to White and Blazevich. The firm was not directly involved in the trial and appeal, but everything crossed Wakefield's desk. He worked on nothing but the pelican case, as it was known. He spent most of his time on the phone with either Mattiece or one of a hundred lawyers working on the case. Morgan averaged ten hours a week on the case, but always on the periphery. His billings were handed directly to Wakefield, and this was unusual because all other billings went to the oil and gas billing clerk, who turned them in to accounting. He'd heard rumors over the years, and firmly believed Mattiece was not paying White and Blazevich its standard hourly rate. He believed the firm had taken the case for a percentage of the harvest. He'd heard the figure of ten percent of the net profits from the wells. This was unheard of in the industry.

Brakes squealed loudly, and they braced for the impact. It barely missed. "We're about to be killed," Darby snapped.

Gray yanked the gearshift into Drive, and pulled the right front wheel over the curb and onto the sidewalk. Now they were out of traffic. The car was angled across a forbidden space with its front bumper on the sidewalk and its rear bumper barely out of traffic. "Keep reading," he snapped back.

Continuing, on or about September 28, Morgan was in Wakefield's office. He walked in with two files and a stack of documents unrelated to the pelican case. Wakefield was on the phone. As usual, secretaries were in and out. The office was always in a state of disruption. He stood around for a few minutes waiting for Wakefield to get off the phone, but the conversation dragged on. Finally, after waiting fifteen minutes, Morgan picked up his files and documents from Wakefield's cluttered desk, and left. He went to his office at the other end of the building, and started working at his desk. It was about two in the afternoon. As he reached for a file, he found a handwritten memo on the bottom of the stack of documents he had just brought to his office. He had inadvertently taken it from Wakefield's desk. He immediately stood, with the intention of returning to Wakefield. Then he read it. And he read it again. He glanced at the telephone. Wakefield's line was still busy. A copy of the memo was attached to the affidavit.

"Read the memo," Gray snapped.

"I'm not through with the affidavit," she snapped back. It would do no good to argue with her. She was the legal mind, and this was a legal document, and she would read it exactly as she pleased.

Continuing, he was stunned by the memo. And he was immediately terrified of it. He walked out of his office and down the hall to the nearest Xerox, and copied it. He returned to his office, and placed the original memo in the same position under the files on his desk. He would swear he'd never seen it.

The memo was two paragraphs handwritten on White and Blazevich internal stationery. It was from M. Velmano, who is Marty Velmano, a senior partner. It was dated September 28, directed to Wakefield, and read:

Sims:

Advise client, research is complete—and the bench will sit much softer if Rosenberg is retired. The second retirement is a bit unusual. Einstein found a link to Jensen, of all people. The boy, of course, has those other problems.

Advise further that the pelican should arrive here in four years, assuming other factors.

There was no signature.

Gray was chuckling and frowning at the same time. His mouth was open. She was reading faster.

Continuing, Marty Velmano was a ruthless shark who worked eighteen hours a day, and felt useless unless someone near him was bleeding. He was the heart and soul of White and Blazevich. To the power people of Washington, he was a tough operator with plenty of money. He lunched with congressmen, and played golf with cabinet members. He did his throat cutting behind his office door.

Einstein was the nickname for Nathaniel Jones, a demented legal genius the firm kept locked away in his own little library on the sixth floor. He read every case decided by the Supreme Court, the eleven federal appellate courts, and the supreme courts of the fifty states. Morgan had never met Einstein. Sightings were rare around the firm.

After he copied it, he folded his copy of the memo and placed it in a desk drawer. Ten minutes later, Wakefield stormed into his office, very disturbed and pale. They scratched around Morgan's desk, and found the memo. Wakefield was angry as hell, which was not unusual. He asked if Morgan had read this. No, he insisted. Evidently he mistakenly picked it up when he left his office, he explained. What's the big deal? Wakefield was furious. He lectured Morgan about the sanctity of one's desk. He was a blithering idiot, rebuking and expounding around Morgan's office. He finally realized he was overreacting. He tried to settle down, but the impression had been made. He left with the memo.

Morgan hid the copy in a law book in the library on the ninth floor. He was shocked at Wakefield's paranoia and hysterics. Before he left that afternoon, he precisely arranged the articles and papers in his desk and on his shelves. The next morning, he checked them. Someone had gone through his desk during the night.

Morgan became very careful. Two days later, he found a tiny screwdriver behind a book on his credenza. Then he found a small piece of black tape wadded up and dropped in his trash can. He assumed his office was wired and his phones were bugged. He caught suspicious looks from Wakefield. He saw Velmano in Wakefield's office more than usual.

Then Justices Rosenberg and Jensen were killed. There was no doubt in his mind it was the work of Mattiece and his associates. The memo did not mention Mattiece, but it referred to a "client." Wakefield had no other clients. And no one client had as much to gain from a new Court as Mattiece.

The last paragraph of the affidavit was frightening. On two occasions after the assassinations, Morgan knew he was being followed. He was taken off the pelican case. He was given more work, more hours, more demands. He was afraid of being killed. If they would kill two justices, they would kill a lowly associate.

He signed it under oath before Emily Stanford, a notary public. Her address was typed under her name.

"Sit tight. I'll be right back," Gray said as he opened his door and jumped out. He dodged cars and dashed across E Street.

There was a pay phone outside a bakery. He punched Smith Keen's number and looked at his rented car parked haphazardly across the street.

"Smith, it's Gray. Listen carefully and do as I say. I've got another source on the pelican brief. It's big, Smith, and I need you and Krauthammer in Feldman's office in fifteen minutes."

"What is it?"

"Garcia left a farewell message. We have one more stop, and we're coming in."

"We? The girl's coming in?"

"Yes. Get a TV with a VCR in the conference room. I think Garcia wants to talk to us."

"He left a tape?"

"Yes. Fifteen minutes."

"Are you safe?"

"I think so. I'm just nervous as hell, Smith." He hung up and ran back to the car.

MS. STANFORD owned a court reporting service on Vermont. She was dusting the bookshelves when Gray and Darby walked in. They were in a hurry.

"Are you Emily Stanford?" he asked.

"Yes. Why?"

He showed her the last page of the affidavit. "Did you notarize this?"

"Who are you?"

"Gray Grantham with the *Washington Post*. Is this your signature?"

"Yes. I notarized it."

Darby handed her the photograph of Garcia, now Morgan, on the sidewalk. "Is this the man who signed the affidavit?" she asked.

"This is Curtis Morgan. Yes. That's him."

"Thank you," Gray said.

"He's dead, isn't he?" Ms. Stanford asked. "I saw it in the paper."

"Yes, he's dead," Gray said. "Did you by chance read this affidavit?"

"Oh no. I just witnessed his signature. But I knew something was wrong."

"Thank you, Ms. Stanford." They left as fast as they'd come.

THE THIN MAN hid his shiny forehead under a ragged fedora. His pants were rags and his shoes were torn, and he sat in his ancient wheelchair in front of the *Post* and held a sign proclaiming him to be HUNGRY AND HOMELESS. He rolled his head from shoulder to shoulder as if the muscles in his neck had collapsed from hunger. A paper bowl with a few dollars and coins was in his lap, but it was his money. Maybe he could do better if he was blind.

He looked pitiful, sitting there like a vegetable, rolling his head, wearing green Kermit the Frog sunglasses. He watched every move on the street.

He saw the car fly around the corner and park illegally. The man and the woman jumped out, and ran toward him. He had a gun under the ragged quilt, but they were moving too fast. And there were too many people on the sidewalk. They entered the *Post* building.

He waited a minute, then rolled himself away.

FORTY-ONE

SMITH KEEN was pacing and fidgeting in front of Feldman's office door as the secretary looked on. He saw them weaving hurriedly down the aisle between the rows of desks. Gray was leading and holding her hand. She was definitely attractive, but he would appreciate it later. They were breathless.

"Smith Keen, this is Darby Shaw," Gray said between breaths.

They shook hands. "Hello," she said, looking around at the sprawling newsroom.

"My pleasure, Darby. From what I hear, you are a remarkable woman."

"Right," Grantham said. "We can chit-chat later."

"Follow me," Keen said, and they were off again. "Feldman wanted to use the con-

568

ference room." They cut across the cluttered newsroom, and walked into a plush room with a long table in the center of it. It was full of men who were talking but immediately shut up when she walked in. Feldman closed the door.

He reached for her hand. "I'm Jackson Feldman, executive editor. You must be Darby."

"Who else?" Gray said, still breathing hard.

Feldman ignored him and looked around the table. He pointed. "This is Howard Krauthammer, managing editor; Ernie DeBasio, assistant managing editor/foreign; Elliot Cohen, assistant managing editor/national; and Vince Litsky, our attorney."

She nodded politely and forgot each name as she heard it. They were all at least fifty, all in shirtsleeves, all deeply concerned. She could feel the tension.

"Give me the tape," Gray said.

She took it from her bag and handed it to him. The television and VCR were at the end of the room on a portable stand. He pushed the tape into the VCR. "We got this twenty minutes ago, so we haven't seen it."

Darby sat in a chair against the wall. The

men inched toward the screen and waited for an image.

On a black screen was the date—October 12. Then Curtis Morgan was sitting at a table in a kitchen. He held a switch that evidently worked the camera.

"My name is Curtis Morgan, and since you're watching this, I'm probably dead." It was a helluva first sentence. The men grimaced and inched closer.

"Today is October 12, and I'm doing this at my house. I'm alone. My wife is at the doctor. I should be at work, but I called in sick. My wife knows nothing about any of this. I've told no one. Since you're watching this, you've also seen this. *[He holds up the affidavit.]* This is an affidavit I've signed, and I plan to leave it with this video, probably in a safe deposit box in a bank downtown. I'll read the affidavit, and discuss other things."

"We've got the affidavit," Gray said quickly. He was standing against the wall next to Darby. No one looked at him. They were glued to the screen. Morgan slowly read the affidavit. His eyes darted from the pages to the camera, back and forth, back and forth.

It took him ten minutes. Each time

Darby heard the word *pelican,* she closed her eyes and slowly shook her head. It had all come down to this. It was a bad dream. She tried to listen.

When Morgan finished the affidavit, he laid it on the table, and looked at some notes on a legal pad. He was comfortable and relaxed. He was a handsome kid who looked younger than twenty-nine. He was at home, so there was no tie. Just a starched white button-down. White and Blazevich was not an ideal place to work, he said, but most of the four hundred lawyers were honest and probably knew nothing about Mattiece. In fact, he doubted if many besides Wakefield, Velmano, and Einstein were involved in the conspiracy. There was a partner named Jarreld Schwabe who was sinister enough to be involved, but Morgan had no proof. (Darby remembered him well.) There was an ex-secretary who'd quit abruptly a few days after the assassinations. Her name was Miriam LaRue, and she'd worked in the oil and gas section for eighteen years. She might know something. She lives in Falls Church. Another secretary whom he would not name had told him she overheard a conversation between Wakefield and Velmano, and the topic was whether he, Morgan, could be trusted. But she just heard bits and pieces. They treated him differently after the memo was found on his desk. Especially Schwabe and Wakefield. It was as if they wanted to throw him up against the wall and threaten his life if he told of the memo, but they couldn't do it because they weren't sure he'd seen it. And they were afraid to make a big deal out of it. But he'd seen it, and they were almost certain he'd seen it. And if they conspired to kill Rosenberg and Jensen, well, hell, he was just an associate. He could be replaced in seconds.

Litsky the lawyer shook his head in disbelief. The numbness was wearing off, and they moved a bit in their seats.

Morgan commuted by car, and twice he was trailed. Once during lunch, he saw a man watching him. He talked about his family for a while, and started to ramble. It was apparent he'd run out of hard news. Gray handed the affidavit and the memo to Feldman, who read it and passed it to Krauthammer, who passed it on.

Morgan finished with a chilling farewell: "I don't know who will see this tape. I'll be dead, so it won't really matter, I guess. I hope you use this to nail Mattiece and his sleazy lawyers. But if the sleazy lawyers are watching this tape, then you can all go straight to hell."

Gray ejected the tape. He rubbed his hands together and smiled at the group. "Well, gentlemen, did we bring you enough verification, or do you want more?"

"I know those guys," Litsky said, dazed. "Wakefield and I played tennis a year ago."

Feldman was up and walking. "How'd you find Morgan?"

"It's a long story," Gray said.

"Give me a real short version."

"We found a law student at Georgetown who clerked for White and Blazevich last summer. He identified a photograph of Morgan."

"How'd you get the photograph?" Litsky asked.

"Don't ask. It doesn't go with the story."

"I say run the story," Krauthammer said loudly.

"Run it," said Elliot Cohen.

"How'd you learn he was dead?" Feldman asked.

"Darby went to White and Blazevich yesterday. They broke the news."

"Where was the video and affidavit?"

"In a lockbox at First Columbia. Morgan's wife gave me the key at five this morning. I've done nothing wrong. The pelican brief has been verified fully by an independent source."

"Run it," said Ernie DeBasio. "Run it with the biggest headline since NIXON RESIGNS."

Feldman stopped near Smith Keen. The two friends eyed each other carefully. "Run it," said Keen.

He turned to the lawyer. "Vince?"

"There's no question, legally. But I'd like to see the story after it's written."

"How long will it take to write it?" the editor asked Gray.

"The brief portion is already outlined. I can finish it up in an hour or so. Give me two hours on Morgan. Three at the most."

Feldman hadn't smiled since he shook hands with Darby. He paced to the other side of the room, and stood in Gray's face. "What if this tape's a hoax?"

"Hoax? We're talking dead bodies, Jackson. I've seen the widow. She's a real, live widow. This paper ran the story of his murder. He's dead. Even his law firm says he's dead. And that's him on the tape, talking about dying. I know that's him. And we talked to the notary public who witnessed his signature on the affidavit. She identified him." Gray was getting louder and looking around the room. "Everything he said verifies the pelican brief. Everything. Mattiece, the lawsuit, the assassinations. Then we've got Darby, the author of the brief. And more dead bodies, and they've chased her all over the country. There are no holes, Jackson. It's a story."

He finally smiled. "It's more than a story. Have it written by two. It's eleven now. Use this conference room and close the door." Feldman was pacing again. "We'll meet here at exactly two and read the draft. Not a word."

The men stood and filed from the room, but not before each shook hands with Darby Shaw. They were uncertain whether to say congratulations or thanks or whatever, so they just smiled and shook her hand. She kept her seat.

When they were alone, Gray sat beside her and they held hands. The clean conference table was before them. The chairs were placed perfectly around it. The walls were white, and the room was lit by fluorescent lights and two narrow windows.

"How do you feel?" he asked.

"I don't know. This is the end of the road, I guess. We made it."

"You don't sound too happy."

"I've had better months. I'm happy for you."

He looked at her. "Why are you happy for me?"

"You put the pieces together and it hits tomorrow. It's got Pulitzer written all over it."

"I hadn't thought about that."

"Liar."

"Okay, maybe once. But when you got off the elevator yesterday and told me Garcia was dead, I quit thinking about Pulitzers."

"It's not fair. I do all the work. We used my brains and looks and legs, and you get all the glory."

"I'll be glad to use your name. I'll credit you as the author of the brief. We'll put your picture on the front page, along with Rosenberg, Jensen, Mattiece, the President, Verheek, and—"

"Thomas? Will his picture run with the story?"

"It's up to Feldman. He'll edit this one."

She thought about this, and said nothing.

"Well, Ms. Shaw, I've got three hours to write the biggest story of my career. A story that will shock the world. A story that could bring down a presidency. A story that will solve the assassinations. A story that will make me rich and famous."

"You'd better let me write it."

"Would you? I'm tired."

"Go get your notes. And some coffee."

THEY CLOSED THE DOOR and cleared the table. A news aide rolled in a PC with a printer. They sent him after a pot of coffee. Then some fruit. They outlined the story in sections, beginning with the assassinations, then the pelican case in south Louisiana, then Mattiece and his link to the President, then the pelican brief and all the havoc it created, Callahan, Verheek, then Curtis Morgan and his muggers, then White and Blazevich and Wakefield, Velmano, and Einstein. Darby preferred to write in longhand. She scaled down the litigation and the brief, and what was known of Mattiece. Gray took the rest, and typed out rough notes on the machine.

Darby was a model of organization, with

notes neatly arranged on the table, and words carefully written on paper. He was a whirlwind of chaos—papers on the floor, talking to the computer, printing random paragraphs that were discarded by the time they were on paper. She kept telling him to be quiet. This is not a law school library, he explained. This is a newspaper. You work with a phone in each ear and someone yelling at you.

At twelve-thirty, Smith Keen sent in food. Darby ate a cold sandwich and watched the traffic below. Gray was digging through campaign reports.

She saw him. He was leaning on the side of a building across Fifteenth Street, and he would not have been suspicious except he had been leaning on the side of the Madison Hotel an hour earlier. He was sipping something from a tall Styrofoam cup, and watching the front entrance to the *Post*. He wore a black cap, denim jacket, and jeans. He was under thirty. And he just stood there staring across the street. She nibbled on her sandwich, and watched him for ten minutes. He sipped from his cup and never moved.

"Gray, come here, please."

"What is it?" He walked over. She pointed to the man with the black cap.

"Watch him carefully," she said. "Tell me what he's doing."

"He's drinking something, probably coffee. He's leaning on the side of that building, and he's watching this building."

"What's he wearing?"

"Denim from head to toe, and a black cap. Looks like boots. What about it?"

"I saw him an hour ago standing over there by the hotel. He was sort of hidden by that telephone van, but I know it was him. Now he's over there."

"So?"

"So for the past hour, at least, he's been moving around doing nothing but watching this building."

Gray nodded. This was no time for a smart comment. The guy looked suspicious, and she was concerned. She'd been tracked for two weeks now, from New Orleans to New York, and now maybe to Washington, and she knew more about being followed than he did.

"What're you saying, Darby?"

"Give me one good reason why this man, who obviously is not a street bum, would be doing this."

The man looked at his watch, and walked slowly along the sidewalk until he was gone. Darby looked at her watch.

"It's exactly one," she said. "Let's check every fifteen minutes, okay?"

"Okay. I doubt if it's anything," he said, trying to be comforting. It didn't work. She sat at the table, and looked at the notes.

He watched her and slowly returned to the computer.

Gray typed furiously for fifteen minutes, then walked back to the window. Darby watched him carefully. "I don't see him," he said.

He did see him at one-thirty. "Darby," he said, pointing to the spot where she'd first seen him. She looked out the window, and slowly focused on the man with the black cap. Now he had a dark green windbreaker, and he was not facing the *Post*. He watched his boots, and every ten seconds or so glanced at the front entrance. This made him all the more suspicious, but he was partially hidden behind a delivery truck. The Styrofoam cup was gone. He lit a cigarette. He glanced at the *Post*, then watched the sidewalk in front of it.

"Why do I have this knot in my stomach?" Darby said.

"How could they follow you? It's impossible."

"They knew I was in New York. That seemed impossible at the time."

"Maybe they're following me. I've been told they were watching. That's what the guy's doing. Why should he know you're here? The dude's following me."

"Maybe," she said slowly.

"Have you seen him before?"

"They don't introduce themselves."

"Look. We've got thirty minutes, and they're back in here with knives to carve up our story. Let's finish it, then we can watch dude out there."

They returned to their work. At one forty-five, she stood in the window again, and the man was gone. The printer was rattling the first draft, and she began proofing.

THE EDITORS read with their pencils. Litsky the lawyer read for sheer pleasure. He seemed to enjoy it more than the others.

It was a long story, and Feldman was busy cutting like a surgeon. Smith Keen scribbled in the margins. Krauthammer liked what he saw.

They read slowly in silence. Gray proofed it again. Darby was at the window. Dude was back again, now wearing a navy blazer with the jeans. It was cloudy and in the sixties, and he was sipping from the cup. He huddled over it to stay warm. He took a drink, looked at the *Post,* looked at the street, and back to the cup. He was in front of a different building, and at exactly two-fifteen he began looking north along Fifteenth.

A car stopped on his side of the street. The rear door opened, and there he was. The car sped away, and he looked around. Limping ever so slightly, Stump walked casually to the man with the black cap. They spoke for seconds, then Stump walked south to the intersection of Fifteenth and L. Dude stayed in place.

She glanced around the room. They were immersed in the story. Stump was out of sight, so she couldn't show him to Gray, who was reading and smiling. No, they were not watching the reporter. They were waiting on the girl.

And they had to be desperate. They were standing on the street hoping somehow a miracle would happen and the girl would emerge from the building, and they could take her out. They were scared. She was inside spilling her guts and waving copies of that damned brief. Tomorrow morning the game would be over. Somehow they had to stop her. They had their orders.

She was in a room full of men, and suddenly she was not safe.

Feldman finished last. He slid his copy to Gray. "Minor stuff. Should take about an hour. Let's talk phone calls."

"Just three, I think," Gray said. "The White House, FBI, and White and Blazevich."

"You only named Sims Wakefield at the firm. Why?" asked Krauthammer.

"Morgan fingered him the most."

"But the memo is from Velmano. I think he should be named."

"I agree," said Smith Keen.

"Me too," said DeBasio.

"I wrote his name in," Feldman said. "We'll get Einstein later. Wait until four-thirty or five before you call the White House and White and Blazevich. If you do it sooner, they may go nuts and run to court."

"I agree," said Litsky the lawyer. "They can't stop it, but they can try. I'd wait until five before I called them."

"Okay," Gray said. "I'll have it reworked by three-thirty. Then I'll call the FBI for their comment. Then the White House, then White and Blazevich."

Feldman was almost out the door. "We'll meet again here at three-thirty. Stay close to your phones."

When the room was empty again, Darby locked the door and pointed to the window. "You've heard me mention Stump?"

"Don't tell me."

They scanned the street below.

"Afraid so. He met with our little friend, then disappeared. I know it was him."

"I guess I'm off the hook."

"I guess you are. I really want to get out of here."

"We'll think of something. I'll alert our security. You want me to tell Feldman?"

"No. Not yet."

"I know some cops."

"Great. And they can just walk up and beat the hell out of him."

"These cops'll do it."

"They can't bother these people. What are they doing wrong?"

"Just planning murder."

"How safe are we in this building?"

Gray thought a moment. "Let me tell

584

Feldman. We'll get two security guards posted by this door."

"Okay."

FELDMAN APPROVED the second draft at three-thirty, and Gray was given the green light to call the FBI. Four phones were brought to the conference room, and the recorder was plugged in. Feldman, Smith Keen, and Krauthammer listened on extensions.

Gray called Phil Norvell, a good acquaintance and sometime source, if there was such a thing within the Bureau. Norvell answered his own line.

"Phil, Gray Grantham with the *Post*."

"I think I know who you're with, Gray."

"I've got the recorder on."

"Must be serious. What's up?"

"We're running a story in the morning detailing a conspiracy in the assassinations of Rosenberg and Jensen. We're naming Victor Mattiece, an oil speculator, and two of his lawyers here in town. We also mention Verheek, not in the conspiracy, of course. We believe the FBI knew about Mattiece early on, but refused to investigate at the urging of the White House. We

wanted to give you guys a chance to comment."

There was no response on the other end.

"Phil, are you there?"

"Yes. I think so."

"Any comment?"

"I'm sure we will have a comment, but
I'll have to call you back."

"We're going to press soon, so you need
to hurry."

"Well, Gray, this is a shot in the ass.
Could you hold it a day?"

"No way."

Norvell paused. "Okay. Let me see Mr.
Voyles, and I'll call you back."

"Thanks."

"No, thank you, Gray. This is wonderful.
Mr. Voyles will be thrilled."

"We're waiting." Gray punched a button
and cleared the line. Keen turned off the
recorder.

They waited eight minutes, and Voyles
himself was on the line. He insisted on
speaking to Jackson Feldman. The recorder was back on.

"Mr. Voyles?" Feldman said warmly. The
two had met many times, so the "mister"
was unnecessary.

"Call me Denton, dammit. Look, Jackson, what's your boy got? This is crazy. You guys are jumping off a cliff. We've investigated Mattiece, still investigating him, and it's too early to move on him. Now, what's your boy got?"

"Does the name Darby Shaw mean anything?" Feldman grinned at her when he asked the question. She was standing against the wall.

Voyles was slow to respond. "Yes," he said simply.

"My boy has the pelican brief, Denton, and I'm sitting here looking at Darby Shaw."

"I was afraid she was dead."

"No. She's very much alive. She and Gray Grantham have confirmed from another source the facts set forth in the brief. It's a large story, Denton."

Voyles sighed deeply, and threw in the towel. "We are pursuing Mattiece as a suspect," he said.

"The recorder's on, Denton, be careful."

"Well, we need to talk. I mean, man to man. I may have some deep background for you."

"You're welcome to come here."

"I'll do that. I'll be there in twenty minutes."

The editors were terribly amused at the idea of the great F. Denton Voyles hopping in his limo and rushing to the *Post*. They had watched him for years, and knew he was a master at cutting his losses. He hated the press, and this willingness to talk on their turf and under their gun meant only one thing—he would point the finger at someone else. And the likely target was the White House.

Darby had no desire to meet the man. Her thoughts were on escape. She could point at the man in the black cap, but he'd been gone for thirty minutes now. And what could the FBI do? They had to catch him first, then what? Charge him with loitering and planning an ambush? Torture him and make him tell all? They probably wouldn't believe her.

She had no desire to deal with the FBI. She didn't want their protection. She was about to take a trip, and no one would know where to. Maybe Gray. Maybe not.

He punched the number for the White House, and they picked up the extensions. Keen turned on the recorder.

"Fletcher Coal, please. This is Gray Grantham with the *Washington Post,* and it's very urgent."

He waited. "Why Coal?" Keen asked.

"Everything has to be cleared through him," Gray said with his hand over the receiver.

"Says who?"

"Says a source."

The secretary returned with the message that Mr. Coal was on his way. Please hold. Gray was smiling. The adrenaline was pumping.

Finally, "Fletcher Coal."

"Yes, Mr. Coal. Gray Grantham at the *Post*. I am recording the conversation. Do you understand that?"

"Yes."

"Is it true you have issued a directive to all White House personnel, except the President, to the effect that all communications with the press must first be cleared by you?"

"Absolutely untrue. The press secretary handles those matters."

"I see. We're running a story in the morning which, in summary, verifies the facts set forth in the pelican brief. Are you familiar with the pelican brief?"

Slowly, "I am."

"We have confirmed that Mr. Mattiece contributed in excess of four million dollars to the President's campaign three years ago."

"Four million, two hundred thousand, all through legal channels."

"We also believe the White House intervened and attempted to obstruct the FBI investigation into Mr. Mattiece, and we wanted your comment, if any."

"Is this something you believe, or is it something you intend to print?"

"We are trying to confirm it now."

"And who do you think will confirm it for you?"

"We have sources, Mr. Coal."

"Indeed you do. The White House emphatically denies any involvement with this investigation. The President asked to be apprised as to the status of the entire investigation after the tragic deaths of Justices Rosenberg and Jensen, but there has been no direct or indirect involvement from the White House into any aspect of the investigation. You have received some bad information."

"Does the President consider Victor Mattiece a friend?"

"No. They met on one occasion, and as I stated, Mr. Mattiece was a significant contributor, but he is not a friend of the President."

"He was the largest contributor, though, wasn't he?"

"I cannot confirm that."

"Any other comment?"

"No. I'm sure the press secretary will address this in the morning."

They hung up and Keen turned off the recorder. Feldman was on his feet rubbing his hands together. "I'd give a year's pay to be in the White House right now," he said.

"He's cool, isn't he?" Gray said with admiration.

"Yeah, but his cool ass is now sitting deep in boiling water."

FORTY-TWO

FOR A MAN accustomed to throwing his weight around and watching everyone flinch, it was difficult to come humbly forward with hat in hand and ask for a break. He swaggered as humbly as he could through the newsroom with K. O. Lewis and two agents in tow. He wore his customary wrinkled trench coat with the belt tied tightly around the center of his short and dumpy physique. He was not striking, but his manner and walk left no doubt he was a man accustomed to getting his way. All dressed in dark coats, they resembled a Mafia don with bodyguards. The busy newsroom grew silent as they walked quickly through it. Though not striking, F. Denton Voyles was a presence, humble or not.

A small, tense group of editors huddled

in the short hallway outside Feldman's office. Howard Krauthammer knew Voyles, and met him as he approached. They shook hands and whispered. Feldman was on the phone to Mr. Ludwig, the publisher, who was in China. Smith Keen joined the conversation and shook hands with Voyles and Lewis. The two agents kept to themselves a few feet away.

Feldman opened his door, looked toward the newsroom, and saw Denton Voyles. He motioned for him to come in. K. O. Lewis followed. They exchanged routine pleasantries until Smith Keen closed the door and they took a seat.

"I take it you have solid confirmation of the pelican brief," Voyles said.

"We do," Feldman answered. "Why don't you and Mr. Lewis read a draft of the story? I think it will explain things. We're going to press in about an hour, and the reporter, Mr. Grantham, wants you to have the opportunity to comment."

"I appreciate that."

Feldman picked up a copy of the draft and handed it to Voyles, who took it gingerly. Lewis leaned over, and they immediately started reading. "We'll step outside," Feldman said. "Take your time." He and

Keen left the office, and closed the door.
The agents moved closer.

Feldman and Keen walked across the
newsroom to the conference door. Two
large security guards stood in the hall.
Gray and Darby were alone inside when
they entered.

"You need to call White and Blazevich,"
Feldman said.

"Waiting on you."

They picked up the extensions. Krauthammer was gone for the moment, and
Keen handed his phone to Darby. Gray
punched the numbers.

"Marty Velmano, please," Gray said.
"Yes, this is Gray Grantham with the *Washington Post,* and I need to speak to him. It's
very urgent."

"One moment, please," the secretary
said.

A moment passed, and another secretary
was on the phone. "Mr. Velmano's office."

Gray identified himself again, and asked
for her boss.

"He's in a meeting," she said.

"So am I," Gray said. "Go to the meeting, tell him who I am, and tell him his
picture will be on the front page of the *Post*
at midnight tonight."

"Well, yes sir."

Within seconds, Velmano said, "Yes, what's going on?"

Gray identified himself for the third time, and explained about the recorder.

"I understand," Velmano snapped.

"We're running a story in the morning about your client, Victor Mattiece, and his involvement in the assassinations of Justices Rosenberg and Jensen."

"Great! We'll sue your ass for the next twenty years. You're out in left field, buddy. We'll own the *Post*."

"Yes sir. Remember, I'm recording this."

"Record all you want! You'll be named as a defendant. This will be great! Victor Mattiece will own the *Washington Post!* This is fabulous!"

Gray shook his head in disbelief at Darby. The editors smiled at the floor. This was about to be very funny.

"Yes sir. Have you heard of the pelican brief? We have a copy."

Dead silence. Then a distant grunt, like the last gasp of a dying dog. Then more silence.

"Mr. Velmano. Are you there?"

"Yes."

"We also have a copy of a memo you sent

to Sims Wakefield, dated September 28, in which you suggest your client's position will be greatly improved if Rosenberg and Jensen are removed from the Court. We have a source that tells us this idea was researched by one called Einstein, who sits in a library on the sixth floor, I believe."

Silence.

Gray continued. "We have the story ready to run, but I wanted to give you the chance to comment. Would you care to comment, Mr. Velmano?"

"I have a headache."

"Okay. Anything else?"

"Will you run the memo word for word?"

"Yes."

"Will you run my picture?"

"Yes. It's an old one from a Senate hearing."

"You son of a bitch."

"Thank you. Anything else?"

"I notice you've waited until five o'clock. An hour earlier, and we could've run to court and stopped this damned thing."

"Yes sir. It was planned that way."

"You son of a bitch."

"Okay."

"You don't mind ruining people, do

you?" His voice trailed off, and he was almost pitiful. What a marvelous quote. Gray had mentioned the recorder twice, but Velmano was too shocked to remember it.

"No sir. Anything else?"

"Tell Jackson Feldman the lawsuit will be filed at nine in the morning, just as soon as the courthouse opens."

"I'll do that. Do you deny you wrote the memo?"

"Of course."

"Do you deny the existence of the memo?"

"It's a fabrication."

"There's no lawsuit, Mr. Velmano, and I think you know it."

Silence, then, "You son of a bitch."

The phones clicked, and they were listening to the dial tone. They smiled at each other in disbelief.

"Don't you want to be a journalist, Darby?" Smith Keen asked.

"Oh, this is fun," she said. "But I was almost mugged twice yesterday. No, thanks."

Feldman stood and pointed to the recorder. "I wouldn't use any of that."

"But I sort of liked the part about ruining lives. And what about the lawsuit threats?" Gray asked.

"You don't need it, Gray. The story takes up the entire front page now. Maybe later."

There was a knock at the door. It was Krauthammer. "Voyles wants to see you," he said to Feldman.

"Bring him in here."

Gray stood quickly and Darby walked to the window. The sun was fading and the shadows were falling. Traffic inched along the street. There was no sign of Stump and his band of confederates, but they were there, no doubt waiting on darkness, no doubt plotting one last effort to kill her, either for prevention or revenge. Gray said he had a plan to exit the building without gunfire after the deadline. He wasn't specific.

Voyles entered with K. O. Lewis. Feldman introduced them to Gray Grantham, and to Darby Shaw. Voyles walked to her, smiling and looking up. "So you're the one who started all this," he said in an attempt at admiration. It didn't work.

She instantly despised him. "I think it was Mattiece," she said coolly. He turned away and took off the trench coat.

"Can we sit?" he asked in general.

They sat around the table—Voyles, Lewis, Feldman, Keen, Grantham, and Krauthammer. Darby stood by the window.

"I have some comments for the record," Voyles announced, taking a sheet of paper from Lewis. Gray began taking notes.

"First, we received a copy of the pelican brief two weeks ago today, and submitted it to the White House on the same day. It was personally delivered by the deputy director, K. O. Lewis, to Mr. Fletcher Coal, who received it with our daily summary to the White House. Special agent Eric East was present during the meeting. We thought it raised enough questions to be pursued, but it was not pursued for six days, until Mr. Gavin Verheek, special counsel to the director, was found murdered in New Orleans. At that time, the FBI immediately began a full-scale investigation of Victor Mattiece. Over four hundred agents from twenty-seven offices have taken part in the investigation, logging over eleven thousand hours, interviewing over six hundred people, and going to five foreign countries. The investigation is continuing in full force at this time. We believe Victor Mattiece to

599

be the prime suspect in the assassinations of Justices Rosenberg and Jensen, and at this time we are attempting to locate him."

Voyles folded the paper and handed it back to Lewis.

"What will you do if you find Mattiece?" Grantham asked.

"Arrest him."

"Do you have a warrant?"

"We'll have one soon."

"Do you have any idea where he is?"

"Frankly, no. We've been trying to locate him for a week, with no success."

"Did the White House interfere with your investigation of Mattiece?"

"I'll discuss it off the record. Agreed?"

Gray looked at the executive editor. "Agreed," Feldman said.

Voyles stared at Feldman, then Keen, then Krauthammer, then Grantham. "We're off the record, right? You cannot use this under any circumstances. Do we understand this?"

They nodded and watched him carefully. Darby was watching too.

Voyles looked suspiciously at Lewis. "Twelve days ago, in the Oval Office, the President of the United States asked me to ignore Victor Mattiece as a suspect. In his words, he asked me to back off."

"Did he give a reason?" asked Grantham.

"The obvious. He said it would be very embarrassing and seriously damage his re-election efforts. He felt there was little merit to the pelican brief, and if it was investigated, then the press would learn of it, and he would suffer politically."

Krauthammer listened with his mouth open. Keen stared at the table. Feldman hung on every word.

"Are you certain?" Gray asked.

"I recorded the conversation. I have a tape, which I will not allow anyone to hear unless the President first denies this."

There was a long silence as they admired this mean little bastard and his tape recorder. A tape!

Feldman cleared his throat. "You just saw the story. There was a delay by the FBI from the time it had the brief until it began its investigation. This must be explained in the story."

"You have my statement. Nothing more."

"Who killed Gavin Verheek?" Gray asked.

"I will not talk about the specifics of the investigation."

"But do you know?"

"We have an idea. But that's all I'll say."

Gray glanced around the table. It was obvious Voyles had nothing else to say now, and everyone relaxed at the same time. The editors savored the moment.

Voyles loosened his tie, and almost smiled. "This is off the record, of course, but how did you guys find out about Morgan, the dead lawyer?"

"I will not discuss the specifics of the investigation," Gray said with a wicked grin. They all laughed.

"What do you do now?" Krauthammer asked Voyles.

"There'll be a grand jury by noon tomorrow. Quick indictments. We'll try to find Mattiece, but it'll be difficult. We have no idea where he is. He's spent most of the past five years in the Bahamas, but owns homes in Mexico, Panama, and Paraguay." Voyles glanced at Darby for the second time. She was leaning against the wall by the window, hearing it all.

"What time does the first edition come off the press?" Voyles asked.

"They roll off all night, starting at ten-thirty," said Keen.

"Which edition will this story run in?"

"Late City, a few minutes before midnight. It's the largest edition."

"Will it have Coal's picture on the front?"

Keen looked at Krauthammer, who looked at Feldman. "I guess it should. We'll quote you as saying the brief was personally delivered to Fletcher Coal, who we'll also quote as saying Mattiece gave the President four point two million. Yes, I think Mr. Coal should have his face on the front, along with everyone else."

"I think so too," Voyles said. "If I have a man here at midnight, can I pick up a few copies of it?"

"Certainly," Feldman said. "Why?"

"Because I want to personally deliver it to Coal. I want to knock on his door at midnight, see him in his pajamas, and flash the paper in his face. Then I want to tell him I'll be back with a grand jury subpoena, and shortly after that I'll be back with an indictment. And shortly after that, I'll be back with the handcuffs."

He said this with such pleasure it was frightening.

"I'm glad you don't carry a grudge," Gray said. Only Smith Keen thought it was funny.

"Do you think he'll be indicted?" Krauthammer asked innocently.

Voyles glanced at Darby again. "He'll take the fall for the President. He'd volunteer for a firing squad to save his boss."

Feldman checked his watch and pushed away from the table.

"Could I ask a favor?" Voyles asked.

"Certainly. What?"

"I'd like to spend a few minutes alone with Ms. Shaw. That is, if she doesn't mind."

Everyone looked at Darby, who shrugged her approval. The editors and K. O. Lewis stood in unison and filed out of the room. Darby took Gray's hand and asked him to stay. They sat opposite Voyles at the table.

"I wanted to talk in private," Voyles said, looking at Gray.

"He stays," she said. "It's off the record."

"Very well."

She beat him to the punch. "If you plan to interrogate me, I won't talk without an attorney present."

He was shaking his head. "Nothing like

that. I was just wondering what's next for you."

"Why should I tell you?"

"Because we can help."

"Who killed Gavin?"

Voyles hesitated. "Off the record."

"Off the record," said Gray.

"I'll tell you who we think killed him, but first tell me how much you talked to him before he died."

"We talked several times over the weekend. We were supposed to meet last Monday, and leave New Orleans."

"When did you last talk to him?"

"Sunday night."

"And where was he?"

"In his room at the Hilton."

Voyles breathed deeply, and looked at the ceiling. "And you discussed with him the meeting on Monday?"

"Yes."

"Had you met him before?"

"No."

"The man who killed him was the same man you were holding hands with when he lost his brains."

She was afraid to ask. Gray did it for her. "Who was that?"

"The great Khamel."

She choked and covered her eyes, and tried to say something. But it wouldn't work.

"This is rather confusing," Gray said, straining to be rational.

"Rather, yes. The man who killed Khamel is a contract operative hired independently by the CIA. He was on the scene when Callahan was killed, and I think he made contact with Darby."

"Rupert," she said quietly.

"That's not his real name, of course, but Rupert'll do. He's probably got twenty names. If it's who I think it is, he's a British chap who's very reliable."

"Do you have any idea how confusing this is?" she asked.

"I can imagine."

"Why was Rupert in New Orleans? Why was he following her?" Gray asked.

"It's a very long story, and I don't know all of it. I try to keep my distance from the CIA, believe me. I have enough to worry about. It goes back to Mattiece. A few years ago, he needed some money to move along his grand scheme. So he sold a piece of it to the Libyan government. I'm not sure if it was legal, but enter the CIA. Evidently they watched Mattiece and the Libyans with a great deal of interest, and when the litigation sprang up, the CIA monitored it. I don't think they suspected Mattiece in the Supreme Court killings, but Bob Gminski was handed a copy of your little brief just a few hours after we delivered a copy to the White House. Fletcher Coal gave it to him. I have no idea who Gminski told of the brief, but the wrong words hit the wrong ears, and twenty-four hours later, Mr. Callahan is dead. And you, my dear, were very lucky."

"Then why don't I feel lucky?" she said.

"That doesn't explain Rupert," Gray said.

"I don't know this for a fact, but I suspect Gminski immediately sent Rupert to follow Darby. I think the brief initially scared Gminski more than the rest of us. He probably sent Rupert to trail her, in part to watch, and in part to protect. Then the car exploded, and suddenly Mr. Mattiece just confirmed the brief. Why else would you kill Callahan and Darby? I have reason to believe there were dozens of CIA people in New Orleans hours after the car exploded."

"But why?" Gray asked.

"The brief had been legitimized, and

Mattiece was killing people. Most of his business is in New Orleans. And I think the CIA was very concerned about Darby. Lucky for her. They came through when it counted."

"If the CIA moved so fast, why didn't you?" she asked.

"Fair question. We didn't think that much of the brief, and we didn't know half as much as the CIA. I swear, it seemed like such a long shot, and we had a dozen other suspects. We underestimated it. Plain and simple. Plus, the President asked us to back off, and it was easy to do because I'd never heard of Mattiece. Had no reason to. Then my friend Gavin got himself killed, and I sent in the troops."

"Why would Coal give the brief to Gminski?" Gray asked.

"It scared him. And, truthfully, that's one reason we sent it over. Gminski is, well, he's Gminski, and he sometimes does things his way without regard for little obstacles like laws and such. Coal wanted the brief checked out, and he figured Gminski would do it quickly and quietly."

"So Gminski didn't level with Coal."

"He hates Coal, which is perfectly understandable. Gminski dealt with the President, and, no, he didn't level with him. It all happened so fast. Remember, Gminski, Coal, the President, and I first saw the brief just two weeks ago today. Gminski was probably waiting to tell the President some of the story, but just hadn't got the chance."

Darby pushed her chair away, and walked back to the window. It was dark now, and the traffic was still slow and heavy. It was nice to have these mysteries revealed to her, but they created more mysteries. She just wanted to leave. She was tired of running and being chased; tired of playing reporter with Gray; tired of wondering who did what and why; tired of the guilt for writing the damned thing; tired of buying a new toothbrush every three days. She longed for a small house on a deserted stretch of beach with no phones and no people, especially ones hiding behind vehicles and buildings. She wanted to sleep for three days without nightmares and without seeing shadows. It was time to go.

Gray watched her carefully. "She was followed to New York, then here," he said to Voyles. "Who is it?"

"Are you positive?" Voyles asked.

"They were on the street all day watching the building," Darby said, nodding to the window.

"We've watched them," Gray said. "They're out there."

Voyles seemed skeptical. "Have you seen them before?" he asked Darby.

"One of them. He watched Thomas' memorial service in New Orleans. He chased me through the French Quarter. He almost found me in Manhattan, and I saw him chatting with another fella about five hours ago. I know it's him."

"Who is it?" Gray asked Voyles again.

"I don't think CIA would chase you."

"Oh, he chased me."

"Do you see them now?"

"No. They disappeared two hours ago. But they're out there."

Voyles stood and stretched his thick arms. He walked slowly around the table, unwrapping a cigar. "Mind if I smoke?"

"Yes, I mind," she said without looking at him. He laid it on the table.

"We can help," he said.

"I don't want your help," she said to the window.

"What do you want?"

"I want to leave the country, but when I

610

do, I want to make damned sure no one follows. Not you, not them, not Rupert nor any of his pals."

"You'll have to come back and testify before the grand jury."

"Only if they can find me. I'm going to a place where subpoenas are frowned upon."

"What about the trial? You'll be needed at trial."

"That's at least a year from now. I'll think about it then."

Voyles placed the cigar in his mouth, but did not light it. He paced and analyzed better with one between his teeth. "I'll make you a deal."

"I'm not in the mood for deals." She was leaning against the wall now, looking at him and looking at Gray.

"It's a good one. I've got planes and helicopters and plenty of men who carry guns and are not the least bit afraid of those boys out there playing hide-and-seek. First, we'll get you out of the building, and no one will know it. Second, we'll put you on my plane and fly you anywhere you want. Third, you can disappear from there. You have my word we will not follow. But, and fourth, you allow me to contact you through Mr.

611

Grantham here if, and only if, it becomes urgently necessary."

She was looking at Gray as the offer was made, and it was obvious he liked the deal. She kept a poker face, but, damn, it sounded good. If she had trusted Gavin after the first phone call, he would be alive and she would never have held hands with Khamel. If she'd simply left New Orleans with him when he suggested, he would not have been murdered. She'd thought about this every five minutes for the past seven days.

This thing was bigger than she was. There comes a time when you give up and start trusting people. She didn't like this man, but for the past ten minutes he had been remarkably honest with her.

"Is it your plane and your pilots?"

"Yes."

"Where is it?"

"Andrews."

"Let's do it like this. I get on the plane, and it's headed for Denver. And no one is on it but me, Gray, and the pilots. And thirty minutes after we take off, I instruct the pilot to go to, let's say, Chicago. Can he do that?"

"He has to file a flight plan before he leaves."

"I know. But you're the director of the FBI, and you can pull some strings."

"Okay. What happens when you get to Chicago?"

"I get off the plane alone, and it returns to Andrews with Gray."

"And what do you do in Chicago?"

"I get lost in a busy airport, and catch the first flight out."

"That'll work, but you have my word we won't follow."

"I know. Forgive me for being so cautious."

"It's a deal. When do you wish to leave?"

She looked at Gray. "When?"

"It'll take me an hour to revise it again, and add Mr. Voyles' comments."

"An hour," she said to Voyles.

"I'll wait."

"Could we talk in private?" she said to Voyles while nodding at Gray.

"Certainly." He grabbed his trench coat, and stopped at the door. He smiled at her. "You're a helluva lady, Ms. Shaw. Your brains and guts are bringing down one of the sickest men in this country. I admire you. And I promise I'll always level with you."

He stuck the cigar in the middle of his chubby smile and left the room.

They watched the door close. "Do you think I'll be safe?" she asked.

"Yes. I think he's sincere. Plus, he has men with guns who can get you out of here. It's okay, Darby."

"You can leave with me, can't you?"

"Sure."

She walked to him and put her arms around his waist. He held her tightly, and closed his eyes.

AT SEVEN, the editors gathered around the table for the last time Tuesday night. They quickly read the section Gray added to include Voyles' comments. Feldman walked in late with an enormous smile.

"You will not believe this," he said. "I've had two phone calls. Ludwig called from China. The President found him there and begged him to hold the story for twenty-four hours. Ludwig said the man was near tears. Ludwig, being the gentleman, listened respectfully, and politely declined. The second call was from Judge Roland, an old friend of mine. Seems as though the boys at White and Blazevich called him away from the dinner table and requested permission to file an injunction tonight with an immediate hearing. Judge Roland listened quite disrespectfully, and impolitely declined."

"Let's run this baby!" Krauthammer yelled.

FORTY-THREE

THE TAKEOFF was smooth and the jet was headed due west, supposedly for Denver. It was adequate but not luxurious, but then it was owned by the taxpayers and held by a man who cared nothing for the finer things. No good whiskey, Gray determined as he opened the cabinets. Voyles was an abstainer, and at the moment this really irritated Gray since he was a guest and dying of thirst. He found two semichilled Sprites in the refrigerator, and handed one to Darby. She popped the top of the can.

The jet appeared to be level. The copilot appeared in the door of their cabin. He was polite and introduced himself.

"We were told that we would have a new destination shortly after takeoff."

"That's correct," Darby said.

"Fine. Uh, we'll need to know something in about ten minutes."

"Okay."

"Is there any liquor on this thing?" Gray asked.

"Sorry." The copilot smiled, and returned to the cockpit.

Darby and her long legs consumed most of the small sofa, but he was determined to join her. He lifted her feet and sat at the end of it. They were in his lap. Red toenails. He rubbed her ankles and thought only of this first major event—the holding of the feet. It was terribly intimate for him, but didn't seem to faze her. She was smiling a little now, unwinding. It was over.

"Were you scared?" he asked.

"Yes. And you?"

"Yes, but I felt safe. I mean, it's hard to feel vulnerable with six armed buddies using their bodies as shields. It's hard to feel watched in the rear of a van with no windows."

"Voyles loved it, didn't he?"

"He was like Napoleon, making plans and directing troops. It's a big moment for him. He'll take a shot in the morning, but it'll bounce off. The only person who can fire him is the President, and I'd say Voyles has control of him at the moment."

"And the murders are solved. He has to feel good about that."

"I think we've added ten years to his career. What have we done!"

"I think he's cute," Darby said. "I didn't like him at first, but he sort of grows on you. And he's human. When he mentioned Verheek, I saw a trace of water in his eyes."

"A real sweetheart. I'm sure Fletcher Coal will be delighted to see this cute little man in a few hours."

Her feet were long and thin. Perfect, really. He rubbed along the top of them, and felt like a sophomore moving up from the knee on the second date. They were pale, and needed sun, and he knew that in a few short days they would be brown with sand permanently stuck between the toes. He had not been invited to visit later, and this was disturbing. He had no idea where she was going, and this was intentional. He was not certain she knew her destination.

The foot play reminded her of Thomas. He'd get half drunk and smear polish around the nails. With the jet humming and shaking softly, he was suddenly many miles removed from her. He'd been dead for two weeks, but it seemed much longer. There'd been so many changes. It was better this way. If she was at Tulane, walking by his office, seeing his classroom, talking to the other professors, staring at his apartment from the street, it would be awfully painful. The little reminders are nice for the long run, but during the mourning they get in the way. She was a different person now, with a different life in a different place.

And a different man was rubbing her feet. He was an ass at first, cocky and abrasive, a typical reporter. But he was thawing rapidly, and under the jaded layer she was finding a warm man who obviously liked her very much.

"Tomorrow's a big day for you," she said.

He took a sip of straight Sprite. He would pay an outrageous sum of money for a ice-cold imported beer in a green bottle. "Big day," he said, admiring the toes. It would be more than a big day, but he felt the need to understate it. At this moment, she had his attention, not the chaos of tomorrow.

"What'll happen?" she asked.

"I'll probably go back to the office and

wait for it to hit. Smith Keen said he would be there all night. A lot of people will be in early. We'll gather in the conference room, and they'll bring more televisions. We'll spend the morning watching it break. It'll be great fun listening to the official White House response. White and Blazevich will say something. Who knows about Mattiece. Chief Runyan will have a comment. Voyles will be very visible. The lawyers will assemble grand juries. And the politicians will be delirious. They'll hold press conferences all day on Capitol Hill. It will be a rather significant news day. I hate you'll miss it."

She gave a little sarcastic snort. "What's your next story?"

"Probably Voyles and his tape. You have to anticipate a White House denial of any interference, and if the ink gets too hot for Voyles, he'll attack with a vengeance. I'd like to have the tape."

"And after that?"

"Depends on a lot of unknowns. After six o'clock in the morning, the competition gets much stiffer. There'll be a million rumors and a thousand stories, but every paper in the country will be wedging in."

"But you'll be the star," she said with admiration, not sarcasm.

"Yeah, I'll get my fifteen minutes."

The copilot knocked on the door and opened it. He looked at Darby.

"Atlanta," she said, and he closed the door.

"Why Atlanta?" Gray asked.

"You ever changed planes at Atlanta?"

"Sure."

"You ever got lost changing planes at Atlanta?"

"I think so."

"I rest my case. It's huge and wonderfully busy."

He emptied the can and set it on the floor. "Where to from there?" He knew he shouldn't ask because she hadn't volunteered. But he wanted to know.

"I'll catch a quick flight somewhere. I'll do my four-airports-in-one-night routine. It's probably unnecessary, but I'll feel safer. I'll eventually land somewhere in the Caribbean."

Somewhere in the Caribbean. That narrowed it to a thousand islands. Why was she so vague? Did she not trust him? He was sitting here playing with her feet and she wouldn't tell him where she was going.

"What do I tell Voyles?" he asked.

"I'll call you when I get there. Or I might drop you a line."

Great! They could be pen pals. He could send her his stories and she could send postcards from the beach.

"Will you hide from me?" he asked, looking at her.

"I don't know where I'm going, Gray. I won't know until I get there."

"But you'll call?"

"Eventually, yes. I promise."

BY 11 P.M., only five lawyers remained in the offices of White and Blazevich, and they were in Marty Velmano's on the tenth floor. Velmano, Sims Wakefield, Jarreld Schwabe, Nathaniel (Einstein) Jones, and a retired partner named Frank Cortz. Two bottles of Scotch sat on the edge of Velmano's desk. One was empty, the other almost there. Einstein sat alone in one corner, mumbling to himself. He had wild, curly gray hair and a pointed nose, and indeed looked crazy. Especially now. Sims Wakefield and Jarreld Schwabe sat in front of the desk with ties off and sleeves rolled up.

Cortz finished a phone chat with an aide

to Victor Mattiece. He handed the phone to Velmano, who placed it on the desk.

"That was Strider," Cortz reported. "They're in Cairo in the penthouse suite of some hotel. Mattiece will not talk to us. Strider says he's over the edge, acting very bizarre. He's locked himself in a room, and, needless to say, he ain't coming to this side of the ocean. Strider says they've told the boys with the guns to get out of town immediately. The chase is off. The fat lady is singing."

"So what're we supposed to do?" asked Wakefield.

"We're on our own," said Cortz. "Mattiece has washed his hands of us."

They spoke quietly and deliberately. The screaming ended hours ago. Wakefield blamed Velmano for the memo. Velmano blamed Cortz for bringing in a sleazy client like Mattiece in the first place. That was twelve years ago, Cortz screamed back, and we've enjoyed his fees ever since. Schwabe blamed Velmano and Wakefield for being so careless with the memo. They dragged Morgan through the mud again and again. It had to be him. Einstein sat in the corner and watched them. But that was all behind them now.

"Grantham mentioned only me and Sims," Velmano said. "The rest of you guys may be safe."

"Why don't you and Sims skip the country?" Schwabe said.

"I'll be in New York at 6 A.M." Velmano said. "Then to Europe for a month on the trains."

"I can't run," Wakefield said. "I've got a wife and six kids."

They'd heard him whine about his six kids for five hours now. As if they didn't have families. Velmano was divorced, and his two children were grown. They could handle it. And he could handle it. It was time to retire anyway. He had plenty of money stashed away, and he loved Europe, especially Spain, and so it was adios for him. He sort of pitied Wakefield, who was only forty-two and didn't have a lot of money. He earned well, but his wife was a spendthrift who had a penchant for babies. Wakefield was unbalanced at the moment.

"I don't know what I'll do," Wakefield said for the thirtieth time. "I just don't know."

Schwabe tried to be a bit helpful. "I think you should go home and tell your wife. I don't have one, but if I did I'd try to brace her for it."

"I can't do that," Wakefield said pitifully.

"Sure you can. You can tell her now, or wait six hours and she'll see your picture on the front page. You have to go tell her, Sims."

"I can't do that." He was almost in tears again.

Schwabe looked at Velmano and Cortz.

"What about my children?" he asked again. "My oldest son is thirteen." He rubbed his eyes.

"Come on, Sims. Get a grip," Cortz said.

Einstein stood and walked to the door. "I'll be at my place in Florida. Don't call unless it's urgent." He opened the door and slammed it behind him.

Wakefield stood weakly and started for the door.

"Where are you going, Sims?" asked Schwabe.

"To my office."

"What for?"

"I need to lie down. I'm okay."

"Let me drive you home," Schwabe said. They watched him carefully. He was opening the door.

"I'm fine," he said, and he sounded stronger. He closed it when he left.

"You think he's okay?" Schwabe asked Velmano. "He worries me."

"I wouldn't say he's okay," Velmano said. "We've all had better days. Why don't you go check on him in a few minutes?"

"I'll do that," Schwabe said.

Wakefield walked deliberately to the stairway and down one flight to the ninth floor. He picked up speed as he approached his office. He was crying when he locked the door behind him.

Do it quick! Forget the note. If you write it, you'll talk yourself out of it. There's a million in life insurance. He opened a desk drawer. Don't think about the kids. It would be the same if he died in a plane crash. He pulled the .38 from under a file. Do it quick! Don't look at their pictures on the wall.

Maybe they'll understand one day. He stuck it deep in his mouth, and pulled the trigger.

THE LIMO stopped abruptly in front of the two-story home in Dumbarton Oaks, in upper Georgetown. It blocked the street and that was fine because it was twenty minutes after midnight, and there was no traffic. Voyles and two agents jumped from the rear of the car, and walked quickly to the front door. Voyles held a newspaper. He banged the door with his fist.

Coal was not asleep. He was sitting in the dark in the den in his pajamas and bathrobe, so Voyles was quite pleased when he opened his door.

"Nice pajamas," Voyles said, admiring his pants.

Coal stepped onto the tiny concrete porch. The two agents were watching from the narrow sidewalk. "What the hell do you want?" he asked slowly.

"Just brought you this," Voyles said, sticking the paper in his face. "Gotta a nice picture of you right next to the President hugging Mattiece. I know how much you like newspapers, so I thought I'd bring you one."

"Your face'll be in it tomorrow," Coal said as if he'd already written the story.

Voyles threw the paper at his feet, and started walking off. "I got some tapes, Coal. You start lying, and I'll jerk your pants off in public."

Coal stared at him, but said nothing.

Voyles was near the street. "I'll be back

in two days with a grand jury subpoena," he yelled. "I'll come about two in the morning and serve it myself." He was at the car. "Next I'll bring an indictment. Of course, by then your ass'll be history and the President'll have a new bunch of idiots telling him what to do." He disappeared into the limo, and it sped away.

Coal picked up the paper, and went inside.

FORTY-FOUR

GRAY AND SMITH KEEN sat alone in the conference room, reading the words in print. He was many years beyond the excitement of seeing his stories on the front page, but this one brought a rush with it. There had been none bigger. The faces were lined neatly across the top: Mattiece hugging the President, Coal talking importantly on the phone in an official White House photo, Velmano sitting before a Senate subcommittee, Wakefield cropped from a bar convention picture, Verheek smiling at the camera in an FBI release, Callahan from the yearbook, and Morgan in a photo taken from the video. Mrs. Morgan had consented. Paypur, the night police reporter, had told them about Wakefield an hour earlier. Gray was depressed about it. But he wouldn't blame himself.

They began drifting in around 3 A.M. Krauthammer brought a dozen doughnuts, and promptly ate four of them while he admired the front page. Ernie DeBasio was next. Said he hadn't slept any. Feldman arrived fresh and hyper. By four-thirty, the room was full and four televisions were going. CNN got it first, and within minutes the networks were live from the White House, which had no comment at the moment but Zikman would say something at seven.

With the exception of Wakefield's death, there was nothing new initially. The networks bounced back and forth between the White House, the Supreme Court, and the news desks. They waited at the Hoover Building, which was very quiet at the moment. They flashed the photos from the papers. They couldn't find Velmano. They speculated about Mattiece. CNN showed live footage of the Morgan house in Alexandria, but Morgan's father-in-law kept the cameras off the property. NBC had a reporter standing in front of the building where White and Blazevich had offices, but he had nothing new. And though she wasn't quoted in the story, there was no secret about the identity of the author of the brief. There was much speculation about Darby Shaw.

At seven, the room was packed and silent. The four screens were identical as Zikman walked nervously to the podium in the White House press room. He was tired and haggard. He read a short statement in which the White House admitted receiving the campaign money from a number of channels controlled by Victor Mattiece, but he emphatically denied any of the money was dirty. The President had met Mr. Mattiece only once, and that was when he was the Vice President. He had not spoken to the man since being elected President, and certainly did not consider him a friend, in spite of the money. The campaign had received over fifty million, and the President handled none of it. He had a committee for that. No one in the White House had attempted to interfere with the investigation of Victor Mattiece as a suspect, and any allegations to the contrary were flat wrong. Based on their limited knowledge, Mr. Mattiece no longer lived in this country. The President welcomes a full investigation into the allegations contained in the *Post* story, and if Mr. Mattiece was the perpetrator of these heinous crimes, then he must be brought to justice. This was simply a statement for the time being. A full press conference would follow. Zikman darted from the podium.

It was a weak performance by a troubled press secretary, and Gray was relieved. He suddenly found himself crowded, and needed fresh air. He found Smith Keen outside the door.

"Let's go eat breakfast," he whispered.

"Sure."

"I need to run by my apartment too, if you don't mind. I haven't seen it in four days."

They flagged a cab on Fifteenth, and enjoyed the crisp autumn air rushing in the open windows.

"Where's the girl?" Keen asked.

"I have no idea. I last saw her in Atlanta, about nine hours ago. She said she was headed for the Caribbean."

Keen was grinning. "I assume you'll want a long vacation soon."

"How'd you guess?"

"There's a lot of work to be done, Gray. Right now we're in the middle of the explosion, and the pieces start falling to earth very soon. You're the man of the hour, but you must keep pushing. You must pick up the pieces."

"I know my job, Smith."

"Yeah, but you've got this faraway look in your eyes. It worries me."

"You're an editor. You get paid for worrying."

They stopped at the intersection at Pennsylvania Avenue. The White House sat majestically before them. It was almost November, and the wind blew leaves across the lawn.

FORTY-FIVE

AFTER EIGHT DAYS in the sun, the skin was brown enough and the hair was returning to its natural color. Maybe she hadn't ruined it. She walked miles up and down the beaches and ate nothing but broiled fish and island fruit. She slept a lot the first few days, then got tired of it.

She had spent the first night in San Juan, where she found a travel agent who claimed to be an expert on the Virgin Islands. The lady found a small room in a guest house in downtown Charlotte Amalie, on the island of St. Thomas. Darby wanted crowds and lots of traffic on narrow streets, at least for a couple of days. Charlotte Amalie was perfect. The guest house was on a hillside, four blocks away from the harbor, and her tiny room was on the third floor. There were no shutters or curtains on the cracked window, and the sun woke her the first morning, a sensuous wake-up call that summoned her to the window and displayed for her the majesty of the harbor. It was breathtaking. A dozen cruise ships of all sizes sat perfectly still in the shimmering water. They stretched in a careless formation almost to the horizon. In the foreground, near the pier, a hundred sailboats dotted the harbor and seemed to keep the bulky tourist ships at bay. The water under the sailboats was a clear, soft blue, and as smooth as glass. It gently curled around Hassel Island, and grew darker until it was indigo and then violet as it touched the horizon. A perfect row of cumulus clouds marked the line where the water met the sky.

Her watch was in a bag, and she had no plans to wear it for at least six months. But she glanced at her wrist anyway. The window opened with a strain, and the sounds of the shopping district echoed through the streets. The warmth filtered in like a sauna.

She stood in the small window for an hour that first morning on the island, and watched the harbor come to life. There was no hurry. It woke gently as the big ships inched through the water, and soft voices came from the decks of the sailboats. The first person she saw on a boat jumped into the water for a morning swim.

She could grow accustomed to this. Her room was small but clean. There was no air conditioner, but the fan worked fine and it was not unpleasant. The water ran most of the time. She decided to stay here a couple of days, maybe a week. The building was one of dozens packed tightly together along streets that ran down to the harbor. For the moment, she liked the safety of crowds and streets. She could walk and find whatever she needed. St. Thomas was known for its shopping, and she cherished the idea of buying clothes she could keep.

There were fancier rooms, but this would do for now. When she left San Juan, she vowed to stop looking over her shoulder. She'd seen the paper in Miami, and she'd watched the frenzy on a television in the airport, and she knew Mattiece had disappeared. If they were stalking now, it was simply revenge. And if they found her after the crisscrossing journey she had taken, then they were not human, and she would never lose them.

They weren't back there, and she believed this. She stayed close to the small room for two days, never venturing far. The shopping district was a short walk away. Only four blocks long and two blocks deep, it was a maze of hundreds of small and unique stores selling everything. The sidewalks and alleys were crammed with Americans from the big ships. She was just another tourist with a wide straw hat and colorful shorts.

She bought her first novel in a year and a half, and read it in two days while lying on the small bed under the gentle rush from the ceiling fan. She vowed to read nothing about the law until she was fifty. At least once an hour, she walked to the open window and studied the harbor. Once she counted twenty cruise ships waiting to dock.

The room served its purpose. She spent time with Thomas, and cried, and was determined to do it for the last time. She wanted to leave the guilt and pain in this tiny corner of Charlotte Amalie, and exit with the good memories and a clean conscience. It was not as difficult as she tried to make it, and by the third day there were no more tears. She'd thrown the paperback only once.

On the fourth morning, she packed her new bags and took a ferry to Cruz Bay, twenty minutes away on the island of St. John. She took a taxi along the North Shore Road. The windows were down and the wind blew across the backseat. The music was a rhythmic mixture of blues and reggae. The cabdriver tapped the wheel and sang along. She tapped her foot and closed her eyes to the breeze. It was intoxicating.

He left the road at Maho Bay, and drove slowly toward the water. She'd picked this spot from a hundred islands because it was undeveloped. Only a handful of beach houses and cottages were permitted in this bay. The driver stopped on a narrow, tree-lined road, and she paid him.

The house was almost at the point where the mountain met the sea. The architecture was pure Caribbean—white wood frame under a red tile roof—and built barely on the incline to provide for the view. She walked down a short trail from the road, and up the steps to the house. It was a single story with two bedrooms and a porch facing the water. It cost two thousand a week, and she had it for a month.

She placed her bags on the floor of the

den, and walked to her porch. The beach started thirty feet below her. The waves rolled silently to the shore. Two sailboats sat motionless in the bay, which was secluded by mountains on three sides. A rubber raft full of kids splashing moved aimlessly between the boats.

The nearest dwelling was down the beach. She could barely see its roof above the trees. A few bodies relaxed in the sand. She quickly changed into a tiny bikini, and walked to the water.

IT WAS ALMOST DARK when the taxi finally stopped at the trail. He got out, paid the driver, and looked at the lights as the cab drove in front of him and disappeared. He had one bag, and he eased along the trail to the house, which was unlocked. The lights were on. He found her on the porch, sipping a frozen drink and looking like a native with bronze skin.

She was waiting on him, and this was so damned important. He didn't want to be treated like a houseguest. Her face smiled instantly, and she set her drink on the table.

They kissed on the porch for a long minute.

"You're late," she said as they held each other.

"This was not the easiest place to find," Gray said. He was rubbing her back, which was bare down to the waist where a long skirt began and covered most of the legs. He would see them later.

"Isn't it beautiful?" she said, looking at the bay.

"It's magnificent," he said. He stood behind her as they watched a sailboat drift toward the sea. He held her shoulders. "You're gorgeous."

"Let's go for a walk."

He changed quickly into a pair of shorts, and found her waiting by the water. They held hands and walked slowly.

"Those legs need work," she said.

"Rather pale, aren't they?" he said.

Yes, she thought, they were pale, but they weren't bad. Not bad at all. The stomach was flat. A week on the beach with her, and he'd look like a lifeguard. They splashed water with their feet.

"You left early," she said.

"I got tired of it. I've written a story a day since the big one, yet they want more. Keen wanted this, and Feldman wanted that, and I was working eighteen hours a day. Yesterday I said good-bye."

"I haven't seen a paper in a week," she said.

"Coal quit. They've set him up to take the fall, but indictments look doubtful. I don't think the President did much, really. He's just dumb and can't help it. You read about Wakefield?"

"Yes."

"Velmano, Schwabe, and Einstein have been indicted, but they can't find Velmano. Mattiece, of course, has been indicted, along with four of his people. There'll be more indictments later. It dawned on me a few days ago that there was no big cover-up at the White House, so I lost steam. I think it killed his reelection, but he's not a felon. The city's a circus."

They walked in silence as it grew darker. She'd heard enough of this, and he was sick of it too. There was half a moon, and it reflected on the still water. She put her arm around his waist, and he pulled her closer. They were in the sand, away from the water. The house was a half a mile behind them.

"I've missed you," she said softly.

He breathed deeply but said nothing.

"How long will you stay?" she asked.

"I don't know. A couple of weeks. Maybe a year. It's up to you."

"How about a month?"

"I can do a month."

She smiled at him, and his knees were weak. She looked at the bay, at the moon's reflection in the center of it as the sailboat crawled by. "Let's take it a month at a time, okay Gray?"

"Perfect."